SONS OF BITCHES

BAD ROAD RISING BOOK IV

MIKE BARON

LET YOUR RIGHT BRAIN RUN FREE

A LIBERTY ISLAND BOOK

ISBN: 978-1-947942-21-9

Sons of Bitches

Bad Road Rising Book 4

©2018 by Mike Baron

All Rights Reserved

Liberty Island

Libertyislandmag.com

Published in the United States of America

CHAPTER 1

Polly

The title *Muhammad* burst from the cover in three-dimensional letters like a Cecil B. DeMille production. A lean, mean fighting machine in a white suit, wraparound shades, beard and turban, with a scantily clad houri clinging to one leg, cigarette dangling from his lip. He was side-kicking a Hasidic Jew with skullcap and phylacteries two feet off the ground.

"It's meant to be satiric," Polly Furst said. "I'm Jewish myself."

"Do you go to temple?" Josh Pratt asked. They were sitting outside at a round metal table adjacent to the sidewalk at the Laurel Tavern, a family-friendly pub on Monroe Street in Madison, Wisconsin. It was late June and the temperature was in the mid-seventies. Josh's dog, Fig, sat at his feet. He flipped through the comic book.

"No. I come from a long line of secular Jews."

"Man, I love comics. Used to read them in prison. This is good art."

"Thank you."

"Where do people pick this up?"

"From my website or at conventions. Capital City and Westfield have it. I asked Diamond and never heard back. I think it was too hot for them."

"Have you received any death threats?"

"Too many to count. I told the police and they said there was nothing they could do. FBI, same thing. It's like they have no interest in protecting me. I had to shut down my Twitter account and block about a hundred people on Facebook."

"Did you report them to the administrator?"

1

"No. I guess I should have, huh."

"Cops don't protect people," Josh said. "They come along after you've been stabbed and try to figure out who did it."

"I have a bunch of shows coming up. I'm not going to be intimidated into hiding! I contacted Executive Security and they suggested you."

"Huh," Josh said. He'd graduated from their seminar last December and hadn't taken any security jobs, although he'd been involved in investigating the Cretaceous murders. "Anything local?"

"What do you mean?"

"I mean, has anyone phoned you or approached you in person?"

"No. I keep my phone number private but now I'm beginning to worry."

"Where do you live?"

"I rent an apartment at Alhambra on the South Beltline."

"I get two hundred fifty dollars a day plus expenses."

Polly goggled. She was a skinny thing with pale skin, a pouf of curly red hair and a Roman nose. She wore a Tank Girl T-shirt over her flat chest, and wire-rimmed glasses. She looked like a gooney bird. She snuffled, pulled a used tissue from her backpack and ran it under her nose.

"Allergies. My cash flow isn't so great, as you can imagine, but I have a terrific collection of original art I've gathered over the years. My grandfather bunked with Charles Addams and Bill Mauldin in World War II. I suppose I could put some of my pieces up for auction."

"I'm sympathetic to your case, Polly, but I don't work for free."

"I know that. People think that because I'm a starving comic book artist that I should do jobs for the publicity."

"You make a living at this?" Josh said.

"Sort of. I got lucky last year when Vertigo tapped me to do a three-issue run of *Fables*. Then I did a fill-in issue of *Wonder Woman*, so I have a little money in the bank. I may have to sell my Mauldins and Addams drawings."

She looked him up and down. "You are festooned with dog hair."

The waitress came with three hamburgers. Josh set one on the ground for Fig. By the time Josh straightened up, it was gone. Polly wolfed hers down, looking around furtively as if some green justice warrior were about to make a citizen's arrest. She brought out two amber plastic bottles from her backpack, opened them and downed two pills.

"Do you have a concealed carry permit?" Josh said.

Polly stared at him like he was a bug. "Don't be absurd! No one should have a gun except the police."

"I'd like to take a look at your place and if you don't mind, I'd like to see your original art."

"Do you know anything about comics?" Polly said.

"I like *The Badger*. I think I have a few floating around."

"Everybody loves *The Badger*," Polly said. "I never wanted to do superheroes."

Josh hefted *Muhammad*. "What's this?"

"It's a satire."

"I don't think Muslims do satire. Tell me something. With everything that's happening in the world, with terrorists flowing over the southern border like a land rush, what made you think this was a good idea?"

"I'm an artist. I can't think about what's politically correct and I can't let prejudice affect what I consider art, or it's the death of art. Every day we hear of another ukase from some idiot that this or that should be off-limits." Polly spoke in a faux low voice. "'There are many proper subjects for humor. Islam is not among them.' Fuck that! Even *Schindler's List* has a few laughs."

Josh liked her. He'd always hated bullies.

"Now they say you can't write *Luke Cage* unless you're a black man. And you can't play a movie Indian unless you're an Indian. There's a reason they're called actors. Edgar Rice Burroughs would have been forbidden to write *Tarzan* because he never went to Africa. Alexandre Dumas could not have written *The Three Musketeers* because he was a black man. They're calling for the death of the imagination."

"I hear you."

"Did you ever see *The Year of Living Dangerously*? Linda Hunt, this little midget woman, won an Oscar for portraying an Indonesian man. What do we do now? Take away her Oscar 'cause she's not Indonesian?"

"Never saw it." Josh hadn't seen many movies, and most of those he had seen he saw in prison. Inmates voted on what they wanted to see, so Josh had intimate knowledge of *Hell Up in Harlem*, *Superfly*, *Buck Town*, *Easy Rider*, *Hell's Angels on Wheels* and *Wild Angels*. The tiny gay contingent never could summon the votes for *The Birdcage*.

"Sorry for the rant. Seems like I gotta justify everything I do these days."

"Not to me."

"So what do you think?" she said, fixing her green eyes on him.

"About what?"

"About protecting me!"

"Let's take a look at that original art. I might do it for the art."

"Great!" Polly said. When the check came she snatched it. "I've got this."

Minutes later the waitress returned, perplexed. "Ma'am, your credit card didn't go through."

"What?"

"We got notice from your bank that it's been canceled."

"That's impossible," Polly said.

It's started, Josh thought as he reached for his wallet.

CHAPTER 2

Be It Ever So Humble

"Don't you have a car?" Josh asked as he loaded Polly's Trek bike into his trunk.

"I have an old Beetle. If I ever make enough money, I'm going to buy a Prius."

With Fig's snout sticking out the rear passenger window, they drove down Monroe and took Seminole Highway to the Beltline. The Alhambra Apartments were a series of vaguely Middle Eastern-style three-story apartment buildings overlooking the Beltline and the Arboretum. All second- and third-floor apartments had balconies. The ground units had patios. There was a clubhouse with a pool and tennis courts. The parking lot was largely empty at 2:00 p.m., because most people were working. Fig dutifully followed Josh a step behind on his left as she'd been taught.

Polly hefted the Trek on her shoulder and walked up the steps to the front door as Josh admired a custom Wide Glide with a pinstriped tank. They entered the foyer, which smelled of Pine-Sol and corned beef. Polly set down the bike and opened her mailbox with a key, withdrawing several envelopes. Josh counted twenty-four tenants.

"There's a laundry room in the basement but no elevator."

Polly climbed the steps with her bike on her shoulder, Josh and Fig following. Two bikes were chained on the third-floor landing, where Polly pushed through a fire door into a carpeted corridor that smelled of Chinese takeout. Josh and Fig trailed Polly as she approached her door in the middle of the corridor and stopped dead, dropping the bike with a bounce.

A red swastika was drawn on her door in felt-tipped marker. Polly started to shake. Josh put his hand on her shoulder while Fig nuzzled her crotch with a worrying whine.

"Anyone come to mind?" Josh said.

"I've always gotten along great with my neighbors. I can't imagine..."

While Polly fumbled with her keys, Josh took out his phone and photographed the door. He looked around. The door opposite was covered with bumper stickers, including COEXIST, PRO-CHOICE AND PROUD OF IT, and HOPE AND CHANGE.

"Who's this?" Josh said.

"That's Maggie. She's cool. We're pretty tight. No way she'd have anything to do with this."

Once inside, Polly leaned the bike against the island separating the kitchen from the living room and opened the sliding screen door to the patio. Fig went out and thrust her snout between the bars, staring across the green expanse of the Arboretum to the capitol building in the distance. Josh followed, his gaze sweeping from the WARF building in the west all the way to the capitol. He looked right and left. Anyone could jump the little fence separating Polly's apartment from her neighbors'. You could toss a grappling hook from the ground and climb up. You could get on the roof and drop down. Josh thought like a criminal because he used to be one. It had taken prison and a compassionate chaplain to turn his life around.

"Can you have a dog?" he asked.

"We can have small dogs but there's an extra security deposit. Why? You think I should get a dog?"

"They can be very useful if you're worried about people trying to get in."

"I'm sorry. I'm just not a dog person."

Josh looked at her drawing board set up in one corner beneath a gooseneck lamp, at a right angle to her computer. A mug on a side table read MALE TEARS. He looked down at a penciled page showing three bedraggled thieves, two men and a woman, sneaking into a tower using a line and grappling hook.

"I thought I'd try my hand at a Conanesque barbarian-type story. It's called 'Ruby Red.' It's for *Dark Horse Presents.*"

"You've got that effortless mastery of line that is the soul of art."

Polly blushed like bad rosacea. "Wow. Thanks! Here. Let me drag out some of my original art."

She went into the bedroom and returned with a big plastic storage tub, translucent with a blue lid. She set it on the cheap coffee table in front of a cloth sofa and popped the lid. Josh sat across from her in a kitchen chair. She pulled out a page, eleven by seventeen, of Thor swinging his hammer at a bunch of insectoid minions. Josh recognized the character from the movies. MARVEL was stamped at the top in blue ink.

"This is an original Jack Kirby. I could probably get five hundred dollars for this."

"That's two days," Josh said, holding out his hand for the art. He handled it reverently by the back and edges, seeing where Jack had erased and redrawn using blue pencils.

"I think Joe Sinnott is the inker," Polly said.

"Are you in a relationship?" Josh said.

"What's that got to do with anything?"

"If you are, that person may be at risk. Some of these nutjobs are pretty sophisticated. They're not above coming at you through your significant other or family."

"No, I'm not seeing anyone, if that's what you mean. And I'm a lesbian by the way."

Josh grunted. "Not crazy about this location. Somebody could just hop the barrier between your balcony and the next."

"I know both my neighbors and believe me, they're not terrorists!"

"Still, there are a half dozen ways in here. I'm not crazy about this. Do you have someplace else you could go while this blows over?"

Polly stared at him. "All my stuff is here! This is where I draw!"

"Can't you draw someplace else?"

She buried her face in her hands and said, "URG! I *suppose* I could ask my uncle Don. He lives in Middleton. He's one of the reasons I chose UW. You'd like him. He's a biker too. But he's gay. So you might not like him."

"How many of your friends and acquaintances know you have an uncle Don in town?"

"Nobody. I never really have occasion to mention him, and I don't have that many friends. There's Dale."

"Who's Dale?"

"Don's BFF. They met in the Marines. Don't ask, don't tell."

"Give Don a call. And I'll have to take a look at his place, of course."

While Polly called, Josh poked around. He wasn't shy. She'd asked him to protect her from a potentially lethal threat. He went into her little bedroom decorated with some of her landscapes and a framed poster of the Student Union. Her queen-size bed was made with a Snoopy blanket. He went into the tiny bathroom and opened the medicine cabinet. Rows of amber plastic pill bottles with names like space aliens: Omalizumab, Deltasone, Kenalog-40—all prescribed by a Dr. Stanley Hebert of Associated Physicians on University Boulevard—and allergy medications and nasal spray.

Also, Trazodone and Clonazepam for anxiety and depression.

The toilet bowl, seat down, had a brown ring. A crumpled towel lay on the floor and soap scum covered the inside of the shower. When he came out, Polly was sitting at her drawing board with pencil in hand.

"He wasn't in. I left a message."

Josh zeroed in on a framed landscape on the wall near the drawing board showing a pond in autumn, flaming leaves reflected in still water. "Did you do this?"

"No, that's my painting guru, Melissa Granville. You'd like her. I take lessons from her a couple times a month."

"Well come on," Josh said. "Pack up. I'll help you. What do you need?"

Polly turned in her seat and squinted. "What, now? I hardly think so!"

"Well I'm not leaving you here alone. Y'know why your credit card was denied?"

"Oh my god," Polly said. "I forgot all about that. I can't imagine. It's got to be some sort of mistake."

"It's no mistake. Whoever's after you is waging cyber-war. Go ahead. Call your bank. I'll wait."

Josh sat on the sofa and flipped through a portfolio of original art while Polly dialed. A few minutes later she grunted. "I hate these fucking automatic things!"

Five minutes passed.

"Thank you Jesus!" Polly roared into the phone. "A real live person."

Josh looked up while Polly explained the problem. She looked over. "I'm on hold."

Josh looked at a Mike Mignola *Hellboy* page. "Nice!"

"I traded him for that," Polly said, then abruptly turned away and listened. "Yes. Yes. No, that can't be right. No! That's not right! May I speak to a supervisor please?"

With an ashen face she folded her phone. "They said that my account is under federal investigation and all my assets have been frozen."

Josh put the art back in the box and stood. "Pack your things. You can stay with me until we get hold of your uncle."

He paused in the foyer to photograph the mailboxes.

CHAPTER 3

Uncle Don

The Harley was gone by the time they came down with two suitcases and a backpack. It took two trips to load her stuff into Josh's car and her beat-up Beetle with a bike rack on the back. Josh helped Polly attach her bike to the rack with bungee cords. Then she followed him and Fig down the frontage road to Fish Hatchery, from which they got on the Beltline heading west.

They had barely reached Midvale when Polly phoned. Josh picked up while driving. "What?"

"Uncle Don called back. He says it's okay to go to his place."

Josh flipped his right turn signal. "Follow me."

They pulled off on Gammon into the Woodman's parking lot and parked at the back, away from the store. Josh got out and went over to Polly. "Where are we going?"

"7328 Elmwood Avenue in Middleton."

Josh took out a small spiral pad and wrote the address down. "You lead," he said, returning to his car.

It was four by the time Polly pulled into the driveway of a grand old two-story with a broad veranda beneath the shade of several majestic elms and oaks. Josh parked on the street in front and got out, opening the passenger door for Fig. A bald, muscular guy in a white wife-beater sat on the porch with his bare feet up on the rail smoking a Cohiba and drinking a bottle of Tyranena IPA. Josh stopped when he saw the bike.

It sat on the concrete between Polly's VW and an open two-car garage containing four more bikes and an old F-150. The bike in the driveway used a spring leaf for the front suspension and a monoshock in the rear artfully concealed by the custom frame. The engine was a Honda 750 Nighthawk, the four tubes intertwining like a Gorgon's locks, or more precisely, like the 1975 Honda F-400's.

Josh turned toward the porch, where Polly and her uncle hugged, Fig thrusting her snout between them. "Did you build that?"

"Yeah," Don replied. "Like it?"

"Sweet! Polly tells me you build bikes."

"Polly tells me you're a detective."

Josh went up three steps and they shook hands. "Sort of." Don was built like a tight end, his biceps inked with the Marine logo and SEMPER FI.

"You want a beer?" Don said.

"Help me drag her shit in your house and then I'll have one."

It took a few minutes to ferry Polly's luggage, drawing table and supplies into the big house, where they parked it in the living room next to a Steinway baby grand.

"You play?" Josh said.

"Sort of. Took lessons when I was a kid. Always loved the blues."

"Me too."

Don sat at the piano and ripped off twelve bars to a boogie-woogie beat.

"I keep telling him he should get a gig," Polly said.

Don got up, went into the kitchen and returned with three beers. Polly and Josh each took one. Don and Josh returned to the porch while Polly transferred her luggage to a spare bedroom.

Josh twisted off the cap. "You know what's going on?"

Don put his feet back up on the rail and tilted his wooden kitchen chair precariously against the wall. "You mean the jihad? I told her it was a dumb idea."

"She tell you about the swastika?"

"Yeah. I'd love to meet the person who did that. I don't go to temple and I'm not sure I really believe in God. But one thing I know—when they come for the Jews, they don't care whether you're devout or not. Never thought I'd see this shit here at home. I was in the sand for two years.

You expect it in some shithole ruled by sixth-century mullahs. You don't expect it on Main Street." He paused to glug.

"You religious?"

"Sorta," Josh said.

"Whaddaya mean? You're not one of those tree-huggers, are you?"

Josh laughed. "No. I came to Jesus in prison. I believe he is the Son of God and that he died for our sins."

Don held up a hand. "Gotcha. My folks weren't religious and neither were Polly's. Her dad's my older brother. Far as I'm concerned, whatever floats your boat so long as you're not bothering anyone."

"Yeah that's the way I feel about it," Josh said. "Polly says none of her friends know about you or this place. Is that correct?"

"Not exactly. I was down on the Union terrace last summer when she introduced me to a friend of hers—Shawna—a babe. But who knows where she is?"

Josh took out a pad and made a note. "It's best if no one knows she's here. I wonder if I could get her to wear a mild disguise."

Don snorted. "Riiiight."

"Sunglasses and a head scarf, like Audrey Hepburn."

"Yeah. She can pretend it's a burka."

From inside they heard Polly setting up her drawing board.

"Hey Polly!" Josh said.

She came out on the porch. "What's up, Josh?"

"You know your friend Shawna? You introduced her to Don last summer?"

"Yeah. What about her?"

"Where is she now?"

"I guess she's back in Vermont. She only came out here for summer school. Why?"

"Just trying to figure who knows your uncle Don."

"Nobody knows uncle Don," Polly said. "Except Dale."

"Who's Dale, again?" Josh said.

"Friend of mine," Don said. "Fellow gyrene."

Josh looked at Polly. "You need to notify your landlord about that swastika. And I need you to bring up your Twitter and Facebook accounts and forward all the death threats to me."

"I told you, I quit Twitter, and I unfriended and blocked anyone who threatened me on Facebook. But I'll see what I can do."

"Excellent," Josh said. "Now if you guys are settled, I have to go feed my dog."

CHAPTER 4

Death Threats

Josh pulled into the driveway of his modest yellow ranch house on Ptarmigan Road on Madison's southwest side. Fig leaped out behind him and ran to the front door. Fig was a supposed German Shepherd he'd adopted last year from Milwaukee gangster Jerell Moore. Josh had named the dog after his dead girlfriend.

Fig looked like the union of a German Shepherd, a cattle dog, a Maine coon cat and a badger. One ear stood straight up. The other was bent like a semaphore signal. Her tail rivaled that of a peacock for sheer splendor. A fine patina of dog hair covered every surface of the house, and tufts of dog hair wafted through the air wherever Josh walked. He got a shop vac at Harbor Freight and was barely able to keep up. So he got another shop vac from Harbor Freight and hooked them up in tandem, the blow hole from the first feeding into the suck hole on the second. It worked better but was still insufficient to keep up with all the dog hair. Josh needed a vacuum with the sucking power of a 747.

"All right Figgers, let's eat!" he said, walking into the kitchen, with Fig dancing, wagging and barking. Josh decanted a can of dog food into a heavy pewter bowl he'd picked up at a garage sale. At first he'd used a light steel bowl, but Fig kept grabbing the bowl in her jaws and leaving it in the backyard. He set the pewter bowl on a footstool. Fig lowered her snout and scarfed.

"Do you even taste anything?" Josh said, grabbing a beer from the fridge and heading out the door to his back deck. He'd built the cedar deck himself and installed the hot tub. Sitting in a padded chair, Josh put his feet up on the round table with the umbrella hole, pulled out his phone and dialed Roland Stoeckle, an NSA agent. Josh left a message to call him.

He'd met Stoeckle the previous year when he'd killed a spook who went by the name of Edward Martin. Martin was a cover for Wayne Culligan, whose brother Phil had belonged to the Insane Assholes MC. Next Josh phoned Aaron Kofsky, CEO of Dovetail Software, a company that specialized in creating and circumventing firewalls for the feds. Josh left another message. These were important men. He was lucky to know them.

Josh had met Kofsky when Steve Fleiss, a lawyer, sent Josh to Cabo the previous year to retrieve Kofsky, a gambler and fetishist who'd embezzled hundreds of thousands of dollars from Dovetail. Kofsky wasn't a bad guy, except for a taste for kiddie porn. Now he was Josh's go-to guy on the internet.

Josh saw that Stoeckle had phoned, and returned the call.

"Sir, I'm working for a woman who published a comic called *Muhammad*. She's getting death threats. Do you have the time to meet with me and review jihadist elements in the Upper Midwest?"

"I'll be in Madison on Saturday. We could get together then."

"Give me a call when you hit town."

"You might check with the FBI."

Stoeckle gave him a number for an Agent Ross Phillips in Chicago. Josh phoned Phillips; the call went straight to voicemail, and he left a message.

Josh went into his office and uploaded the photograph of the Alhambra mailboxes to his computer. All but two of the twenty-four of them sported plastic labels. Some were only last names but Josh got their full names by entering them into the Madison white pages along with the addresses.

Most of them were on Facebook. Of these, Mustapha Abed, Fatima Khoury and Fayeed bin Sa proudly proclaimed their Muslim faith. Mustapha Abed was a twenty-five-year-old factory worker. Fatima Khoury was a twenty-six-year-old grad student in chemistry and Fayeed bin Sa managed a Burger King. None of them had criminal records. Josh would get the remaining two tenants' names from Kofsky via property management.

Josh checked his email and found that Polly had forwarded her Facebook and Twitter account information. Although she'd canceled her Twitter account, Josh found the whole history when he logged in.

We will rape you and cut off your head, Jew bitch.

DIE JEW DIE! ALLHAU ACKBAR!

Jew cunt: you may think you're smart mocking the Prophet but Allah will have the last word.

There were dozens. Sickened, Josh logged out. With all the noise about hate speech, trigger warnings and micro-aggressions, he wondered how a business like Twitter could permit this. Josh was against censorship. He was a First Amendment absolutist, but this was beyond free speech. These were death threats.

His phone rang. It was Aaron Kofsky calling him back.

"Just the man I want to see!" Josh said.

"What do you need?"

Josh gave Kofsky a brief outline. "Is there any way to trace these Twitter accounts, to find out who is really behind them?"

"Funny you should ask. We're developing a program to trace the provenance of Islamic terrorist sites. These people are web-savvy and often hide behind multiple screens and bouncers. You trace it to a server in Bratislava. You trace that to a server in Colombia. You trace that to a server in Syria. It's like *The 500 Hats of Bartholomew Cubbins*. You've got to lift a lot of hats to get to the scalp.

"That said, if the threat were credible or against someone like a senator or the president, the FBI can get everything Twitter knows, such as login ID and the internet protocol address of the computer that made the post. They can then get a court order for the internet service provider to tell them who pays for that connection. From there it's just regular police work to come up with the person who posted.

"If you don't have the FBI, you can still figure out within a reasonable level who someone is by profiling what time of day they post, who they follow on Twitter, and try to infer data from what they say and who follows them."

"What about you, Aaron? Could you trace these posts?"

"I could if I had the time. But we're slammed here. Tell you what. Things should loosen up by the end of the week. Give me a call then and we'll see if we can get together."

"Thanks, Aaron. I'll be in touch."

Josh called Polly.

"Uncle Don wants me to pack a pistol," she blurted.

"Something to think about."

"As if!" Polly snorted. "You know I'm signing at Westfield Comics on Saturday."

"I'll be there," Josh said.

Fig laid her head on his lap and wagged her tail against his plastic trash bin, thumping bass.

Josh pushed back from the computer and stood. "Okay! Okay!"

Somehow the dog knew it was Monday. And Monday meant *The Sing-Off*. They went into the living room and sprawled on the sofa, Fig's head upside down in Josh's lap, her legs in the air, as he turned on the big flat-screen television. Ben, Shawn and Sara sat at the judges' table flashing their ivory. First up was an a cappella group from Natchez called Grouper, consisting of four young black men. As one provided a bass with hands and a mouth that was indistinguishable from Ron Carter, the others harmonized on "I Heard It Through the Grapevine." Fig leaped off the sofa, sat, tilted her snout and howled.

Josh clapped his hands. It was as funky as he got.

At the commercial break, a thick old guy in a work shirt said, "I was injured by a garbage truck, and the insurance company only wanted to pay me $10,000. I knew that wasn't right so I contacted Steve Fleiss and he got me $250,000!"

Fleiss appeared earnest and combative, looking like Gary Shandling circa *The Larry Sanders Show*. He barked:

"Big corporations are the scum of the earth! They treat the little guy like garbage! And insurance companies are the worst! They employ armies of lawyers to deny people their benefits. Well, I'm Steve Fleiss, 'The Hammer.' I was a judge for twelve years, and they don't frighten me!

"Have you been in an accident and believe that you were short-changed by the insurance companies? Call me, Steve Fleiss, The Hammer. I recently settled several cases. My clients received $200,000, $300,000 and $2.3 million! Now I can't guarantee you $2.3 million. Every case is different. But if insurance companies are giving you the runaround, call The Hammer and I promise to get you every cent you deserve."

"You see?" Josh said. "This is how you get rich."

They went to bed. Josh lay awake thinking about what might have been, until Fig had had enough and burrowed her muzzle into his armpit and whined.

"I'm sorry, Fig. I didn't mean to upset you."

CHAPTER 5

Bricklin

The next morning Josh and Fig ran five miles, passing his neighbor Phil Bass in his Lexus driving to work as they headed back. They exchanged waves even though Josh had served Phil with a summons from his ex-wife last December. Phil had loaned Josh his SUV to drive to Iowa last Christmas to confront Wynn Houtkooper, former drummer for Cretaceous, who'd been traveling around the country chopping off heads.

Last week a dude asked Josh, "When's the last time you saw anyone but a Muslim posing with a human head?"

"Wynn Houtkooper," Josh said. Then he had to explain.

And there was the unresolved matter of Bass's group wanting to buy Josh out of his house and build a clubhouse on his property. The latest offer was a half mil. Before Stoeckle had put Josh on the NSA payroll, he probably would have sold out. Never in his wildest dreams did he envision a sum of that magnitude. But now NSA had him on retainer for six figures so that he would keep his mouth shut about "Edward Martin." Money was not an issue at the moment, which was why he was able to take on Polly.

Like most bikers, Josh envisioned himself as a knight in tarnished armor, a brawler and a gentleman who went out of his way to help widows, orphans and stray dogs. Most of the bikers Josh had known were good guys despite their abrasive appearance. A lot of those hairy, leather-clad, patch-wearing, tatted-up crowd were lawyers, doctors and architects. Who else could afford $25,000 for a new Harley?

Josh showered, running his HeadBlade ATX over his scalp. It had two tiny rubber wheels in front to negotiate the skull and looked like a Can-Am Spyder. He dressed and checked his email. There was a message from maybe a woman named Limpho: "my name is limpho, i hope you are fine, after i view your pictures on facebook then i decide to keep in touch, please feel free to respond to my mail. i have something serious to tell you then we can get acquaintance ok."

"YOU'RE A BUM!" he wrote back. "GET A JOB!"

He deleted her email and looked at the FBI's list of terrorist organizations operating in the Upper Midwest. These included the Posse Comitatus, the NRA and the Constitution Party. There was no mention of any groups affiliated with Islam. He threw a Jimmy Dean breakfast sandwich in the microwave and ate it on the back deck while orioles sang and Fig barked at the Labrador who lived in back. Josh threw some sweats and hand wraps in a leather overnighter, bungeed it to the back of his Road King and rode downtown, through the isthmus, out East Washington to the Zhong Yi Kung Fu Academy situated in a strip mall that also contained a laundry and a liquor store. It was eleven o'clock.

Josh leaned the bike in front, put his cell phone in the tank bag and walked through the glass front door into the polished wood interior. Sunlight slanted in through skylights illuminating millions of dancing gold motes. The room was thirty-five by fifty, with kung fu wooden men lined up against the wall next to a half dozen free-standing heavy bags filled with water. Sifu Nelson Ferreira was sitting on the floor with his legs at one hundred eighty degrees, wearing a traditional black kung fu outfit with double-breasted frogs. Nelson came from Brazil and weighed three hundred pounds. He looked like a teapot with legs. Josh had been training with him for four years.

"Josh," Nelson said.

Josh bowed. "Sifu!"

"Go change. Let's work out."

Josh went into the men's room, took off his civvies and put on a strap and cup, loose-fitting sweatpants and an Indian T-shirt. Out on the floor he took a few minutes stretching and warming up before turning to Nelson, clicking his heels together and bowing.

"Sifu!"

"Want to do sticks?" Nelson said, walking to a wall covered in weapons stashed in cubbyholes and hanging from hooks. He chose four rattan batons from a wastebasket made from faux elephant skin and handed two to Josh, who gripped them with two inches of butt sticking out.

"Double *seda wale*," Nelson said. The sticks moved like Gatling guns, almost too fast for the eye to follow—in the traditional Filipino pattern. Forehand, backhand, loop. Josh and Nelson moved around the floor smacking sticks like two drunken hockey players with exquisite control.

Nelson pulled back breathing hard. There were droplets of sweat on his forehead beneath his tight helmet of curls. It wasn't Josh's place to tell Nelson he ought to lose weight. It wasn't as if the big man didn't know. But a lifetime of habit was hard to change, even for a kung fu master.

"Now let's do box pattern."

"Nelson, do you know any Muslims?"

"We had some Muslims come in here last week, wanted to train. They wanted to take a class, but were insistent that they could not bow before the altar. I told them that the bow of the heart is not the same as the bow of the head. I quoted the Koran to them. They still didn't want to bow, but wanted to take class, just didn't want to obey the class etiquette. I told them to take a hike, and they accused me of being a racist. I laughed and said, 'This is a Chinese cultural practice. If you do not want to participate, then you don't have to. Have a great day.'"

Josh got down to business. "I'm guarding this chick who drew a comic about Muhammad and now she's getting death threats. Did you know any in Rio?"

"No. I'm sure they were there but we never saw any. Do you know any Muslims?"

Josh shrugged. "I knew some black Muslims in the joint, but they weren't the type to get bent out of shape about a comic. They loved Black Panther, Luke Cage and Punisher. There was a Son of Silence, called himself 'The Sheik,' but I think he was just a meth addict."

They heard the roar of a V-twin as it backed to the curb. The roar went silent and a minute later the door opened, admitting a big woman wearing carpenter pants, a gray sweatshirt and a black leather vest, and carrying a gym bag. Her name was Bricklin Beasn.

"Hello boys!" she boomed.

"Hey Bricklin," Nelson said. "Bricklin, this is Josh."

She pumped Josh's hand with a man's grip. "You're the guy who had the shootout in your driveway."

Josh cleared his throat. He wished it would all just go away. "Yeah."

"That's tough, buddy. I feel for ya."

"Thanks."

"Bricklin was in Desert Storm."Nelson said.

"Oh?" Josh said. "What branch?"

"Army,"

"See any action?"

"A little."

"You ever see one of those camel spiders?"

Bricklin shot him a look of stupefaction, disbelief and umbrage.

"Oh honey, don't let me commence! One of those fell out of my boot one morning, and I about shit a camel!"

The door creaked open and two more women entered carrying gym bags, both with buzz cuts. One had a floral tattoo creeping up her neck. Josh looked at Nelson. As Bricklin turned to greet them, he saw her colors. DEATH TO ISIS, said the top rocker over a picture of crossed Colt 45s and a skull. The bottom rocker said LET'S ROLL.

"Bricklin runs a self-defense class for women on Wednesdays," Nelson said.

"You can work out with us if you like," Bricklin said.

"No thanks. I gotta fly," Josh said, turning to Nelson. "Gotta fly."

They bopped fists. Josh had thought of asking Nelson to help with the guard duty, but Nelson had a family and worked full-time as a kung fu instructor. Besides, Nelson had helped Josh before.

Outside, Josh stopped to admire Bricklin's ride, a full-dress Indian with saddlebags. The all-new, all-authentic Polaris Indian. It was a lot of bike, but she was a lot of woman. He waited until he was home before he checked his phone.

Kofsky had called, inviting him for a cookout Friday evening.

Ross Phillips had returned his call. He called the agent back.

"Thanks for returning my call, Agent Phillips."

"Stoeckle told me you might call. What's up?"

Josh described the Polly situation. He heard Phillips inhale through his teeth.

"A couple years ago a similar situation arose in Seattle," Phillips began. "A young woman announced on her Facebook page Everybody Draw Muhammad Day. She was forced to change her identity and go underground."

"What do you mean she was forced? Who forced her?" Pause.

"It was recommended by several government agencies."

"So you got nothin'."

"Mr. Pratt, we're stretched to the breaking point."

"I see. Well, thanks for your time."

"Sorry I couldn't be of more assistance."

CHAPTER 6

Reconnoiter

Josh cruised Westfield Comics in the High Point shopping center on Madison's West Side, cheek by jowl with Pier 1, Weight Watchers and Planet Fitness. Josh backed his bike into a slot in the lot and approached. The store had a big picture window and a bright red roof. A hand-lettered sign in the window said, POLLY FURST SIGNING HER COMIC MUHAMMAD, SATURDAY, TEN TO FIVE. Posters advertising *Convergence*, *Blood Shot* and *The Avengers* faced out from the glass door. Josh pushed inside to a clean, well-lighted space filled with wall racks and free-standing shelves. A young woman who appeared as if she'd been sandblasted with freckles, her hair in a topknot like Taras Bulba, looked up from the front desk.

"Hello!"

"Hi."

"Looking for anything in particular?"

"Just browsing, thanks," Josh said. He rode the perimeter, marveling at the explosion of color, brawn, fantastic creatures, hot buns and costumed superheroes that screamed silently from the walls. He pulled out a copy of *Rat God* by Richard Corben, an artist whose work he'd come to appreciate in the joint via much-traveled copies of *Weird Tales*, *Neverwhere* and *Underground*.

Josh had never been a comics guy. His father, Duane, didn't encourage reading or any type of "book larnin." Josh had barely glimpsed comics throughout his peripatetic adolescence, usually in the hands of others then quickly stashed. It wasn't until he was sentenced to nine years for various felonies that he truly discovered comic books.

Graphic novels, action figures and statues filled the free-standing shelves. Everyone from Witchblade to a one-sixth scale Iron Man.

He completed his circumnavigation. "Got any *Badger*?" he said to the girl behind the desk.

"Maybe in the back issues. I don't think it's currently being published."

"I understand you're having a signing tomorrow."

"Yes! Polly Furst will be signing her comic *Muhammad* here from eleven until five."

"Aren't you afraid of terrorist attacks?"

The girl smiled quizzically, unsure. "Are you serious? This is Madison, not Paris."

Josh took out a card and laid it on the table. "I'm Josh Pratt."

The girl picked up the card and grinned at it. "Dorothy Little," she said, sticking out her hand. "Wait a minute. You're that guy..."

"I am that guy. Polly has asked me to provide security here tomorrow. I'll just be hanging around. I won't be in the way."

"You're not going to bring a gun, are you?"

Josh threw his hands up and looked shocked. "Oh heavens, no! Guns are icky."

"They're awful."

"What kind of a crowd are you expecting?"

While they spoke, the door opened and three young men entered, skinny, unshaven. Two of them wore glasses. They went wordlessly to the new-arrivals shelf and examined the latest titles with Talmudic attention.

"Oh maybe a couple hundred. We had Neil Gaiman here last month and people were lined up around the block! He didn't leave until he'd signed the last book, at two-thirty in the morning."

"No kidding! How are you advertising?"

"*Isthmus*, WMAD, online."

"I'll see you tomorrow then."

"Looking forward to it!" Dorothy said.

Josh went home, played with Fig, did what he could online and at five, loaded Fig into the Chrysler and headed toward Aaron Kofsky's house in Zebrawood, a luxe development west of Madison, and home to bankers, athletes and dot-com millionaires. Josh rolled with his elbow in the wind,

Fig's snout deployed like a radar detector, the honeyed smells of spring wafting through the open windows.

Josh turned at the stone gates and followed the winding tarmac through small stands of alder, walnut and birch, past Tudor mansions, Taliesin rock caves and huge American Bland houses with three- and four-car garages. He turned in at Kofsky's, a confused but impressive jumble of Southwest adobe, mansard roof and bay windows. It looked like a house designed by a committee. Josh parked in front and went in through the arched oak front door, Fig at his heels. Hearing music playing from the patio, he walked through the voluminous living room, past the walk-in fireplace, out the sliding glass doors, where Kofsky and his sometime girlfriend, Sandy Meyer, were dancing to Graham Central Station. Sandy had the stringy look of an aging female athlete, her platinum hair cut short. She wore a halter top and shorts. Kofsky, pale and bulbous, greeted Josh with a smile, sweat beading on his forehead.

Sandy knelt to nuzzle Fig, stood and hugged Josh.

"Good to see you, Josh!"

"You too, Sandy."

Kofsky lifted the stainless steel hood on his outdoor gas grill. "We'll eat and then after dinner I'll show you what I was able to find from your client's Twitter and Facebook accounts."

Fig lay under the table while Kofsky served grilled steak and corn on the cob. Sandy slipped Fig a sliver of steak and winked at Josh.

"She's not my dog."

After dinner Sandy excused herself to do the dishes. Josh and Kofsky went into an office covered with framed black-and-white photos of Muddy Waters, Son Seals and Otis Rush. Kofsky sat at his desk while Josh looked over his shoulder.

"So you're seeing Sandy again?" Josh said.

"Giving it the old college try."

"That's great. Hope it works out for you guys."

Kofsky grunted. Since discovering a disc of kiddie porn in Kofsky's desk, Josh had kept a close eye on him, trying to discern if Kofsky was still addicted. It went without saying that if Josh ever discovered Kofsky acting on his darker impulses, Josh would kill him.

Kofsky brought up Polly's Twitter page and stroked some keys, producing a window on the left filled with computer code. "I was able to trace five of these to a server in Iran. That tells you all you need to know. Five different accounts, but they could all be the same person. I'm trying to locate another six but they're damned good, whoever they are. I'm afraid that of these, some might be in the United States. They could be next door for all I know. The problem is in navigating backward through a series of domain names and robots. I forwarded my findings to the FBI."

"What about Facebook?" Josh said.

Kofsky brought up Polly's FB page, stroked some keys. The window appeared and within it, the death threats Polly had deleted. "I notified Facebook about these accounts. I assume your client did too because none of them are still on Facebook. Nevertheless, this one here?"

He indicated Bashir Asi.

"I traced this to 237 Allied Drive, apartment 29."

"Great," Josh said. Allied Drive off the South Beltline was a center of gang activity. "What do we know about Bashir Asi?"

"Works as a waiter at Croissanwich on Monroe Street, immigrated from Lebanon in 2007, not a registered voter. He is twenty-nine years old, single, and regularly visits child porn sites."

"What about the other Facebook threats?"

"I'll get to 'em as soon as I can. We're swamped right now with two projects."

It was nine by the time Josh and Fig returned to his house. Josh checked his messages. Stoeckle had written, "I can meet with you Saturday."

Josh wrote back, telling the agent about Polly's signing and suggesting they meet at seven at the Edgewater.

"C U there," came the reply.

CHAPTER 7

The Signing

After he and Fig had run, showered and eaten breakfast, Josh phoned Polly.

"I will pick you up. I don't want you driving your car."

"Why not?"

"Just a precaution. I'll pick you up at nine thirty."

Josh arrived at Don's house at nine fifteen. He parked at the curb, got out and went over to Polly's red VW Beetle in the driveway. It was first-generation, front-wheel drive with the vase on the dash. Josh got down on his back and shined a tiny LED flashlight up under the chassis. There were no add-ons. The brake lines appeared intact. The car was locked so he couldn't check under the hood. He ran his hands beneath the bumpers searching for a tracking device. He'd look inside when he had more time.

As Josh went up the front steps to the porch, the front door opened and Polly came out wearing a yellow-and-white sundress and a broad-brimmed straw hat, with a heavy leather briefcase looped over one shoulder. She pointed to two cardboard boxes on a glider.

"Would you mind?"

Josh reached in his pocket and handed Polly a keychain, a five-inch hexagonal steel rod with two steel spikes. "Here's your new keychain."

Polly instinctively grasped it in her fist so that the two parallel spikes protruded above her knuckles. "Cool! Is this some kind of karate thing?" She struck a wide stance and threw a few punches. "Hoo! Ha!"

"Did you contact your bank?"

"Yes. They acknowledge that my account was hacked and are reinstating it with new security measures. They're sending me a new card."

Josh picked up one of the boxes. It was heavy and filled with copies of *Muhammad*. They put the boxes in the trunk. Polly got in the passenger seat.

"Where's Don?" Josh said.

"He's at work."

"What work?"

"Carson's Craft Spirits. They used to be Carson's Discount Liquor until the city forced them to take down their sign. Now it's like..." Polly stuck a finger under her nose and held up her pinkie. "Ooh la la!"

Josh parked close to the comics shop's entrance, and they each carried a box inside. The staff had set up a table near the front with a poster on an easel: POLLY FURST, CREATOR OF ULTRA PIGEON, WEIRD GIRL, AND MUHAMMAD. A plump, balding young man greeted them at the door.

"Good morning, Polly. I'm sorry to tell you this but we may have to cancel this event."

"What?!" Polly squawked, still holding the box.

"Someone phoned in a bomb threat."

"Did you notify the police?" Josh said.

"Right away. They said they'd send someone over later to take a statement. I have it on the recorder."

"Could I hear it?" Josh said.

"I'm sorry, you are?"

"Josh Pratt. Polly has hired me to provide security."

"I'm the manager, Wally. Come on back."

Josh wished he'd brought Fig. Then he was glad he hadn't.

Josh followed Wally to an office in the back decorated with posters of superheroes and movies: *Age of Ultron, Scott Pilgrim Saves the World, Badger*. Wally pressed a button on a call monitor on the desk, fast-forwarded through some stuff, played a blip, backed up and pressed the button.

"You host the Jew-bitch Polly Furst and we will burn down your store." Click.

The voice sounded Middle Eastern.

"That's not a bomb threat," Josh said.

"What the fuck, man! Bombing, burning, what's the dif?"

"I get your point, but it's probably just a bluff. Do you have a record of the phone number?"

Wally pushed some buttons and a number with a 608 exchange came up. "I gave it to the cops."

Josh exited the office and went into the warehouse in back, a room with a ten-foot ceiling, cinderblock walls and a concrete floor. Steel shelves lined the walls and marched in orderly ranks through the room, filled with cardboard boxes marked with titles and numbers. Many of the boxes said QUEBECOR. The rear door was solid steel, held shut by a deadbolt and a slide bolt. Josh tried the door and found it unlocked. He looked out the rear of the shop across a service area and a road that ran down the back of the mall.

Up front, undaunted by the threat of cancellation, Polly had set up shop at the table, laying out stacks of comics, her backpack by her side. Dorothy gave Polly a Starbucks cup and turned to Josh.

"Can I get you anything? Coffee? Soda?"

"I'd love a coffee. Cream and sugar."

Dorothy left through the front door, where visitors were lining up: two young dudes spouting fountains of hair and holding skateboards, and a goth woman with pink hair and nose and chin studs. By the time Wally opened the door, there were a dozen people in line. The board punks bypassed Polly and went straight to the new-arrivals rack. Josh stood by a spinner rack pretending to peruse the titles. Polly plastered a smile on her face and waited hopefully. It was ten thirty before a young man with a bookish face and rimless glasses came up to her.

He pointed to *Muhammad*. "I'll take one of those."

"Sure!" Polly chirped. "Can I sign it for you?"

"Yeah. Make it out to Matt. And I really admire what you're doing, you know? Too many cartoonists are afraid of offending people."

Polly wrote on the splash page. "I'm not trying to offend people, I'm trying to point out the absurdity of trying to control an image and an idea shared by billions of people."

The man forked over five bucks. "I know. *Charlie Hebdo* tried the same thing."

Polly smiled. "This is America. They won't try that shit over here."

"I hope you're right."

The purchaser went over to the new comics rack. Next up were some admiring young girls, both toting drawing pads. More people showed, most bypassing Polly to check out the new releases. Josh went to the used-issue boxes in the back and looked up *Badger*, finding several he didn't have.

A steady stream of visitors trooped in all morning. Polly greeted everyone, garnering perfunctory responses save for a handful who had come to support her. At noon Dorothy asked what kind of pizza they'd like, and by one the pizza was gone. Josh went outside every fifteen minutes and scanned the parking lot. College students surged around two o'clock and a lively scene developed out front on the sidewalk with board punks stunting, a juggler on some kind of one-wheeled Segway, and comics fans comparing titles and dishing about the new *Avengers* movie. A food truck sold tacos.

The promised cop never arrived.

Josh went inside. "How we doing?" he asked Polly.

"Better than I'd hoped. I've sold twenty copies!"

Josh looked up. He'd caught a scent, a flicker, a movement that should not have been there, and here came trouble in the form of a thin, intense young man with a shock of black hair and a G.I. Joe beard. He elbowed rudely through the scrum outside the door. Josh took up position behind Polly as the young man bore down on her with laser intensity. He glanced once at Josh and his demeanor subtly changed to something less confrontational. He picked up a copy of *Muhammad*, glared at it and ripped it in two.

"Blasphemy!" he hissed.

"That's five bucks you owe her," Josh said.

"I will never pay this Jew-bitch whore." He spat in Polly's face.

Josh was on him in two steps, throwing him to the ground on his face and jacking his arm up behind his back.

"Call the police. That's assault."

Polly used a tissue to wipe her face. "Just let him go, Josh. It's not worth it."

Josh looked up, his knee planted in the small of the man's back. "You sure? It might discourage him from future jihad."

"Just let him go," Polly said.

Josh looked over at Wally, who nodded. Josh removed his knee and let the man go. The spitter got to his feet without meeting their gaze and slunk out. Josh watched him wend his way through the crowd outside the door. People were hesitant. They knew something had happened but not exactly what. Wally went outside.

"Come on in, folks! Nothing to fear. Just a disgruntled customer. Come on in and meet writer/artist Polly Furst!"

Their mood changed and they stepped forward, eager now to be part of the scene, the action, whatever it was.

Josh could not ignore a strand of worry that tugged at the back of his lizard brain and kept his eyes on the parking lot. Five or six people crowded around Polly examining her comic, asking questions and reaching for their wallets. A line waited at the cashier's counter. In addition to Dorothy, a young man wearing a Hulk T-shirt worked the second register.

There it was again, that wire of anxiety tugging at his occipital lobe. The whine of an engine drifted faintly through the open door. Josh went outside, stood on his tiptoes and saw the vehicle approaching the shop at high speed.

He turned and bellowed, pushing customers to either side. "GET AWAY FROM THE DOORS! GO! GO!"

Some looked at him quizzically but most—raised on a steady diet of *Avengers* and the phrase "Move it people!"—bolted. Josh ran inside.

"GET BACK! GET AWAY FROM THE DOORS! HE'S GOING TO RAM THE STORE!"

He boosted Polly from her seat and hustled her straight back between the racks, through the back door and sat her down in the office.

"Stay here. Don't come out until I tell you."

"Why?" she said, but Josh had already locked the door and shut it behind him. He was halfway to the front when the vehicle leaped the sidewalk and smashed into the plate glass window, sending a tsunami of shards straight back. People screamed. The old black Chevelle stalled four feet in after knocking down a portion of the front wall.

Wally dialed 911.

The car was too old to have an airbag and the driver hadn't fastened his seatbelt. Even if he had, there was nothing to prevent him from smashing his head into the steering wheel. He lay back, dazed, with blood streaming from a gash in his forehead. Josh yanked open the door, dragged him out, placed him face down on the floor and jammed a knee in his back.

An ashen-faced young woman said, "He yelled '*Allahu Akbar*' just before he hit."

Josh heard sirens.

CHAPTER 8

Stoeckle

Officer Abe Nagal, whom Josh had met the previous year just after the Insane Assholes shootout, bent over the dazed perp. Nagal, who was built like a fireplug with red hair, cuffed the prostrate driver and removed his wallet.

"Abdul Al Sayeed," Nagal said as he went through the wallet. He pulled out a green card. "Originally from Libya. Here since 2007."

Another cop interviewed Polly in the office as more police arrived, followed by an ambulance. The crowd dispersed except for the spectators, watching from fifty feet away as the cops set up a perimeter. Detective Sobol, a cadaverous middle-aged man with a widow's peak, interviewed Josh in the shop. He regarded the *Muhammad* comic at arm's length.

"Not very smart," the detective said, "baiting jihadis like this."

"Why is it okay to bait Christians, call them racist, intolerant homophobes, sue them for not baking gay wedding cakes, but you can't say boo about Muhammad?"

Sobol looked up. "I hear you. I'm just saying she had to know this was coming."

Josh sighed. "My client's a little naive."

"We can't protect her. Cops are reactive. We show up after the crime has been committed, never mind what the mayor says."

"What's going to happen to Al Sayeed?"

"He'll be charged with attempted manslaughter. The DA will move to have him deported and the usual suspects will crawl forth from the sewers

34

to try and get him off. Look, regarding the young lady, I'm glad you're watching her. You get a lead on any more of these crackpots, you call me. I'm not unsympathetic here."

It was six by the time the cops let them go. Dorothy and Polly helped nail sheets of plywood over the gaping hole in the front wall, their hammer blows reverberating like distant cannon shots. Grateful he'd parked his car far back from the building, Josh loaded the box of comics into the trunk. Polly had sold an entire box—thirty issues.

"I am so glad I hired you!" Polly said. "You saved my life!"

"Maybe. That piece of shit he was driving died on the way in. What's the next event?"

"I'm signing at FemCon, the annual feminist science fiction convention. It's at the Edgewater Saturday and Sunday. I'll be there both days."

"Are you staying there?"

"They gave me a room. Why?"

"Just covering the angles." Josh was certain he could get a strong police presence at the hotel, which lay on the isthmus fronting Lake Mendota. Someone would phone in a bomb threat. It was inevitable.

"Where are your parents in all this?"

Big sigh. "We don't really get along. They wanted me to go into medicine, and when I switched my major to art my dad cut me off. He's a big linoleum wholesaler. Furst Floors? You heard of them?"

"Yes. Siblings? Mom?"

"My mother died of cancer when I was twelve."

"I'm sorry."

"I have an older sister who's an executive for First Wisconsin. We're not close."

"Have you spoken to your father since the threats began?"

"No. We don't really talk. I suppose I should tell him."

"Where does he live?"

"Whitefish Bay. 'White Folks Bay,' we used to call it in high school."

"Could you go there if you had to?"

"I suppose. But my dad's place isn't any better protected than Don's."

"Don't you think you ought to tell him what's going on?"

"I suppose."

They drove to Don's house, where Josh carried the box of comics inside, went out on the porch and phoned Detective Heinz Calloway of the Madison Police Department.

"Calloway," the cop said.

"You hear about the contretemps at Westfield?"

"Hell yeah. Can't say I'm surprised. I would advise your client to cancel her public appearances."

"Come on, Heinz. She's not going to do that. I just wanted to give you a heads-up. She'll be at FemCon next weekend, Saturday and Sunday. It's at the Edgewater."

"I suppose you'd like a police presence."

"That would be nice."

"I'll see what I can do but that's also Marathon Weekend, so we're going to have cops all over the city."

Josh saw that Agent Stoeckle had phoned. He called back.

"I'm staying at the Residence Inn. Meet me in the bar."

Josh drove to the West Side hotel, parked in the lot and went inside. The Lamplight Lounge was dim and cool. Stoeckle sat at the copper-topped bar nursing a martini, his laptop open next to him. Josh took a stool and ordered a beer.

They waited until his beer came and silently clinked.

"Was that you at the shopping mall?" Stoeckle said.

"Yeah. Polly was signing. Some jackass tried to drive his car right through the front window."

"Yeah," the agent said. "Abdul Al Sayeed. Sudden Jihad Syndrome. Read a paper about it in the *American Psychiatric Journal*. There are thousands like him all over the country."

"Do you have a list?"

Stoeckle drained his martini and signaled for another. "Of course we have a list. There are thousands of names. So does the FBI. Go take a look at their Ten Most Wanted. Six of those guys are jihadis. What do you want to know?"

"I'd like a list of anybody on your list who lives in the Upper Midwest—Wisconsin, Minnesota, Illinois, Michigan. And I'd like to know if there are any terrorist training camps up here."

"Sure, but those two Texas shooters, they drove from Arizona."

"I'm aware."

"Let me see," Stoeckle said, stroking his laptop. He moved through several screens before a map of the Upper Midwest appeared with tiny red icons hovering over Minnesota. He clicked the icon and an aerial photograph appeared of what appeared to be a summer camp, with a block of text.

"Ever hear of Jamaat ul-Fuqra? They are a paramilitary organization dedicated to jihad. They used to be mostly African American, but they've welcomed participation by Middle Eastern immigrants. This one here in Minnesota is the closest. Kanebec County. We've been keeping tabs on them, but they're not a high priority."

"Could you run a background check on Abdul Al Sayeed? And on anyone on the list within two hundred miles of Madison?"

Stoeckle made a note on his laptop. "ISIS also claims to have a Wisconsin presence, but we don't know what that is. I'll send you that list. And if you come across anything new you'll tell me, right?"

"You bet."

"How're things? I heard somewhere you were involved in Wes Magnum's resurrection; is that right?"

"Yeah. This broad hired me to prove she owned a song Wes wrote. Well she didn't really hire me, since she didn't pay me anything. Then we had these fakakta ninja crawling out of the woodwork."

Stoeckle's cell phone chimed. He looked at it.

"Gotta go. Keep me posted."

"Will do. Later."

CHAPTER 9

Deliberate Provocation

Fig thumped her tail against the leather sofa back as Josh entered shortly before eight.

Josh headed straight to the kitchen, Fig at his heels. "You've been very patient. You're a good doggie!"

He decanted an entire ten-ounce can of Purina moist "beef" into Fig's bowl. Her snout was in it before it hit the ground, and by the time Josh walked back through the living room, she'd finished. He went outside and got his mail. According to *Motorcyclist*, BMW was about to produce a W3 cruiser with three cylinders arranged in a V. Zero's new e-bike had a two hundred-mile range and a one hundred fifty-mile-per-hour top speed. BMW's new e-bike featured two small electric engines hanging off the side of the frame like its classic boxer. It was a brave new world. No matter what else went to shit, there were always new motorcycles. The Middle East would erupt in flames but the sedulous engineers at Honda, Kawasaki, KTM, Ducati and a dozen other manufacturers would burn the midnight oil creating new machines and expanding markets.

Josh saved most of his money in a bank but handled his own stock investments in Harley and Polaris. Harley was down; Polaris was up. He collapsed on the sofa. A second later Fig leaped up and curled into a ball next to him. Josh flicked on Headline News to learn that an earthquake in Nepal had killed six climbers on Mount Everest, and that the country was seriously considering banning all future climbs. Stock footage panned across some of the frozen bodies that had been up there for decades. No one could get them down because the air was so rarefied that helos couldn't fly and people were exhausted.

Josh flashed back to Garden in the Sky outside Nederland, Colorado, where Wynn Houtkooper had killed Space Cadet. It was hard enough at twelve thousand feet, never mind twenty-nine thousand. Video of bearded men with scimitars marching a line of prisoners in orange jumpsuits along a beach. Josh turned to the Speed Channel running a documentary about the Fish Carburetor, one of the greatest flimflams of modern times. Attaching the Fish Carburetor to your late-model Ford, Chevy or Dodge was guaranteed to increase mileage to at least one hundred miles per gallon.

Local news didn't come on until ten, so he'd have to wait to see the damages. His phone rang. He'd been expecting Katy Varner's call all afternoon.

"Hello, Katy."

"Hello, Josh. Could you give me a statement regarding this afternoon's mayhem?"

"Are you recording?"

"Yes."

"I was providing security for Polly Furst, who writes the *Muhammad* comic. This dude came in, cursed her, tore up her comic and spit on her. We let him go. Five minutes later he tried to drive his piece-of-shit Chevelle through the store and knocked himself out. Jihadis zero, Polly one. He still owes her for the comic."

"You're referring to the alleged perpetrator, Abdul Al Sayeed?"

"That's right."

"Thank you. Okay, we're off the record. I'm not recording. How about we get together so you can fill me in on the background? I'd like to buy you a drink."

"Katy, there is no background. We have enough publicity, don't you think?"

"Come on. What have you got to lose? I've got an idea I'd like to run past you."

"Next week. I'm beat."

"How about Monday at six? Meet me at the Madison Club."

"I didn't know they let women into the Madison Club."

"The times they are a-changin'. See you then."

Josh sat in the dim room with Fig's snout in his lap. Katy wanted to get in his pants. She was very attractive, but he had no illusions it would involve anything long-term. Katy was a young lady on the make. She'd made a splash on national TV with her exclusive about the resurrection of rock legend Wes Magnum.

But after a month of Fig Newton—the woman, not the dog—he'd reassessed what he wanted in a woman. It was no longer a simple matter of getting laid. Fig had shown him what a real relationship could be, what it was like to have someone you not only loved, but really liked, in your life. Maybe if she hadn't died, they might have married. Had kids. Maybe they'd sour on each other and start blaming each other for their disappointments. Josh didn't think that would have happened, but it had happened to him before, before he went to prison.

Prison had made him re-evaluate his life. He wouldn't have made it without Pastor Frank Dorgan. Dorgan didn't push Christ; Josh willingly accepted Christ into his heart and soul. He prayed often and silently. He didn't speak much about his faith.

The ten o'clock news led with the mall attack, showing footage of the smashed shop and interviews with locals. Thankfully, there was no mention of Josh, but they did interview Polly, referring to her as a local artist. The reporter, a man with hair like a sculpted platinum eighteenth-century wig, said, "The assailant's motives remain unclear."

The anchor, a middle-aged Latina with luxurious black hair, asked the platinum-wigged correspondent, "I understand she's published a comic called *Muhammad*, David. Do you think this was a deliberate provocation?"

"Definitely," David said.

Josh switched it off and dragged his weary ass into his bedroom, with Fig running ahead and leaping on the bed. Josh got down on his knees to pray. He said the Lord's Prayer softly while Fig licked his face, and then he looked under the bed. It looked as if the futon stashed there had exploded. Tufts of white everywhere interspersed with shredded frozen-food packaging, half a label from Swanson's Frozen Chicken Pot Pie, a strip from a Godfather's Pizza box, several mismatched socks.

He looked Fig in the eye. "Did you have anything to do with this?"

Fig whined softly, quizzically.

"I didn't think so." Josh crawled into bed, turned off the lamp and pulled up the covers, but he was a long time falling asleep. His mind raced like a wild mouse. It was always like this when he was on a case. He was just one man. He didn't know if he was up to the job. There were wackos all over the country just looking to take offense. Any slur, real or imagined, on the Prophet was a license to kill.

Josh could not legally carry a gun because of his past convictions. But he would if he had to.

CHAPTER 10

The Edgewater

On Sunday Josh and Fig did five miles, showered, shaved and had a breakfast of Jimmy Dean Frozen Breakfast Sandwiches. One for Josh, one for Fig. Stoeckle had forwarded the files on twenty-two jihadis in the Upper Midwest, including two in Madison. One of them was Polly's neighbor, Mustapha Abed.

On his Facebook page, Abed described himself as "a loyal soldier of Islam" whose interests included soccer, MMA and *The Jon Stewart Show*. He was from Lebanon and worked as a steamfitter for Alliant Energy. Josh downloaded and printed Abed's FB photo, showing an angry-looking man with curly brown hair. Josh checked police records but thus far Abed was clean. He'd posted several photos, taken on different occasions, of himself at the High Noon Saloon with a beer in his hand.

Photo in hand, Josh headed downtown at noon, rolling into The Edgewater's garage and parking in a yellow triangle. He entered the hotel through the front door, thanked the doorman and went up to the events calendar. FemCon was a two-day event, Saturday and Sunday, beginning June 10 in the Grand Ballroom. At this hour nothing was happening, and no one stopped Josh from walking down the hall and entering the Grand Ballroom. A curving wall with floor-to-ceiling windows looked out on the bright blue Lake Mendota, with Governor's Island in the distance.

Outside was a balcony, which someone might conceivably use as an entry point. Josh opened a sliding door and stepped into the sunlight.

It was a beautiful day in the mid-seventies with a breeze wafting in off the lake. Already there were dozens of white sails spreading out from the Hoofer's pier at the Wisconsin Union. Josh walked all around the big room, peeked behind the bar and checked out the restrooms. One good thing—there was nowhere a sniper could stand, since the hotel faced the lake.

An old man with a few tufts of white hair wafting over his pink scalp came up to him. The name tag on his blue blazer said JOHN PERKINS. "Can I help you, sir?"

"Just getting the lay of the land. I'll be at the FemCon event next week. Do you get many people via the lake?"

"Ah, on a warm summer night, sir, there can be fifty boats docked or tethered out there."

"Is there any other way to gain access to your lakeside?"

"Just through the hotel, sir. We used to have a little outdoor grill down there, but it got torn up two remodels ago."

"How long have you been here, Mr. Perkins?"

"Thirty years. Worked my way up from bellhop. I'm the general manager."

Josh shook hands. "Josh Pratt. I'm providing security for Polly Furst. She's the young lady who drew the *Muhammad* comic."

"We all know who she is, Mr. Pratt. A feminist science fiction convention. Well, well. That's something new. Y'know, two remodels ago, there used to be a room right beneath us. The Brigadoon Room. It had a nautical theme with aquariums and portholes, and it was the most perfect little bar because nobody knew about it, you see. Not to say it wasn't profitable. The place was jammed on weekends. You know what's there now? The workout room, with four ellipticals, four treadmills, a sauna and free weights."

"Progress I guess," Josh said.

"Bush, Carter, and Reagan have all stayed here. Not Nixon though. He stayed at the Park when he came to town. I met Paul McCartney here, and Tom Jones, Elvis and Count Basie. You'll find their photographs in the boathouse."

"I'd like to speak to your security manager."

"The front desk will direct you. We'll see you next week."

Josh went to the front desk, where a young woman with a honey-colored ponytail, wearing a blue blazer with THE EDGEWATER in gold script over the breast pocket, twinkled, "How can I help you?"

"May I see your security manager?"

"Is there a problem?"

"No, ma'am. It's about FemCon."

"I'm excited! Wait one minute."

She picked up the phone. A minute later a trim, shaved-skulled black man who could have been anywhere from thirty to fifty came out of a suite of offices wearing creased gray slacks and a blue blazer with a blue-and-gold tie over a sky blue shirt.

"I'm Andre Dalton," he said, extending his hand.

They shook. "Josh Pratt. I provide security for Polly Furst, the young woman who made the *Muhammad* comic."

"Come with me, Mr. Pratt."

Josh followed Dalton back through the suite of offices to a cubicle looking out on the front garden. Dalton sat behind an oak desk while Josh took the fabric sofa with buttressed legs. It looked like a Taliesin design.

On a wall of shelves was a framed photo of Dalton with a stunning black woman and two kids, a photo of Dalton with a bunch of GIs in the sand, some framed certificates and high school and college wrestling trophies.

Dalton slid a business card across the desk. "I just found out about Ms. Furst. She presents a security challenge."

Josh picked up the card and slid one of his. "Yes sir. I wanted to give you a head's-up on the situation."

"I appreciate that, Mr. Pratt. Tell you the truth, I would just as soon she didn't come. The general manager feels the same way. And the chief of police. And the mayor."

"Well she's gonna come. Things didn't work out so well for that camel jockey yesterday, so I kinda doubt anything's going to happen at FemCon, but we can't assume that. Will you have extra security?"

"We will, plus at least one uniformed police officer. And the good Lord knows who else. The organizers tell us we can expect five thousand people. Several groups have already filed for demonstration permits, not that they're going to let a little thing like that stop them. This is Madison.

The Religion Is Evil Foundation. Students for Justice in Palestine. You can't gas them; you can't shoot them."

"Play Lynyrd Skynyrd."

Dalton smiled. "Please don't bring a firearm."

"I won't. You were in the military?"

"Two tours in Afghanistan."

"How'd you end up in Madison?" Josh said.

Dalton turned a frame around his desk so Josh could see the black-and-white photo of his wife. She reminded Josh of Lena Horne.

"Benita was going to grad school here. We met online. Christian singles."

Josh stood. "Thank you for your time, sir. I will keep you appraised."

CHAPTER 11

Katy

On Sunday afternoon Josh dropped by Don's place. Don came out to admire Josh's Road King.

"Noice! What did you do to her?"

Josh recited by rote: "Engine: 88 with oil cooler. Changed the cams to S&S gear drives with .510 lift. Took out the fuel injection and replaced it with an S&S Super E, Yost Power Tube, S&S manifold and Pingle high-flow petcock. S&S teardrop air cleaner cover with a K&N filter. Screamin' Eagle Hi-Performance ignition unit with a 6200-rpm rev limiter. Accell Super Coil, FireWire plug wires and spiral wound metal core wires. Accell platinum-tip plugs. Five-speed tranny with Barnett Kevlar clutch, self-adjusting hydraulic chain tensioner. Screamin' Eagle dualies. Progressive springs in front with higher viscosity, Progressives in back. Changed the rear swing-arm bushings to STA BO nylon high density. SBS semi-metallic disc brake pads, and the brake lines are stainless steel braids. Went to tubeless wheels."

They went into Don's open two-car garage, which contained four bikes, including the custom Honda 750. Don swung a leg over and sat, his ass twenty-five inches off the concrete.

"This is my latest. Picked the engine up at an estate auction, added the springer front end."

"Sweet," Josh said. "I once rode a hardtail to Sturgis and back. Never again."

"I hear ya," Don said. "Gonna sell it."

He pointed to Fig. "What's with that ear?"

"She came that way. Where's Polly?"

"She's inside working on commissions."

"Do you have any firearms?" Josh said.

"This house is armed, if that's what you're asking."

"Maybe you could teach Polly to shoot."

Don laughed. "I'll try."

Inside, Polly was bent over her drawing board, which she'd set up in a corner of the living room with the gooseneck lamp. She wore cat's eye glasses. Josh looked over her shoulder as she sketched with a blue pencil.

"How's it going?"

"My dad called. He's totally freaked out. Says he'll pay your bill but can't understand what I'm doing."

"That's great. You get any threats via Facebook, make a note of who they are, notify the FB administrators and tell me."

"Okay."

"What about your phone?"

"Nobody knows my number but my friends. Believe me, I'll let you know."

Josh went home and worked with Fig, putting a slice of cheese inside a hollow ball and throwing it. After Fig brought the ball back a dozen times, and Josh rewarded her with treats, he held the ball down.

"Find!"

Fig went around the yard like a mine detector, snout stopping behind a juniper bush. She sat back and barked. Josh went over, dug up the paper-wrapped cheese and gave it to her.

"Good dog."

Monday was filled with trepidation and excitement. On the one hand he didn't want Katy Varner poking into his life. On the other hand, he'd be happy to fuck her. He decided to play it by ear, so to speak, and hear what she had to say before making a decision. He rode downtown, leaving his bike in Fleiss's parking lot two blocks down from the tony Madison Club, which occupied a prime spot on East Wilson adjacent to the Monona Center. The three-story, redbrick Federalist building showed its age with a stone engraving: 1905. Until recently it had been the bastion of old white men—leaders of industry, academics, sports figures—but like every other institution devoted to staying behind the times, the Madison Club had been under relentless media attack for exclusivity and had actively sought to recruit women and minorities.

Josh wore khakis and a striped gray-and-white crew-neck pullover. The prim young beauty behind the reception desk greeted him with a dazzling smile. "Good evening! How can I help you?"

"I'm meeting Katy Varner."

"Go right in, Mr. Pratt. She's expecting you."

Katy was waiting at a table in a corner of the main dining room, with expansive windows looking out on Lake Monona. She rose and waved as Josh entered the big room. She was wearing a low-cut strapless plum-colored evening dress that clung to her rounded body.

She stuck out her hand. "Thanks for coming, Josh. Would you like something to drink?"

"I'm on my bike, so I can't get snockered. But I could have a beer."

A waiter in a white apron took Josh's order, nodded toward Katy's gin and tonic.

"I'll have another," she said.

They looked out on the lake, where dozens of triangular white sails flitted like water bugs.

"Beautiful evening," Katy said.

"Yes it is."

"You just can't stay out of trouble, can you?"

"Trouble is my business."

Katy's laugh sounded like silver coins falling into his hand.

"So it is. *Madison Magazine* has asked me to write a feature about Polly."

"You'd have to talk to Polly about that."

"I was hoping you could put me in touch."

"I'll give you her phone number."

Katy rested two warm fingers on Josh's wrist. "I'd like to interview both of you."

"Come on, Katy. I said what I had to say."

The waiter brought their drinks and took Katy's empty. "Would you like to order something off the menu?"

Katy looked at Josh. "How about it? My treat. The buffalo burgers are to die for."

"Give us a few minutes," Josh said, picking up his menu. He waited until the waiter left. "What's your idea?"

"I was hoping to get a few drinks in you first."

"You may not need them."

She took his wrist again. "I already have a publisher committed to doing a book about you. All I need is your cooperation and he'll issue a contract."

Seeing the horror creep across Josh's face, she quickly added, "Hear me out please. I know how much you hate publicity, but this would be a huge thing for you! I'm talking consulting jobs, paid interviews, endorsements. Movies."

Josh shook his head, his mouth a grim line.

"You'd be famous."

Josh slugged beer. "No thanks."

"It would be a huge step for your career."

"My career is fine, thanks."

"It would be a huge step for my career."

"I've done enough for your career."

"Think about it. It would open you up for the big time. Who knows where it could lead?"

Saved by the waiter.

"Have you come to a decision?"

"I'll have the grilled coho salmon with the rice pilaf," Katy said.

"And you, sir?"

Josh was starving, but he'd be damned if he'd let Katy buy him a meal and grill him throughout dinner. Ambition burned behind her eyes.

"I think I'm gonna pass."

Katy looked stricken.

"You're sure?" the waiter said. "Perhaps one of the appetizers."

"No thanks. I just have no appetite."

"Delay my order a minute, will you?" Katy said.

The waiter read her body language and withdrew. Katy laid a hand on Josh's thigh. "How about if we just go back to my place and I'll fix you something? I only live a block away at the Federal."

Josh felt the heat rising in his groin, but he'd learned not to start anything he couldn't finish, and he wasn't sure he could finish this.

"Katy, if I thought you'd give up on the book idea and leave me out of your stories, I'd fuck you in a New York minute. But you can't so I won't. Thank you for the drink."

He got up and left.

CHAPTER 12

Boat

On Tuesday afternoon Josh sat on his front stoop with Fig on a blanket at his feet, reading Conn Iggulden's book about Genghis Kahn. Dave Lowry arrived home in his Audi SUV and turned up his gently curving blacktop toward his three-car garage. Josh closed the book, set it on his chair and headed across the street with Fig at his heels. Dave saw him coming and waited beside his car.

"What's up, Josh?"

"Dave, could I borrow your boat this weekend?"

Dave looked surprised. The third garage was for his Chris-Craft runabout with a one hundred ten-horsepower Mercury engine that he put in Lake Mendota to entertain prospects. Dave was a fundraiser for the University of Wisconsin.

"Well sure, I guess. Do you have a trailer hitch?"

"I'll have one Friday. I just need it Saturday or Sunday. Don't worry about gas or any of that stuff. I'll top everything off."

"You ever operate a boat like that?"

"Sure, but any tips would be welcome."

"Well okay. Give me a minute to tell Louise I'm home and I'll be right out."

"Thanks, Dave."

Lowry was Josh's most steadfast neighborhood friend, the only dissident regarding Phil Bass's plan to buy Josh out and build a clubhouse on his property. One of Josh's first jobs had been rescuing the Lowrys' two schnauzers from a dog-fighting ring. Josh walked back to Dave's garage and looked at the sleek red-and-white boat as Fig did a perimeter check and then stepped outside and watered the Lowrys' lilies.

A minute later Lowry emerged sans jacket and tie. "Louise says you should stay for dinner."

"Aw, you guys keep having me over for dinner."

"Louise wants to fix you up with our friends' daughter Dianne."

"Thanks for the head's-up."

Lowry showed Josh how to turn on the fuel, run the pump so the fuel wouldn't explode and handed him the key. They went inside where George and Gracie, the Lowrys' schnauzers, immediately play-attacked Fig, who stuck her butt in the air, wagged her tail and chased them.

"You might as well just use the Jeep. It's already hooked up. The key's in the ignition."

"Thanks, Dave. Really appreciate it."

They sat on the back patio listening to the burble of the fountain while Louise grilled pork chops and the dogs chased each other. Lowry got a vodka gimlet for himself and a beer for Josh.

"Tell us about your latest adventure."

"You mean Westfield?" Josh said.

"I have to say, and I'm not meaning to be confrontational here, that the young lady's decision to produce a Muhammad comic wasn't very wise."

"Why? Because terrorists?"

"Well, yeah."

Josh shrugged. "It's a free country."

"Well now you have your work really cut out for you, because other nut-balls across the nation hear about what happened and they think it's a good idea to kill your client."

"I know."

"How do you fight something like that?"

"Dear," Louise said, spatula in hand, "don't start arguing with Josh."

"I'm not. I'm just trying to understand what's going on. How do you fight something like that?"

"Damned if I know," Josh said. "You try to anticipate—alert the authorities to potential threats. Problem is, so many people are crying wolf that one hundred twenty-four national security agencies can't deal with it all. And the police, they're not really trained to handle this sort of thing."

Lowry dug out his smartphone and poked. "Jesus. You're right. There are one hundred twenty-four national security agencies." He held up the phone. "You have one of these?"

"Yeah. Got to, don't I? The internet is now your modern investigator's primary tool. We can access arrest records, root around in private e-mails, dig up your past."

"You know how to do that?"

Josh smiled ruefully. "Sorta. I got a guy does the heavy lifting. When I went in the joint, computers were a thing but they weren't everything. I come out, everybody's texting and tweeting and selling shit online. You don't have a computer, you may as well not speak English. And all these guys say they don't need a computer, you know what they're really saying? They don't know how to type. Thank God I took a typing class in prison."

Louise returned from the kitchen and plopped chops and salad in front of the boys and sat at the round wood table. Lowry raised his glass.

"Happy belated Mother's Day, my love."

Josh raised his too.

Louise looked at him. "Do you miss your mother, Josh?"

"No. I never knew her. I don't even know her name. Whenever I asked my old man about her, he had a different story. One-night stand. Heroin addict. Christ knows why he didn't just give me up to an adoption agency. I think way down deep inside, fatherhood must have touched him. Or the idea of fatherhood. He wasn't very good at it."

"Do you forgive him?"

"Sure, what the hell. It's the Christian thing to do."

"Are you in contact with him?" Louise said.

"Nope. Don't know if he's alive."

"Have you ever looked at your father's arrest record?" Lowry said.

"Nope. No interest."

George, Gracie and Fig made out like bandits on leftovers. Lowry brought out the Scotch.

"Hey guys," Josh said. "I have to go to San Diego in a week for five days. Would you look after Fig?"

"Of course," Louise said. "We love Fig."

"What's going on?" Lowry said.

"San Diego Comic Convention. I'm accompanying my client."

"Oh!" Louise said. "We see it on the news! How exciting!"

"I'm excited," Josh said.

Josh went home thinking about his dead girlfriend and masturbated, wondering if he should have taken Katy up on her offer. He lay in bed with Fig, watching a boxing match. His phone rang.

"What's up, Polly?" he answered.

"Katy Varner's interviewing me tomorrow."

"Great."

"Do you know who Abdul Alhazred is?"

"Nope. Should I?" Josh said.

"That's not his real name of course. He's an apostate Bosnian Muslim who's made a career of exposing radical Islam, an artist and pamphleteer. The dude is fearless. He just contacted me via FB and offered to share a table with me at C2E2."

"Whazzat?"

"It's the biggest comic convention in the Midwest, at the McCormick Center in Chicago. I've had a table reserved since last year."

"Yeah? So?"

"This is huge! He's been on Fox, MSNBC, writes for *FrontPage Magazine*. If I sit with him it could be the start of a movement! Not that many people in the comic community are willing to support me."

"Do they support him?"

"Hell no! But the way I figure, both of us together is news, and it can't hurt to get our message out."

"What's the message?"

"That a pluralistic Western society cannot coexist with radical Islam."

"So you think this is a good idea?"

"Hells yeah!"

"Okay," Josh said. "I'll check him out and talk to you tomorrow. Hey, did you know it was Mother's Day?"

"That was last month, Josh." Beat. "I'll talk to you tomorrow, Josh."

CHAPTER 13

WMAD

Katy wanted to interview Polly at Don's house but Josh nixed that. They arrived at the WMAD studios on the Beltline at three o'clock Wednesday afternoon. Polly wore a black leather vest over a white shirt and tan trousers. While Josh waited with Polly in the green room a tech came in, fastened a small wireless microphone to her shirt and handed her a clipboard and a pen.

"Please sign that release. It states that you agree to appear on WMAD and that the resulting segment is the property of WMAD."

Polly signed and handed it back.

"You're on shortly. Just be yourself."

They had the room to themselves along with a snack and vegetable spread in circular plastic trays that still had the Woodman's sticker. Josh helped himself to celery, crackers and a pecan-encrusted cheddar cheese ball.

Katy poured herself a plastic cup of water and sat in an institutional chair with plaid upholstery, eyes on the big flat-screen TV, which showed a line of cops in riot gear clashing with a wild mob.

"Police clashed with demonstrators again today at the G3 summit in Brussels. Thousands of self-described anarchists have descended on the Belgian capital to voice their displeasure with what they see as international banking practices. Our correspondent Jean Petier caught up with some of them outside the Hall of Justice."

The camera focused on a demonstrator, a dark-haired young man wearing a bandanna over his mouth, dressed in distressed black leather and surrounded by jumping, jockeying, shouting demonstrators.

"Down with banks! Down with America! Down with the Jews!" they chanted.

Jean Petier, a middle-aged man in a suit, asked the leather-clad demonstrator, "Sir, what exactly are you protesting?"

The young man pulled down his bandanna. "We are here to protest a cabal of rich and powerful bankers manipulating currency for short-term profits at the expense of the common man."

Faint pops could be heard. Petier looked to his right and hurriedly addressed the camera. "It looks like they're firing tear gas. We're going to have to move." He yanked a handkerchief from his jacket and began coughing, moving with the herd.

The anchor was new. It used to be Katy, but since the Wes Magnum exclusive she had moved up to special events producer. The new anchor was a café-au-lait young woman with a cap of black hair and square rimless glasses. "In local news, the City Streets Commission has released a list of road-repair projects that will begin on the fifteenth of this month and continue on into August."

"The happiest time of year," Josh said.

Katy entered in full diva mode, glad-handing and kissing Josh on the cheek. "Thank you so much for doing this! If it goes well, we'll lead off the local news with it. See you in a few minutes. Josh, you'll have to watch from in here."

"That's fine."

Katy breezed out.

"She likes you," Polly observed.

"Tell me about it."

A minute later the tech returned and used a remote to switch from the broadcast to a live feed from the studio. "Polly, you can go in now."

Josh settled back on the sofa to watch.

"Local artist Polly Furst caused a sensation recently with the release of her *Muhammad* comic book. Many Muslims, indeed many Americans, consider her comic a needless provocation against adherents of one of the world's great religions. Many are calling it a hate crime. Polly, how do you respond to this?"

Polly smiled and faced the camera. "Well this is Madison, so people expect to be offended. But seriously, it's not my intention to offend. It's my intention to entertain. If you don't like it, don't read it! It's satire, folks! Like Bugs Bunny."

In a mock baritone Polly sang, "I'm going to kill the...kill the wabbit..."

The camera cut to Katy. "Last Saturday a man drove his car into the front of Westfield Comics while you were signing, sending three people to the hospital. Yes, we have the right to free speech, but weren't you, in effect, crying fire in a crowded theater?"

"This is America," Polly said. "We don't censor ourselves for fear of what some nut will do! By the way, this is what my comic looks like."

Polly whipped *Muhammad* from her vest and held it to the camera.

"Cut!" Katy yelled, standing and tearing off her mic. She stormed off camera, her mouth turned down.

Josh barked. Polly re-entered the green room laughing and flushed.

"Wow! I guess I won't make the evening news!"

Josh held a finger up and phoned Kofsky.

"What?" Kofsky said.

Josh told him what had happened. "Can you tap into their databank and retrieve that video before it's deleted?"

"I'm trying to run a business here."

"I'm sorry, man. I wouldn't ask you if it wasn't important."

"I got fifteen minutes until my next meeting. I'll give it a shot but if I come up *bupkis*, you're on your own."

"Thanks, Aaron. Appreciate it."

The producer, a thin, balding NPR type with glasses, came in. "Katy wants to thank you for coming in and to let you know she'll be in touch."

"I'll bet," Polly said.

Josh found himself liking her more and more.

Polly whooped and stuck her arm out the window as they drove away like a couple of successful bank robbers. "All right! Rock and roll! Let's get a drink! I feel like celebrating!"

"Why? You just screwed yourself out of a news segment."

She rounded on him. "Oh no I didn't! I heard you talking to your friend the net guy. You get that tape. I know you can."

"So what if I could? It belongs to the station. You show that and they'll sue you."

"You know what? I don't care. What are they going to get? My Beetle? My savings account? This is war, buddy!"

"I thought you were just doing it because you could."

"I was. But now I'm doing it because I must! Come on. Take me to the Laurel. I'll treat."

"What the hell," Josh said.

CHAPTER 14

At the Laurel

They took a table outside across the street from a coffeehouse and an art center and watched the parade of humanity while drinking from glass steins. Moms with strollers, board punks, bikers in black and yellow spandex, the late-lunch crowd—they walked, rolled and glided by while hidden speakers softly played Randy Newman's "Birmingham."

"Why'd you whip it out, Polly?" Josh said.

"For the same reason I draw Muhammad."

"A-huh."

The waitress came and they ordered cheeseburgers, and Josh had another glass of beer.

"I've got an interview with Kira Davis tomorrow."

"Who dat?"

"She's a conservative blogger. Don't worry. It's over the phone. Or Skype, to be precise."

A lanky blond teenage girl glided by on a longboard, did an abrupt flippy and came back, board in hand. "Are you that cartoonist lady?" she said.

"That's me," Polly said.

The girl grinned goofily. "Wow! I saw you on the news the other day! All I can say is right on!"

"Thank you very much! What's your name?"

"Ashley. Where can I get your comic?"

"Westfield has it."

"If I get a copy will you sign it?"

"Sure."

"Great!" she said. "I'm going right now! I'll be back in fifteen minutes."
She zoomed away. Josh looked at Polly.

"Think she's old enough to drive?"

He gazed up the street. If Ashley recognized Polly, so could somebody
else. He looked back at Polly. Wraparound shades and a ball cap to hide
that red furze would help. A tan wouldn't kill her either. Or maybe it
would.

The waitress brought their burgers and for a while there was no talking.
Josh watched the dandelion-thin Polly wolf hers down and wondered if
she ate like that all the time. Josh was halfway through his second beer
when a tricked-out Honda roared up and squeaked to a halt at the curb
ten feet away, back end covered with bumper stickers like a nest of Band-
Aids: BLACK FLAG. DEAD KENNEDYS. RAGE AGAINST THE MACHINE.
Ashley piled out with another girl and two boys, each clutching a copy of
Muhammad. Both boys had sleeve tats. One had a neck tat, a silver ring
the size of a key holder through his nose and quarter-sized ear inserts.

"Hi!" Ashley sang. "These are my friends Marsha, Lars and Terry. I
told you I'd be back!"

"I think your comic is heinous," said Lars, the boy with the ear inserts.
"And I loved your run on Wonder Woman."

"Thank you!" Polly said, signing the comics with a gold-tipped marker.

"Except you could have made her boobs bigger."

Ashley swatted him on the shoulder. "Lars!"

"I wish you'd draw Dr. Strange," Terry said.

"I would love to draw Dr. Strange! Know anybody at Marvel?"

"What did you think of *Avengers: Age of Ultron*?" Marsha said. She
was a chunky girl with pink hair and a butterfly tat on her bicep.

"Haven't seen it yet."

"Why won't they make a Black Widow action figure?" Lars said. "The
People demand a Black Widow action figure!"

"I think they're afraid of what you'd do with it," Polly said.

At the edge of his radar Josh picked up a disturbance. The woman at
the next table was glaring at them. She was taut, tight, fortyish, in runner's
shorts and shoes, sipping a double latte ordered off the new menu. The

old menu featured all-you-can-eat Friday-night fish boil. The new menu featured wild Pacific coho salmon.

While Polly talked shop the woman became irate, growing subtly in stature like a long-dormant volcano filling with gas. Josh looked around for the waitress, anxious to be gone.

Too late. The woman leaned over, tapped Polly on the shoulder. "I think it's terrible what you're doing! Insulting an entire religion like that. It's offensive, it's deliberate and it's not the American way!"

Josh stood, put a hand on Polly's shoulder. "Let's go."

Polly turned to confront her accuser knee to knee. "Listen. If you think—"

Josh put his hands beneath Polly's elbows and lifted her out of the chair, gripping her biceps and propelling her through the door into the bar, which they had to pass through to get outside. He dropped a twenty on the counter and marched Polly out the front door into the sun.

"Let go!" Polly demanded.

They exited and turned west, where Josh had parked. He glanced back once. The woman was arguing intensely with the four kids.

Polly shook herself loose and rounded on him, red-faced. "Don't you manhandle me like I'm a child! That woman was no threat to me!"

Josh held his hands up, placating. "Okay. I'm sorry I grabbed you like that. But if you want me to run interference for you, you're gonna have to trust me. I'm the expert on security. You know how to draw comics."

Polly pouted but the fire had gone out. "Stupid bitch! I'll bet she equates Israel with Nazi Germany."

"We'll never know."

"Okay. I was gonna treat."

Josh held out his hand. "Gimme twenty bucks."

Polly rummaged in her backpack, pulled out her wallet and dropped a twenty in Josh's outstretched hand. Josh drove to Don's house, preceded Polly up the stairs and opened the front door.

"Does he always leave this door unlocked?"

"Yes."

"Not anymore. You need to keep it locked when nobody's home, and you need to lock it at night when you go to bed."

"Don won't like that."

"Tough titty!"

Polly tossed her backpack down on the sofa and picked up the remote. "The five o'clock news is on."

"There's no point looking for your segment, and now Katy Varner hates your guts."

"No biggie. There are plenty of other news organizations."

Josh trotted upstairs and checked the bedrooms. He went through the kitchen down into the basement. When he came upstairs Polly was sitting hunched over her drawing table, pencil in hand.

"What are you drawing?"

"It's a short story about a sixties girl who gets a huge beehive bouffant and refuses to let anyone touch it for a week because it took so long and cost so much, and then she wakes up screaming in the middle of the night from thousands of spider bites. They've been breeding in her hair!"

"Noice. When does Don get home?"

"He should be home any minute but honestly, Josh, you can go. I'm fine here. It's not like armies of crazed militia are tracking me night and day."

"It's not like they're not."

The rumble of a V-twin made the windows rattle. Minutes later Don bounced up the back stairs and entered through the kitchen, grabbing two beers on his way through to the living room.

"Whassup, rockers?" he said, handing a beer to Josh.

Josh waved his hand. "I've had enough."

Polly stuck out her mitt. "Gimme."

Don gave her the beer. "How'd the interview go?"

"It was great until she whipped out a copy of her comic," Josh said. "They threw us out."

Don laughed.

Josh went out on the porch, motioning Don to follow him. "I want to ax you something about your bike." They went into the garage, where Don had left his V-Rod.

"Do you keep a loaded firearm close at hand?"

"Yeah. Why?"

"You know why."

"Yeah, but I try not to let paranoia spill over, know what I mean?"

"The times they are a-changin', Don."

"I hear ya. Let's go for a ride sometime."

"You bet."

"Hey, I'm gonna make a mess of spaghetti. Want to stay?"

"Some other time. I've got a hungry dog at home."

CHAPTER 15

The Sin of Pride

Josh sat in his car at the Alhambra with a telephoto lens focused on the front door. It was seven thirty Thursday morning. He photographed everyone leaving. There were a couple of Middle Eastern dudes he photographed several times. He'd positioned himself in such a way that he could read the license plates of anyone entering or exiting. He wrote them down in his notebook next to a capsule description: "white Civic, horsey blond woman," "blue Pontiac,

acne kid."

Out came a guy who screamed *wrong*. Josh had spent much time observing deviant behavior and knew the signs. The guy was black, clean head with a goatee, wearing camo trou and a pea jacket. He emerged on the stoop, jerked to a halt, looked back the way he'd come, turned around and walked to an ancient multi-hued Corolla, stopping every now and then to look around some more. Josh buried his face in the latest *Motorcyclist* but the guy clocked him. Josh got one clear shot before the dude started looking around.

Paranoid schizophrenic maybe.

Josh sat until nine, returned home, printed his photos and tacked them to the big bulletin board in his office, which he'd turned into a war room. He sought to match the photos with the names on the mailboxes.

He sent his picture of the jerky dude to Kofsky.

"See if you can match this mug with whatever they got in the National Crime clearinghouse database."

In addition to the Alhambra residents, he'd posted pictures of the FBI's Ten Most Wanted Terrorists, including two who lived in the Upper Midwest. According to the FBI:

Ahmad Achmed Rasin was indicted after taking multiple trips to Pakistan and Yemen, where he allegedly attempted to obtain military training for the purpose of killing American soldiers overseas. On November 5, 2014, a federal arrest warrant was issued for Achmed Rasin in the United States District Court, District of Illinois, after he was charged with conspiracy to provide material support to terrorists; providing and attempting to provide material support to terrorists; conspiracy to kill in a foreign country; conspiracy; and false statements.

Achmed Rasin grew up near Chicago, and also has ties to the Detroit, Michigan, area. Achmed Rasin is thought to be at large somewhere in the Upper Midwest. He is to be considered armed and extremely dangerous.

Husayn Muhammad Al-Akkaba was indicted for his alleged role in the August 11, 1992, bombing of Pan Am Flight 830, while it was en route from Japan to Hawaii. He is alleged to have prepared the bomb that was placed under a seat on Flight 830, resulting in the death of a 16-year-old passenger and injuring 16 other passengers.

Al-Akkaba has thin lips, a cleft chin, and a wide mouth. He wears a mustache, glasses, and dresses very well. Sudan Al-Umari is a Sunni Muslim and doesn't drink or gamble, but smokes Cuban cigars. He has a high school education and is a mechanic and an explosives expert. Al-Umari formed the 15 May Organization in 1979. Its mission was to promote the Palestinian cause through violence toward supporters of Israel. Al-Umari has a Lebanese passport.

His last known address was 1867 Borquardt Street, Midlothian, IL.

Meanwhile, Stoeckle had come through and provided Josh with a list of one hundred twenty-two men and women on the terrorist watch list in the Upper Midwest. Three lived in Dane County, four in Milwaukee. Two of the Milwaukee symps were black Muslims. None lived at the Alhambra.

Josh phoned Detective Calloway, in charge of Madison's Gang Unit.

"What?" the detective answered.

"You know I'm guarding this comic book chick."

"Oh yes. The whole city knows."

"Could you run some license plates for me?"

"No I can't. The chief just sent out a memo. Does not want us interfacing with private investigators."

"Well, fuck."

"Sorry, broheem. Should your interests coincide with an ongoing investigation, that's another story."

"Well, don't you fear a terrorist attack here? I mean, Madison's about as ungodly as it gets."

"I say thee nay, friend Pratt. The DA says this Al Sayeed bird is a lone gunman, case closed."

Kofsky called while Josh was on the phone. Josh signed off with Calloway and called him back.

"I need to see you ASAP," Kofsky said.

"What did you find?"

"I got shit but this isn't about your case. I need your help. Can you come over?"

"Meet me at the Golden Arches at one."

The Golden Arches was a classic McDonald's in Middleton with two huge gold arches. When Josh arrived on his Road King, Kofsky got out of his Tesla. They went inside and got coffee, took it outside and sat at one of the round metal tables.

"I'm being blackmailed."

"What?" Josh said.

Kofsky pulled out his latest-model Droid, dialed up and turned it around. One glance and Josh looked away. Kiddie porn. Pre-pubescent Southeast Asian boys and girls posing nude, their faces uniformly glum. It was the same garbage Josh had dug up in Kofsky's office, and which Josh used to keep Kofsky in line.

The accompanying message on the Droid said, "We will contact you shortly to arrange payment. Do not involve the police. Such would not be appropriate."

There was room for only one blackmailer in Kofsky's life.

"Odd locution. Can you trace it?"

"I tried. This guy's clever. I backtracked through a half dozen servers before I gave up. He's using comsats and scramblers."

Kofsky looked off. A moment later: "He's better than me."

"Okay, where did he get this shit? Didn't you wipe your server clean?"

"I transferred everything I needed to a new server and dismantled the old one. Whoever did this got it before I changed hard drives, which was last August."

"Was there a demand?"

Kofsky put his hand in his unkempt hair. "No. I'm waiting for the other shoe to drop."

"You're not still messing with this shit, are you Aaron?"

Kofsky looked up with desperate eyes. "Absolutely not! I'm seeing a therapist and Sandy and I are getting along great! We even have sex!"

"I'm praying for you, brother."

"Yeah, well you're mostly responsible. I call it your intervention."

Josh wished he had another internet expert to snoop on this one. "Any idea who might have sent this?"

"Thinking about it. Hate to say it, but the only people I can think of are my partners. But I'm the one who created the software on which we depend. I'm the tech guy. So on one level it doesn't make any sense."

"Anyone in particular?"

Kofsky folded his hands and stared off into the distance. "Henry Baxter. He's consistently voted against me. He's a major investor, owns twenty-five percent."

"Well you're the tech guy. If you can't find who sent it, how do you expect me to do it? I can barely operate my phone."

"You're the detective! Come on, man."

"Do you want me to use my national security contacts?" Josh said.

Kofsky went white. "Hell no. We'll lose the contract."

"You're the one working on a defense contract."

"I can't go to them with this! They'd cancel our contract." "Not necessarily, Aaron. Did you sign a morals clause?"

"No! I don't want this to come out!"

"Well what about darknet? Surely you've met some expert hackers there."

Kofsky's eyebrows did a *pas de deux*. "I'll look but these guys hide behind aliases and God knows how many servers and transfers."

"Can you put me in touch with Anonymous?"

Kofsky's eyes narrowed. "Maybe. I'll send you a link. But watch out for those guys. They could go either way."

"I get two hundred fifty a day plus expenses."

"No prob."

"Let me know as soon as the blackmailer contacts you."

Kofsky buried his face in his hands. "I'm ashamed of my past behavior. Not a day goes by I don't burn with shame."

"Give me your hand, Aaron. Let's pray together."

Kofsky stared at him like he was a spider but he took Josh's hand. They bowed their heads.

"Heavenly Father, please give this good man Aaron the strength he needs to fight his demons and help me find this blackmailer, if you don't mind. Amen."

"Amen," Kofsky murmured.

Josh bowed his head again. "Lord, let me not be so prideful."

Kofsky picked up his coffee. "Knock it off or we'll be here all day."

CHAPTER 16

Black Widower

Josh debated whether to contact Stoeckle but ultimately deemed it too risky. Josh liked Kofsky, had prayed for him and wanted to believe him. Josh was a big believer in second chances. All he had to do was look in the mirror.

He went home and worked with Fig for an hour in the yard. He put a tiny amount of C4, obtained from an ex-military buddy, in a hollow ball and threw it. Fig ran after it and each time she found it, Josh gave her a treat. He bought Oscar Mayer hot dogs by the dozens. They had done this enough times that Fig was familiar with C4's signature odors. Next, Josh hid the ball containing the C4 in the yard.

"Find!" he commanded and Fig took off, snout down, tail up, until she located the prize, stood by it and barked. She snatched the tumbling hot dog from the air.

Inside, Josh checked his email and found two messages. The first was from someone named Ekaterina:

> Good day, My name is Ekaterina. I am that type of person who generally has good mood every day, and I do not need to have much reason to be happy. I myself have a good intuition and sometimes I prefer to trust to my feelings at current moment in order make a decision, than take my time and hardly think about all pluses and minuses.
>
> I currently do not have any priority about the country where

I would like to build my future, and I am not searching for a man from exactly this country. I am sure if you will find me interesting, you will find a way to win me, and make me be interested at you. I like you profile very much. I'm from Russia. I think you know it's country of long winters and snow. But our country is also famous for great hospitality. I'm 29 years old .I'm family-oriented and I would found a close-knit family. In my free time I'm reading, listening to music, cooking and learning foreign languages. Please tell me about yourself: what do you like most of all and what are your aims and ambitions? What kind of books, music do you like? I would like to know about you more. I'll try to tell about myself more in my next mails. I'm waiting for your reply so much.

Best wishes, Ekaterina

"YOU'RE A BUM!" Josh wrote. "GET A JOB!" Then he blocked her.

The second was from Kofsky and contained an encrypted code.

"Enter this at your own risk," Kofsky wrote. "Should put you in touch with Anonymous."

Josh took a deep breath. He entered the code. His monitor went blank and he was reaching for the shutdown button when a pinprick of white light appeared in the center. It soared toward him, resolving into a grinning skull, white on black, with red lettering in the eye sockets: "Enter freely and of your own will."

Josh clicked the icon and his screen dissolved into a psychedelic swirl, which turned into a riotous assortment of icons against a constantly shifting green-yellow background that made him queasy. One of these icons, some kind of lizard, was labeled "chat rooms." Josh clicked on it.

Hackers Unanymouse, War on Windows, Rotten Apples, Kill All Zionists and Against Corporate America were some of the titles. They were countless. The screen only showed twenty-four. Josh scrolled and scrolled until he came to a white circle with a black spider with a red hourglass on its back. BLACK WIDOWER/THIS GUN FOR HIRE. He clicked it on.

"Black Widower is Lochinvar in a black hat, Robin Hood in camo, Zorro in white tights. If you have a David and Goliath situation, and you are David, contact me. Rates negotiable, guaranteed effective. Warning. Trolls or govt. stooges need not apply."

"Moving to Montana" played over Josh's speakers. He clicked on the "contact" icon.

> *Dear Black Widower: I am a private investigator from Madison, WI, working on a blackmail case. My client is gay* [a little fudging here, but Josh figured anyone who would advertise on such a site would sympathize with underdogs] *who is being blackmailed by parties unknown via the internet. I need someone who can uncover the blackmailer's identity and am willing to pay market rates. Yours sincerely, Josh Pratt.*

He enclosed his phone number. It had a message-in-a-bottle feel to it. Next he went to FemCon's site.

> *This is the world's leading feminist science fiction and comic convention. FemCon encourages discussion and debate of ideas relating to feminism, gender, race, and class. FemCon welcomes writers, editors, and artists whose work explores these themes as well as their many fans. We have panel discussions, academic presentations, and readings as well as many other uncategorizable events. FemCon is primarily a book and comic-oriented convention... with an irrepressible sense of humor.*

No mention of Muhammad. But the chances a Muslim would come within ten miles of this affront to all the Quran holds dear were slim. Unless. And it was that "unless" with which Josh dealt. He checked the guest list and found that Polly was listed as "popular *Wonder Woman* artist."

His phone rang, an unknown number. "Josh Pratt."

"Greetings, Mr. Pratt. This is Black Widower. You're an interesting guy."

"That was quick."

"I live online, Mr. Pratt."

Josh outlined the case, leaving out nothing.

"You believe your client is on the straight and narrow?" Black Widower said.

"I do."

"Any competent sociopath appears sincere. I could not in good conscience protect a pederast."

"I understand. You have my word."

"I believe you, Mr. Pratt. Your background indicates you're a man of your word. I will undertake to identify your blackmailer for ten thousand dollars."

Josh swallowed. It was a lot of money. "I'll have to check with my client."

"He'll go for it, Mr. Pratt. Mr. Kofsky is worth fifteen million dollars."

"How the hell—"

"I'm very good at what I do. I can do it from here or I can do it from there. It would be better if I did it from there. Dovetail has everything I need. It would be better if we did it from there."

"I'll have to check with my client," Josh said. "Where are you?"

"Arvada, Colorado."

"Can I reach you at this number?"

"For the next twenty-four hours."

"I'll get back to you."

Kofsky was in a meeting. Josh left a message. He wondered if the feds knew about Black Widower. Had to. They had an entire cyber-crime unit dedicated to Anonymous. Josh couldn't ask. He didn't want to be responsible for tipping off the feds. But to live outside the law you must be honest.

CHAPTER 17

Take It Down

Josh was a creature of ritual. Every morning he and Fig ran five miles, same route, up and down Ptarmigan, then showered, ate and went to work. As a security expert, Josh knew that such routines were anathema to his personal safety. If anybody wanted to kill him, all they had to do was lie in wait by the side of the road. Yet Josh sensed no imminent threat. He didn't believe in astral projection, psychics or horoscopes, but he believed in some hidden sixth sense. It had worked for him before. He knew he should alter the routine but where else could he run? Ptarmigan was the only through street.

He put on jeans, a Norton T-shirt and a black leather vest covered with patches. Everything but a flash.

At 7:00 a.m. he crossed the street holding an air pump with a gauge. He checked the tires on Lowry's Jeep, pumped them up to forty, got behind the wheel and slowly eased the boat out of its berth, down the tarmac and onto the street. Pulling into a service station on University in Middleton, he topped off both the Jeep and the boat and headed toward Don's house. Car and boat were too long for the driveway so he parked on the street, went up the steps and knocked. A moment later a sleepy-eyed Polly opened the door wearing a pink terrycloth robe and rubbing her eyes.

"Is it Saturday already?"

"What time do the doors open?"

"Ten a.m. We should get there at least an hour early to set up." She peered past Josh, squinting. "Where's your car?"

"We're going by boat."

A goofy grin appeared. "Really?"

"Fer reals. Got any coffee or doughnuts?"

"Come on in."

While Polly gathered her stuff, Josh sat on the front porch with his feet up on the rail sipping coffee and eating a Kellogg's Frosted Strawberry Pop-Tart that tasted like cardboard. Polly came out in jeans and a Tank Girl T-shirt, shouldering her backpack.

"Can't get my comics wet."

"We won't. You could always put them inside a plastic garbage bag, but it's a calm day and I see no reason why they'd get wet."

They carted her goods to the car, got in and drove to the ramp adjacent to the Rusty Scupper, a quasi-nautical-themed restaurant on the west end of the lake. At a quarter to eight the queue stretched all the way back to Allen Boulevard. They waited in line behind a sleek fiberglass inboard.

"Are you happy?" Polly said.

"Excuse me?"

"It's a simple question."

"I guess."

"You guess? Don't you know?"

"You sound like the prison shrink."

"Do you have a girlfriend?"

"Not at the present." Josh felt uncomfortable under Polly's gaze. He was not someone who shared his feelings.

"Want me to fix you up? I have a dozen girlfriends who'd die to have a boyfriend like you."

Josh grimaced. His last two girlfriends had died. "I appreciate the offer, Polly. I really do. But I'll find my own."

"I hope I'm not being intrusive, I honestly want to know. I like you, Josh. I also think a lot about what it means to be happy. I know people who have everything—good health, wealth, a loving mate, but they're not happy. They're unfulfilled."

"A lot of people don't have happiness in them," Josh said. "I used to be like that. Anxious. Always trying to prove myself. Looking for the next score, the next fuck, the next high."

"What changed?"

"Went to prison. Straightened out. Found Christ. Did I ask if you went to temple?"

Polly barked. "I come from a long line of secular Jews. In fact, my parents are shocked and disgusted with my comic. 'Why do you have to insult them? What if they come after you?'"

"Well, they are coming after you."

Polly scooched over and put her arm over Josh's shoulders. "That's why I have you!"

The line moved. Josh started the engine and followed. It was eight thirty by the time he backed the Chris-Craft into the clear blue waters of Lake Mendota, and already dozens of craft were sailing, buzzing and roostering across the surface. Most of the tiny white sails emanated from the Hoofer's pier, seven miles to the east. Josh parked the Jeep while Polly waited in the boat, roped to the municipal pier.

Josh got in the boat, opened the gas, primed the fuel injection and started her up. LOUISE was written in gold script on the stern. They headed east across the glass-smooth lake at a brisk clip, Polly grinning like a dog with her face in the wind.

"Wheeee!" she said.

"You water-ski?" Josh said.

"Ha! I'm as unathletic as it gets."

The boat had a water ski roll bar to which a wakeboard was attached like an elevated spoiler. The skis were still in Lowry's garage. They buzzed a plumb line toward the Capitol's white dome directly over The Edgewater, arriving just after nine. While Josh tied up, Polly procured a cart from the bellhop and loaded her trade goods.

They took an elevator up three floors to the ballroom, unloading in a broad hall lined with tables. Each table had a banner: GUEST REGISTRATION, REGISTRATION, PURCHASE CELEB PHOTO TICKETS, GIRL SCOUT COOKIES. While Polly obtained lanyards for her and Josh, Josh wheeled her trade goods into the ballroom, which had been transformed into a bustling souk exploding with banners and bright art. Signs on easels framed the entrance to the ballroom.

Attendees must respect common sense rules for public behavior,
personal interaction, common courtesy, and respect for private

property. Harassing or offensive behavior will not be tolerated. FemCon reserves the right to revoke, without refund, the membership and badge of any attendee not in compliance with this policy. Persons finding themselves in a situation where they feel their safety is at risk or who become aware of an attendee not in compliance with this policy should immediately locate a member of security, or a staff member, so that the matter can be handled in an expeditious manner. FemCon is a designated SafePlace. Microaggressions are not permitted.

Today's panels: "Fisking Your Filk and Vice Versa, Feminist Icons in Science Fiction; The Role of the Dragon in Smashing Male Hierarchy; Putting Down Rabid Puppies; and Guest of Honor: Joan Vinge."

Josh stopped a woman wearing a FemCon Volunteer T-shirt.

"Ma'am, where's Polly Furst's table?"

She consulted a chart. "Follow me."

Polly's table backed up against the floor-to-ceiling windows overlooking the lake. Josh unloaded her books from the cart and returned it to the bell station. When he returned, Polly had set up her free-standing vertical banner: POLLY FURST! CREATOR OF MUHAMMAD THE COMIC! ARTIST FOR WONDER WOMAN AND VERTIGO'S FABLES! The banner featured an eleven-by-seventeen full-color repro of the *Muhammad* cover. Josh walked around the room while Polly set her merch on the table. Most of the tables were devoted to science fiction and trade goods such as steampunk paraphernalia, everything from bowler hats to chronometers, to jewelry made from watch gears to leather valises. Several tables sold T-shirts: A WOMAN'S PLACE IS IN THE HOUSE AND SENATE, I SQUAT SO I CAN CRUSH THE PATRIARCHY WITH MY POWERFUL THIGHS, a pink clenched fist over the feminine symbol superimposed over a red star, TRAMPLE PATRIARCHY, and DRAGONS DON'T KIDNAP PRINCESSES, THEY RESCUE THEM.

One table sold nothing but homemade dragon plushies in all sizes. When Josh rounded the last corner, two women and Polly were facing off over the table. The two volunteers looked like Tweedledum and

Tweedledee. The larger one wore a FemCon T-shirt; the other wore a T-shirt that said SHUT THE FUCK UP.

Polly was red-faced and her hands were on her hips. The two volunteers glared at Josh when he came up.

"What?"

"They're telling me I have to take down my banner! And I can't sell my comic!"

"I'm sorry," said the volunteer built like a tractor. "It's a matter of liability. We can't take the chance that your exhibit will offend someone. They could report us and we could get hit with a lawsuit."

"For what?! Hurting their feelings?"

"For posting hurtful and inflammatory material," said the other volunteer. Both women were stocky, wore shorts, had calves like beer kegs and short hair.

"Whose feelings?" Polly demanded. "Muslims? You think a Muslim's going to come to a feminist science fiction convention?"

"People post pictures. Instagram. Facebook. That's all we need," said the stockier one. Her badge said MARGE. She turned on Josh.

"Who are you?"

"Josh Pratt, ma'am. I'm Polly's friend."

"I'm sorry," said the other, whose name was Canada. "You're here as our guest and if you want to stay, the banner has to come down and the *Muhammad* comics have to go back in the box."

"But that's most of my trade goods!" Polly said. "How am I going to make any money?"

"Did you pay for this table?"

"No." Like most exhibitors, Polly hadn't thought she would need the preferred treatment for doing so.

"You're going to have to abide by our orders or you're outta here."

Polly was close to tears. Josh stepped behind the table and tapped her on the shoulder.

"Do as they say. I have an idea."

He rolled up the banner and put it away while Polly sullenly removed her comics from the table and put them in a cardboard box. Several stacks of comics remained, including *Wonder Woman*, *Fables* and *Jostlin' Jocylen*, an earlier self-published effort. Josh picked one up and flipped through it. It wasn't nearly as polished as her later work.

"Thank you," Marge said. The two women rolled on down the aisle like a pair of bowling balls.

Polly turned on Josh. "Do you believe that shit? Feminists afraid to offend Muslims? Helloooo! Don't they know how women are treated in Muslim—"

Josh put his finger to his lips.

"What?" Polly said quietly.

"Just keep those comics handy. Nothing says people can't ask for it."

CHAPTER 18

Art Critics

Josh took a copy of *Muhammad*, rolled it up and put it in his vest. At ten to ten, the lobby was filled, with more people waiting outside, many of them in costume. A lot of women with plush unicorns or dragons affixed to their shoulders, some in spandex, most with backpacks. About a third of the audience was men, mostly bearded, toting packs. Josh went outside the front door, held up the copy of *Muhammad* and walked slowly down the line.

"Folks, Polly has these but you have to ask for them. Get your *Muhammad* comic from Polly Furst."

A woman gasped. Another squeaked. A young man with a chin stud stepped out as if to confront Josh, who stopped and looked at him. The young man stepped back, muttering to himself. Others expressed interest. Josh got an idea.

He went back inside and suggested Polly go out front with a stack of comics and sell them there. She was off in seconds. Josh settled down behind her table, picked up a copy of *Fables* and read. The story was called "Pegasus," only instead of ancient Greece the action took place on the planet Olympus, where physics precluded the use of firearms or fast projectiles such as arrows. Thus Olympus became a hotbed of hand-to-hand combat, masters studying the native fauna for inspiration. Bell, with his mighty winged steed, operated the Flying Horse Kung Fu School. One day he received a challenge from the nefarious Chimera.

"S'cuse me."

Josh looked up at a young Asian man with smooth features and a Beatles cut.

"Yes sir."

"Is Polly here?"

"She's out front but she'll be back in as soon as she runs out of comics."

"Do you still have copies of *Muhammad*?"

Josh plucked one from the box, stood, looked up and down the corridor and flashed it at the fan. "We're not supposed to have these."

"Why not?"

"You know why not."

"That's bullshit," he said. "Can I buy it?"

"Why don't you go out front and buy it from Polly? We're not supposed to sell it in here."

The young man took off. Josh bent to Pegasus's kung fu exploits.

"Josh!"

He looked up to see Bricklin the Desert Storm vet heading his way with a tall, thin friend wearing a dragon on her shoulder. Bricklin wore a gray sweatshirt with the sleeves cut off, revealing fully tatted arms, and cargo shorts. Her right foot was a prosthetic.

"Hi, Bricklin. Are you a comics fan?"

"More sci fi. This is Ros."

"Hi Ros."

"We're here for the dragons and the unicorns," Ros said.

Josh stood and motioned Bricklin close. "You know who Polly is?"

"Who doesn't? It was all over the news."

"There's always a chance some nutjob is gonna come in here and try something. You know who I'm talking about?"

"I got an idea."

"Just asking you to keep an eye out."

"Will do, chief."

"'Preciate it. Polly's out front now hawking her wares."

"I'll go take a look."

"Thanks, Bricklin."

He went back to Pegasus. People kept asking when Polly would return, and when Josh looked at his watch he saw that it was eleven. He looked up to see Bricklin coming back his way.

"She needs more comics."

"Would you mind sitting here for a minute while I go out there?" Josh said.

Bricklin moved behind the table. "No prob."

Josh grabbed a stack of comics and fought his way through the thickening mass toward the front door. Sci-fi freaks mingled with wedding guests in the lobby. Josh weaved his way through the crowd out front, where the line to get in stretched up Pinckney Street. Polly worked the crowds halfway up the block. As Josh approached, she was signing a comic on a boy's back.

"That's the last one," she said.

"I got reinforcements," Josh said, handing her the fresh stack.

"I want one!" said a middle-aged woman in a black corset and top hat.

"Me too!" cried another.

Laughing, Polly worked her way farther down the line. "Okay, okay!"

Josh scanned over her head and across the street. There was a disturbance in the making. Four young men were glaring at them from in front of the four-story redbrick Ambassador, home to state legislators, philanthropists and university regents. They were dressed alike in baggy camo trou and loose-fitting pea jackets or hoodies, working themselves up to make a move. Josh turned to Polly.

"Got your phone?"

"Sure. Why?"

"You see those guys across the street? I want you to start filming as soon as I leave the curb."

"What? Those guys?"

"Don't point. Keep your camera on them. Can you do that?"

Polly set her pack down and removed her phone. "On it."

Josh faced the line and cupped his hands. "Folks! We're gonna have a little excitement here! You might want to film this with your phones."

As the four men strode across the street, stopping traffic, Josh scanned their flat bellies for suicide belts. They were all fingering things in their jacket pockets, and when they were halfway across, Josh went to meet them, not looking at them, walking diagonally as if heading past them. For an instant he was three feet from the leader.

"Muhammad blows dead pigeons," Josh said in a low voice.

The man turned on him in rage. "What? What did you say?"

Shock of recognition. It was Polly's neighbor Mustapha Abed.

"You heard me. Muhammad blows dead pigeons. That means he sucks their tiny pricks."

Abed was in his mid-twenties with thick, curly black hair from which his eyes, nose and mouth appeared like burrowing animals. He went bug-eyed. His unibrow flexed and straightened as he drew a hunting knife from his pocket. Josh kicked him in the nuts hard enough to lift him off his feet, and as a second assailant rushed at him clutching a pipe, Josh ducked to his left, elbowed Pipe in the diaphragm and kicked his legs out from under him at the back of the knee. The last two got Josh between them as traffic stopped and people yanked out their cell phones. Josh focused on one, juked and jived, whirled and rushed the other, coming inside the swing of the guy's crowbar, smashing his right elbow into the hawk-nosed face, kicking backward as the last one closed in, catching him high in the chest, splintering something.

Police sirens wailed. They were kitty-corner from the Department of Public Safety and the city jail. Josh went to the curb where the line stretched, and sat down. Several people cheered and broke into spontaneous applause. In seconds the place was swarming with cops. Polly came over and sat beside Josh.

"That was so groovy."

"Get back in the hotel right now or you may not be able to."

Polly got the message and booked. Showing his hands, Josh stood at the approach of a uniformed officer wearing a body camera. His tag said CARSON.

"What happened?"

"I was walking across the street when one of them suddenly attacked me with a knife. I defended myself."

Carson looked at the sprawled bodies with exaggerated slowness. "May I see some identification please?"

Josh produced his driver's license and his private investigator's license. Carson stared at it.

"Josh Pratt. I should have known."

"I'm working security for one of the artists at FemCon. We have reason to believe she may have been targeted."

"I see," Carson said as a plainclothes officer approached. "These guys attacked you first?"

Josh gestured to the long line of supplicants, many of them still recording. "Ask anybody."

"It's true, officer," a woman dressed like Poison Ivy said. "That one guy pulled a knife and attacked him first."

The plainclothes looked at Josh with distaste. He was short with snow-white hair covering his skull. "You didn't say anything to set them off?"

"Maybe they're on drugs. You should test them."

Cops asked questions. There were many eyewits, and the consensus was as Josh had said. Four men of vaguely Middle Eastern persuasion had suddenly and for no apparent reason attacked him in the middle of the street.

"Ahmina ask you to come down to the station," Plainclothes said, "and give us a statement."

"I'm sorry, sir, but I'm providing security for my client. I'll be happy to speak to you here."

The cop held up a finger, walked over to his shop, conferred with someone, came back. "Okay. Whyn'tcha have a seat in my office and tell me what happened."

Josh slid into the Crown Vic opposite the cop, who pulled out a small tape recorder and set it on the armrest between them. "This is Detective Walt Pfeiffer. It is May 10, twelve thirty, speaking with—please state your name."

"Josh Pratt."

"What happened?"

Josh repeated his story, exchanged cards and went back inside. By this time most of the line had entered the building and the four assailants had been handcuffed and booked. The cops had more than enough to convict all four for assault. Just as Josh entered the building he saw the WMAD news van pull up in front and out bounced Katy Varner, her cameraman and her producer. Josh hastened inside without looking back. Polly's table was mobbed. Josh walked between two tables several places down and came up behind her. The tabletop contained only a handful of her issues as Polly signed and made change.

"That was awesome, Josh," she said over her shoulder. "Thank you!"

"My pleasure."

"I'm almost sold out! And I have enough commissions to keep me busy for a month! I have a couple hundred issues left, but we'll have to go back to my apartment to get them. They're in the basement storage locker."

Josh spotted the cameraman bobbing through the crowd. Katy Varner emerged from the wall of humanity in stunning contrast to the unkempt crowd.

"Polly! Can you tell us what happened?" she said, thrusting her microphone in Polly's face.

"Sure! I can't say for sure, but I believe those guys were jihadis. We'll have to wait and see. They want me dead because I've blasphemed the Prophet!"

She whipped out a copy of *Muhammad* and held it before the camera. Katy didn't bat an eye. She could always edit it out later.

"Polly, in view of the fact that there have been two attempts on your life in a week, do you regret publishing your comic?"

"Are you kidding? This is America. We're protected by the First Amendment, right?"

"Don't you have a responsibility to innocent bystanders who may be caught up in your situation?"

Polly held up the comic. "We're protected by the First Amendment, right?"

"Answer the question, Katy," Josh chimed in, instantly regretting it. He didn't want to be part of the story, but he knew it was inevitable. He was a human lightning rod.

"The Supreme Court has argued there are limits on the First Amendment. You can't cry fire in a crowded theater," Katy said.

"You want an interview, show my comic." She held it up again.

Katy's producer, a balding wan PBS type in glasses and a plaid shirt, whispered in her ear.

"You know we can't show that because of security reasons," Katy said.

"You can't show it because you're afraid Muslims will chop off your head."

Katy said to her cameraman and producer, "Let's go, boys. We're done here."

CHAPTER 19

The Usual Suspects

By 4:00 p.m. Polly had sold everything. She could have sold her socks if she wanted, and still people had lined up holding issues of *Wonder Woman* and *Fables* they'd bought from the sole back-issue booth. The two FemCon volunteers were back, Marge and Canada. Marge bulled her way to the front of the line.

"Polly, I'm very sorry, but we're going to have to ask you to leave."

Polly looked up, startled. "Why?"

"We can't take a risk that some other nutjob won't try to disrupt the convention."

"What kind of feminist are you?"

"The kind who wants to keep her head."

Canada beefed her way alongside Marge. "Islam is one of the world's great religions. How would you feel if they constantly portrayed Jews in a negative light?"

"They do!" Polly said brightly.

Josh leaned down. "Come on. Let's get the hell outta Dodge."

With a tight smile Polly stood. "Folks, friend me on Facebook! I'll be at C2E2 with plenty of copies. Thanks for coming!"

Several people applauded. Polly simply left the empty boxes beneath the table. She pointed to the aluminum canister containing her banner. "Josh, will you carry that?"

Josh would have preferred to keep his hands free, but he didn't want to become obsessive-compulsive. He picked it up, carrying it easily by its handle. Marge and Canada walked with them like a couple of rolling boulders to make sure they didn't sneak back into the con. They took the lobby elevator to the lake level. It was five, and the sun was still high in the sky. White triangles flitted across the surface of the lake, most heading toward the Union.

Josh and Polly walked through the chattering cocktail-hour crowd, oblivious to the action upstairs, and loaded what was left into the boat. They powered west, leaving a wake in the otherwise still, glassy green water. By six, Josh had returned the boat and vehicle to Lowry and driven Polly to Don's house in his own car.

Don was on the porch, beer in hand, boots on the rail. "Boy howdy, son! You went through them camel jockeys like a hot knife through butter!"

He reached down, snagged a bottle and tossed it to Josh, who caught it one-handed, popped the cap and tilted a plastic captain's chair carefully back against the wall.

"I don't know for sure they were after Polly, but it's a good bet. I told them Muhammad blows dead pigeons. That's why they attacked me."

Don arfed. "Sweet! Now what? Do I need to keep a gun next to my bed?"

"Well that's always a good idea, but I don't think anyone knows Polly's here. We took a boat to and from. Guarantee we weren't followed."

Don uncapped a bottle of beer and handed it to Polly. "What if somebody recognizes you?"

"Out here?" Polly said.

"It wouldn't hurt for you to wear a cap and sunglasses," Josh said.

"You could dye your hair," Don said.

"I'm not dying my hair! I have more cons this year!"

"You could dress like a pig," Josh suggested.

Polly whirled on him with balled fists. "Youuuu!"

"If you're okay, I'll go feed my dog."

"Go," Polly said. "Wait a minute."

She gave him a big hug. "Thanks for saving my life, Josh."

"For all I know those guys were just jaywalking."

"Yeah. Right."

Josh drove home, fed Fig and phoned Calloway.

"Mr. Pratt," Calloway said with lip-smacking relish. "Did you know all of man's problems can be traced to his inability to sit still in a room?"

"What did they find?"

"Amir Zakirali, Rachman Sidi, Mustapha Abed, Larry Qab. Qab had a flask filled with hydrochloric acid in his pocket."

"Mustapha Abed is Polly's neighbor," Josh said.

"I did not know that. Abed is on a terrorist watch list along with Qab."

"Larry Qab?"

"Yeah. You know him?"

"No. Have you searched Abed's place?"

"Not yet."

"Can I come?"

Beat. "Meet us there at eight. Don't tell anybody."

It was still light out when Josh kicked out his stand in the Alhambra parking lot. Two plainclothes Crown Vics, as obvious as ketchup on white bread, were parked in front of the main entrance while the usual group of the dully curious formed a semi-circle. A uniform at the door stopped Josh.

"Josh Pratt, officer. I'm here at Detective Calloway's invitation." The uniform waved him through. Josh went up the steps into the corridor, where two cops were standing outside an apartment three doors down from Polly's. Josh showed them his ID. A cop handed him a pair of food bags with rubber bands and latex gloves.

"Hands and feet."

Josh put them on and stepped into Abed's apartment as an officer walked out carrying Abed's laptop in gloved hands. A frisson of shock rippled down Josh's spine. A Nazi flag covered one wall, like Nuremberg Rally decor. On the night table sat a copy of *Mein Kampf* in Arabic, a jumbo jar of petroleum jelly, a box of tissues and a stack of stroke books. While Calloway looked through Abed's closet, Josh flipped through the stroke books. *Big Tits*, *Black Ass* and *For Your Eyes Only*, which contained pictures of nude, underage boys. There were videos on the lower shelf: *Fuck Me Up the Poop Chute*, *Anal Antics*, *Weenie-Waggin' Daddy*, and *Vagina, Queen of Qunts*.

Josh cautiously pulled out the table's drawer, revealing a copy of *The Holy Koran* and *The Protocols of the Elders of Zion* in Arabic. A forensics tech dusted a can of red spray paint on the kitchen counter.

"Ten bucks says it's a match for the swastika on the door," the tech said.

"Dude loves Hitler," Josh said.

Calloway turned, holding a paper bag in both hands. "Look at this shit." He held it out so Josh could see the five sticks of dynamite wrapped in rubber bands. "Works as a machine operator at Baltec Paving and Roads. They use dynamite to build roads."

"What about his vehicle?" Josh said.

"It was parked in the Doty Street garage. We're going over it right now."

Josh pointed to a sleeping bag, a tent and a backpack against the wall. "What about that?"

"Don't know. You see what you need?"

"I'd like to go through his things if you don't mind."

"Sorry. You shouldn't even be here."

Josh held his hands up. "I'm outta here. What about meeting me on the terrace Tuesday for lunch? I'll buy."

"Two o'clock. And I'll buy."

"Thanks, Detective."

"Get out of here."

CHAPTER 20

Church

Josh fed the dog, got the mail and dialed Black Widower.

"This is Black Widower. Tell me why."

"Josh Pratt. The client has approved your expenses. If you give me a routing number I will deposit half the amount now, half upon completion."

"Cash will be fine. You can pay me when you see me."

On Sunday Josh and Fig attended the First Baptist Church of Mount Horeb, an old wood country church with a steeple and a bell. They sat in the back row. Pastor John, an aging longhair in shirt and tie, delivered a stem-winder from the wood podium.

"My friends, Proverbs tells us, 'They have sharpened their tongues like a serpent.' We've all been guilty of gossip at some time. Even the best of us can't resist passing on lurid news about a friend, a relative, an acquaintance. The Lord loves a wise tongue but we live in an age of confessions. How many of you are on Facebook?"

Josh raised his hand along with dozens of others.

"Mark Twain said, 'A lie can travel halfway around the world while the truth is putting on its shoes.' Never been truer than today, when social media can make or break a person in a matter of minutes. Used to be we got our news from the town crier, and if there was a shooting in Tarrytown, citizens in Manhattan wouldn't know about it until the next day when someone rode in on a horse.

"Then came the Pony Express and all of a sudden people were getting their news a mere three weeks after it happened! Next you got radio, may

God bless that good Catholic, Marconi. Soon you had the George and Gracie Show, Amos and Andy, the Shadow! You got Orson Welles scaring the crap out of people with a fake broadcast called 'War of the Worlds'! You know what that was about? Martians invading New Jersey. They say some people were so terrified that they leaped to their deaths rather than stay and face the Martians.

"And you know what came next."

"TV!" a kid shouted. Everybody laughed.

"That's right. Now things are moving faster and faster. Now you got your choice of five hundred different channels, everything from a history of the bungee cord to the vilest pornography. You know what came next."

"The internet!" the kid shouted.

"Give that boy some medical marijuana! Yes! The internet and all those social media sites that suck our life force like space vampires. Facebook. Twitter. Instagram. Lies can travel halfway around the world while the truth is putting on its shoes. And they do! You kids who are still in school, ever have your feelings hurt by something somebody said on social media? Of course you have! Bullies love Facebook and Twitter! So I guess what I'm saying, a wise man holds his tongue. Better to be thought a fool than to open your mouth and remove all doubt. I often say to my wife, Sarah..." He gestured to a good-looking babe sitting behind the upright Yamaha electric keyboard behind him. "Before I met my wife, I was a Gatling gun of opinions. You name it, I had an opinion on it. What's the best breakfast cereal? Grape Nuts, and anyone tells you different is a damn fool! Who makes the best car? Ford. Case closed. Do you run the toilet paper top over or underneath?

"And I haven't even mentioned politics."

Sarah played a bluesy riff.

"Uh-oh. That's Sarah's version of the hook. So let me close with the Apocrypha: 'How can he get wisdom whose talk is of bullocks?' Thank you and God bless. Amen."

Everyone said, "Amen!" like they meant it.

Josh hoped to slip away and was at his car when Sarah, the pastor's copper-haired wife, touched him on the arm.

"Josh, Pastor John would like to speak with you."

"Sure," Josh said, ruffling Fig's ears as she sat behind the wheel. He looked over Sarah's shoulder to see Pastor John talking with his parishioners. He held a woman's hand and spoke to her intensely, then excused himself and beelined for the truck. Fig barked once in celebration.

Josh shook the pastor's hand.

"Josh, this business you're involved in, this *Muhammad* comic, well, the sermon was partly about you. This young woman is stirring up a lot of trouble."

"I understand, sir, and I appreciate your concern."

"How do you feel when you hear someone maligning Christians? It's the same for Muslims."

"I hear you."

John held Josh's hand in both of his and looked at him with his honest blue eyes. "I just pray you're doing the right thing here, son."

"I do too."

"I just want you to know that I'm here, if you need to talk to someone."

"Thank you, sir."

John seemed reluctant to let him go, but Josh got in the car and shut the door. The pastor turned to his church with a smile and raised his arms. All the way home, Josh thought about what Pastor John had said. Josh had never been a talker, not one of those guys who had an opinion on everything and insisted on sharing. At parties he hung back and observed. He kept his opinions to himself and would no more gratuitously insult someone than urinate in public.

Josh wondered if Pastor John was sending him a message. Don't make trouble. Don't arouse the head-choppers. Let that stupid girl fend for herself. It's her mess; let her deal with it. Josh didn't support causes he deemed unjust or inappropriate. He remembered the underground comics they had passed around in Waupun—*Jiz Comics, Young Lust, Zap, Hy-Tone*, Frank Stack's *The Adventures of Jesus*—comics that made fun of all the square values. There'd been a few obscenity busts and border seizures back in the day, but by the time Josh had gotten out, nobody cared.

Josh pulled into his driveway. There was an older Subaru Outback with Colorado plates parked at the curb and a man on his stoop relaxing in a lawn chair with his boots on a planter, poking at a handheld device. The man had long hair, a beard, wore aviator's glasses and a Broncos cap. As Josh got out, Fig leaped out after him and ran up to the man, tail wagging. The man put down his device and petted the dog.

"Good doggie!" He stood and took off his sunglasses, revealing wide-set brown eyes. "Josh Pratt? I'm Randall Kleiser."

He stuck out his hand. Josh stared at it. "Who?"

"Black Widower!"

CHAPTER 21

Unexpected Guest

"Oh!" Josh pumped his hand. "What are you doing here?"

"I'm here to help you with your project."

Josh opened the front door and they went inside.

"Did you drive straight through from Colorado?"

"No biggie. I felt like a change of pace."

"You're running from something."

Kleiser grinned and spread his hands. "That's why you're a detective!"

Josh went into the kitchen, seeing the dirty dishes in the sink, junk strewn across the table. He pulled two cans of Coke from the yoke, went back into the living room and tossed one to Kleiser. "Where ya gonna stay?"

Kleiser popped the top and swigged. "I was hoping to stay here. I can't check into a motel."

Josh laughed. "Randall, I admire your nerve. You drive fourteen hundred miles overnight and show up on the doorstep of someone you don't know from a hole in the ground expecting to be let in."

"I'll give you a thou for putting up with me for a week. If it takes any longer we'll talk about that then. You got the money?"

"No. Didn't expect you so soon. I can get it tomorrow."

Fig sauntered over and licked Kleiser's pants.

"Don't lick the pants, Fig," Josh said.

"Can I stay?"

"No cigs, no women, no drugs."

"No prob."

"Okay. You can sleep in the guest bedroom."

"This is where the shootout happened, isn't it?" Kleiser said.

"Right out there."

"And the neighbors loved it."

"Yes they did."

Kleiser went out and returned with a plastic laundry tub filled with five tablets, six cell phones, a five-port USB hub, a laptop and about a hundred feet of cords and cables. "I'll need access to the client's computer. Kofsky does legally what I do illegally."

"He's starting a game division and bringing you in as a game designer. That's your cover."

Kleiser clapped his hands together. "Great! I don't want to be in your way. Just give me your wireless password and I'll set up shop in the spare bedroom."

Josh showed him the room and went for a walk with Fig west on Ptarmigan. Josh glanced up White Oak Court and saw Phil Bass's Infiniti parked in the drive. Last winter Bass had loaned Josh his 4x4 to drive to Iowa during a snowstorm, not because he was a good neighbor but because he wanted to buy Josh's property and turn it into a clubhouse.

When Josh got back, Kleiser was in the kitchen wiping off the counter. The kitchen was sparkling clean. "Hey if you like, I could clean up your hard drive, get rid of the cookies and crap that's slowing it down."

"I have Webroot," Josh said.

"Worthless," Kleiser spat. "Up to you. I usually charge fifty dollars an hour."

"Yeah go ahead. I'll go to the store and get some food. You eat pork chops?"

"Anything you want to cook, hoss."

Josh drove to Woodman's and loaded up. Three grizzled, middle-aged men in surplus army gear stood at the intersection holding cardboard signs: HUNGRY, PLEASE HELP. U.S. VETERAN NEEDS TO FEED FAMILY. Josh rolled down the passenger window and handed out five-dollar bills.

"God bless you," one man said.

"Thanks, man," said another.

The homeless swelled in the spring and peaked around August, when they either moved to warmer climes or stayed indoors at shelters. Back home Josh ferried the groceries into the kitchen and went out back to prep the grill. Minutes later Kleiser appeared holding two bottles of beer.

"Hope you don't mind."

"That's why I got 'em."

"I used to ride back when I was in college. Thinking about getting a bike."

"What did you ride?"

"A Honda 600. I know you ride Harleys."

"There comes a time in a man's life when he must switch from crotch rockets to cruisers. Actually, I've been a cruiser guy my whole life. Why do you call yourself Black Widower?"

"My girlfriend, Patty Ivan. She liked to dress up like Elektra at comic conventions. You know, the Marvel superhero. In 2012 she boarded a Southwest flight from Denver to Austin. They singled her out for extra security. She texted me from the plane. They waved through a bunch of Arab women in hijabs. The plane blew up."

"Was it a bomb?"

"They never did announce the cause, so my guess is yeah. It was a bomb."

"You know what I'm working on?"

"Guessing it has something to do with that *Muhammad* comic."

"You learn that by reading my e-mails?"

Kleiser leaned back in a lawn chair with his hands behind his head. "Naw. I follow the news. I just put two and two together."

"Was my name mentioned?"

"Yeah. It was on the ABC nightly broadcast, toward the end. Just a bit about you busting up some jihadis outside FemCon."

"Fuck. They actually said my name?"

"Yeah, but all it said was that local investigator Josh Pratt who was involved in a shootout with a cycle gang last winter acted in self-defense. Why'd they attack you in the first place?"

"I told them Muhammad blows dead pigeons."

"But how did you know they were jihadis?"

"Four scowling young men of Middle Eastern extraction heading for a feminist science fiction convention? They weren't there to collect *Lulu*."

"Awesome."

Josh went inside, marinated the pork chops in condensed orange juice, garlic and teriyaki sauce. He threw a package of Knorr's Red Beans and Rice in a pot of water and turned up the gas. He went back outside, sat in a chair and slugged beer. "So how you gonna track this fucker?"

"Your client's computer logged the IP address. We start there. But do you really want me talking technical? How computer-literate are you?"

"Not very. I can barely operate my smartphone. I'm good with a wrench."

"See, I would come to you to fix my bike. You come to me to fix your computer."

"Yeah okay. Listen, man. About your girlfriend. I know how you feel."

"I know you do."

"I'd just like to pray for a minute in their memory. Yours and mine."

"Go ahead."

"I'd like you to join me." Josh sat up and held out his hands.

After a second Kleiser stuck his out and they joined hands. Josh bowed his head.

"Dear Lord, thank you for bringing these women into our lives and please watch over them on their spiritual journey. Amen."

"Amen," Kleiser echoed, clearing his throat.

CHAPTER 22

Gamer

With his backpack, long hair and beard, Kleiser looked like a gamer. He arrived at Dovetail's Middleton HQ Monday morning and was immediately given a pass and sent to Kofsky's office. Kofsky welcomed him warmly and bade him sit. Kleiser looked around at the framed posters: *Avengers: Age of Ultron*, *Hellboy*, Call of Duty.

Kofsky sat behind his desk, which was an oval glass slab sitting on rusted industrial pylons. "Before we proceed, you have to sign this confidentiality agreement." He slid it across the desk. Kleiser picked it up and read it.

"No prob." He signed with a flourish.

"I want to assure you that my perversion never went beyond looking. You understand that, don't you?"

Kleiser held up his hands in a placating manner. "Ain't here to judge. Here to find the fucker."

"They've sent a demand. They want a half mil."

"When?"

"This morning. Haven't had time to tell Josh. You have your own office here down the hall, with a view of the parking lot, your own air-gapped server and your own blade. You set it up however you like. All I ask is that it remain completely independent of the house system. Don't email me. Don't email Josh. You learn something, you tell us in person. I'm sorry to act so paranoid but we have a Defense Department contract. We all had to sign not only confidentiality but loyalty oaths."

"Seriously?"

"Yeah. I know, right? You'd think we were back in the fifties. You want to look at this here, or you want me to send it to your machine?"

"Put it on a flash drive," Kleiser said. "I'll check it for viruses or worms before I install it."

"How will you do that?" Kofsky said.

Kleiser grinned. "Does Toyota tell Honda?"

Kofsky took a blank disc from his desk, inserted it into his computer and went to work. Minutes later the disc popped out. Kofsky put it in a plain white envelope and handed it to Kleiser. Kofsky stood. He was a puffy man with a halo of curly hair. "Well, come on. I'll show you to your office."

They went down the quiet, darkened halls past spotlit framed posters for *Alien*, *Blade Runner*, *Star Wars* and *Pacific Rim*. At the end of the corridor Kofsky opened a door on a tiny room with a desk on which sat a monitor, cordless keyboard, server and blade. A lone framed *John Carpenter's The Thing* poster hung on the back wall. A horizontal window looked out on the shaded parking lot, where Kleiser counted two Infinitis, a Mercedes, a new Corvette and a Lexus. Business was good.

"Anything you need, give Iva a holler. She's the woman at the front desk."

"Will do."

Kleiser waited until Kofsky clicked the door shut behind him, whipped his backpack up on the industrial steel gray desk and pulled out his laptop, which he'd made himself from bits and pieces of other computers. It was Frankenstein's monster, with a louvered carbon fiber body. It was two inches thick, grotesque by modern standards. It was fully charged and ready to go, so Kleiser didn't even have to plug it in. He booted up, took Kofsky's blackmail disc and slid it in the slot. He gazed nonchalantly at images of children in seductive and obscene poses and read the email: *We are your worst enemy. We know your sins. It will cost you $500,000 to prevent us from sending these files to the Defense Department. Do not contact the police, for such would not be meet.*

He checked the disc for malware and sure enough, it contained a file-eating Trojan. Kleiser grabbed his pack and quick-walked down the hall to Kofsky's office. The door was open and Kofsky was on the phone. Kleiser waited until he was finished.

"It contains malware. It's probably infected your entire system now. I need to have access to your system."

"Can you get it out?" Kofsky said, rising from his desk, face crinkled with worry.

Kleiser set his backpack on the desk and took the boss's seat. "Almost certainly. The question is how long it will take. You got someplace else you can work?"

"I'll be in the boardroom."

Kleiser entered a command and the Dovetail home page was replaced by a bewildering scroll of code. Kleiser had built his first computer when he was fifteen and had subsisted on the fringes of internet culture since. For a while he had made a living as a fix-it man, wiping computers of viruses, malware and dead space so that they functioned as a computer ought—instantly. He'd never been particularly political, although he'd always had libertarian leanings because he had authority issues and couldn't hold a regular job. He'd never wanted a regular job. He'd always viewed himself as an outsider, a bandit, a fringe character exploiting loopholes in time and space to survive.

He'd learned by going into computer guts and getting his hands dirty. He took several programming courses at Denver Technical College, his only formal education post-high school. He was even a Comcast service rep for a month before they fired him.

Kleiser had always had a fascination with darknet and other gray-area matters, and was an early supporter of Anonymous—if for no other reason than it made him feel like a dashing revolutionary. That was before he met Patty. Patty was a medical billing technician, but in her spare time she volunteered for soup kitchens, was a Big Sister and brought home stray dogs. She was a totally good person and Kleiser had fallen helplessly in love with her. He'd even bought an engagement ring, although he'd been terrified about bringing it up.

But then it was too late. Patty got on that plane bound for Austin and some fucking Arabs blew it out of the sky. Oh, they didn't know for sure. There wasn't enough plane left to prove anything. The press coverage completely ignored what everyone was thinking. Even when Al-Qaeda took credit, thoughtful-looking talking heads said to one another, "We may never know what caused this tragedy."

Kleiser became serious about Anonymous. He went after the Transportation Safety Authority, revealing the names of hundreds of TSA officials who'd been arrested for theft and bribery, outing TSA officials who subscribed to the Ashley Madison cheating site, revealing hundreds who were delinquent on their taxes or had been hired despite criminal records for drug-dealing, domestic violence and rape.

Kleiser now headed the TSA's "no fly" list.

Miraculously, Kleiser had not yet showed up on the FBI's Ten Most Wanted Cyber-Terrorists list. Since Patty's death, he had learned everything he could about radical Islam and had helped take down several Islamic hackers in Eastern Europe and Iran. It took Kleiser four hours to remove the malware from Dovetail's system.

"How you doing?"

Kleiser jumped. He hadn't heard Kofsky come in.

"I think I cleared it out. It was hella clever. Used an algo I've never seen, but I got it."

"Yeah, listen, it's five thirty. I'm outta here, but if you want to keep working, go ahead. We have a security guy. I'll just let him know you're here."

"I'm on a roll, hoss. I'll keep working."

"Great. I hope you're not still here when I arrive tomorrow morning."

"You got a sofa bed?"

"Use the couches in the boardroom. See ya."

Kofsky left, closing the door behind him. Kleiser got up, stretched, opened the little cube fridge and took out a Red Bull. He wasn't hungry. He was skinny as asparagus. He often went ten to twelve hours without eating. He went down the hall to the men's room, then up to the foyer, where the security guy stood looking out at late-afternoon traffic.

"Hey," Kleiser said.

The security guard turned. He was a young black man with military bearing. He wore a sky blue shirt and navy trousers held up by a Batman's utility belt draped with tasers, fazers, canisters, cuffs and sprays. "Yes sir."

"I'm Randall Kleiser. I'm working on Kofsky's computer."

"Figured. I'm Tyrone Scott."

They shook hands.

"Ex-military?" Kleiser said.

"Yes sir. Army."

"They got any doughnuts or like that around here?"

"You might try the break room."

Kleiser found a stale doughnut and a brown banana in the break room, took them back to Kofsky's office and finished them off. He went to work uncovering Kofsky's blackmailer by exposing the full domain address.

A legitimate citizen might obtain a court order demanding that the web company give him the real domain of the sender. But Kleiser was not legitimate. The blackmailers were obviously using slave computers they'd taken over. Kleiser assumed that one of the IP addresses in the headers of the email belonged to a computer the sender had control over, or that actually controlled Kofsky's computer. With the safeguards Dovetail had installed, that was next to impossible. Dovetail had a superb safety record, which is why the Defense Department trusted it with secrets.

Kleiser copied the code and went into darknet using an IP address known to fewer than a dozen people. He entered the address into an Anonymous program that cataloged every known and unknown terrorist group in the world.

And got lucky.

CHAPTER 23

On the Terrace

On Tuesday, as on most every other day, Josh and Fig ran, ate and trained in the backyard. As always, if Josh wasn't quick enough with the training moves, Fig would paw his thigh and bark. They came back in the house at nine, Fig grinning and wagging. Polly had phoned while they were outside. He called her back.

"Do you know who Abdul Alhazred is?!" she gushed on the phone.

"Yes, you told me."

"He goes by Zlatko. He's the guy who won that Draw Muhammad contest in Florida! He's a reformed Bosnian Muslim who emigrated and became a staunch defender of liberty and the West. He's been fighting radical Islam for years. He contacted me! He wants to share a table with me at Chicago!"

"Oh yeah that's right. You told me."

"Zlatko is fearless. He's a black belt in karate."

"Do me a favor. Hold off on that until we see how San Diego goes. How's it goin' over there?"

"Fine. I've laid out my next project—eight pages for *Dark Horse Presents*. It features Highly Slicey, the Rasta Assassin. I'm writing and drawing three episodes; isn't that cool?"

"Who's Highly Slicey?"

"The Rasta Assassin! He and he smoke de ganja den go out and take care of bidness. Did you know the word 'assassin' comes from '*hashishm*', from the Indian cult of Thuggee that smoked hash before going out and killing people?"

"No slow drives by the house, hard stares?"

"Nope. I walked around the neighborhood yesterday and everybody was cool."

"Did you wear shades and a hat like I asked?"

"Yes. I felt like Lauren Bacall."

"Call me if anything happens."

"Yes, Dad."

Josh went to his computer. Abdul Alhazred, the so-called "Mad Arab" author of the *Necronomicon*, a fictitious book that was the repository of all evil, was created by H.P. Lovecraft. The artist's real name was Zlatko Dzelko, raised in a Muslim household in Dearborn. He and his parents were often at odds because he refused to attend mosque. Dzelko's turning point came at age twelve when his older sister Fatima began dating an infidel boy. One night her father waited for her to return home and attacked her with a cast iron skillet, giving her a concussion.

Amir Dzelko refused to take his daughter to the hospital. "Let the whore die!" he told his family.

So Zlatko carried her to the family car himself, and when Amir tried to stop him, Zlatko knocked him down. He never returned home. At the hospital, he called the cops and told them what had happened. The cops were sympathetic, but unless Fatima pressed charges there was nothing they could do. Zlatko begged Fatima to seek emancipation but she dutifully returned to her family.

A year later Amir burned Fatima alive for dating a Christian. By that time Zlatko had moved to Chicago and embarked on a life as a cartoonist, supporting himself by working at Best Buy. 9/11 was a turning point for him. Whereas previously he'd wanted to draw Batman, now he saw that it was his calling to become a modern-day Thomas Paine pointing to the danger of radical Islam. He created Al Qabong, a grotesque hybrid of Wonder Wart-Hog and the Punisher whose sole purpose was fighting radical Islam. He wrote pamphlets and drew posters, often depicting Muhammad as a sinister killer.

Josh sent him a Facebook friend request along with a message: I'M PROVIDING POLLY FURST'S SECURITY AT SAN DIEGO."

Zlatko responded immediately. NICE! I CAN'T MAKE SAN DIEGO. I'LL BE AT A CONFERENCE IN TEXAS. LOOK FORWARD TO MEETING YOU IN CHICAGO.

MAYBE WE CAN GET TOGETHER BEFORE THEN. I WOULD BE HAPPY TO MEET YOU HALFWAY, SAY IN BELOIT.

NO NEED. I'VE BEEN MEANING TO VISIT THE UNIVERSITY FOR A WHILE. THIS IS THE EXCUSE I NEED. LET ME LOOK AT MY SCHEDULE AND I'LL GET BACK TO YOU. They exchanged phone numbers.

Josh checked out the San Diego con and learned that it had been sold out for over a year. He called Polly back. "How am I going to get in?"

"Don't worry. We'll figure something out."

"Send me your travel info. I need to book a ticket."

San Diego was in three weeks. Josh went online and booked a ticket via United, arriving midday Thursday. The biggest comic con in North America, San Diego was four days long, not counting the Wednesday-evening preview. Polly was renting a house with four other cartoonists and offered to put Josh up.

He'd never been to San Diego.

At noon, Josh saddled up and rode into town, parking in a slot across from the Memorial Union. He made his way through the buskers and "informational tables," and up the steps into the east entrance. He worked his way around the crowd in line for Babcock Hall ice cream, through the subterranean and vaguely Germanic Rathskellar out onto the terrace, where a band entertained the lunch crowd. The band—two guys and a gal—were set up on the little stage with its back to the lake, facing the building. Most of the colorful round metal tables were taken but as Josh watched, two girls in sunglasses, shorts and ponytails got up, shouldered their backpacks and left. Josh swooped on the table like a hawk, tossing his own backpack on top to claim it.

He was early. He faced the lake and watched the little white triangles dart to and fro. The lightly amped band was playing blues that barely broke the surf of chitchat. Undergrads, grads, faculty, businesspeople, tourists—they all came to the Union Terrace. It was the place to see or be seen and had been for sixty years.

Josh recognized a bearded grad student reading Sartre. He was there every time Josh came down and had to be at least sixty. At another table three cute coeds poked and stared at their phones. Josh went to the open-air grill and picked up two brats, chips and two big Cokes and carried them back to his table on a cafeteria tray.

Calloway came around the edge of the building and Josh waved to him. Calloway, Madison Police's gang expert, was a six-foot-three black man in an elegant gray seersucker suit, light blue shirt and red tie with a tiny gold pig pin. Calloway had a wandering eye that stared upward like a searchlight. Josh stood and they bopped fists. They sat.

"Did you buy me a brat?" Calloway said.

"No. I got two for myself but now I realize I can't eat both. I give it to you."

Calloway grabbed the brat and stuffed half in his mouth. They ate while the band played.

Calloway daintily wiped his lips with a paper napkin. "Tell me about your latest shitstorm."

"Are you aware of any jihadist gangs operating in Dane County?"

"No. Students for Justice in Palestine is a registered student group, but as far as I know they're not committing felonies. Al Sayeed and Mustapha Abed are loners. There are sullen, resentful, mentally unstable people all over. Whatcha gonna do."

"Could you check for any Mustapha Abed types? Anybody in the past year who was cited for jihadist activity? Verbal threats, online threats, vandalism?"

"You want a lot for a brat. You get a name, run it by me. Otherwise I'm not going to do your job for you. Where's your client now?"

"At an undisclosed location."

"That reporter, Varner, contacted me. She wants to write a book about you."

"I know."

"You fuckin' her?"

"No," Josh said. "Not that she hasn't tried."

"You're a better man than I, Gunga Din."

Calloway had been happily married to the same woman for thirty years.

"There was an incident in Jackson County in February," the detective said. "Dude sees a van in a ditch, pulls over to help. Four sketchy guys, barely speak English, very grateful for his helping to pull them out. They gave him a jar of ginseng. He got a glimpse in the van and saw a lot of boxes, said it smelled of patchouli."

"Do you know his name?"

Calloway pulled a spiral pad from inside his jacket and made a note. "Email me later."

"Why do you even know about that?" Josh asked.

"The dude phoned it in. He said it was just odd. Got the license plate. Turns out it was stolen. They found it the next day burned in a field."

"Did you know there was a Jamaat ul-Fuqra training camp in Kanabec County in Minnesota?"

"How you spell that?"

Josh spelled it.

"I'll check with Clark and get back to you."

"Thanks, Heinz."

CHAPTER 24

Melissa

Josh felt his cell tingle as he rode home but couldn't answer it. It rang again as he kicked out in his garage. It was Polly.

"Josh, Melissa my painting guru just called. She wants me to help her put a closet door back in and fix her garbage disposal. I'm going out there."

"Hang on, I'll go with you. I'll pick you up in a half hour."

"Great! Thanks, Josh!"

Josh fed Fig and took the car. Polly skipped down from the porch when she saw him, carrying a black portfolio. She slid in the car and put her portfolio in the back.

"Thanks, Josh!"

"I need to meet this guru."

"You'll love her. Melissa is seventy-eight, lives alone, paints, still drives herself to church on Sundays. I don't know why she doesn't move into an assisted-living place. I worry that she's going to fall and break something."

"She should get one of those bracelets."

"I told her that. Maybe you can convince her."

Polly directed Josh west on 14 until they got to Cross Plains and turned north. Melissa lived in one of those odd little neighborhoods that sprout in rural areas, usually around a common well. White Tail Lane was the name of the cul-de-sac, surrounded by five homes. Melissa's was farthest back, nearly hidden by trees. Josh followed the pitted blacktop to a fifties-style ranch, not unlike his own house. An old black dog stood in the yard barking. An old woman with a cane and a broad-brimmed straw hat came out onto the veranda.

Josh wrote the address down on his spiral pad.

"Orville, come!"

The old hound turned and went to his mistress with a suspicious backward glance. Melissa started to come down the three steps but Polly rushed to her before she could descend, embracing the older woman in a bear hug.

"Hello my dear," Melissa said in a gravelly voice. "Who's your friend?"

Josh came up the steps. "Josh Pratt, ma'am."

Melissa looked from Josh to Polly with a puzzled expression. "Are you..."

"No, silly!" Polly said. "You know I'm a muff diver. Josh is just a friend." Melissa gripped Josh's arm. "Too bad. I like this one. If I were sixty years younger, I'd want him to fuck the socks off me. Well, come on in and have some lemonade."

They turned and followed the old woman into the house, which smelled of lavender, oil paint, turpentine and cats. A big Siamese met them at the door and twined between Josh's legs. Two more loafed on the back of the sofa. Tufts of animal fur flitted over the hardwood floor. Trophies lined the mantel above the redbrick fireplace. Josh read the labels. First place, Sonoma Invitational Plein Air contest. First place, Durango Wild West Days. Above the trophies was a big painting of a group of Indians hightailing it across the plains in front of a huge storm front, lightning touching down in the distance. The Indians were so real, Josh could almost reach out and touch them. Foam sprayed from their horses' mouths. They seemed to be in motion. Josh looked at the signature in the corner. GRANVILLE.

Polly went with Melissa into the kitchen to get lemonade while Josh looked at the other paintings in the room. Most were Western landscapes—some of animals, some with just the land. In an alcove jutting into the yard was an easel next to a table holding several palettes, jars, tubes and brushes. Stacks of paintings leaned against the wall. Josh was entranced. He wondered how one of her paintings would look over his fireplace, instead of the semi-naked broad on the Harley.

The ladies returned with glasses. Josh and Polly sat on an old brocade sofa, while Melissa took a creaky wooden rocking chair. A cat immediately leaped into her lap and she absent-mindedly stroked it.

"Thank you for coming. Young man, there's a sliding closet door in my bedroom which came off its rails, and for the life of me I can't get the damn thing to fit right. Would you take a look at it?"

"Certainly," Josh said, carrying his lemonade down the hall. The bedroom looked like the aftermath of an explosion on a fashion runway. Clothes were heaped carelessly over a love seat, a bedside table, a dresser. Josh had to move several pairs of shoes away from the closet to make room for the door, which slipped easily back into place.

He returned to the living room.

"Polly says you can fix my garbage disposal. My neighbor gave me some kale and Swiss chard. Do you know how to prepare kale and Swiss chard? You put it down the garbage disposal! Well I must have put too much because now the damn thing is stuck."

Josh set his lemonade on the mantel and smiled. "Let me look."

The garbage disposal was jammed. Josh returned to the living room. "Do you have a plunger?"

"There should be one in the bathroom closet."

Josh retrieved the plunger and worked the drain with a great sucking sound. He turned on the water and the disposal, and it swooped clean.

"You're a genius!" Melissa declared. "I understand you're protecting this girl from crazed jihadis."

"I do my best."

"When Glen was alive we toured all through Egypt and the Middle East. All the Arabs we met were so nice to us! I don't know what's happened to the world."

"Crazy people have taken over," Polly said.

"What else needs fixing?" Josh said.

Melissa reached to a crowded table at her elbow, pulled out a silver flask, opened it and poured several ounces into her lemonade. She held the flask up.

"Wodka?"

Josh held up his hand.

"No thanks," Polly said.

Melissa took a swig. "Oh I have a laundry list, much more than you could hope to fix today, even if I were paying you. I have cracks that need to be spackled and painted, a ton of shit that needs to be hauled to the landfill, litter boxes..."

Polly got up. "I can at least clean out the litter boxes."

"Thank you, my dear! Melville, Bailey and Jagger thank you! Did I tell you I fucked Mick Jagger forty years ago? He said I was damn tight for an old broad!"

Josh colored. Melissa laughed like a guinea pig, a series of delighted squeals.

Polly swatted at the old woman. "Be good!"

The old lady reached into the pile at her elbow and brought out a bag of marijuana and pack of Zig-Zags. She held the papers up.

"Did you know Jesus was a head? Just look at this pack of Zig-Zags!"

She handed the works to Josh.

"Roll me a doobie, would you dear?"

"Ma'am, do you sell your paintings?"

Melissa looked up, surprised. "Not anymore. Why? Are there any that strike your fancy?"

Josh went into the studio and retrieved a painting of a cowboy in chaps and ten-gallon hat kneeling next to a desert oasis while his horse drank. The still water reflected the red buttes in the background.

"Ah. 'Drink at Dusk.' You take it, young man."

"Oh I couldn't do that! Let me pay you for it."

"Nonsense! I don't need your money, and you were kind enough to come out here and humor an old lady. Take it! I won't take no for an answer."

CHAPTER 25

Fantasy Mushrooms

On July 8, Polly and Josh flew to San Diego on separate flights. Polly flew United in the morning, arriving at noon. Leaving Kleiser in charge of Fig, Josh flew United in the evening, arriving at ten thirty. Once on the ground, he grabbed his bag from the overhead compartment, emerged from the gate and spotted his scheduled Uber driver, who was holding up a hand-lettered cardboard sign that said PRATT.

The driver was a short Asian man with a brush haircut and horn-rimmed glasses.

"Hi!" he said. "I'm Pak. Thanks for choosing Uber."

They shook hands and Josh got in the passenger seat of Pak's old Miata.

"Small car," he said.

"I would have brought the Bronco if you had more luggage. This is easier to drive."

They drove through the warm, scented night.

"You here for the con?" Pak said.

"Yup."

"First time?"

"Yup."

"Prepare for culture shock. One hundred twenty-five thousand people in one room. Are you a comics guy? A movie guy?"

"Neither. I'm providing security to a young lady artist."

"She must be hot stuff to need security here."

"She is."

"Got a pass?"

"No. She said she could get me one."

Pak laughed. "Rotsa ruck! There are scalpers out front. Starting price is a thousand dollars."

"Are you shitting me?"

"Man, it's been sold out for over a year. Ever since the fucking movie people discovered it, excuse my French."

"Fuck the movie people!" Josh said.

"You know anything about comics?" Pak said.

"I like *Badger*."

"Yeah, man! I dig the Badger man myself! Let me cue you into a little event that's not on the books. Saturday at noon, right? They hold the Fanboy Slalom. A bunch of cosplayers race from the southwest corner of the room to the northeast corner. They're not allowed to shove anybody or knock anybody down. The record stands at twelve minutes fourteen seconds. Watch for it."

"Okay."

The rental was a two-story wood frame on Genoa Street in Mission Bay, entrance book-ended by a pair of royal palms. The lights were on and "Suite: Judy Blue Eyes" drifted through the open windows along with sounds of laughter.

"Sounds like a party," Pak said as Josh paid him. "Take my card."

Josh went up the steps and banged on the screen doorframe, but the music was blasting so hard no one could hear him. He went inside, found four people partying around the living room but no Polly.

An older dude in a dirty white shirt and a vest, with glasses and unkempt hair, approached. "You must be the detective."

They shook hands. "Josh Pratt."

"Sven Rickard. This is my house. I rent it out every year."

"Where's Polly?"

"She went to the preview."

Josh was irritated. He'd told her not to go anyplace without him. "Great. How far away is it?"

"About ten miles."

The door opened and Polly entered laughing, with a woman friend dressed like Catwoman, if Catwoman weighed one hundred eighty pounds.

"Josh!" she exclaimed, dropping her backpack and embracing him. "Hey everybody, this is my friend Josh."

"Hi," Catwoman said. She had a silver bead protruding from her nose like a chrome zit. Josh suppressed an urge to pluck it.

"I'm Kat, with a 'K,'" she said.

"I'll remember that."

"Anybody tell you you look like Jason Statham?" Kat said.

"Maybe if they're blind," Josh said.

The rest were Joe, Jean and Shirley, all in their late twenties. Joe wore an Ethan Van Sciver Batman T-shirt and had freckles. Jean wore a faux-fur bra and panties, her face made up like a chipmunk. A gray cloth tail hung from her ass. Shirley wore a dress made out of huge Valiant Comics swag bags sewn together.

Josh picked up his bag and turned to Rickard. "Where do I bunk?"

"There's a futon in the attic. Just pull on the rope and the ladder will come down."

"Great."

Josh woke to Talking Heads and the smell of bacon. He grabbed his phone and called Kleiser.

"Yeah," Kleiser answered.

"Randall, it's Josh. How's Fig?"

"She's fine. I took her for a walk and she shat on the neighbor's lawn. Don't worry, I got it. I'm changing phones after this call. Let me give you the new number."

Josh visited the second-floor bathroom and went downstairs, where everybody was buzzed on coffee. Rickard served up pancakes and bacon.

They boarded a bus at nine thirty and as they neared the Convention Center, the streets filled with costumed superheroes, families with strollers and backpacks, all manner of freaks.

"Did you get me a ticket?" Josh said.

"Don't worry! I'll get you in," Polly assured him.

The mob was so thick around the convention center, it took the bus fifteen minutes to crawl the final hundred yards. Uniformed cops stood in the street directing traffic. Hawkers and street theater performers surrounded the con. Clowns paced with sandwich boards: WEEHAWKEN! THE FUTURE OF COMICS! STOP BY THE WB BOOTH! SNEAK PREVIEW

THIS AFT OF THE NEW JAMES BOND. A guy dressed like The Goon was scalping tickets: "Getcher day pass here—only three hundred dollars!"

The line to pick up tickets was a quarter mile long. Polly expertly navigated her way through the mob to the professional registration desk inside, where hundreds of people were standing in line. Polly tugged at Josh's sleeve.

"Look! There's Erik Larsen! And Matt Wagner!"

As they stood in line dozens of people hailed Polly. She introduced Josh as her "male escort" to much amusement and eye-rolling. Finally they made their way to the counter, where a woman wearing an XXL San Diego Comic Con Volunteer shirt looked up and smiled.

"How can I help you?"

"Polly Furst. I'm a working professional, and this is my male escort."

The woman looked through her files and produced a laminated pass on a lanyard. "I have your registration but nothing for your friend. What's his name?"

Polly looked around furtively and leaned in. "Don't you recognize him? This is Jason Statham."

The woman did a double take and smiled. "Oh! Oh of course! Just a minute."

She entered something into the computer and produced another pass on a lanyard showing a drawing of Nexus by Steve Rude. "Here. I left the name off. Your secret is safe with me. And Mr. Statham? I loved you in *Safe*."

"Thank you," Josh said in a bad Limey accent. "That's my best movie."

Along with their passes they received a large swag bag decorated with a Hellboy image and containing the program booklet, invitations to several parties and five complimentary rubber ninja throwing darts. The program cover featured Dan Schkade's Spirit, courtesy of Dynamite Comics.

As it was ten fifteen Thursday morning, it took fifteen minutes just to get through the doors into the convention hall, a vast room that was already SRO. Volunteers went through their backpacks, fastening a yellow tag to the vetted bags. They passed two sword vendors on their way to the table. Everything from katanas to orc axes weighing five pounds.

The crowds were worse than at Sturgis, where at least it was mostly outside. Immediately inside the door was a two-story pavilion with an immense billboard advertising DISCO—THE HEARTWARMING STORY

OF A BOY AND HIS DOG! The graphic showed a small black dog sailing through the air grasping a Frisbee in its jaws, while Asa Butterfield and Jennifer Lawrence looked up beaming.

Next to that was the Warner Bros. booth with an immense graphic touting NEW JUSTICE LEAGUE starring Gabourey Sibide as Wonder Woman, Jack Black as The Flash, Michael K. Williams as Superman, Neil Patrick Harris as Batman and Lena Dunham as Catwoman. Several thumping basslines competed with one another.

"You could faint in here and never fall down," Josh said.

"WHAT?" Polly said.

"I SAID, YOU COULD FAINT IN HERE AND NEVER FALL DOWN!"

Polly leaned in and spoke directly into Josh's ear. "Don't laugh, this really works. Do as I do and follow me."

She put both her hands out in front of her as if she were diving, palm to palm, and plowed ahead. Sure enough, the human crowd-splitter worked and they passed people right and left. It was no place for epileptics. Lights flashed and sirens wailed. An Imperial Stormtrooper platoon marched through the crowd single file. Here came Groot, eight feet tall, followed by seven Deadpools and nineteen Harley Quinns. There were svelte Harley Quinns and Harley Quinns that looked like road barrels, all carrying massive mallets.

Artist Alley stretched on forever, hundreds of artists seated behind long tables, many with banners advertising their wares. Polly consulted her program.

"We're at D-37."

They went down D aisle looking at the numbers, coming to a stop before D-37. There sat a young man who looked like he'd been attacked with an industrial stapler, piercings running from eyebrow to cheek, through the nose, lip and tongue, with ear inserts the size of nickels. No normal skin showed on his fully tatted arms and halfway up his neck. Before him on the table was a collection of grotesque hard plastic dildos in primary colors, some with spikes.

"Fantasy Mushrooms," he said. "Go ahead. Pick one up."

CHAPTER 26

Day One San Diego

"This is Polly's table," Josh said.

The kid looked up with a sneer that magically morphed into a zero. "Oh. Yeah. Sorry. Didn't think you'd get here until tomorrow." He stood, swept his "mushrooms" into a wheeled suitcase and booked.

"How does that shit even get in here?" Josh said.

"There's nothing wrong with that," Polly said, moving behind the table and uncorking her banner cylinder. It only took a minute to set up a vertical banner headlined POLLY FURST! in bright comic book lettering over ARTIST: WONDER WOMAN, FABLES, MUHAMMAD.

On their left was Drednox Comix with a display of amateurish color comics. Polly introduced herself to the slim black man behind the table.

"Duane Albright!" he said.

To the right sat Tsui Mak, a Filipino kid selling posters of his superhero paintings. Polly introduced herself and Josh, whose eyes zeroed in on a painting of a lissome blond draped across a chopper with a leaf-spring front end, a small Honda four-cylinder set longitudinally in the hand-built chassis and a uni-shock rear end.

Josh pointed. "Like it."

"Thanks."

"Do you ride?"

Tsui laughed. "Ah hell no. I made it up!"

"You won't believe this, but this dude I know in Madison actually made that bike."

Mak brightened. "Seriously? Dude! I would love a picture of that!"

They exchanged cards.

Polly laid out her wares, including copies of comics and a pamphlet, *Polly Furst Sketchbook*, five dollars. Josh stood on the extra chair and surveyed the crowd. All he could see was rank upon rank of undistinguished humanity, with every fifth person made up as an alien. People purchased comics and had them signed. Polly sold five copies of *Muhammad* before eleven.

A man stopped to glare. He was in his late thirties with a dot-Indian complexion, wearing a plaid cotton shirt, tail pulled out. He pointed at *Muhammad*.

"Do you have any idea how offensive that is?"

"Don't like it?" Polly said. "Don't buy it."

"That's hate literature," the man hissed.

"How is it hate literature? Muhammad's a stud!"

"It should be banned!"

Polly stood and put up her dukes. "Fight me, ban boy!"

The man's face swelled and he whirled. Since every path was blocked by a solid wall of humanity, he stormed slowly away. A gawky *Big Bang* type in glasses with a cowlick approached purposefully and gushed.

"Polly Furst! You're the man! I love your art so much! I bought one of your originals off e-Bay!"

"Thank you very much. What page did you buy?"

"*Wonder Woman*, that story with the Penguin. Page 17 with Wonder Woman swooping in through the window!"

"That's a good one."

He plopped his backpack down on a patch of table and rummaged. "Would you mind signing a few comics?"

"That's why I'm here."

He brought out hard rectangles of Mylar and backing board holding five *Wonder Woman* issues, carefully filleted them and handed Polly a gold-tipped marker. "Would you mind signing the covers?"

"Not at all."

As she signed each comic with a flourish, supplicants piled up behind the young man.

Josh had to visit the men's room. It was two o'clock. He leaned down.

"I'm going to the men's room. Why don't you go with me."

Polly stared. "What?"

"Not to come in! Just to get away from the table while I'm gone. I don't want to leave you unattended."

"Don't be ridiculous. Go. I'll be fine."

Josh looked around. It was against policy to leave the client unattended in a high-profile situation like this, but he had to visit the john. The problems of being a sole proprietor.

"If you get a situation, call me."

"Go."

Josh headed for the nearest men's room, against the north wall eighty yards away. It was like throwing himself into the banzai pipeline. A solid sea of humanity rose up against him. His progress was glacial. He put both hands together as if he were praying, extended them in front and as if by magic, the crowd density receded by 50 percent. People saw "the wedge" and instinctively turned sideways or waited.

Even so, it took him ten minutes to get to the men's room. Inside, Tony Stark pissed next to Robb Stark. At the sinks, Wolverine carefully set his claws on the counter and washed his hands next to an Imperial Stormtrooper. Every urinal was taken. Every urinal had a line. It was like Sturgis. When a stall opened next to Josh, he took it, breathing through his mouth. The previous tenant had pissed all over the seat. Josh wanted to chase after him and smash his face. Using the toe of his shoe he carefully raised the seat.

It was another fifteen minutes before he returned to Polly, pleased to see her signing. A fan had brought her a drink and a sandwich. Josh's stomach whumped. He edged his way behind the table and leaned down.

"You want to take a break?"

"Good idea!" Polly said.

Josh handed her wraparound sunglasses and a ball cap. "Wear these."

Polly dutifully put them on. "Back in fifteen!" she shouted to the faithful as she rose and headed north. Soon a fresh batch replaced them.

"Where's Polly?" asked a woman with a round face.

"She'll be back in twenty," Josh said.

"Okay, I'll take a *Muhammad*."

Josh put the five bucks in Polly's change box.

"Will she sign my comic if I wait?" the woman said.

"Almost certainly."

He sold five comics in the next ten minutes. A Black Widow character slunk up. She had the shape and red hair and wore an orange-nozzled Uzi on her hip.

"Where's Polly?" she growled.

"Back in ten."

"Who're you?"

"I'm her male escort."

The corner of Black Widow's mouth turned up. She handed Josh a white envelope. "That's an invitation to Michael Davis's party at Tucci's Saturday night. Be there or be square."

"Okay," Josh said, slipping it in the money box.

An eight-foot-tall orc trucked past, accompanied by six trolls. The Avengers slowly conga-lined toward the celebrity autograph chutes. They were very good except for the Flash, who weighed three hundred pounds. Josh fielded a dozen inquiries before Polly reappeared a half hour after she had left.

"You'll never guess who I ran into in the ladies' room!"

"You got people asking about you. I sold twelve *Muhammads*. They'll all be back for your autograph."

Polly took her seat. "Do you know who I ran into in the ladies' room?"

"Who."

"Nichelle Nichols! I almost died! I made a complete fool of myself."

"Who's Nichelle Nichols?"

"She was Lieutenant Uhura in the original *Star Trek*! Don't tell me you haven't heard of *Star Trek*."

"I've heard of it. Some gal stopped by and left this." He handed her the invite.

Polly's face lit up. "How cool is this? Michael Davis's parties are famous! We're going."

"Do I have to dress up?"

"No, silly. Not unless you want to. Just tell everybody you're Jason Statham."

It was 5:00 p.m. when the administrators came, a large woman with a Prince Valiant cut and a knobby geek in flood pants, both wearing SDCC Administration T-shirts. They swooped by the line of supplicants. The woman picked up one of the few remaining *Muhammad* comics on the table.

"You must stop selling this."

Polly looked up startled. "What?"

"We've had several complaints. SDCC promises a safe environment for all comic fans."

"There are one hundred fifty thousand people here. How many complaints?"

The woman looked uneasy. "I'm sorry, that's our policy. Either you stop displaying it or we're going to have to ask you to leave."

Josh watched the arguments well up in Polly's mouth, puffing out her cheeks, as her forehead wrinkled in anger and frustration. He reached past her, grabbed the small stack of *Muhammad* issues and put them beneath the desk.

"No problem."

"Thank you," the woman said. She and her marching companion walked away. A gawky young man was next in line.

"Can I buy one of those comics?"

Polly looked around to make sure they weren't being observed. "You want it signed?"

"Yes please."

Polly picked up a copy, set it on her lap and signed it, furtively exchanging the pamphlet for a five-dollar bill. By five thirty she had run out.

"Got any more?" Josh said.

"I have a hundred more back at the house."

"Let's call it a day. I'm exhausted."

"What about the DC party tonight at Croce's?"

"I'd like to take a nap."

"Forget it. We're going straight through."

CHAPTER 27

Jade

At 8:00 p.m. the crowd outside Croce's approached mob levels, with anxious supplicants, producers and hangers-on hoping to somehow be admitted to the Warner Bros. bash. Polly wore jeans and a Punisher T-shirt. Josh wore jeans and a Sturgis T. It took twenty minutes to get to the gatekeeper, built like a nose tackle in a gray suit with sunglasses. Polly showed him her invite and he waved them through the door.

The inside was chock-a-block, freelancers surrounding the open bar like bees struggling to get to the queen. Josh followed Polly, who used the wedge to gain access to the bar, squeezing in between Bane and Batman.

"What do you want, Josh?" she yelled over the boiler room ambience.

"I'll have a Coke!" Josh shouted back.

Polly got herself a beer and handed Josh the Coke. She dropped a five in the tip glass.

"Oh!" she exclaimed. "There's Jim Lee!"

Josh followed her to where a diminutive Asian man was holding court in a banquette. To his left sat Poison Ivy. To his right sat Daenerys Targaryen with a dragon on her shoulder.

"Polly!" he said, rising and offering his hand.

"Hi Jim! This is my bodyguard, Josh."

They shook hands.

"Bodyguard?" Jim said.

Poison Ivy said, "She's the one who does that *Muhammad* comic!"

"Oh sure," Jim said, sitting back. "How you doing?"

"They told me I had to stop selling it because someone complained."

"That's rough!" Jim said. "Hey, let's catch up later."

As they turned around, fresh supplicants rushed into the gap. Josh surveyed the crowd. They certainly looked menacing. Several Wolverines with steel claws protruding from between their knuckles vogued through the bar, as well as a really scary Cyborg and a four hundred fifty-pound Nightcrawler. Others were their own creations, bedecked with leather, bandoliers, orange-tipped assault rifles and facial piercings. A slim young woman with a brunette pageboy appeared before them.

"Are you Polly Furst?"

"Yup."

"Oh gosh! I love your work! I have all your *Wonder Women*! I wish I'd known you were here tonight I would have brought them to get signed!" She put her hands to her mouth. "Is that all right?"

Polly laughed gleefully. "Come by the table tomorrow. I'm in Artist's Alley."

Josh spotted a bruiser cruising their way with dagger eyes. He was about six two with a shock of black hair, fashionable stubble and a steel hoop the size of a teething ring through his nose. He wore a gray sweatshirt with the sleeves cut off, revealing fully tatted arms: the Punisher, Batman, Wolverine, skulls, daggers, a flying eyeball. He looked angry.

Josh loomed at Polly's side, giving the guy an angle. The man saw Josh and a ripple of doubt washed through him. He confronted Polly.

"You draw that vile *Muhammad* comic, don't you?"

"I wouldn't call it vile."

"You don't think it's vile to insult one of the world's great religions?"

"Well I could argue with you about that but I won't."

"Because you know you can't win that argument."

Josh stepped up. "Move on, buddy."

"Or what?" the big guy sneered.

Josh put his hands up in a placating manner. "We're here to enjoy the party. We're not here to argue."

"Too bad. This bitch has disrespected millions of people."

Josh tapped Polly on the shoulder. "Come on." He stepped aside for her to precede him.

"Not so fast!" the big guy said, putting his hand on Polly's shoulder.

Josh grabbed the hand in both of his, turned and bent it backward with his thumbs crossed on the back, and took the man to the ground. A ripple of shock radiated outward. People stepped away. A minute later the bouncer appeared—the big guy from the door.

"Call the cops!" the inked dude bellowed from the ground. "He assaulted me!"

Josh turned to the bouncer. "Sir, that's not true. He put his hands on Polly first."

A tall woman with long black hair in a braid and green eyes stepped up. "That's true, Phil. They were trying to get away from this guy."

The bouncer turned on the inked dude, who was on his feet. "Okay. You gotta go."

Inked Dude was defiant. "What the fuck? I never laid a hand on him!"

The bouncer stepped in close. "Outside or I call the cops."

Inked Dude truculently turned and stalked toward the exit.

"You know who that was?" the tall woman said.

"No," Polly said. "Who was that douchebag?"

"Kane Owsley. He writes for Groovacious."

"Oh fuck," Polly said.

"What's Groovacious?" Josh said.

The tall woman turned emerald eyes on him. "It's a pop culture site like Ain't It Cool or Icv2.com. Very influential. They also have a newsstand magazine and have begun publishing comics."

"What does that douchebag do?" Polly said.

"He's their chief comic reviewer. Owsley has the power to make or break stars."

"Kane Owsley my ass," Polly said. "I'd love to see his birth certificate."

"Is he an Arab?" Josh said to the woman with green eyes. "I'm Josh Pratt, by the way."

Her hand was cool. "Jade Kamal."

"Are you Eye-talian?"

Jade smiled with amusement. "Sort of."

"What do you do?"

"I'm a writer. I write *Bismillah* for Vertigo."

Polly went wide-eyed. "Oh! You write *Bismillah*! Have you received any death threats?"

"No. But we're careful not to show Muhammad."

"What's *Bismillah?*" Josh said.

"*Bismillah's* an Arab superheroine who flies through the desert on a magic carpet," Jade said. "Sort of like *Route 66* for the Middle East. She's got a genie sidekick named Gruber. It's also the name of my band."

"You a musician?" Josh said.

"Like the Gorillaz. They're a studio band. Nobody knows who they really are. Bismillah sings love songs to goats and camels and children."

"How do you get away with this?"

Jade shrugged. "We've gotten some pushback on the level of six-year-olds whining. The book does pretty well. It's not mean-spirited or anything. We're just trying to entertain."

"Me too," Polly said.

"Yes, but it's a matter of degree. My criticism of Islam, if any, is pretty mild. Whereas you've gone whole hog, so to speak."

"I never thought I'd get so much negative reaction."

"Well I admire your courage. I wouldn't have the guts to do what you did."

"Are you a Muslim?" Josh asked.

"I think so. Depends who you ask."

"Maybe you could say something about my comic to your fans."

"I'll get back to you on that." Jade drifted away.

Josh called Kleiser.

"She's fine, Josh. I'm changing phones at midnight. Here's the new number."

CHAPTER 28

SDCC Day Two

The scene outside the convention center Friday morning resembled Mecca during the haj. Tens of thousands of fans, many of them in cosplay, had lined up. Using the wedge, Polly and Josh made their way to the pro entrance and squeezed in. When they got to Polly's table, they found that the administrators had covered the title of her *Muhammad* comic on the banner with duct tape.

"Oh for God's sake," Polly said.

"No, this is good," Josh said. "Kinda jumps out at you, doesn't it? People will want to know what's beneath the tape."

Polly unloaded her last hundred copies of *Muhammad* beneath the table as a voice came over the intercom: "Attention, dealers and artists! The doors will open in ten minutes! Gird your loins!"

"Get out your brass knuckles," Josh said.

Polly sighed. "They took those away at the airport."

"I'll give you another one when we get back."

The crowds flooded in. Young men with twelve-inch Mohawks and enough facial piercings to build a particle-beam accelerator. A platoon of Harley Quinns marching in rank. The morbidly obese with their walkers, canes and carts. Families dressed like the Incredibles. Service dogs dressed as Bat Hound. A dead ringer for Walter White.

Walter White stopped at the table, picked up Polly's convention sketchbook and flipped through it. "Nice work."

"Thanks!" Polly said. "Anyone tell you, you look like Walter White?"

The man winked. "All the time."

They watched him go.

"That was Bryan Cranston," Josh said.

A kid in a Deadpool T appeared. "Do you have *Muhammad*?"

Polly looked furtively around and reached under the table. "Do you want it signed?"

"Yes please."

"How do you know she has it?" Josh said.

"Jade Kamal told me. I love *Bismillah*!"

The day ground on, with fans bringing Polly and Josh lunch. At two thirty a volunteer came by and reminded Polly she was on a panel at three: "Women in Comics." It took them twenty minutes to exit the main hall and take the escalator to the second floor, another fifteen to work their way down the corridor to the meeting room. The line stretched all the way back into the second-floor hall. A cluster of volunteers in SDCC's characteristic blue-and-yellow T-shirts stood at the doors, which had not been opened.

The same woman who'd insisted that Polly remove her comics came toward them with a grim expression. "You're no longer required for this panel."

Polly opened her mouth. "What?" she squeaked.

"The board had an emergency meeting and asked Bonnie Dart to replace you."

"But I've been listed for this panel for over a year! I wrote a speech!"

People gathered around. Josh noticed the odious Owsley filming them with his camera. Josh casually moved between him and Polly.

"Please try to understand," the woman said. "This is a family-friendly, all-inclusive event. We're not used to this kind of controversy. There have been threats."

"Those nutjobs won't know she's been deep-sixed," Josh said. "If they're gonna bomb, they're gonna bomb."

The woman put a finger to her lips, leaned in and snarled, "Please! Do not mention anything like that!"

Josh looked around. "Are we in America?"

Polly grabbed his arm. "Come on, Josh. Let's go."

They headed back toward the escalator.

"Hater!" someone shouted.

They kept going.

"Jew bitch!" someone shouted.

Josh whirled, eyes scanning the crowd. A shoving match broke out ten feet away. A thick-lipped man shaped like a weather balloon, wearing a Hellboy T-shirt and with Marty Allen hair, had pushed a wiry red-haired kid in wire-rimmed glasses to the ground. Sides formed as volunteers tried to separate them.

"Come on, Josh!" Polly pleaded, pulling him toward the escalators.

They booked. It took a half hour to get back to the table in Artist's Alley. Polly stared at the blank space where her display had been. Even the banner was missing. She turned to Drednox Comix.

"Duane! What happened to my stuff?"

"Two guys came by. They said you'd asked them to pack it up! Oh shit—"

"What did they look like?" Josh said?

"Slim, dark, beards."

"Would you know them if you saw them again?"

Duane looked spooked. "One of them wore a Hitler T-shirt. I didn't want to say anything, you know, he may have been trying to be ironic or something..."

Polly rushed behind the table and gasped. "Oh no! They took my original art!"

Josh looked around as if he could spot the perp but it was a hallucinatory display: Iron Man staggered by, blinking and clanking; a woman hunkered down behind a double-wide baby pram, preparing to play ice breaker; Groot staggered through the crowd on stilts.

"We've got to report this," Josh said.

"To who?" Polly said. "The con?"

"Fuck the con. We'll go outside and talk to the police. Do you have photocopies of the stolen pages?"

"Photocopies?! Oh Josh! Yes, I scan everything but the originals are worth a lot of money. I sold a page for a thousand dollars last year to a collector in Spain."

"Come on. We'll tell the con later."

They sliced their way slowly toward the exit. It was a struggle, the pressure slowing them and weighing them down as if at the bottom of the sea. It took them twenty minutes to step outside into the brilliant afternoon sun, where the scene was even busier than before, with uniformed cops standing in the middle of Harbor Drive blowing whistles and directing traffic like Roman legionaries.

"Was it insured?" Josh said, waiting at the curb with two hundred others for the cop to wave them across.

"Fuck no," Polly said.

The cop blew her whistle and motioned them forward. She was a slight Hispanic woman in a light blue short-sleeved cop shirt, wearing a shiny black-brimmed officer's cap. Her nametag said FAVELA. "Officer," Josh said, "we'd like to report a theft."

"Not right now, sir. Give me a minute. Please go stand at the curb and I'll come to you."

They returned to in front of the convention center while Favela spoke into her shoulder unit. Another cop strolled to the middle of the intersection as Favela joined them, leaning in to hear them over the crowd. Polly told her what happened.

"I can give you copies of the stolen pages."

"Ma'am, I'll be happy to take a report, but as you can see right now we're overwhelmed." She handed Polly her card. "Please visit this station to file your complaint."

"Can I email you?"

"No, ma'am. You must be present."

Favela's shoulder unit squawked and she was immediately distracted, walking away speaking to her shoulder.

"Great," Polly said.

"Come on. Let's tell the organizers."

They fought their way inside to the pro registration table, where they spoke to a sympathetic volunteer wearing a Battlepug T-shirt.

"I will alert our security staff," she said.

They wedged their way through the mob. It took twenty minutes to reach Polly's table, where a mousy woman with hair in her face sat arranging crudely drawn posters of the *Game of Thrones* crew.

"This is my table," Polly said.

"This guy said I could have it," the woman answered without looking up. "I paid him two hundred dollars."

"What?!"

"Come on," Josh said. "You've got nothing else to sell, and now they won't know where to find you."

"Fine," Polly said. "Let's go find DC."

CHAPTER 29

The Fanboy Slalom

The DC table was surrounded by a hardened reef of freelancers wielding their portfolios like Roman shields. Polly took one look.

"FUGGEDABOUDIT! Let's get out of here before we go mad!"

They went upstairs and left the convention center on the ocean side, like blind cave creatures stumbling into sunlight. They found a bench and collapsed in the shade of an oak tree that had dodged two hundred years of waterfront improvement.

"Oh my God!" Polly exclaimed, shrugging out of her backpack and flopping onto the bench. "I'd forgotten what a zoo it is! It's like a John Brunner novel! All those people!"

"What are we going to do for the rest of the con?" Josh said.

"We're going to roam the floor incognito. They can't very well keep me out. Not enough people know what I look like to stop me from going to panels, and in the evening, we'll go to the cool parties. Tonight it's the 1st/Devil's Due party at Gnocci's."

"Who they?" Josh asked.

Polly looked at him with a funny grin. "*The Badger*, dope!"

Josh smacked his palm against his forehead. "Duh! Will the Badger be there?"

"No doubt."

Gnocci's, a nouveau Italian joint, was within walking distance. Josh and Polly arrived at a quarter of eight. Freelancers were two deep at the bar as a piano trio danced through "Nica's Dream."

Polly got two beers while Josh swooped by the bulging buffet, carrying platters filled with cold cuts and vegetables to a booth in the corner. By the time they hoovered up the food, the room was at near capacity, the babble of conversation drowning out the band.

"Oh!" Polly said. "There's Bill and Linda Reinhold!" She popped up and rounded on a diminutive man with glasses and bangs, and a Junoesque woman. Josh trailed along.

"When are you going to draw another *Badger*?" Polly said.

"Well I've been working on a script..." Reinhold started to answer.

"For three years," Linda filled in.

Josh was awe-struck and tongue-tied. He loved Reinhold's *Badger*, which he'd read in the joint. He eavesdropped and followed Polly as she worked the room like Huey Long, slapping biceps and pumping arms. Josh's gaze swept like a lighthouse, on the alert for any anomaly, darkness or disruption. But the crowd was already dark and disruptive by nature, living in worlds of their own imaginations.

Josh felt a hand on his shoulder and turned.

"Hi," Jade Kamal said. She wore a long purple shift off one shoulder that covered her feet, as if she'd just walked off the set of *Rome*.

"Hello, Jade. How are you?"

"I'm good. I heard you had a little drama today."

"You mean the stolen pages? Or the nutter who closed us down?"

"Why do you keep looking around like that?"

Josh looked into her green eyes. "It's my job."

Polly turned and sparkled. "Hi Jade!"

Jade unslung her mauve Gucci shoulder bag and pulled out a phone the size of a postcard. "I want to show you something." She poked, found and turned it around.

"This is a discussion board to which I belong, on Western images of Islam. This is a screen capture because they deleted it about five minutes after they posted it."

Josh and Polly stared at the screen.

All those who wish to join me in destroying the Jew bitch who defiles our Prophet. You know how to get in touch with me. –Hashim Rashad

"That's it?" Polly said. "No address?"

"They're using darknet," Josh said. "It's the internet you don't see."

"I notified the moderator and asked that that person be banned from the group. He is."

Josh handed Jade his card. "Would you email me that?"

Polly grabbed Josh's arm. "Now what?"

"Well, we'll notify the FBI and Homeland Security. I may have a little suck there. By the way, you standing and not sitting at a table makes my life a lot easier."

Polly turned to Jade. "Are you doing something for First/Devil's Due?"

Jade batted her thick eyelashes. "I'm doing an issue of *Badger*."

Josh brightened. "What's it about?"

"Ham's three-legged pig Senator Kasten sets out on a cross-country hike to raise awareness for the other white meat."

Polly shook her head in disbelief. "Wow. So much to process."

"Are you gonna be able to draw a pig?" Josh said.

Jade smiled. "No sweat. I like bacon too."

It was one by the time they returned to Genoa Street in a cab, which Polly paid for from her reams of cash. They slept late and returned to the convention shortly before noon beneath a ceramic blue sky. Seagulls squawked as Josh and Polly queued up at the pro entrance.

Inside was cool despite a hundred thousand people in one room. Josh grabbed Polly's hand. "Come on! It's almost time for the Fanboy Slalom!"

They snaked their way to the northeast corner of the enormous space, standing at the tail end of Artist's Alley next to girls who were drawing pink dragons and cats, and guys offering YOUR ZOMBIE CARICATURE. Power Girl stood in the corner with her arms crossed. A young mother with a double-wide pram attempted to make her way down the aisle. Gripping the handle in both fists, she put her head down.

"Ramming speed!" she cried, thrusting forward.

"Ramming speed!" her two adorable girls shrieked, laughing.

People yelped and cursed. The young mother emerged in a momentary clearing and shook her head, her hair flying. "Thank you!"

Josh looked at his watch. "It's ten past noon. They should be breaking any second now."

Several dozen people had gathered in a sort of semi-circle at the corner, grudgingly allowing browsers to sift through their ranks for the irritated artists who'd rented tables to sell their wares. Half the expectant crowd were cosplayers, including two Deadpools and two Harley Quinns. Pleasurable tension vibrated through the crowd.

"Here they come!" someone yelled from the sea of people, and seconds later Spider-Man squeaked between two human boulders, zigzagged past the few remaining obstacles and smacked into the very corner of the room, whirled and sank to one knee with arms upraised in triumph. A steady flow of lithe young things filtered through the mob to follow suit as Power Girl made notes on a clipboard. Participants continued to trickle in like at the Tour de France three hours after the winner has crossed the finish line.

Power Girl had a powerful set of lungs. "HEAR YE, HEAR YE! SPIDER-MAN, A.K.A. SIMON GROSS OF ALEXANDRIA, VIRGINIA, HAS WON THE FANBOY SLALOM AT TWELVE MINUTES, FOUR SECONDS IN THE YEAR OF OUR LORD 2017!"

Overwhelmed by the noise, chaos and crowds, Josh and Polly wedged their way out of the main hall and went outside toward the harbor. Polly sat on the concrete steps and opened the con program on her knees. The cover was a Nick Runge painting of Batman and the Punisher arm-wrestling in a bar.

"There's a panel at three I want to see. 'Wonder Woman—Empowering or Stereotype?'"

"I can hardly wait."

"Oh wait," Polly said. "I have money. Let me pay you."

"What about the original art?"

Polly looked up. "Do you want original art?"

"Sure. Hang on while I call my NSA guy."

Josh sat in the shade on the patio, back against the railing, and called Stoeckle. No answer, so Josh left a message regarding the threat and forwarded the message. They walked up the esplanade to Seafront Village—a collection of faux-quaint shops, including art galleries, coffeehouses, souvenir shops and a Subway. They got subs and sat under an umbrella in the sun looking across the waters to the aircraft carrier USS *Theodore Roosevelt*.

"I feel liberated," Polly declared. "It's kind of a relief not to have to fight my way in there anymore. From now on I declare my independence from the con! From this day forth, I'm free to see the other San Diego—

the zoo, Mission Bay! We may even go to Tijuana!" She pointed at Josh with her sub.

"Have you ever been to Tijuana?" she said.

"Nope."

"Want to go?"

"Nope."

"Why not?"

"Because it's not safe, from what I've heard. Even bikers I know say it isn't safe."

Polly stuck out her lower lip. "Pooh. You're no fun. So what do you want to do until tonight? We can't miss Michael Davis's party!"

"Who's Michael Davis?" Josh said.

"He was a founding member of Milestone comics and created *Static*, along with Dwayne McDuffie."

"Who's Static?"

Polly used a finger to peel down her lower eyelid. "Did you grow up under a rock?"

Josh shrugged.

"Doesn't matter!" Polly said, stretching her arms. "Look at that sea! Smell that air! Aren't you just glad to be alive?"

"Yes I am."

"Good. Are you happy? I mean right now."

"I guess."

Polly plucked at his sleeve. "Oh come on, Josh! You guess?"

"Sure. I'm happy. If you're happy, I'm happy."

"I know! Let's go see a movie!"

CHAPTER 30

To the Con!

Tucci's was a block inland from the Hyatt, an old-style Italian restaurant with red-and-white checked tablecloths and pictures of Florence, Genoa and Sicily on the wall. It was 9:00 p.m. and the line stretched down the block and around the corner, most supplicants poking and staring at their handheld devices. Josh and Polly got in line. Polly pulled out her sketchpad, leaned on a rail and drew the people around them in quick, sure lines.

They reached the front of the line, where a tanned middle-aged man in a tux was almost in tears at being refused entrance.

"Don't you know who I am?" he wailed.

The doorman, who looked like Yaphet Kotto, said, "I don't know and I don't care. Next!"

Polly presented her invite and the doorman waved them through.

An electric buzz hovered over the crowd inside—famous faces everywhere, a thousand expensive scents in the air, the tinkle of glass, the sound of laughter, the throbbing of a live band somewhere in back. It was a big room, every place setting marked with a swag bag. Josh picked one up. Inside was a bagged copy of the latest issue of *Static*, a DVD of *Standing in the Shadows of Motown*, a Milestone coloring book and pack of crayons, and a pair of oversized, pink-framed cat's-eye sunglasses.

Polly grabbed his hand and pulled him toward the bar, where four bartenders were moving constantly, like one of the mechanical bands at the House on the Rock in Wisconsin. Polly wedged herself between a tall black man with beard and glasses wearing a porkpie hat and the slim, middle-aged man whom he was talking to. She elbowed the black man in the ribs and he turned.

"Michael!" Polly said.

"Polly!" Michael Davis replied, giving her a hug.

"This is my bodyguard, Josh."

Davis coolly appraised Josh. "So it's come to this."

They shook hands. Davis turned and brought the other man up. "You know Bill Sienkiewicz, right?"

Polly's eyes grew wide. "You're like a god to me!"

Sienkiewicz blushed. "A false god."

They cooed over each other's work while Josh scanned the room. He was uneasy in these crowd settings, because the mob could conceal someone intending to do harm until it was too late. But how many people even knew Polly was here? Odds were just the immediate handful. Josh relaxed a little. He spotted Oliver Stone talking to Christian Bale. He spotted the actor who played Clay on *Sons of Anarchy*. He spotted Lady Gaga drinking champagne from a slipper.

"Josh!" Polly said. She handed him a beer.

He spotted Scarlett Johansson heading toward him in a strapless black dress. As she approached he saw that it wasn't the movie star, but the woman who'd handed him the invite two days ago. He looked around to see who she was really after, but she came right up to him.

"You're not Jason Statham."

"And you're not Scarlett Johansen."

They regarded each other for a minute.

"Are you a comic guy?"

"Josh Pratt. I'm Polly Furst's security."

Scarlett stuck out her hand. "Shelley Schultz. I'm a cosplayer and a dancer. I was in The Shazam's video 'Maserati' and The Foreign Films' 'Arcade on the Beach.'"

Josh hadn't heard of either group. "Are those available?"

"They're both on YouTube. So what are you, like a bodyguard?"

"Yes."

Josh followed Shelley's gaze as she turned toward Polly, holding court among a clutch of eager fanboys.

"I admire her courage," Shelley said. "I could never put myself out there like she does."

"She's standing up for what's right."

"I don't know what's right anymore. Maybe I never did. You want to do a line?"

Josh smiled. "No thanks. I had enough of that shit."

"What're you drinking, sailor?"

"Beer."

"You a biker?" Shelley said.

"Yeah."

"You look like one. What do you ride?"

"A modified Road King."

"Modified how?"

Josh slugged beer and inhaled. "Engine: 88 with oil cooler. Changed the cams to S&S gear drives with .510 lift. Took out the fuel injection and replaced it with an S&S Super E, Yost Power Tube, S&S manifold and Pingle high-flow petcock. S&S teardrop air cleaner cover with a K&N filter. Screamin' Eagle Hi-Performance ignition unit with a 6200-rpm rev limiter. Accell Super Coil, FireWire plug wires and spiral wound metal core wires. Accell platinum-tip plugs. Five-speed tranny with Barnett Kevlar clutch, self-adjusting hydraulic chain tensioner. Screamin' Eagle dualies. Progressive springs in front with higher viscosity, Progressives in back. Changed the rear swing-arm bushings to STA-BO nylon high density. SBS semi-metallic disc brake pads, and the brake lines are stainless steel braids. Went to tubeless wheels."

Shelley clapped. "Outstanding!"

"Do you ride?"

"No, I just dig bikes and bikers. I was Miss Daytona two years ago. Y'know, we should blow this Popsicle stand and find someplace quiet. Where are you staying?"

"The Hyatt. Can't leave my client."

Shelley pointed. "Look at her. She's not going anywhere. Think someone's going to make a move on her here?"

Polly bubbled like a fountain amid a crowd of fans.

"Hang on a sec." Josh went to Polly.

"Hey. I'm thinking of breaking away for a couple hours. That all right with you?"

Polly looked past him to the redhead. "Sure. Nobody knows where I am. I mean nobody who's out to get me. Go on. Take the rest of the night off. I can make my way back to the hotel all right."

"You're sure?"

Polly pushed him on the shoulder. "Go on! But I'll expect you to work extra hours in the morning. Keep your phone on!"

Josh started to turn.

"Josh!"

He turned back.

"Practice safe sex!"

Josh laughed.

As he and Shelley left the restaurant, Shia LaBeouf was in the doorman's face.

"I told you, I lost it! Just check the guest list."

Shelley took Josh's hand and led him down the street, across the Pacific Highway back to the Hyatt. Bar con was in full cry as they made their way through the lobby. Shelley grabbed his arm like a life preserver.

"There's that scumbag Spiegelman. What a liar."

Josh followed her gaze to a thin, gray-haired man at the bar surrounded by courtiers. Shelley looked at him.

"You know who Spiegelman is, don't you?"

"No."

"Wow. You're probably the only person here who doesn't know who he is."

"Maybe."

She pulled him toward the elevators. "Better you don't know."

They waited with twenty conventioneers, some in costume, watching the elevator dials. They stood back as an elevator disgorged Red Sonja, some kind of Mad Max mash-up, Deadpool and a morbidly obese man wearing black pants, shirt, suspenders, top hat and round sunglasses. A dozen people squeezed into the elevator, all the guys giving Shelley the look-over through the mirrored walls. They got off on eleven and Josh led her down the corridor to his room, inserting the card into the slot. As soon as Josh closed the door, Shelley was on him like a lamprey. His lizard brain took over. He hadn't been laid since Fiona Fab last December. His hands squeezed her up and down like a shopper feeling peaches as she thrust her groin into his.

"I have a diaphragm," Shelley whispered.

They tore each other's clothes off and stumbled to the bed, where he entered her at once, cradling her face in his hands.

My luck's about to turn.

"Wow," he said with his arm around her. "Where have you been all my life?" He didn't really mean it. She was just a quick fuck. Who knew?

Afterward, Shelley sat up and pointed to the green-and-yellow dragon spiraling around his torso. "What's this?"

"A dragon."

She pointed to the crucifix and bleeding heart. "And this?"

"Christ's heart."

"Can I raid your servy bar?"

"Sure."

"Want a beer?"

"Sure."

She got up and he watched her pad naked into the bathroom, emerging a minute later wearing one of his Sturgis Ts. She knelt before the servy bar and took out a bottle of wine and a can of beer.

"I'm going to put these in glasses," she said, taking them into the bathroom. She returned a moment later with two glasses, one filled with wine, one with beer, and sat on the edge of the table. Handing a glass to Josh, she held hers up.

"To the con!"

Josh clinked. "To the con!"

CHAPTER 31

That Sinking Feeling

Josh woke with sunshine on his face and a head full of cotton. He lay there staring at the ceiling trying to remember what had happened, each heartbeat imparting dull pain to his temples. Shelley's scent was on him but Shelley was gone. He looked at the clock. Ten thirty! His message light flashed and as he reached for the phone it rang. He picked it up.

"Hello."

"Wake up, sleepyhead! I've been trying to get hold of you for an hour," Polly said. "You must have had a hell of a night!"

Josh got a bad feeling in his gut. "Where are you?"

"I'm down in the lobby! Some friends told me they saw you following that hot redhead like a jackass after a carrot."

"Give me twenty. I'll meet you in the lobby."

"You sound rid hard and put away wet."

"Urg." Josh hung up and sat stupidly on the edge of the bed for a minute before snagging his jeans with his foot and dragging them close. He checked his wallet. Everything was intact. He wondered if he should change phones. He wondered if he was being paranoid. He called Kleiser.

"She's fine, Josh. I'm changing phones, so let me give you the new number."

Josh wrote it down and looked around. There was no trace of Shelley. He checked the closet, the bureau and the bathroom. Except for the bed and the empty glasses, there was no sign she'd ever been there. He stumbled into the bathroom, banging his toe on the bed frame, then endured a cold shower. He had a faint metallic taste on his tongue and an oppressive undertow in his head.

He dried off and methodically went through his things. Everything was in its place. He couldn't shake the feeling that he'd been drugged.

At least she'd fucked him first. Josh pulled on his pants and a yellow BSA shirt, and joined five disturbingly chipper attendees as they rode to the lobby.

"Did you see Stan Lee yesterday? Man that was so awesome!"

"Yeah he looks great for ninety!"

Polly was waiting for him in the lobby wearing a white dress and cat's-eye sunglasses, her red hair sprouting like a dandelion, fists on her hips. Little Miss Attitude.

"Look what the cat dragged in!" she crowed.

"Shut up. I need coffee."

Polly poked at her phone while a hostess seated them. She didn't look up until Josh had his coffee.

"Kane Owsley says I'm an intolerant Jew bitch making jihad on innocent Muslims."

"Seriously?"

"Not in so many words. You should see the comments. Over a hundred fifty already, pretty much split between Jew bitch and freedom fighter."

"Shelley Schultz. Know her?"

"No. Should I?"

Josh leaned forward, resting his face in his palm, staring through his fingers at a paper place mat depicting Deadpool and Harley Quinn in mortal combat.

"Catwoman. She's the babe I bagged last night."

"Who bagged whom?" Shelley said, studying the menu.

"She bagged me."

The waitress returned. Polly ordered yogurt and fruit; Josh ordered an omelet. He took out his phone.

"There are dozens of Shelley Schultzes on Facebook."

"There's only one that looks like that," Polly said. "Check the profile pics."

"Help me out here, will you?"

Silently they poked at their devices. The waitress returned and laid down their orders. Ten minutes later Josh looked up.

"I can't find her."

"Do you think that's her real name?"

Josh kneaded his eyes with a fist. "Fuck."

"Let me ask Michael. He'd know her."

"Michael Who?"

"Michael Davis! The guy who threw the party! DUH!"

"Go ahead."

A minute later Polly was on her phone saying, "Michael! Fab party!" and turned away. Josh stared at his omelet, picked up knife and fork and consumed it. Polly turned back.

"Michael doesn't know who she is. He gave me the number of his friend Ward, who was in charge of invites. He thinks Shelley's one of Ward's friends."

"You know Ward?"

"I've met him."

"Why don't you call him?"

Minutes later Polly looked at him, perplexed. "Ward says he gave some invites to his friend Sabrina, and that Sabrina might have given them to Shelley."

"Do we have contact info for Sabrina?"

"All he said, she's on Facebook."

Josh pulled out his phone. "What's her last name?"

"Maus." She spelled it.

There were several but none from the United States.

"Call Ward back. See what you can learn about Sabrina."

Polly spoke for a minute and handed her phone to Josh. "He wants to talk to you."

"This is Josh."

"This is Ward. What's this about?"

"You know Shelley Schultz?"

"Not really. She's a friend of Sabrina's. What's this about?"

"You know Polly does that *Muhammad* comic, don't you?"

"Sure."

"Well jihadis are coming out of the woodwork trying to kill her. I stupidly went with Shelley last night. I think she drugged me. I think she was searching for a way to get at Polly. I need to find her."

"Excuse me, who did you say you were? Polly's bodyguard?"

"Yes sir."

"Maybe you need the bodyguard."

"Ward, I was a dumb fuck."

"Okay. Give me your contact info and I'll ask around."

"Thank you, sir."

He handed the phone to Polly.

Josh pictured his disheveled bed. Maybe she'd left some hairs. Maybe she'd worn a wig. Josh had a feeling her name wasn't Shelley and nobody really knew her. But how had she figured to target him? And why?

Or was it another California Miracle, like last year, like Fiona Fab? Josh had a hard time believing he was God's gift to women. He poured himself another cup of coffee.

"Are we through with the con?"

"Yes! Let's go to the zoo! Let's go to Mission Bay and rent WaveRunners! I'll pay!"

"When's your flight?" Josh said.

"Six thirty. I get into Madison at ten forty-five. You?"

"Outta here at eleven, into Madison at three thirty. Who's picking you up at the airport?"

"Don."

"Okay. Good. Give me fifteen minutes. I need to check something."

Polly looked around. "There's Leila del Duca. I'll talk to her."

When Josh got off on the eleventh floor, he saw a short Mexican maid outside his room bundling linens into a hamper. He broke into a run.

"Wait! Stop!" He realized the maid was looking at him with fear. He forced a sickly smile across his face.

"I'm sorry. *Lo siento*. I didn't mean to scare you! Wait..."

He dug in his wallet and handed her a twenty. "I just want to check something," he said, reaching into the bin. He pulled out the white sheets and smoothed them over the hamper. Yes! There! Several long, coppery strands. He plucked them, picked up a tiny cardboard box, ditched the soap and stuck in the hairs. He recognized her glass by the residue of wine. Real glass. He shucked a fresh glass from its plastic envelope and put in Shelley's.

As he walked away, sweating and smiling, he wondered if the maid even spoke English.

CHAPTER 32

Cherchez la Femme

They went to the zoo. The otters entranced Polly on the Hippo Trail, and a red orangutan sitting in a hemp hammock bared its teeth.

"He reminds me of my first boyfriend," she said.

While she flitted from exhibit to exhibit, Josh followed, bringing up videos on his phone: The Shazam's "Maserati" and The Foreign Films' "Arcade on the Beach." There was a redhead in both who might have been Shelley, but he couldn't be sure. He sat on a bench while he searched for credits. The dancers were not credited, so he "liked" both groups on Facebook and sent each the same message. "Can you identify the red-haired dancer in black spandex that performs on your video?"

It was a beautiful sunny day filled with the sounds of children laughing, parrots screeching, lions roaring and a calliope. Airplanes left crisscrossed contrails in the sky, while vendors sold hot dogs and souvenirs. Thousands of visitors of every race and creed wandered the broad avenues. They stopped at Poppy's Patio for a gourmet funnel cake. Josh watched with distaste as Polly consumed the volcanic confection.

She held it out. "Want some?"

Josh waved it away.

"You don't eat much, do you?" Polly said.

"I eat enough."

Josh followed Polly to the hippo bin, where she leaned over the railing aiming her cell phone, while his gaze swept three sixty like a lighthouse until *bam*. That girl! That blond girl pointing and laughing. A missile to the heart, she reminded him so much of his Fig Newton.

She turned and motioned to her boyfriend, and it wasn't Fig.

The weight of loss fell on him so hard he staggered, sat on a bench and buried his face in his hands. The smell, feel and sound of her—gone forever. The howling void in his soul turned into dry heaves, and suddenly Polly was sitting next to him with her arm around his shoulders.

"Josh, what's wrong? What is it?"

He inhaled deeply and shucked it off. "Nothing. Bad moment."

"What? Why? Tell me."

"I saw a girl who looked like Fig. I'm alright now."

Polly touched the tear slick running down his cheek. "Be happy, Josh. I want you to be happy."

He forced a grin. "I'm all right. Really. It happens now and then. I'll get over it."

They returned to Genoa Street at four, packed and took a taxi to the airport. Josh saw Polly off, went to Phil's Barbecue in Terminal 2, ordered a pulled-pork sandwich and settled down with his book, *The Deep Blue Goodbye*, by John D. MacDonald. Danny Bloom had given it to him several years ago, and he'd brought it along just in case. It had lain fallow until Josh had learned that Christian Bale, his favorite actor, was going to play McGee.

Folding the book, he phoned Don.

"This is Don."

"The eagle has flown," Josh said.

"I'll be there. Any trouble?"

"The usual horseshit. Some asswipes complained and they shut down her booth. She'd sold everything anyway. Call me when she gets there."

"Will do."

Don called back at ten. "The eagle has landed."

"Great. See you tomorrow."

Josh boarded his United flight at ten thirty. Because he'd booked late, he sat between a fat businessman in a blue serge suit who smelled of Brut, and a teenage girl wired into her device so she didn't have to react to reality. During the safety message, Josh wondered how United had gotten their hooks into Gershwin's "Rhapsody in Blue" accompaniment and what could be done to save it.

Once they leveled off, Josh went online and checked his messages. Hans Rotenberry of The Shazam had responded to his query about the dancer.

"That was Shelley Schultz. She was a sweet girl, a great friend and a shining light to all who knew her on the Nashville music scene. Shelley died four years ago in an auto accident. A drunk driver crossed the centerline. She was driving alone. We're still trying to recover."

Josh wrote back. "Did she have a sister?"

Rotenberry was online. "No. Why?"

"Ran into a woman claiming she was Schultz at the San Diego Comic Convention. Do you have any idea who would do that?"

"That's fucking unbelievable!" the singer responded. "I have no idea, but it's wrong. There was only one Shelley."

Josh found Schultz's obituary in the *Nashville Daily Corridor*. She was survived by her brother, Al, and her parents, Leslie and Ralph Schultz. There were too many Alan Schultzes on Facebook to contact, and of the Ralphs and Leslies, none were from Nashville or its environs.

Josh searched the Nashville white pages and found three Ralph Schultzes in Nashville, but it was too late to call them. He wrote their numbers and addresses on his spiral pad. When he looked up, the girl next to him stared at him with bemusement.

"What?" Josh said.

"Why don't you just use the phone, dude? You know you can make notations there."

"I'm old-fashioned."

"Whatever." She put her earbuds back in.

Josh arrived in Madison at three thirty in the morning and took a taxi to his house on the far Southwest Side. His taxi driver had framed his master's in comparative religion on the dash. He was also an ordained minister of the Universal Life Church. Sensing Josh didn't want to talk, he just drove, listening to Bob Marley.

The light was on when Josh got home, Fig barking from inside at the sound of the car door. Josh let himself in and knelt to embrace his dog. Kleiser's door was open. Josh could see him inside sawing logs, but as Josh started stashing his stuff, Kleiser appeared wearing only jeans, revealing a bony torso with tatted arms and chest. One of the tats was PATTY in cursive on a scroll surrounded by tiny cupids.

"How was the trip?" Kleiser said.

"Pretty smooth. Find anything?"

"Yeah. I was gonna phone you but I thought about it. I only made headway this afternoon, so I just waited to tell you in person."

The kitchen doggie door went whump and Fig appeared clutching a stick.

"Who is it?" Josh said.

"Don't know yet but I've traced the message through six slaves in six countries and guess where it originated? Jackson County, Wisconsin."

CHAPTER 33

A Godly Man

"How'd you do it?" Josh said.

Kleiser smiled. "I'd tell you, but you'd go into a coma. Tricks I've picked up along the way. To tell you the truth, I'm not sure myself how I did it. I just kept poking and pulling strings. It helps that I have access to Dovetail's network and servers. I also patched into the Pentagon's Skynet system. Hopefully, they won't trace that back to Dovetail."

"Does Kofsky know?"

"No. You're the client, not Kofsky."

"Can you backtrack into the system? Whoever sent it?"

"Maybe."

"Can you give me an address?"

Kleiser's grin was wall to wall. "The original message inadvertently included a tagline from OldMacDonaldsfarm.com, a purveyor of organically grown ginseng and other herbs. On a hunch I fed the info into the Dish network's database and found a subscriber in Jackson County, one Steven MacDonald, 2247 Ralston Road. He has a website."

"Old MacDonald."

"Yup."

Josh headed for his office. "Show me."

Kleiser held out his hand. "That will be five thousand dollars please."

Josh smacked Kleiser on the forehead. "You'll get your money. Show me."

Kleiser followed Josh into the office, sat at the computer and brought up Google Maps. He entered an address and the screen zeroed in on Jackson County, showing a red pin on a winding rural road.

"Great fucking work, Randall! Take the rest of the night off."

"Thanks."

Josh showered and collapsed into bed as the sun was rising, with Fig at his side. He wrapped his arms around her and inhaled her fur. As always, he was surprised by how sweet she smelled. When she was wet she smelled like a wet dog, but when she was dry she had her own sweet smell. One thing about Fig, she was always down for a nap.

Josh woke at ten not fully rested but eager to start the day. He and Fig ran five miles. By the time he'd showered and had breakfast it was eleven. Kleiser was still asleep.

Josh went into his office and started phoning Ralph Schultzes. On the seventh call he hit pay dirt.

"This is Ralph Schultz," said a phlegmy voice.

"Mr. Schultz, this is Josh Pratt. I'm a private investigator from Madison, Wisconsin. Several days ago, at the San Diego Comic Con, I was approached by a young woman who claimed she was Shelley Schultz from Nashville."

"That's impossible. Our Shelley died four years ago. Who did you say you were?"

"Josh Pratt. I'm a private investigator. I think it's possible someone has stolen your daughter's identity."

"Is this a joke?" Schultz demanded.

"No sir. I'm serious. I'm an accredited private investigator. You can check with the Professional Association of Wisconsin Licensed Investigators. Josh Pratt. Spelled just like it sounds. If you like, take some time to check me out. I'd like to call you back. I believe this young woman has malicious intent."

"You're damned right I'm going to check you out. What's your phone number?"

Josh told him. Josh guessed Schultz still used a rotary phone. "I'll get back to you."

"Thank you, sir."

Josh rode to Don's house in Middleton. Don had left for work but the front door was unlocked. He went inside and up the creaky wooden steps, and opened doors until he found Polly asleep in the back.

"Polly."

She opened her eyes. "What?"

"Get up! It's noon already."

Polly flopped around. "Why?"

"So we can review and discuss your security arrangements."

"All right. Why don't you make some coffee? I'll be down shortly."

Josh went into the kitchen and revved up the caffeinator. He went into the living room and looked at the page taped to Polly's drafting table. It was the same page she'd been working on before SDCC, showing a werewolf crouching in a tree looking at a city in the distance at night. Josh admired the way she'd delineated a convincing werewolf with only its outline, the way she'd made the city come alive with pinpricks of light. He heard the shower.

Minutes later Polly came downstairs toweling her hair, wearing a Badger T-shirt and blue jeans. She went straight into the kitchen, pulled a mug and filled it with coffee, cream and sugar. Josh filled a cup and followed her out onto the porch, where they sat on a bench.

"I thought I told you to keep the front door locked."

"I did! Don must have left it open."

"Didn't you tell Don?"

"I forgot. What's the skinny on Black Widow?" Polly said.

A flush of shame crept up from Josh's toes. It had nothing to do with morality. It had everything to do with security. "I'm working on that. Hopefully, she was just a kook."

"A randy kook."

"Chicago's next week. Have you heard anything from the organizers?"

"Not yet, but the day is young. I expect to be disinvited at any minute."

"You're sharing a table with that Arab guy."

"Zlatko's not an Arab. He's Bosnian."

Josh phoned Zlatko. "Chicago's next week. You coming up? You want to come up, I'll put you up for the night and we can all drive down together."

"I think that will work out," Zlatko said. "Let me check my schedule and I'll get back to you."

Polly stared at her device. "The organizers are asking me not to advertise or sell *Muhammad* at Chicago. There's a clause in my contract stipulating that they can remove me and keep my money. 'CFP may terminate this Contract immediately upon written notice if Exhibitor breaches any of its obligations under this Contract, in which event CFP shall retain any deposit or other payments previously made by Exhibitor, and this Contract shall be null, void and without any further force or effect.' Blah, blah, blah."

"Whadja pay for the table?"

"Five hundred bucks."

Josh whistled.

"I won't lose money. I'll make that much the first day on commissions. It's just that these people are so fucking gutless and they're all, like, we're for the First Amendment, but..."

"Faggots," Josh said.

"Hey."

"Sorry."

Josh's phone sang "Lawyers, Guns and Money."

"Mr. Pratt, this is Ralph Schultz."

"Thank you for calling me back, Mr. Schultz."

"I did as you suggested. We're not very tech-wise here so I asked my young neighbor Gary for help. He's one of those kids who's got his head stuck in a computer or a game, but he's a good kid. We don't even have a computer. There is quite a bit of information about you, Mr. Pratt."

"I wish there wasn't."

"I don't doubt that. Said you found Jesus in prison. Is that true?"

"Yes sir."

"Everything I've read indicates that you are a godly man; God knows they're rare enough these days. I talked this over with Leslie and we think we might know who this girl is, who's claiming to be Shelley. Shelley had a friend named Cat, Cat Lowenstein. We never approved of Miss Lowenstein. She came from a wild, godless household with hippie parents, and she's always been a wild child."

In the background a woman said, "She got Shelley to smoke that dope."

"Do have contact information for Cat?"

"No. And I really don't feel comfortable discussing this on the phone. You know, nothing's private these days. Would it be possible for you to come by our house?"

"I'm sorry, sir. I'm in Madison working a security detail. I understand your concern. Could you put me in touch with her parents?"

"All I know, they lived in Memphis and the father's name was Abe. Abe Lowenstein. I don't have to tell you what kind of people they are."

"Yes sir. Do you happen to have any pictures of Cat Lowenstein?"

"We might. I suppose I could send them to you."

"I would really appreciate that." Josh gave Schultz his address.

"What kind of mischief is she up to, if you don't mind my asking?" Schultz said.

"All I can say, it's very serious."

"I'll take your word for it, because I know you to be a godly man."

CHAPTER 34

Old MacDonald

"Go!" Polly said. "I'm fine! Nobody knows I'm here. I can't have you hovering over my shoulder. Go. I'll call you later."

"If you're sure."

"Go!"

"Lock the door!"

Josh got on his bike and looked at the map he'd placed in the window on top of his tank bag. It was a map of Jackson County with 2247 Ralston Road circled in red. Twenty minutes later Josh was headed northwest on the interstate, dicing with trucks, campers, commuters and vacationers. He was occasionally overtaken by groups of bikers, who flashed the universal biker salute. The only guys who didn't were on crotch rockets. Josh hated the interstate and avoided it when possible, but he just wanted to get this over quickly. He wanted to take a look at Old MacDonald's Farm. Turning off the interstate at Black River Falls, he headed north on a county road. It was one thirty when he pulled over on Ralston, a winding blacktop dairy farm road that was shaded by forest on both sides. He paused at the top of the hill to look at a flyer tacked to a telephone pole: "Lost dog! Murphy is a bulldog/cocker spaniel mix. If found, please call..." There was a black-and-white picture of the pup.

The road opened up below, and through the trees he saw the farm. The main house, a white two-story with green trim, was set fifty yards back from the road. A red barn and silo lay to the east. Cattle grazed in a field.

Josh rolled his ride down a dirt trail that soon became invisible from the road. He retrieved his binocs from his tank bag and climbed an accommodating elm, finding a perch ten feet off the ground. Zeroing in on the house, he saw an old beige Ford pickup out front and a line of laundry in back. Josh raised the binocs, following the field up to a tree line about a half mile away, where he thought he saw movement.

The sound of an approaching vehicle grabbed his attention, and he looked down as an old white Ford panel van roared by, leaving a dense cloud of gray smoke behind. Josh followed its progress all the way up to the farm, where it turned in and stopped as a man got out and opened the gate. Josh focused on the man. He was tall, dark and bearded, wearing a white guayabera and a cylindrical hat. The truck drove through the gate; the man closed it, got in and drove into the barn.

A moment later the man emerged from the barn, accompanied by a muscular black man wearing a black muscle shirt and baggy camo trou. They entered the farmhouse via the back door. Josh could barely hear the sound of the door shutting. He would have dearly loved to creep into the barn, see what was there, but not in broad daylight. Who knew how many people were at the farm or what defensive measures they'd set in place?

Josh retrained his binocs. There were video cams fixed high on the barn's exterior and one in front of the house atop a flagpole. Josh perched for a half hour. A series of shots rang out from beyond the tree line to the north and continued to pepper the afternoon as he let himself down, rolled out his bike and cruised slowly past the farm, pausing in front to photograph the sign.

"Old MacDonald's Fresh Organics! Ginseng, cucumbers, squash, Fuji and Red Delicious apples! Since 1974. Steven MacDonald, proprietor. Visit our website at www.oldmacdonaldsfarm.com."

A diagonal white banner two feet tall with the word CLOSED in red slashed across the sign.

Josh snapped a picture.

When Josh returned home around four, Kleiser and the car were gone, but Josh knew he'd be back. He hadn't been paid yet.

Josh went straight to the web page. It had an old-timey, *Farmer's Almanac* look to it, with old magazine-style illustrations of ginseng, cucumbers, tomatoes, etc. There were detailed descriptions of growing, harvesting, storing and ordering. Josh clicked on "About." There was a picture of MacDonald and his wife, Eleanor, posing in front of the farmhouse like in "American Gothic," MacDonald with the pitchfork and hat, Eleanor holding a cornucopia of produce in the hem of her long dress, which was long enough to still fall to the knees.

Josh would dearly love to tour the place, but he feared making contact. If the blackmail had indeed originated at Old MacDonald's Farm, there were some sharp hackers onboard. All he had to do was give them a handle—his name and email—and they would know everything about him down to his bank balance.

Josh called Kofsky.

"Meet me at MacDonald's in Middleton."

"Why?" Kofsky said. "What's up?"

"Things I can't discuss on the phone."

Twenty minutes later Josh pulled into the retro restaurant with the giant golden arches on Greenway Boulevard to find Kofsky sitting at an outside table wearing a seersucker jacket over a black T and sunglasses, with two frosties in front of him. Dovetail was five minutes away.

Josh kicked out his bike and joined Kofsky, who looked disheveled, hair sticking out like Larry Fine's.

"Did you find him?" Kofsky asked.

Josh sat down, checked his frostie to see it was chocolate and swallowed. "Maybe. We've traced it to a property in Jackson County. Maybe some jihadist involvement."

"What?!" Kofsky squawked.

"Maybe. I'll know more after my hacker gets back."

"Kleiser did this?"

Josh nodded.

"Maybe I should hire him."

"Randall's not too fond of regular employment, but go ahead. He's a handy guy to have around."

"Where'd you find him?"

Josh tilted back the cup and glugged, setting it down empty. "Anonymous."

"Huh," Kofsky said.

"Pay the man," Josh said. "Five gees."

Kofsky reached inside his jacket and pulled out his checkbook and wrote out a check for Kleiser's fee. "Now what? Can you take care of them?"

"Oh yeah, Aaron. They'll stop the blackmail and they'll regret they started it. I promise you that. Has there been any subsequent contact?"

"No. That worries me even more."

Josh stood and clapped Kofsky on the shoulder. "Don't worry. Be happy."

Kleiser's car was parked in front when Josh got home. Josh found him in the cool, dark office, Fig's snout on his thigh, looking at an aerial view of a rural property. Josh stared over Kleiser's shoulder.

"MacDonald's Farm?"

"Yup."

Josh pointed at a rectangular pit north of the tree line he'd observed. "Can you close in on that?"

Kleiser zoomed in. "Great conditions—a clear day and Skynet is almost directly above us."

They looked down from about a half mile at a grainy color image. There appeared to be a shaded cupola and one of those portable fiberglass outhouses at one end. The other end was a granite shelf, in front of which there were three tiny white dashes, about five feet apart.

"Beehives..." Kleiser said.

"Targets. That's a gun range."

CHAPTER 35

Drone, Sweet Drone

Josh brought up the Old MacDonald web page. "See what you can find out about Steven MacDonald, the proprietor. I don't want them to know they're being scoped. Can you do that?"

"No prob," Kleiser said, leaving the office. "I'll use my laptop."

Fig followed Kleiser out of the room.

"Have you been feeding Fig?" Josh said.

"Well yeah, I gave her a few snacks."

Josh reached inside his vest. "Oh by the way." He handed the check to Kleiser, who held it up, kissed it and handed it back.

"You'll have to cash that for me. Just give me four thou. The other's for your hospitality."

"Will do."

Kleiser grabbed his laptop and flopped on the living room sofa. Josh returned to his office and searched for Abe Lowenstein in the Memphis white pages. There were three. The listing for one of them was for Abe Lowenstein and Mandy Lowenstein. He called them first.

"Hello," a woman answered in a smoker's contralto.

"Ma'am, this is Josh Pratt in Madison, Wisconsin. I'm looking for Abe Lowenstein, the father of Cat Lowenstein."

The woman coughed. "Abe's dead. Cat's gone."

She hung up. He phoned her back but she didn't respond.

Josh googled "Abraham Lowenstein obituary."

Abraham Lowenstein was an artist, poet and social activist beloved by friends, colleagues and followers, a positive effect on all who knew him. He was born in Fayetteville, AR, and attended Eugene Field Elementary School, Foss Junior High and Norman Beauchamp High, where he first made his mark as editor of the school paper, The Clarion. Young Abe soon found himself in hot water, the first of many occasions, for reprinting the works of Allen Ginsberg.

He studied philosophy and sociology at the University of Tennessee, where he was active in campus politics, as president of the local Students for a Democratic Society, and as an organizer of protests against the Granada Invasion. This led to his first arrest. There would be many others. The Board of Regents eventually asked Abe to resign his position as editor of the campus paper, the Tennessee Bugle, for his editorials excoriating Ronald Reagan.

After graduation Mr. Lowenstein founded Gimme Shelter, a halfway house for at-risk youth, particularly those being released from the juvenile detention system. He begged, wheedled and cajoled friends and acquaintances into donating time, money, and furniture to his non-profit, which occupied an old wood-frame house on Garreth Street.

Mr. Lowenstein is survived by Mandy Lowenstein, his partner of many years, and by his children, Catherine, Morris and Adrian. In keeping with Mr. Lowenstein's wishes, there will be no services, but a celebration of his life, which is scheduled for August 14 in the Low Life Lounge in Mapleton.

There was only one Morris Lowenstein on Facebook, in Atlanta, a mortgage broker. Josh sent him a friend request, then went into the garage, opened the door and gazed at his bikes. Looking at motorcycles always had a calming effect. Fig Newton's Hawk stood on its centerstand. Her father had given it to Josh following her death at the hands of the madman, the Jesuit. The Hawk was as light and as lithe as Fig. Josh wished more motorcycle manufacturers would put centerstands on their bikes.

The trouble started when they began routing the exhaust directly under the frame instead of off to the side. Now hardly any motorcycles came with centerstands, which made chain and wheel maintenance more difficult.

The door to the house opened and Kleiser came out.

"I've always wanted to get a bike."

"Why don't you?"

"Probably kill myself. Haven't ridden since college. Turns out your man Steven MacDonald was something of a firebrand and libertarian celebrity back in the day. Founded the Ashland County Irregulars, sort of a posse comitatus, but the cops kept raiding and rousting, and he gave it up. Took over the family farm in '74, started growing organic vegetables and ginseng. Incidentally, it takes seven years for ginseng to mature and produce, so this is a long-haul operation. Used to publish a newsletter, *The Journal of Objectivity*. The last issue was in 2006."

"Is he still alive?"

Kleiser walked over to the Hawk. "Do you mind?"

"Go ahead."

Kleiser threw a leg over and sat on the Hawk, hands on the grips. "MacDonald's wife, Eleanor, left him in 2001. He has two grown kids, a boy and a girl, who refuse to have anything to do with him. He has *The New York Times*, the *Wisconsin State Journal*, and the *Milwaukee-Wisconsin Journal Sentinel* delivered every day. Or someone does. Bills get paid. The farm web page is no longer available. The domain name oldmacdonaldsfarm is available."

"It was there yesterday."

"They took it down."

"Can you recover it?"

"I can try."

"And no one's seen or heard from MacDonald in how long?"

"I don't know. Calls are going in and out of the house all the time, but I don't know who's talking to whom. Say, would it be possible for me to ride this? Just around the block or something."

"Have you ever ridden a motorcycle?"

"Back in college. Lucky I didn't kill myself."

"Forget it."

Kleiser crouched low on the bike and made a guttural vrooming noise. He downshifted, matching rev to rev with full sound effects. He sounded like Mel Blanc imitating a dragster.

"Is there any way you can turn on the computers and laptops in the house to take a look? It you could, that would be cool."

Kleiser screeched to a halt, sat up and looked at Josh. "I thought of that. But I haven't been able to breach their system."

"I wished there were some way to take a look around that farm," Josh said.

"What about a drone?" Kleiser said.

"What do you mean?"

"A remote-controlled drone with a camera. I've got one in my car."

"Explain."

Kleiser got off the Hawk and walked toward his car. "Better to show than tell, right?"

Josh walked out of the garage and saw low, scudding gray clouds rolling in from the west. Kleiser opened his trunk and removed a black plastic carrying case with rounded corners the size of a dorm refrigerator. He carried it into the garage and set it on the concrete floor, stooping to undo the clasps. Inside, nestled in custom-cut black packing foam, was a four-rotor device that looked a little like a piñata laid on its side. A clear plastic bubble covered the center portion, which housed four tiny electric motors, batteries and transmission devices. The remote was a converted game yoke. It looked like something from *Mad Max: Fury Road*.

Kleiser gently lifted the object out of its nest and carried it over to the workbench, where he set it down. It was about two feet, axle to axle, made of black carbon fiber.

"May need to charge it," Kleiser said, "but it has a two hundred-yard range and is virtually silent. It carries a camera with a zoom lens and microphones."

Josh stared. "Holy shit."

Kleiser pulled a meter from the crate and clipped it to two leads. "It's got a half charge. That's enough to show you what it can do."

Kleiser tucked it under his arm and followed Josh out the garage door into the fenced-in portion of the backyard. Fig popped out of the doggie door as Kleiser set the drone on the picnic table. Kleiser picked up the remote and flipped a couple of toggles, and tiny lights flashed beneath the clear plastic dome: red, blue and green. Four green lights went on in sequence and the device radiated a low hum that Josh could feel through the table.

Kleiser shut it all off and set down the remote. "Hang on." He went into the house and returned a minute later with his laptop, which he set on the workbench, opened and poked. A gray screen appeared. Kleiser picked up the remote, switched all the toggles and waited for it to light up. He wrestled with the yoke, and the drone zoomed straight up. A second later, a color image appeared on the laptop and Josh was looking down at himself from fifty feet.

He looked up. The drone was directly above them. A tiny screen on the control yoke showed the same thing.

"I've also got Fat Shark goggles," Kleiser said. "They offer a submersive experience with no distractions."

Josh watched Kleiser manipulate the drone via remote. "Can I try?"

Kleiser handed him the control yoke. "Small motions until you get the hang of it."

Fascinated by the moving scene, Josh flew the drone south over the strip of trees until it hovered above his backyard neighbor's house, a five thousand-square-foot Prairie-style pile. Numbers on the tiny monitor showed the direction it was flying and the altitude. Slowly, Josh lowered the drone until it hovered next to a second-floor window. He turned until he was looking in the window, where he saw a teenage girl sitting on her bed with earbuds, poking at her device.

"You can also switch on the night-vision feature," Kleiser said, reaching over and pushing a button. The screen turned green. Josh felt like a perv, so he brought the drone up and back toward the house.

He handed the yoke to Kleiser. "Here. You take it."

"Alrighty then," Kleiser said. "Get ready to catch it. I'm going to drop it right into your arms."

It wasn't until the drone was a foot or two above Josh's head that he heard the rotors whirr.

"Ready?" Kleiser said.

"Ready."

Kleiser flipped a switch, the rotors went still and the drone dropped into Josh's waiting hands. It weighed less than five pounds.

"Show me those Fat Shark goggles, will you?"

CHAPTER 36

Blackmail

Tuesday dawned gray and overcast, with rain in the forecast. Josh and Fig did their five and returned to find Kleiser unwrapping breakfast sandwiches from McDonald's. He laid an Egg McMuffin on the floor for Fig, who scarfed it down in two bites.

"I'm off to Dovetail, see if I can backtrack this fucker into his home system."

"You got anyplace to go, Randall?"

"Why? Getting tired of me?"

"Just wondering."

"Not really. My folks live in Florida, but I don't want to bring any heat down on them."

"Is someone looking for you?"

"Well yeah! I think I'm on some watch lists. Say the word, I'm gone."

"Where will you go?"

"I got pen pals all over through Anonymous. Thinking of visiting this cat in St. Louis."

"You're welcome to hang around, but I may have another houseguest this week. He can sleep in the basement."

"No prob."

After Kleiser left, Josh sent Special Agent Stoeckle an email alerting him that Old MacDonald's Farm might be a front for a terrorist training camp. He went online and found that Morris Lowenstein had accepted his friend request.

"Dear Mr. Lowenstein: I am a private investigator from Madison, WI. Last week at the San Diego Comic Con I met a young woman who claimed to be Shelley Schultz. Subsequently, I learned that Miss Schultz is deceased and the person claiming to be her might be your sister Catherine. Have you been in touch with her recently? Sincerely..."

Fifteen minutes later Lowenstein responded.

"What is this about?"

Josh explained.

"What is your phone number?" Lowenstein responded. Josh gave it to him. Josh's phone rang.

"This is Josh."

"Mr. Pratt, this is Morris Lowenstein. I'm very concerned about my sister. We haven't heard from her in two years. I even considered hiring a private detective to track her down. Ironic, isn't it? What kind of trouble is she in?"

"I don't know that she's in any trouble, Mr. Lowenstein, but she may be. Has she ever shown any tendency toward radical causes?"

Lowenstein woofed like a seal. "Like the song says, she was born radical. She came out of the womb waving the black flag of anarchy and clutching a list of demands. Like the bad seed or something. Don't get me wrong, I love my sister. She was the baby by several years. I don't think the folks expected her. We all grew up without much parental guidance. Oh I mean the folks were there, physically, but never seemed to have time for us. Dad was always away at some meeting. Adrian and I rebelled at his rebelliousness, and we grew up fairly conventional. We used to compare our family to others we knew, and ours always came out looking weird. I think deep down in our bones, both Adrian and I realized that our folks were just playing at adulthood and still harbored the emotions and convictions of teenagers. When people asked me what Dad did for a living, I told them he was a professional rabble-rouser, which he was.

"Cat idealized him, begged him to take her to protests. You know that old joke, 'What are you protesting?' And the answer is, 'What have you got?' That was my dad and Cat. He started taking her to protests when she was seven years old. Adrian and I seemed to have been born with an innate maturity and common sense that warned us away from those kinds of activities, but Cat loved it.

"I'll never forget the first time she brought home her black boyfriend. Dad didn't know whether to shit or go blind. His paternal instincts surfaced for a nanosecond, but he couldn't say a damn thing, not after lecturing us all our lives about racism."

"How did your father die?" Josh said.

"Heroin overdose. They left that out of the obit."

"Is there any possibility Cat is mixed up with jihad-related terrorists?"

Silence.

"I wouldn't be surprised."

"Do you have any way of getting in touch with her?"

"No, unfortunately."

"Do you have any pictures of her you could send me?"

"I might," Lowenstein said. "What are your intentions if you do?"

"Let me tell you what happened," Josh said.

"Doesn't surprise me," Lowenstein said when Josh finished. "She's always been sexually aggressive. Maybe it was just your lucky night. She didn't take anything?"

"No, but she had access to my phone while I was conked out. I'm concerned she may have gotten a lot of data."

"You don't even know if she's mixed up with any of these groups," Lowenstein said. "I would like to get in contact if you find her."

"What about Adrian? Would he have any insights?"

"I'll ask him. Adrian's not as tolerant as me."

"Would you send me his contact info?"

"Let me check with Adrian. I'll get back to you."

They exchanged addresses and phone numbers.

At eleven, Kofsky phoned. "The blackmailer called. He wants a hundred grand this afternoon."

"Did he call you on your personal phone?"

"No. He went through the switchboard. He had some kind of accent."

"Hang on. I'll come over."

A half hour later Josh kicked out in Dovetail's employee parking lot in Middleton. The receptionist handed him an ID on a lanyard, he went back to Kofsky's office and they went out the back door to the picnic table by the koi pond.

"He wants a hundred thou to be delivered today at 6:00 p.m."

"Where?"

"He said for me to hang by the checkout lanes at Woodman's and he'd call me."

"What assurances does he offer that this is the end?"

"HA!"

Josh watched a lissome brunette exit from a different portion of the building, lean against a picnic table and take out her phone.

"Do you want me to deliver the ransom?"

Kofsky pulled a cigarette from behind his ear and lit it with a yellow Bic. "What ransom? Do you think I can just lay my hands on a hundred Gs? I told him it would take time. He told me I either get the money or he was forwarding those videos to my board of directors."

Josh steepled his hands and leaned forward to touch them with his mouth. "Is Kleiser here?"

"Yeah. He came in this morning."

"Let's get him."

Kofsky took out his phone. Minutes later Kleiser came out and joined them, wearing aviator shades and a Broncos hat. Josh told him the situation.

"I'd like to bug the briefcase. You have anything like that, Randall?"

"Yeah," Kleiser said. "Got a couple of things might work. Want me to go get them? They're in the car."

"Go ahead," Josh said.

Kleiser walked out of the park around the back of the building, returning fifteen minutes later with two fiberglass cases, which he set on the picnic table and opened. Each held dozens of tiny electronic devices nestled in black foam cutouts. Kleiser grabbed a small aluminum wafer and held it up.

"Self-contained—broadcasts up to ten miles. I can track it with any common oscillating meter."

"Yeah but what happens if he gives me the slip and gets over ten miles?"

Kleiser carefully lifted out a black foam tray revealing another tray underneath. He picked up a tiny aluminum cylinder with two wires protruding from each end. "This little baby sends out a signal that can be read from orbit, any place on earth. Since I don't have any satellites, I patch into Skynet. That's not a problem."

"Excuse me," Kofsky said. "Isn't Skynet a fictional artificial intelligence system from the *Terminator* movies?"

Kleiser grinned, his beard twitching. "Used to be. Now it's what the CIA et al. call their satellite spy system."

"You got something in there we can use to talk to each other? Other than cell phones, I mean?"

Kleiser reached into his case and pulled out two clam-like cell phones, handed one to Josh. Josh opened it and turned it around in his hands. It had no brand or identifiable markings. "I'll enter some numbers," Kleiser said, opening his phone. "You press here and here. It will automatically dial me."

Josh stood. "Meet me back at my place at four. There are a few things I need to pick up."

The sky rumbled and the first drops hit.

CHAPTER 37

Down by the River

Josh went into the basement, Fig at his heels, and unlocked the gun cabinet in the furnace room. As a convicted felon he was not allowed to have guns. He opened the safe and took out his well-worn .45, dropped the mag, checked that it was full, checked to make sure the chamber was empty and slammed it home. He looked at it lovingly and put it back. When you had a gun, all problems looked like a gunfight.

Upstairs he heard the front door open and close. Josh followed Fig upstairs, where Kleiser was standing in the foyer holding a briefcase and shaking off the rain.

"What's the plan, man?" Kleiser asked.

"You have any experience with this sort of thing?"

Kleiser shrugged out of his black nylon jacket, went into the kitchen and pulled a beer from the fridge. "Want one?" he called.

"No thanks."

Kleiser came back to the living room, twisted off the cap and drank. "What, you mean paying the blackmail money? Not really, but I do have a little experience with spy shit. Last year I helped a guy get out of federal detention at a hospital. I'm pretty cool under pressure."

Josh opened the briefcase on the living room table. Inside was a salted roll—stack after stack of singles with hundred-dollar bills on top. It was the best Kofsky could do on short notice. Josh hoped it would fool the blackmailer at least until he headed back to his lair.

"That's ten Gs in there," Kleiser said.

By now the rain was a steady drumbeat on the roof.

"I'm mainly concerned with tracking this guy back to wherever."

"You think it's that farm?" Kleiser said.

"Maybe, although it would be an astounding coincidence."

"Would it? You know Kofsky's Jewish, and he's involved in high-level security. Maybe this blackmail is a feint to control him in some way."

"You know, Randall, you have the makings of a good investigator."

"Don't think I haven't thought about it. Kofsky already offered. The only problem is, I'm wanted for a few felonies and I'm on a few lists."

"Maybe I could help you with that."

"How?"

"I know some feds. Here's what I want you to do—tag along with me but out of sight. When I meet with this guy, maybe you sneak up on his vehicle and plant the satellite bug. I'm putting the other one in the briefcase, just in case. Wear that black jacket. Are you carrying?"

"No, but I got one in the car. Should I bring it?"

"Nah."

"Why don't I ride with you, and you drop me off a quarter mile from the exchange."

Josh pointed a finger at him. "Let's do it."

They drove to the west side Woodman's in Josh's Chrysler. Kleiser stayed in the car while Josh went inside and hung around the customer service desk. At six o'clock the phone behind the desk rang and a clerk picked it up, looked puzzled, looked up.

"Are you Aaron Kofsky?" she said.

Josh took the phone. "Thanks." He walked over to the restrooms where no one could eavesdrop. "What's the plan?"

"Is this Kofsky?" said a man with a slight Middle Eastern accent.

"I've got your money. Where do you want it?"

"We want Kofsky to deliver it."

"Well Kofsky ain't coming. He's a cowardly Jew. He hired me to deliver the money."

"Yes. Of course. Drive to Sauk City. Drive into August Derleth Park. Go down by the river and wait. We are watching you."

Josh returned the phone, went outside and got in the car. "August Derleth Park down by the river. They're planning to make their getaway by boat."

Josh reached into the back seat and pulled out his Wisconsin atlas, opening to the page containing Sauk City. Rain spattered against the roof and windows. "Here's the park. I'll let you out about a quarter mile toward town. Walk to the park, stay in the shadows, go down to the water and see if you can find the boat."

"Want me to plant the tracer?" Kleiser said.

"Only if you can do so without being discovered. Even with this rain it's still light out, so I don't know how you're going to sneak up on them, but see if you can get the boat's name or registration number. It has to have a registration number."

"How can you be so sure they're going to use a boat?"

"It's what I'd do. It's what I did."

Kleiser brought up a map of Sauk City on his phone. "I may have to go in the water."

They drove north on 12 and 19 through rolling hills barely visible through the mist and rain. The rain had settled into a steady deluge, splattering off the asphalt, droplets rising on Josh's waxed windshield. They crossed the river and drove slowly through town, past bars and antique stores. Josh pulled over a few hundred yards south of the park, went behind a building and let Kleiser out.

The park was deserted because of the rain as Josh pulled in and followed the winding path down to the river. He parked in a small lot at the end of the path, the river visible to his right, and waited. He couldn't see a boat, but it could easily be moored to the shore beneath his line of vision. A figure detached itself from the trees in his rearview and approached. Josh studied him in the mirror—medium height, dressed entirely in black, including a balaclava. He waited until the man was at the rear bumper before opening the door.

The man jumped and jammed a hand inside his black leather jacket. Josh showed him his hands.

"Easy."

The black-clad man stepped back, pulling a small automatic. "Where's the money?"

"It's in the back seat."

The man gestured with the gun. "You get it. Get out of the car."

Josh got out of the car, opened the rear door, pulled out the briefcase. As the man reached for it Josh kicked him in the groin hard enough to lift him off the tarmac. The man made a high keening noise and dropped. Josh stomped on his gun hand and kicked the gun under the car, then dropped down with his knee on the man's ribs, feeling one of them snap. The man screamed.

Josh peeled off the balaclava, revealing a young man with pale skin and a mustache. Josh slapped him side to side. Seconds later he heard the sound of an outboard motor starting and receding upriver.

"Why pick on Kofsky?" Josh said to the defiant creature beneath his knee.

"Fuck you!" the man spat. Josh knocked him senseless, dug through his pockets and found a cheap wallet containing an "undocumented worker" driver's license, a food stamp card, a debit card from Kohl's, three credit cards belonging to three different people and twenty dollars. According to the license, the man's name was Heilel Ben Shahar. Josh got up, opened the trunk, picked the man up by his jacket, dumped him inside and shut the lid. A moment later Kleiser appeared, dripping wet.

"I jammed it inside the gunwale. Dude was looking at shit on his phone. I left my phone on shore so it wouldn't get wet. What happened?"

"I grabbed him. He's in the trunk."

"What? Why? Aren't they going to trigger the nuclear option?"

"Probably. But now we got this dude for extortion and gun charges, so maybe we can open up Old MacDonald's Farm. Hang on."

Josh dialed Calloway and told him what had happened.

"So what?" the detective said.

"So what should I do with him?"

"You're in Sauk County. Better take him there."

"This dude may be part of a terrorist training camp. I don't want the locals to screw it up."

"I know Chief Harris. I'll give him a call. They can at least hold him until we get some feds in there."

"Heinz, do you have any feds in mind? 'Cause I know a couple."

"No, let me make a few phone calls. They may want to talk to you."

"Will do."

They drove three blocks to the Sauk City Police Department and parked in the visitor's lot. "Wait here," Josh said.

Inside, a big, uniformed cop with the nametag PATTERSON was chatting with a middle-aged woman sitting behind the desk. Wisconsin law enforcement came in two sizes: big and bigger. They both looked up.

"Officer," Josh said. "I got a guy in my trunk who tried to extort one hundred thousand dollars from my client. I think he's Middle Eastern and may be connected to terrorists."

The cop and receptionist exchanged a look. What fresh hell was this?

"Name?" the cop said.

"Josh Pratt. I'm a private investigator from Madison."

"Aren't you the guy—."

"Yeah."

Patterson turned to the woman. "This is the guy who had the shootout with the cycle gang last year."

"Sir, I was in my house when that happened and didn't fire a shot."

The cop reached over the counter and placed a small recording device on top. "Okay. Tell me what happened."

CHAPTER 38

The Rain

Officer Patterson sent a car to retrieve the gun. He went outside and returned a minute later with the dripping Kleiser and Ben Shahar, who was in handcuffs. Other cops gathered, including Sauk County Sheriff Lemuel Garrett, whom Josh knew from biker charity events. Ben Shahar and Patterson went into an interrogation room. Josh told Garrett about the suspicious farm.

"I know Sheriff LaBute. I'll give him a call."

Josh sat in a wooden chair in the police department next to Kleiser while Garrett called and spoke. He hung up and came over.

"Sheriff says they occasionally hear gunshots but otherwise, the farm has all applicable licenses, pays all taxes and fees, and he sees no reason to suspect them. That's a rural county and lots of people shoot guns."

"When was the last time Sheriff LaBute spoke to Steven MacDonald?"

"I didn't ask him that."

"Sir, it's possible MacDonald is either dead or being held captive by this gang that's taken over his farm."

"What gang?"

"Well I'm not sure, but we traced the blackmail threat to a site in Jackson County. There's a possibility they're affiliated with a terrorist group."

Garrett grinned, his dark tan face cracking into seams. "What, like Al-Qaeda? Here?"

"Sir I don't have to tell you about terrorist activity in Minnesota, right over the river."

"You got a point, son, but law enforcement needs more than that to go in there. And suppose it is a terrorist training camp? Are we going to go in there in our Smokey hats with our service automatics? Isn't this a job for Homeland Security or something?"

"Sir, it's my understanding the feds already know. You should be hearing from them."

"You sure are polite for an ex-con."

"Is the sheriff at least going to go ask what's going on?"

"That was my understanding."

Josh thanked Garrett and he and Kleiser returned to the car, where Josh phoned Kofsky.

"What happened?"

Josh told him.

"What?" Kofsky shouted. "You fucking idiot! What am I going to tell the board?"

"You're going to tell them you have a problem and that you're getting help. I will vouch for you."

"You?" Kofsky barked in disbelief.

"So will others—Sandy, any rabbi if you ask him, any priest for that matter."

"Great!" Kofsky wailed. "Now the whole board will know I'm a perv!"

"Aaron, if you are truly intent on making a change, this should help."

"Yeah. Thanks a lot." Kofsky hung up.

"Well that went well," Josh said, starting the car. They returned to Madison in the driving rain. "I have to accompany my client to Chicago Thursday afternoon. Can you stay and look after Fig?"

"Sure. I got no place to go. I got no plans."

Josh wondered if he should tell somebody about Kofsky's reaction. Could he be considering suicide? Should Josh phone Sandy? Had Josh endangered one client by helping another? No. He'd done what he thought was right. Fucker had pulled a gun on him. They drove in silence save for the hiss of the tires on the wet highway.

"Mind if I turn on the radio?" Kleiser said.

"Go ahead."

Kleiser fooled around, found a classic rock station out of Milwaukee. "Hotel California."

"What's the problem, hoss?" Kleiser finally said.

"Nothing. I tend to overthink things. You ever read that Ray Bradbury story, 'A Sound of Thunder?' It's about a big-game hunter who goes back in time to kill a dinosaur..."

"Are you shitting me? I love Bradbury! I've read everything he's ever written. I even saw the awful movie."

"Well if that hunter had a conscience and an imagination, that would be me. I go back over every fucking action in the day trying to decide if I've helped anyone or hurt anyone."

"No one is that altruistic," Kleiser said. "Quit beating yourself up."

"Hotel California" segued into The Byrds' "The Christian Life" and Josh laughed. God had a sense of humor.

Fig was ecstatic to see them. Josh went into his office. Abdul Alhazred had sent a message: "Will be at your place tomorrow. What's the address?"

Josh phoned him.

"Alhazred," the artist answered.

"Abdul, it's Josh Pratt. I'd rather not post my address on the internet."

"That's cool. Just tell me."

Josh told him. "I hope you don't mind dogs."

"I love dogs," Alhazred said. "See you tomorrow late afternoon. I'll phone when I hit town."

Kleiser's nose was buried in his laptop.

"Where's the boat?" Josh said.

"Merrimac. Man, I'm famished," Kleiser said. "Let's get a pizza. My treat."

"I like Rocky Rococo," Josh said, tossing Kleiser the Yellow Pages. "Something with lots of meat. No fucking anchovies." He went to his wall of discs, pulled out Paul Butterfield's *The Resurrection of Pigboy Crabshaw* and slid it in the Bose. Kleiser leaped up and boogied around the room snapping his fingers.

"What is that?!"

Josh handed him the CD case. It was nine o'clock when the pizza arrived. Josh opened the box on the coffee table and gave Fig a slice. Kleiser slobbered over the CD case.

"You weren't even born when this came out," he said.

"I learned about it in the joint, from Chaplain Dorgan. I learned a lot of things from Chaplain Dorgan. You a religious man, Randall?"

Kleiser flashed a toothy grin. "Not me, pal. Never had much use for it. My folks were Lutherans but they didn't drag me into it. I always thought religion was for the weak-minded, no offense."

"None taken. Works for some, not everyone."

"But you believe in God, don't you?" Kleiser said.

"Yup. And I believe Jesus is his son."

Kleiser regarded him for a minute with hooded eyes. "When's the last time you talked to Chaplain Dorgan?"

A wave of shame and self-loathing washed over Josh. Dorgan was the closest thing to a father he'd ever known. He looked at his watch. Too late to call. But maybe Dorgan was on Facebook. Josh went into his office and checked. No Facebook. Josh googled Chaplain Dorgan. Zipco.

He pulled the little spiral pad from his pocket and wrote, DORGAN. When he came out, Kleiser was in the shower. Josh went to his bath and did the same. Toweling off, he caught sight of himself in the mirror. He needed a shave. Why hadn't he shaved in the shower? Exhaustion overcame him as he stumbled to his bed. Seconds later, Fig jumped up and lay down at his feet.

Josh dove into a dream, following Chaplain Dorgan down a long, shaded, Gothic hall as in some old-world cathedral. Dorgan was a sandy-haired mesomorph who pumped iron and participated in triathlons. The faster Josh ran after him, the farther Dorgan retreated, finally disappearing into a tiny black dot in the distance.

Josh paused, panting in the dark. A voice rasped from right behind him.

"Hello, son."

Josh turned around.

It was his father. Duane.

CHAPTER 39

Zlatko

Zlatko Dzelko, aka Abdul Alhazred, loved America almost as much as he hated Islam. He'd had more death threats than George W. Bush and Al Sharpton combined, and had obtained the impossible, a concealed-carry permit in Illinois, through a political favor from a Republican state senator. Zlatko made no secret of his mission: the destruction of Islam. His weapons were satire and brushes. When some statist creep raised his ugly head to bray for more government and higher taxes, Zlatko was there to paint him in the worst possible light. Zlatko's propaganda was extremely effective. He'd been profiled by *Juxtapoz*, *The Weekly Standard* and *Rolling Stone*.

He was just one guy, a pamphleteer, a graffiti artist, but he had made a difference. He could tell by the death threats. Every time he appeared, the death threats multiplied. Under the current administration, neither the FBI nor Homeland Security was sympathetic, urging him to change his name, go underground and stop provoking those Muslims.

One of his posters showed a smirking moppet turning toward the viewer with a burning house in the background. It said, THEY BURNT THE AMERICAN FLAG. SO I BURNT THEIR SECTION 8 HOUSING.

Zlatko had tried enlisting three times, but each military branch had turned him down, ostensibly for flat feet when in fact they simply feared the attention and death threats he would inevitably attract.

Zlatko's fuzz buster had been silent since he'd crossed the state line, and he gradually pressed the accelerator of his 2006 Boss Mustang, the big V8 surging ahead as "Sweet Home Alabama" boomed through the Harman Kardon speakers.

God bless America! Where else could a poor boy from Bosnia grow up to be that most American of creatures, a comic book *auteur*? Sure there were great French, Spanish and Japanese comic book creators, but the art form itself had sprung from the pages of the American tabloid—Richard Outcault's *The Yellow Kid*, the *New York World* in 1896. *The Kid* was printed in yellow ink because the newspaper publisher had barrels of it sitting around. Hence the term "yellow journalism."

Zlatko had wanted to be a comic book artist since he first picked up a copy of *Conan the Barbarian*, by Roy Thomas and Barry Smith. It transported him into a world far beyond the mean, peeling walls of the underheated tenement he shared with his family. When his father found the comic hidden beneath Zlatko's mattress, he called Zlatko in, slapped him twice and forced him to burn it.

"Western influence," his father had called it.

Jeez, Pops, if you hate Western influence so much, what the fuck are we doing in America?

Zlatko knew full well what they were doing in America. Getting ahead, improving themselves at others' expense. The whole fucking world wanted to get to America and feast off the endless bounty of American freedom and largesse, not the least of which was the government. Zlatko's father played the social services like Zubin Mehta. Subsidized housing. Food stamps. Medicaid. When he worked, driving a taxi, Gorlik Dzelko had refused service to drunks, those with service animals and Jews.

At the dinner table Gorlik had railed against the crassness of American culture, browbeat his family, ostentatiously prayed and hid stroke books at the back of his closet.

Following the death of his sister, Zlatko left home at seventeen, took a job doing construction and studied art at night at a community college. He worked hard, became a manager, lived simply and worked on his art. He published his first comic, *Al Qabong*, at twenty-five. *Al Qabong* was a man-boar who rode a camel named Oscar Mayer and waged a one-man war on jihad, a sort of anti-jihad Punisher. Al Qabong was seven feet tall, carried a solid-body Strat over his shoulder to hit bad guys, a Rhino revolver with bullets dipped in bacon fat, and bacon bombs. He wore a broad flat-brimmed black hat, hand-tooled boots and pigskin gloves.

"How in halal y'all doin'?" Al Qabong greeted jihadis before lobbing his bacon bombs and unlimbering the Strat. He called his band Filthy Swine.

The one hundred twenty-page graphic novel garnered Zlatko nominations for Russ Manning and Eisner awards, and industry attention.

BEEP! The fuzz buster shrieked and pointed. Zlatko slowed from eighty to about sixty, seeking camouflage among a group of trucks. He caught a glimpse of a county Mountie whipping past the Janesville turnoff.

He hit the Beltline at three thirty and pulled into Josh's driveway on Ptarmigan Road twenty minutes later. The door opened before he got there and a big, shaggy mutt ran up to him, sniffing. He crouched to scratch her ears. A fit, tatted-out dude with a shaved head appeared in the door.

"Abdul?"

"Call me Zlatko," he said, walking up to Pratt and shaking hands. "Thanks for inviting me. Stoked to meet Polly. I meant to get in touch with her earlier, but life got in the way."

"Come on in," Pratt said, holding the door. "I'll see if I can get her over here."

Zlatko entered the living room, eyes drawn to the landscape over the fireplace. A bearded dude in Bermuda shorts and a NOT LAME T-shirt set his laptop aside, rose and shook his hand.

"Randall Kleiser."

"Zlatko Dzelko."

Zlatko was a wiry little guy with an eagle-beak nose and a gleaming black pompadour that looked like it belonged on a bigger man. He clapped his hands together.

"Diggin' on how you kick jihadist ass! That scene two weeks ago at the con, that was heinous, man!"

"You want a beer? Randall?"

"Hells yeah," Zlatko said.

Josh went into the kitchen and got three beers, handed them out.

Zlatko twisted off the cap and held up the bottle. "Point—the beer Badger made famous. When you're out of town, you're out of Point."

"Come on out on the deck, you guys," Josh said, leading the way.

They settled in plastic chairs and a chaise lounge.

Josh slugged the beer. "Zlatko, how do you deal with death threats?" Zlatko lifted his shirt, revealing the butt of a black automatic in a pancake holster. "Bring 'em on. They know I'm armed. They know I'm ready to go down fighting. If those two fuckheads who died in Galveston had gotten by the security guard, I would have tapped 'em."

He pointed to his temple.

"Oh yeah, man," Kleiser said. "You won that Draw Muhammad contest."

"How is it that you haven't been disinvited to Chicago?" Josh said.

Zlatko flashed Gene Kelly teeth. "I'm on the board. We had a meeting last night that got pretty rowdy, but in the end, nine of fifteen board members backed me. We've laid on extra security for the show, including dudes in cosplay. We've got eight agents roaming the floor disguised as superheroes."

"Are you going to draw Muhammad?" Josh said.

"Fuck yeah, if people ask! I'm charging twenty bucks a sketch, and all proceeds go to the Charlie Hebdo Fund."

"Let me see if we can get Polly over here," Josh said, picking up his phone and walking around the hot tub, Fig at his heels. He returned a moment later. "She'll be here in an hour with her uncle Don."

"Great!" Zlatko said.

An hour later the roar of an unmuffled V-twin wrapped around the house. Josh, Kleiser and Zlatko went inside as Polly and Don reached the door. Josh made introductions.

Zlatko opened his arms. "Polly!"

"Abdul!" Polly said, embracing him.

"Call me Zlatko. Y'know, I've always wanted to show Wonder Warthog going after Islamists. I wrote Gilbert Shelton but I never heard back."

"I still have my *Wonder Warthog* comics," Kleiser said. "And my *Fabulous Furry Freak Brothers.*"

"You're coming to my panel, right?" Zlatko said.

"What panel?" Polly said.

"'Are We Still *Charlie Hebdo*?' After the initial outrage and outpouring of sympathy, how many in the comics community will stand up and tell jihadis, 'No, you won't tell me what do draw?'"

"Wait a minute," Josh said. "You think that's a smart idea? Advertise where you're gonna be?"

Zlatko looked at him with disdain. "Dude, this is America. The whole point of what I do is to reaffirm American values. The First Amendment."

"They won't let you bring a gun in there. Do they screen for weapons?"

"Of course they screen for weapons. They check every backpack."

"And you know what's the first thing you see when you get in the door?" Polly said. "A dude selling samurai swords and zombie axes."

"Who's paying for the extra security?" Josh said.

"The con," Zlatko said.

"They must be thrilled about that," Josh said.

"It's not a problem. The board stands behind me."

"That's refreshing," Polly said.

Zlatko stood. "So are you gonna feed us or what? I'm so hungry I could eat a deep-fried rat."

"I'll call KFC," Polly said.

CHAPTER 40

Arrival in Chicago

Josh grilled burgers on his Weber, and they ate out back at the picnic table.

"So what?" Zlatko said to Polly. "Are you an observant Jew?"

Polly laughed. "No, I'm one of those secular Jews they warn you about."

"Yet you draw Muhammad."

"It seemed like a good idea at the time."

Zlatko grinned snarkily. "You draw him because they tell you not to draw him."

"I know, right? This is fuckin' America, raghead! You don't tell us what to draw."

Zlatko turned to Don. "What about you? Go to temple?"

"I'm a fag biker. I go to fag bars. What about you? Ever wear leather?"

Zlatko was amused. "You're not my type."

"What is your type?"

"The young Sophia Loren." Back to Polly. "What do your folks think when you draw Muhammad?"

"They are appalled. We don't talk much. They're second-generation immigrants whose ancestors came from some stinking shtetl in Eastern Europe. They're the type of Jews who lie low, mind their own business and hope nobody notices. They've been stigmatized by centuries of pogroms. It's in their blood. My brother went off to join the Israeli Air Force. You'd think they'd be proud but they're not. They're ashamed."

Zlatko looked at Josh. "What about you?"

"I have accepted Jesus Christ into my heart and soul."

"Don't get him started," Polly said.

After dinner Josh, Kleiser and Zlatko went out front to see Don and Polly off. Don rode a customized Heritage Softail, with a hand-painted tank featuring Lady Death, art by Monte Michael Moore. Josh cringed at the sound of Don's 75-inch engine. He'd been around loud bikes his whole life, but out of deference to his neighbors he'd reinstalled his baffles.

The shootout with the Insane Assholes last year had alerted his neighbors to the fact that they had a biker in their midst. Funny thing. Josh had lived on Ptarmigan Road for four years before the gilded finger of the developers touched down, surrounding his modest ranch-style house with mega-mansions. Now he was an eyesore and possible safety hazard dragging down property values. The neighbors had taken up a fund to buy him out, but so far they were only up to six hundred Gs, more money than Josh had ever seen but not enough to cause him to pull up stakes.

Josh, Kleiser and Zlatko returned to the backyard with three glasses and a bottle of bourbon.

"Old MacDonald's gonna have to wait 'til next week," Josh said. "I'm in no condition to drive."

"What's Old MacDonald's?" Zlatko said.

Josh told him. Zlatko bared his teeth.

"A terrorist training camp? Wouldn't you love to go in there guns blazing?"

"We don't know it's a terrorist training camp," Josh said. "It's just fishy."

"Do you shoot?" Zlatko said.

"I'm an ex-con. I'm not supposed to."

"But you do, don't you?"

"Sometimes, if someone loans me a gun."

"Do you know about the Rhino? Wait. Let me show you."

They stayed up talking until midnight. Josh showed Zlatko the pull-out in the basement. In the morning everyone slept in. Josh was first to rise, and took Fig on a run. They left for Chicago at noon Thursday, Josh following Zlatko's Mustang. The Donald E. Stephens Convention Center was on River Road in Rosemont, across the street from the Hyatt, where the con had put Polly. She was a guest because they'd chosen her over a year ago, before *Muhammad* came out. It was too late to back out now. If they disinvited her, they would be reviled.

Josh couldn't get a room so Polly agreed to share. The room had two queen-size beds and a nice view of the convention center across the street, long lines already forming. They dumped their stuff and headed across the street, Polly pulling a wheeled suitcase filled with trade goods. They stood at the guest registration table behind Tony Moore, original artist for *The Walking Dead*.

Long lines stretched from three entrances as security guards searched backpacks and wanded people.

The convention hall was the size of a blimp hangar. They'd given Polly a table next to Abdul in the middle. To their left was Zach Howard, to their right, Steve Butler. Abdul Alhazred's banner looked like a biker's upper rocker: AL QABONG—THE HOG WITH THE SHLONG, and underneath, BY ABDUL ALHAZRED, THE MAD ARAB. Polly had left her banner at home since *Muhammad* was too inflammatory, but the con had put her name up in big block letters on white cardboard stock, stapled to the backdrop behind her.

Only professionals and vendors were allowed in the night before the show, and the big hall was a busy hive. DC, Marvel and Valiant constructed two-story pre-fab pavilions, while merchandise vendors erected twenty-foot kiosks. Sure enough, they passed a blade vendor on the way in with a display that put "The Night Watch" to shame. While Polly set up, Josh kept an eye out, noting several cosplayers who appeared to be armed with real steel. At least one of them was dressed like a twelfth-century Crusader. Josh wondered who was really behind the steel mask.

Polly set out copies of her sketchbooks and *Wonder Woman* work, leaving the *Muhammad* comics under the table, and covered the whole thing with a tablecloth. They went across the street and had dinner in the Hyatt. Polly looked like a bobblehead.

"Oh my god," she said, "there's Art Spiegelman dining with Neil Gaiman! I think I'm going to die."

Her words reminded Josh of Shelley's peculiar reaction in San Diego. "Who's Spiegelman?"

"He created *Maus*, about the Holocaust, using mice for Jews and cats for Nazis."

It was eight by the time they finished. Josh was wiped from the previous night and looked hopefully at Polly.

"Go to bed, Josh! I'll be fine." She took Zlatko's arm. "Zlatko will protect me."

Zlatko held up a fist. "Fuckin' A, Bob!"

Josh looked from Zlatko to Polly. He needed sleep. "Awright, fuck it. I'm going to bed."

"I'll try not to wake you when I come in."

Josh rode the elevator with eight crazed conventioneers to the tenth floor as talk swirled. Stan Lee looked good for his age. Tom Hiddleston was rumored to be making an appearance. Marvel canceled twenty-four titles and announced sixteen new ones. Josh got off with several others and let himself into his room. Music pounded faintly from the adjacent room.

Josh stretched, stripped, brushed his teeth and screwed wax earplugs into his ears. He was asleep within minutes.

CHAPTER 41

Chicago—Friday

Josh never heard Polly come in. When he woke at ten, she lay wrapped in a sheet like a mummy, sawing away. Josh went down to the fitness room and worked out with weights for a half hour, returned to the room, where Polly was still sleeping, and took a shower. When he came out she was sitting on the edge of her bed poking at her phone.

She did a double take.

"Whoa! Who did that dragon?"

Josh pirouetted.

"Kasamura Oda. Anything good happen last night?" Josh said.

"I met Guillermo del Toro!"

"Who is that?"

"I forgot, you grew up under a rock. He's a film director. He did the best *kaiju* movie ever, *Pacific Rim*!"

"What's a *kaiju*?"

"It's a giant monster! Jesus! Don't you know anything?"

"I guess not."

"Let's head over. The show already started."

Josh looked out the window. Lines stretched from the convention center's main entrance to the end of the massive building and around the corner. It looked like a casting call on Mars—eight-foot aliens vying for space with gremlins, Hawkmen, trolls, dragons, ninja, Iron Men, Wonder Women and the de rigueur Deadpools and Harley Quinns.

Polly carried a backpack filled with cereal bars, raisins, almonds, bottled water, sketchpad, pens, pencils, sharpener, brushes, inks and a book should she find herself momentarily bored. They picked up program booklets. The cover was a Bill Reinhold Badger body-slamming a mime. Inside was a list of all special guests, events and sponsors, and a map of the convention floor.

Polly led with the wedge, Josh right behind her. Zlatko was holding court when they arrived at their table, with a dozen people standing in line to buy his latest *Al Qabong*. Polly took the seat next to him and uncovered her wares, including a hand-lettered sign: DRAWINGS $50. People immediately formed a line in front of her table, and she was busy until 1:00 p.m. selling sketches and comics. A pale woman with frizzy hair wearing a dress made of two giant Warner Bros. swag bags leaned in. Polly leaned forward.

"You got any of those *Muhammad* comics?" she said quietly.

Polly looked all around like a drug dealer, reached beneath the table and pulled the comic out facedown. She surreptitiously signed it, took the woman's money and said, "Thank you."

The woman stuffed it in her booty bag and melded with the crowd.

Polly thrust cash at Josh. "I'm starving. Get us something to eat."

"Okay, I'm going to get food. Zlatko, you want something?"

"Yeah, get me a hamburger, man. Ketchup and pickles."

"Watch after the girl."

Zlatko patted his abdomen. "No prob."

"How'd you get that in here?"

"I came in through the service entrance."

Josh shouldered his way to one of the many indoor vendors and stood in line behind Captain America. Burgers were seven bucks a pop but they were big. By the time he got his order and returned to the table it was one forty-five.

"Thank God!" Polly exclaimed, unwrapping her burger and wolfing it down. As they ate, a boneless Riddler vamped in front of their table, twirled his cane and said in the fruitiest voice imaginable, "When is a room not a room?"

He looked around expectantly, but no one paid him the slightest attention.

"WHEN IT'S A MUSHROOM!" he crowed.

A mother with two little boys in tow approached. "Excuse me, sir, can I take a picture of you with Scott and Terry?"

"Certainly. I charge twenty dollars per photo," the Riddler chirped.

"Captain America let us take a picture for free!" one of the boys piped up.

The Riddler did an elaborate double take and placed his hand on his chest, fingers spread. "I am not Captain America!"

"No shit," the mother said. "Let's go, boys."

By two thirty Polly had sold twenty-six copies of *Muhammad*. A man with Bob's Big Boy hair, weighing about 350 pounds and wearing an XXXL Chicago Comic Con T-shirt, bulled his way in front of Zlatko, who was working on a commission showing Al Qabong cold-cocking a sinister jihadist in suicide vest with his Strat.

"Hello, Ron," Zlatko said, without looking up.

Ron leaned on the table. Josh smelled his B.O. "I just saw someone walking through the hall with a *Muhammad* comic!"

"Didn't get it from me."

"I warned you this would happen."

Zlatko looked up. "What would happen, Ron? The dissemination of controversial material? Last time I checked, the First Amendment had not yet been repealed."

"Hey," Polly said. "I sold it to him. If you have a problem, speak to me."

Ron steered his gut toward Polly. "If it were up to me, you wouldn't be here."

Polly pointed at herself. *"Moi?* Little old *moi?"*
"It's nothing personal. I support the First Amendment, but there are exceptions. You can't cry fire in a crowded theater. That's what you're doing."

Polly faked a massive yawn.

"Move along, Ron!" Zlatko said. "You're blocking our tables."

Ron wagged a bratwurst-size finger. "This isn't finished." He turned and started to waddle away.

Zlatko stood and cupped his hands. "Nice to see you're back! Especially after seeing your front!"

Ron held up his middle finger without turning around.

"What a charming fellow!" Polly said.

"He's on the board," Zlatko said. "A real pain in the ass."

Polly looked beneath the table. "Good thing I brought two hundred copies!"

Josh was like a dog in a thunderstorm for the rest of the day, expecting some crazed berserker to rush them with an ax. Polly drew commissions when she wasn't signing comics. Several pros came by to support her, including Bob Layton, Gail Simone and Paul Guinan. Zlatko drew Muhammad. He drew Hulk Muhammad, Bat Muhammad, Spider-Muhammad and Hellboy Muhammad.

At six forty-five the PA system blasted, "ATTENTION! THE HALL IS CLOSING IN FIFTEEN MINUTES." The crowd had thinned to the point where you could actually see past the closest people. Josh looked past the mob in front of their tables and noticed a tall, thin, intense young man with the unhinged look of a maniac staring intently, dressed all in black with ninja climbing claws and an over-the-shoulder sword. Josh's alarms went off.

He tapped Zlatko on the shoulder. "Bug fuck at two o'clock."

Zlatko casually looked around. "I see him."

Polly leaned in. "What are you talking about? He doesn't look any crazier than anyone else here."

"Looks like he's getting ready to explode," Josh said.

Zlatko reached for his phone. "I'll call security."

"Could be nothing," Josh said.

"I trust your instincts."

While Zlatko dialed, the ninja snaked through the crowd, reaching over his shoulder for the sword. "DEATH TO INF—" he shouted before Josh leaped on the table and kicked him in the jaw, sending him over backward. He hit the floor hard.

"Ouch," Zlatko said.

"Fuck!" Josh said, leaping down and kneeling next to the unconscious ninja. His pulse was steady. Josh thanked God he hadn't killed the man. Minions, hobbits and Brother Bones stood in a circle snapping pictures.

"Is he all right?" someone said.

"What happened?"

Minutes later two security guards came up. One pulled out a transceiver. "We're gonna need an ambulance."

"That's it," Zlatko said, covering his table with a white tablecloth. "Let's go."

CHAPTER 42

Ad Hoc

The ninja's name was Howard Lutz Jr., a twenty-four-year-old student at Northwestern majoring in comparative religion with a minor in journalism. He'd dropped out, to his parents' disgust, fallen in with some radicals and become increasingly alienated over the past year. Howard Lutz Sr. was Vice President of Sales for Day-Tech, a company that made anesthesia machines, headquartered in Sweden. He lived on the North Shore with his third wife, Heidi. Junior was an only child.

Junior had recently started dating one Fatima Rouhani, president of the local Students for Justice in Palestine. Afterward, as a result of the attack, police had raided Junior's apartment and found seven unregistered firearms and a mini bomb factory, as well as cases of *The Protocols of the Elders of Zion* and *Mein Kampf* in Arabic.

Zlatko knew a Chicago PD lieutenant, who gave him the skinny. "Dude wouldn't shut up," Zlatko said over dinner in the Hyatt's American Grill over drinks. Zlatko had a martini, Polly red wine, Josh a beer. "Apparently he'd been planning something for months. His neighbors said he was squirrelly as hell and that he and his girlfriend made so much noise they called the cops on them a couple times.

"Said he'd planned to buy a samurai sword off the floor the whole time. Who cares about weapons checks at the door when you can pick up a nice samurai sword or zombie ax?

"Said he intended to kill both me and Polly for blasphemy." Zlatko lifted his glass and toasted Josh. "And you get three points for the kick."

"Lucky kick," Josh said.

"The Bears are sending a scout."

While they were eating, a gamine girl with a blue hairband and wearing yoga pants came up. "Hi, excuse me, I'm Mona Ashburton for Comics Source. What the hell happened today? At your booth? I heard there was an arrest."

"Some loony bird came at us with a samurai sword," Polly said. "But Josh here jumped on the table like some kind of superhero and kicked that sucker right in the teeth!" She grabbed Josh's arm and scooched close.

Josh leaned toward her ear. "I don't think we should make a big deal of this."

"There's a con paper they put out every day," Mona said. "They've already got the story."

"What story?" Zlatko said. "No one talked to us. Except the police."

"They say it was because you draw Muhammad. Care to comment?"

"You can draw your own conclusion," Zlatko said, polishing off his martini. He signaled to a waiter for another.

Mona held out a tiny recorder. "Tell me what you think happened."

Zlatko smiled. "It's not what I think happened, it's what happened. Some nut came at Polly and me with the intent of cutting off our heads because we draw the Prophet."

"Aren't you needlessly antagonizing millions of peaceful American Muslims?" Mona said.

Zlatko shrugged. "Listen, we're eating. You got a card? Give me your card and I'll call you after dinner. We'll set something up."

Mona reached into her feedbag, pulled out a wallet and removed her card. "Promise?"

Zlatko made the Scouts sign. "Swear to God."

"Thank you, Zlatko!" Polly said as the waiter arrived with their dinner.

Zlatko watched Mona sashay through the crowd. "Not a problem." He looked at his phone. "Fuck."

"What?" Josh said.

"They're convening an emergency board meeting. I have to go."

"What's it about?" Polly said.

"You know what it's about," Josh said. "It's about whether they're going to allow us into the convention tomorrow."

"Maybe I should go too," Polly said.

"Can we finish dinner first?" Josh said.

Zlatko stood. "They're meeting right now. We have to go." He threw a fifty on the table and trooped out, followed by Josh and Polly. The board was holding its ad hoc emergency meeting in the Frank Lloyd Wright Room on the mezzanine, a quasi-Prairie-style ballroom. The board sat at a big round table in the center of the room. The top of the table was unfinished plywood. Josh counted eight board members as they walked in. Conversation ceased. Ron, still wearing his volunteer T-shirt, stood.

"Who invited him?"

A black-haired woman with thick glasses and a plush dragon perched on her shoulder said, "I did. Zlatko's a founding member of this con and deserves to be here."

Zlatko spread his arms in greeting. "My friends! What calamity could possibly persuade you to forgo hobnobbing with George Takei to meet in this dismal place?"

A thin old dude with white hair and beard said, "Zlatko, it's exactly as we predicted. You two together constitute an unacceptable risk to ordinary congoers who just want to look at comics and have fun."

"Nothing happened," Zlatko said.

"If you consider some nut with a samurai sword nothing!" Ron said.

Zlatko snagged a spare folding chair from an adjacent table and dragged it over. "It happened late in the day. Nobody was hurt. Our security measures worked perfectly."

Ron pointed at Josh. "What security measures? That hood?"

"Mr. Pratt is a licensed private investigator."

"He's a thug," Ron said. "We looked him up. Served seven years for, what was it? Oh yeah, I remember, atrocious assault. What the hell is atrocious assault?"

"Chainsaw," Josh said.

"Folks," Polly said. "Can I speak for a minute?"

"No way," Ron said.

"Let her speak," said the dragon woman. Others murmured ascent.

"Folks," Polly said, "I never had any intention of drawing a fuss. I grew up reading underground comics. *Pudge*, *Girl Blimp*, anything by Crumb and Foolbert Sturgeon's *Adventures of Jesus*. Anyone remember what fun those comics were? That frisson of forbidden pleasure you got just from looking at the pictures? I also grew up believing that in America you can say what you like, so long as it's not hateful or incendiary. How many of you have actually read my *Muhammad* comic?"

Two dudes and the dragon lady raised their hands.

"Then you know there's nothing disrespectful about it. I'm just having a little fun, reimagining Muhammad as a playa, a swingin' dude, a black James Bond."

"You know Muslims regard any depiction of the Prophet as blasphemy," Ron insisted.

"Have you seen how Muslims caricature Jews?" Polly asked. "Have any of you looked at official Iranian websites? Do you know what they teach in Palestinian schools? Seems to me the Muslims are in no position to demand respect from others."

"Do Muslims even read comics?" Josh said.

"That dude's name is Howard Lutz Jr.," Ron said. "I seriously doubt he's a Muslim. The point is, you two are an attractive nuisance. You're attracting every sick son of a bitch in Chicago."

Zlatko held up a finger. "One guy."

The white-haired dude said, "I got off the phone with our insurance rep a little while ago. He phoned me to tell me that they're not responsible for incidents caused by deliberate provocation."

"What provocation?" Polly said. "All I'm saying, if you believe in the First Amendment, and you believe this is still America and we can say what we want regardless of threats from Third World savages, it shouldn't even be an issue."

A thin black girl with a wild pouf of hair hunched forward. "Excuse me...Third World savages? To whom, exactly, are you referring?"

"Not you, Doris," the dragon lady said. "We all know you're a First World savage."

Doris looked like she wanted to kill for an instant, but everybody else laughed and she laughed too.

"Okay," Ron said. "Enough of this crap. We need to take a vote. All those in favor of asking Zlatko and Polly to give up their tables—with a full refund—say aye."

"Wait a minute!" Zlatko said. "The First Amendment is part of our charter! Do you really want to read about this on Icv2.com on Monday?"

Ron slapped the table. "I move we cut off debate."

"Second," White Hair said.

"All those in favor of asking Zlatko and Polly to give up their tables for a full refund, raise your hand." There was a second of inactivity. Time stopped. The board's faces reflected anxiety, fear, anger, bewilderment. And then the hands shot up. It was over in an instant. Only Zlatko and the dragon lady held back.

"Gutless cowards!" Zlatko spat and headed for the exit. Josh and Polly followed him.

"Some of us have families, Zlatko," White Hair said.

CHAPTER 43

The Road to Radical Rage

Bar con was in full swing. Zlatko led the way. When the sweet young Indian bartender came over, he said, "Three shots of bourbon, please." He turned to Polly. "What will you have?"

"I'll have two shots."

"One shot," said Josh.

"There's no hope," Zlatko said. "No hope for this country."

"I'm thinking of emigrating to Israel," Polly said. "You want to come with me?"

"Let me think about it."

The bartender returned with their drinks. Zlatko and Polly did a one-two. Josh held his in his hand. "Now what?"

"We still have that panel tomorrow," Polly said.

"I doubt they're going to allow that," Josh said.

"Too late to cancel. What are they going to do? Announce over the PA that the *Charlie Hebdo* panel has been canceled? And embarrass every half-assed penciler, inker, editor and letterer who posted that stupid meme on Facebook?"

"Superhero comics are all about standing up for the little guy," Polly said. She punched the air. "Fight the powa!"

Zlatko framed the crowd with his hands. "Gilbert Shelton did this savage drawing—'Three Most Admired Americans.' Billy Graham, Spiro Agnew and Richard Nixon. Savage shit, like Goya's portraits of the Spanish Crown. Billy Graham didn't belong there, but I didn't know that at the time. Shelton threw him in because, you know, white preacher on television, he's got to be evil. Spiro Agnew was a piece of shit. Nixon? Nixon was Nixon.

"This is just gonna drive me to draw more outrageous pictures of Muhammad. Muhammad butt-fucking a camel. Muhammad shredding Jewish babies. Muhammad vamping in leather lingerie..."

Polly held up a hand. "Stop."

Zlatko stared at her as if seeing her for the first time, inhaled deeply and let it out in a controlled stream through his nose. His honker looked like the conning tower on a submarine.

A café au lait-colored young man in Clark Kent glasses edged up to Polly. "Excuse me, Miz Furst? I just want to say you're incredibly brave and I love your comic and I hope DC asks you to take over *Wonder Woman*."

"Thank you! What's your name?"

"Haydar Hassan."

"Where you from?"

"Pakistan."

"Are you Muslim?" Zlatko said with an edge.

"I don't know. It just doesn't make any sense over here, know what I mean?"

Zlatko pointed at Haydar in triumph. "Behold! An enlightened man."

"I have Christian friends. In Pakistan, you couldn't have Christian friends."

"A Christian's devotion to Jesus causes him to embrace love and forgiveness as he follows in Christ's path," Zlatko said. "But the only way to advance in Islam is through increasingly radical demonstrations of submission. I've seen it happen over and over, and this is why we'll never be free of jizlamists so long as we permit unfettered immigration. We need to kick out every Muslim."

"What's a jizlamist?" Haydar said.

"That's what I call 'em. 'Jihad' plus 'Islam' equals 'jizlam.' Only I spell it with a 'z' because it's really all about their jiz. What is jizlam but the most fucked-up attitude toward sex and women imaginable?"

"What do you mean?" Haydar said. "What happens over and over?"

"You start by praying daily. Then you grow a beard. Then you go to the mosque. Then you demand your woman, if any, to stop behaving like a harlot and cover herself. Maybe a good beating so she doesn't forget. Then you seek out your radical imam until the only thing left is to shoot a bunch of infidels and blow yourself up.

"If you must prove your devotion to God over and over in ever-increasing efforts, sooner or later there's nothing left but to blow yourself up. Plus a lot of these dudes actually believe they'll have access to seventy-two virgins in Paradise. Jizlam.

"Look at the Church of LDS. Another fake religion contrived solely so that Joseph Smith could fuck as many broads as he liked without incurring the wrath of the community."

"I have a girlfriend," Haydar said defensively.

"I'm not talking about you," Zlatko said. "Jizlam is as much sexual perversion as anything else. I know how these guys think because I know them! They're like Ted Bundy—obsessed with pussy every waking minute! Islam gives them a channel to work off their sexual frustration—otherwise they'd be out raping and killing women like Ted Bundy! Instead, they submerge their sexual frustration into hatred for the infidel and that dream of seventy-two virgins. They really believe that shit!"

"Not all Muslims think that way," Haydar said. "There are lots of moderate Muslims."

"Know any?"

"A few."

"Who are they?"

"That's not fair. You're extrapolating these characteristics to billions of people!"

"So what are you saying? That there are billions of good Muslims who don't want to kill the infidel? Where are they?"

Jade Kamal emerged from the crowd like Moses parting the Red Sea. "What's going on?" she said brightly, embracing Polly and then Josh.

"Jade," Polly said, "do you know Abdul Alhazred?"

Jade regarded Zlatko like the Hope Diamond. "The notorious Double A! A pleasure."

They shook hands.

"We're talking tribalism," Zlatko said. "Haydar here thinks it's unfair to characterize most Muslims as bloodthirsty savages."

"That's reasonable," Jade said.

"It's ninety percent of Muslims who give the rest a bad name," Zlatko said.

"That's ridiculous," Haydar said.

Jade stuck out her hand. "Jade Kamal."

"Haydar Hassan."

"Tribalism makes you say that," Zlatko said.

Josh scanned the crowd, catching a glimpse of red hair. Thinking he saw Cat Lowenstein, he set his glass on the bar and applied the wedge, apologizing as he parted the crowd. By the time he emerged from the bar she'd disappeared. He caught a whiff of her scent. Or was it his imagination?

Just the thought of her gave him a boner. He didn't know whether he wanted to confront her or throw her in the sack. Yeah he did. But he wanted to ask her if she'd drugged him, and if she had, what was the point?

Like she'd tell him. Josh chuckled. Used and abused. Story of his life. Polly et al. had commandeered a bar table and now sat on tall stools with their drinks. Josh pulled up a stool.

"Muslims need a sense of humor," Polly said.

"Muslims have a sense of humor," Jade said.

"Really," Polly said.

Jade smiled demurely. "I went to see a Muslim tribute band called Bomb Jovi last night at a mosque in London. They sang "Losing My Head Over You," "Rocket Launcher Man" and "You're Six, You're Beautiful and You're Mine." Their last song, "Living on a Prayer Mat," almost brought the house down! Then this guy bragged about how he had the entire Koran on a DVD. I asked him, 'Can you burn me a copy?' That's when the trouble started."

Everyone laughed.

Josh's phone vibrated. He went through the lobby out front to take the call. It was a warm August night and bar con had spilled out front. Josh had to walk halfway up the block, to a four-foot replica of the Eiffel Tower near the parking lot, to answer. It was agent Ross Phillips.

"Mr. Pratt, Stoeckle tells me you think there might be some kind of jihadist training camp in Wisconsin. Is that right?"

"Yes sir. No one's seen the proprietor in ages. He was a bit of a libertarian crank, I understand. I went by the place and I saw some dudes who looked Middle Eastern, and some black dudes."

"What are the chances you could get in there, take a look around?"

"Pretty slim. Those boys are all stirred up. They tried to blackmail a client of mine and it backfired. We got one of 'em in the Jackson County jail. Heilel Ben Shahar." Josh spelled it.

"I'll check him out. We have no agents to spare, what with this Kentucky shooting. Are you sure there's no way you can get in there and take a look? They tell me you're a very resourceful man."

"Sir, we'll give it a try in the coming week."

"I appreciate that, son."

Josh phoned Kleiser.

"She's fine, Josh."

CHAPTER 44

Charlie Hebdo

Polly, Zlatko and Josh met in the American Grill at nine for break-fast. The waiter put them in an end booth next to Mark Nelson, Bob Schreck, Cliff Biggers and Adam Hughes, who looked like four bunker busters in a bomb bay.

The waiter came and filled their cups. After they ordered, Josh excused himself, stepped outside the hotel and phoned Kofsky.

"How'd it go with the board?" Josh said.

"Well I'm still here. They took it pretty well. I told them you'd put the fear of God in me, and that I've been going to counseling and I'm making progress. They were impressed with the fact I came forward. Only that prick Baxter wanted me to step down."

"You mentioned me. What do they know about me?"

"What everybody else knows. You're a crazy motherfucker. I told them you were my security consultant. They want to talk to you."

"What for?"

"They have questions. It's legit. Now I'm gonna have to put you on the fuckin' payroll. You might as well do some work."

Josh snorted. "What about Kleiser?"

"Fucking Kleiser is a gold mine. We're making him an offer."

"He'd have to settle down, get a social security number."

"Well, I do have some clout."

By the time Josh returned to the restaurant his waffle had arrived. At nine thirty the restaurant emptied out as fans and pros returned to the convention center. Josh, Polly and Zlatko remained seated. There was no rush—nothing until the panel at four, "Are We Still *Charlie Hebdo*?"

"I vote we split for Wisconsin right after the panel," Polly said. "I can save on the hotel room."

"Fine with me," Zlatko said. "I'll just go home."

"Where do you live?" Polly said.

"Evanston. I keep a low profile."

Polly checked out, leaving her and Josh's stuff with the bell captain. They crossed the street at noon and had to stand in line fifteen minutes just to show their pro passes. They found Zlatko in the cavernous, booming lobby conferring with his security chief, a tall Latino with a rogue's mustache. Josh did a double take.

"Enrique?" he said.

The man in the sky blue security shirt and navy blue tie looked at him and cracked into a grin. "Ese...! I might have known! Whatchoo doin' here, *hermano*?"

Josh punched Enrique on the arm. "Same as you, bro. Security work. Enrique Vaca, this is Polly Furst."

Zlatko was astonished. "You know this guy?"

"We met last year at the Executive Security Foundation seminar in Madison," Enrique said. "Then this fool goes and digs up a dead rock star and two ninja."

"And now," Polly said, "the ninja are dead and the rock star lives!"

"You're in charge of security at their panel?" Josh said.

Enrique grinned. He looked like a young Tyrone Power. "That's right."

Josh grunted. Polly grabbed him by the arm.

"Come on. I want to shop for steampunk. Zlatko, we'll meet you at the panel."

Zlatko waved as Polly dragged Josh through the main doors onto the convention floor, which resembled the inside of Galactus's clothes dryer filled with action figures and toys. Several incomprehensible basslines vied for dominance. A man with a plummy voice squawked incoherently through the PA. Cosplayers vamped and posed. Money changed hands.

It was worse than Sturgis. At least at Sturgis you were outside, surrounded by your own kind. The scene on the con floor was *Mad Max* and Fellini's *Satyricon*. Epileptics didn't stand a chance. Josh's eyes swept the floor on the lookout for telltale signs of trouble. It was like looking for flyspecks in a mound of pepper. *Everybody* looked suspicious. And yet, most of these people were self-described nerds and geeks whose only brush with action came via movies or computer games. Sure, the odd bodybuilder roamed the floor garbed as Conan or someone from *Game of Thrones*, and there were a surprising number of stunning women decked out as their favorite characters.

A platoon of Imperial Stormtroopers stomped by. It was the same platoon he'd seen in San Diego, the 231st.

Polly bought a brown felt top hat, leather goggles and a corset from We Be Steampunk. Shortly before four they went upstairs for the panel. An immense scrum had formed outside the room, and when the previous panel ended, it looked like Grand Central Station as people rushed to get in even before the room had emptied. Enrique and another Executive Security guard wanded people as they entered, causing a line to form down the hall into the main gallery.

When Josh and Polly finally made it inside, the room was already SRO and uncomfortably warm. Zlatko was sitting at a table on the raised dais next to a thin woman in a tank top, with a buzz cut and glasses, and an obese, bearded man with glasses. Polly worked her way to the front of the room and joined them on the dais. Josh stood against the wall with his arms crossed.

Zlatko tapped his microphone. There were four other microphones, one for each speaker, and pitchers of water and plastic cups.

"Okay, welcome to 'Are We Still *Charlie Hebdo*?' Our panelists are Polly Furst, creator of the *Muhammad* comic..."

"BOO!"

Josh looked. A zit-faced young man wearing a Che Guevara T-shirt stood and cupped his hands. "BOOOO!"

Enrique cut through the crowd like a great white, took the guy by the elbow and escorted him out.

"JEWS HAVE CAUSED EVERY WAR!" he shouted just before he was ejected.

"Please hold the booing and catcalls until after I've announced the guests," Zlatko said. "Next to Polly is Rich Meldrum from the Comic Book Defense Initiative; to my left is Freda Goldrick-Rab, creator of *White Bitches Be Like*; and I'm Abdul Alhazred, creator of *Al Qabong*. A couple years ago the French satirical magazine *Charlie Hebdo* held a Draw

Muhammad contest with predictable results. Humor-impaired Muslims stormed the building and killed twelve people. It used to go without question that terrorist murder was an unacceptable form of 'protest.'" Zlatko used quote fingers. "Here in the enlightened West we used to have a tradition of free speech. But what has happened in the years since the attack?

"*Charlie Hebdo* itself has waved the white flag of surrender and will no longer publish cartoons of the Prophet..."

A woman stood and unfurled a sign: THE FUTURE MUST NOT BELONG TO THOSE WHO SLANDER THE PROPHET MUHAMMAD! "Please put away your poster and sit down, ma'am," Josh said. "This is a panel discussion, not an Occupy moment."

"Free speech!" the woman yelled. Several others stood and joined her. Enrique and the other uniformed security guard escorted them out.

"Free speech for me but not for thee," Zlatko said. "That pretty well sums up the Islamic point of view. Freda, what's your take?"

"Abdul, I could not disagree with you more. Yes, we have a tradition of free speech in the West, but we also have a tradition of respect for religion. You wouldn't stand for someone saying that Jews are evil and need to be exterminated. Why do you think it's all right to insult hundreds of millions of Muslims?"

A third of the audience clapped and shouted. But Zlatko interrupted them.

"Well let's look at the way Muslim countries deal with unpopular viewpoints. If you insult Muhammad in Saudi Arabia, they cut off your head. If you do it in Iran, they throw you in prison for life. If you insult the Prophet in Syria..."

The lights flickered on and off. A uniformed Rosemont cop stood at the door flicking them. "Folks," he boomed, "we're going to have to evacuate the convention center. Please stand and file out in an orderly manner. Do not use the elevators; please use the stairs."

"What?" Zlatko boomed over the mic. "Why?"

"Folks, please obey our orders," the cop repeated. "I know it's a drag, but it's better to be safe than sorry."

Zlatko's eyes burned with unholy fervor and a Cheshire grin plastered itself across his chin. He was enjoying himself.

Josh walked to the service entrance at the back of the room and opened the door on a service corridor. "Come on, Polly. Let's go."

The other panelists joined them as a volunteer led them through the labyrinth.

"Someone phoned in a bomb threat," the volunteer said.

Polly turned to Josh. "Well, that deteriorated quickly."

CHAPTER 45

Maybe Baby

The panelists debouched into a service parking lot chockablock with flustered pros, volunteers, firefighters, cops and service vehicles with flashing lights. A cop with a German Shepherd on a leash entered the building behind them.

Polly clapped her hands together. "Great! Just what comics needs."

"Yeah," Zlatko said. "And you thought comics were escapism! Hey, look. Obviously the con is through for the day, and maybe for the whole weekend. I'm going back to my crib and try to get some work done. Don't know if I'll see you tomorrow, but it's been great finally meeting you. You too, Josh. You know where to find me."

Zlatko embraced Polly, who hugged back enthusiastically. He switched his embrace to Josh, stepped back and disappeared into the crowd.

Josh looked at Polly. "Now what?"

"Like to hang around for the Boom! party at Carlucci. I want to pitch Ross Richie."

"What's the pitch?"

"It's a kiddie book, but for adults too. Dagnabbit Rabbit and Upchuck Duck. Dag suffers from Tourette's syndrome, only he cries 'Racist!' Upchuck's a bulimic duck."

"Faboo."

They returned to bar con at the Hyatt until the shuttle bus took them to the party, a few miles down River Road. Carlucci's was an elegant, old-world-style place with family crests, photographs of Palermo and Sicily on the wall, and a fenced-in patio, where the party was taking place as a string quartet sawed away at "Welcome to the Jungle." Colored lights hung from tree to tree, imparting a warm glow.

They cruised the buffet and found some empty seats next to the wall. Josh surveyed the patio: industry types; au courant young men in fadeaways, earrings and nose studs; artsy young women clutching portfolios; dealers; retailers; editors, some in suit and tie, most in shirts advertising their love and/or affiliation. Josh and Polly ate Mongolian barbecued pork ribs. Everybody was talking about the evacuation and what had caused it. Polly looked up, smiled and stood.

"Linda!" she said.

A statuesque woman with long hair came over and embraced her. "Polly! How are you?"

"I'm good."

"Bill and I were at our table when they suddenly decided to evacuate the hall. Do you know why? We haven't been able to get a straight answer."

"Someone phoned in a bomb threat."

Linda covered her mouth. "Really? Who? Why?"

"Well, I don't know for sure but it may have been to shut down our panel, 'Are We Still *Charlie Hebdo*?'"

"Oh," Linda said. "What a shame. You're not in any danger, are you?"

Polly turned to Josh, who hurriedly set down his rib and wiped his hands on a paper napkin. "This is my bodyguard, Josh. Josh, Linda."

Josh stood and offered his hand. "Hi."

"Linda's husband drew *The Badger*."

"Seriously?" Josh said.

"Yes. He drew a lot of issues in the eighties. Bill Reinhold?"

Josh's jaw dropped. "Is he here?"

"He's here somewhere," Linda said. "I'll drag him over."

"Oh there's Ross Richie!" Polly said. "Wait here while I go bug him."

Josh sat to finish his plate. He finished the ribs and was on the coleslaw when he felt a presence and caught the scent of her perfume. Just like that, he had a boner. Like a dog that sees a slice of pizza. The feel of her. Her textures and smell.

"Hi, stranger," the redheaded demon said as she sat next to him wearing a different little black cocktail dress.

"Cat Lowenstein, I presume," Josh said.

Cat dimpled like Elizabeth Montgomery. "You are a detective!"

"Why'd you take your best friend's name, Cat?"

"Believe it or not it's because I loved her. I did it to honor her. It gave me a chance to start over. You've started over, haven't you Josh? You know what it's like."

"I changed a few things. What about you, Cat? Did you get religion?"

She warbled. "I don't believe religion makes you a better person. I believe you become a better person by admitting your past mistakes and not repeating them."

"Did you put something in my drink?"

Cat looked at him wide-eyed. "What?"

"Did you slip me a mickey?"

"Why would I do that?"

"I don't know."

"I hardly think I needed to drug you! What are you talking about?"

"I woke up with a splitting headache and a drug hangover."

"Well I didn't do it!"

"And then you just disappeared without a note or anything."

Cat put her fingers on Josh's wrist. They burned. "I thought I'd made a mistake and I was ashamed."

"Did you?"

Her hand dropped to his thigh. "No. Why don't you meet me back at my hotel? I'm at the Marriott, suite 460. I'll show you it wasn't a mistake."

Josh's throat went dry—the same reaction he'd had as a teenager when he met a pretty girl. He stood and looked around, couldn't see Polly. "Let me just check with my client."

Cat let her fingers trail as she stood. "Goody! Meet me in a half hour."

Josh was on a mission. He cruised the patio until he located Polly happily regaling a ring of fanboys. He worked his way to shouting distance.

"Hey, mind if I take off for an hour?"

She looked past his shoulder to where Cat was waiting expectantly. "Oh no!" she said. "She's back!"

She pushed him. "Go. I'm fine. I'll see you back at the hotel. I'll take the shuttle."

Josh went out front, waited for the shuttle to disgorge its load, and jumped aboard. The Marriott was the second stop. Josh got out and went inside. He wondered who was bankrolling Cat at the suites-only hotel.

In the men's room off the lobby he checked himself, washed his face and hands, sniffed his pits. Good to go.

He waited for the elevator with a dozen conventioneers, half in costume. He squeezed into the elevator with two Batmen.

"I'm Batman," one said.

"I'm Batman," said the other.

A funny-looking old dude with a big nose wearing a Nexus T-shirt said, "My friends, you can both be Batman."

Josh got out on the fourth floor and walked down the chilled, hushed corridor to suite 460. He raised his hand to knock and heard something scrape from just inside the door. His knuckles froze two inches from the door and the hair on the back of his neck stood up. He held his breath, straining to hear through the heavy door. Absolute silence.

Feeling a black tide rip through his chest he turned around, took the elevator down, waited for the shuttle and returned to the Boom! party at the restaurant.

CHAPTER 46

Wonewoc

People on the patio were shimmying and bopping as the string quartet sawed away at "Sweet Little Sixteen." Josh found Polly holding court at a table with three Eisner Award winners. He tapped her on the shoulder.

"Back so soon?" Polly said. "That was fast!"

"I had second thoughts."

Polly reeled back as if struck. "No! You?"

"What do we do now?" Josh said.

"Aw fuck it," she said. "I sold most of my inventory. Let's go home."

"Tonight?"

"Why the hell not? There's no point in hanging around. I'm not going to get any work from DC or Marvel. They won't have Polly Furst to kick around!"

"The hotel's gonna charge you for the room."

"I want to walk in Wonewoc! I want to go to Mukwonago! We'll take off first thing."

Josh shrugged. "Let's go."

As they left the restaurant, two news vans sped past, passing a howling ambulance going in the opposite direction. Polly checked con comments on Facebook on the bus.

"This is the biggest thing to happen in comics since Superman landed in Kansas. Social Justice Warrior says Zlatko and I are racist hatemongers who should be banned forever from all comics, shunned by decent society and possibly burned at the stake. Crabcake El Dweek says we are heroes and should make our panel a regular event."

"Are those real names?" Josh said.

"They're the names they use on Facebook. Farley Harrison, creator of *Evangelista*, is calling for a boycott. That's funny. *Evangelista* depicts Christians as hateful hypocrites and calls for the end to tax-exempt standing for churches and synagogues."

It took them a half hour to get back to the hotel, which was jammed with displaced comic geeks. The feast had moved to the hotel lobbies.

Polly drooped. "I'm beat. Let's leave in the morning. It's no big deal."

Once in their room, Polly went into the bathroom to prepare for bed. Josh caught glimpses of her in her slip. She had a nice figure. He was acutely aware of her proximity and his own frustrated libido. She was lesbo. Did that make her more attractive? Josh was afraid of his mind swamps. His father, Duane, appeared like the imp of the perverse on his shoulder and told him to go for it.

"You grab every piece of pussy you can."

Josh had dated a nurse once, who told him that catatonic and unconscious patients sometimes displayed boners, and the way to get rid of them was to slap your hands together over the boner.

Polly closed the bathroom door. Josh slapped his boner. He didn't sleep well that night. He dreamt he followed a redheaded demon through a forest, catching glimpses of her diaphanous gown, traces of her exquisite perfume, as he chased her through the woods. A monstrous creature reared before him. Dog Boy. A werewolf. Eugene Moon.

He woke with the sweats, showered and was dressed by the time Polly woke. They checked out at seven and hit the road, grabbing breakfast at a McDonald's halfway to Madison. They crossed into Wisconsin at nine. Polly stuck her arm and head out the window like a dog.

"WHEEEEE! I feel better already!"

"The media is coming after you," Josh said. "I hope you're ready."

"Are you kidding? I'm going to flash my *Muhammad* comic on every station that interviews me. And if they don't like it, I won't do the interview."

"Try to keep my name out of it."

Polly turned on the radio and searched for an all-news station, but it was Sunday. The news stations were on autopilot, running come-to-

Jesus meetings and canned programs about UFOs and giants returning to inhabit the earth. They pulled into Don's driveway shortly after eleven. Don and a friend with a wild shock of white hair were wrenching on a hardtail with an S&S engine.

Polly piled out, ran to Don and embraced him. "Uncle Don! Uncle Don!"

Josh got out. "What's going on?"

Don turned to his friend. "This is Dale. Dale, Josh. Josh is Polly's bodyguard."

Dale shook Josh's hand warmly. "Oh dear! I knew she was hot, but a bodyguard?"

"On account of the Muslims," Josh said.

"Muslims lust for our dear Polly?" Dale said. He wore a sweatshirt with the sleeves torn off, revealing buff tatted arms including the Devil Dog insignia.

"You're a stitch." Josh turned to Don. "She gonna be okay with you boys? I need to go home and do some work."

"I think so," Don said. "We're both strapped."

Dale grabbed his crotch. "Fags with guns!"

Josh went home, picking up his *Wisconsin State Journal* off the driveway. Fig greeted him ecstatically. Kleiser was asleep. Josh sat on the sofa and went through the Sunday *Journal*. There was an article on page two about a bomb threat forcing the closure of the Chicago Comic Con. The con would reopen Sunday with heightened security.

Josh went online and googled CHICAGO EVACUATED. There were hundreds of hits. Comicbookresources reported that the bomb threat "may have been due to the presence of controversial creators Abdul Alhazred and Polly Furst, whose drawings of Muhammad have upset many in the industry." Josh figured Polly's phone and internet were lighting up with queries and condemnations.

He checked Groovacious. Kane Owsley suggested that if Muslims took out Polly, it would be her own fault.

Josh went for a run with Fig, and when he got out of the shower, Kleiser was pecking away at his laptop on the back deck with a mug of coffee. Josh joined him.

"I want to take a look at Old MacDonald's tonight with the drone," Josh told him.

"Kofsky offered me a job."

"You gonna take it?"

Kleiser stretched and looked at the sky. "I'm tempted, but then I'd have to go back on the grid, cough up a social security number. I have enemies."

"You know what Robert E. Howard said about enemies. If you don't have 'em you're not living right."

"Oh I got 'em. Trouble is, some of them are government agencies."

"The feds have a long tradition of hiring miscreants. I'll talk to my guy. I'm sure they'd be delighted to have you working for their side for a change."

"Much appreciated," Kleiser said, poking at his laptop. A few minutes later he said, "Look at this." He tilted the screen toward Josh.

It was a satellite view of the MacDonald farm in full color. A tree line snaked north to south on the east side of the property, backing up against a state wildlife area.

Kleiser pointed to the tree line. "Their property ends east of this creek. If we can get into this wildlife area, the whole farm will be within drone range."

"What about audio?"

"Yup."

"Fantastic. Why don't you chart a route for us from that wildlife area. We'll take off around six, get in position while it's still light."

Josh got up.

"Where are you going?" Kleiser said.

"I'm going to take a nap. This could be an all-nighter."

CHAPTER 47

Circle of Hell

They took the interstate in Kleiser's car, heading north on Buford Road toward the Black River State Forest, which abutted the farm. They brought hip waders and massive backpacks, because much of the forest was a swamp. They were in position by eight on a slight rise just east of the farm, concealed by a line of cottonwood, elm, maple and locust trees that followed the creek. Kleiser removed his drone from the backpack, checked the systems and set it on a rock. He carefully set his controls and laptop on the rock as well.

"It'll record everything straight to my hard drive. I've also got it set up to record straight to yours."

Josh opened his backpack and pulled out Arby's sandwiches and four bottles of water. They settled down with their backs against trees, each lost in his own device as they waited for the sun to go down. Mosquitoes attacked. Josh pulled out a bottle of Off! bug spray. Sprayed his hands and rubbed it on the back of his neck and handed it to Kleiser. At eight the crackle of gunfire came from the west.

"Target practice," Josh said.

They ate, leaned back and watched birds flit across the cobalt blue.

"You ever think about Patty?" Josh said.

Kleiser's hands were behind his head as he looked up. "All the time. Every day. It's like a ghost limb. They cut off your leg but you still feel it itching. What about you?"

"I can't get her out of my mind. It's like God was taunting me by offering this perfect woman that I don't deserve, and then taking her away and laughing, with that deep God laugh the way He does."

"You don't believe that."

Josh sighed. "No. I try to have a good attitude. I try to stay busy—that's the key. But every now and then...I mean, like every night, I think about her. We were only together a couple weeks. Who knows what might have happened if she lived? You been with other women?"

"Nope. Not in six years. What about you?"

Josh looked back on his recent series of one-night stands. "A couple. No biggie. They weren't like Fig."

The western glow faded and night crept up on them. Looking through the tree break at the farm they saw lights twinkle, heard dogs barking in whining, unintelligible imprecations.

"I thought Muslims didn't like dogs," Kleiser said.

"Let's get that drone up."

Kleiser laid out his equipment and did a quick run-through. He turned a switch on the drone and thumbed his control yoke, and the four rotors buzzed to life like locusts. The drone rose straight in the air and a minute later, Kleiser's open laptop showed the green glow of night vision as the drone crossed over the tree line and entered Old MacDonald's Farm airspace. White lines appeared on the video indicating direction and scale. The view slid by, like the aerial view of a shag carpet, until it overshot the unmistakable form of a man carrying a gun. The gun, some kind of shortened rifle, was immediately evident.

The drone hovered. The gun dude leaned against a fence post, slung his gun over his shoulder, pulled a cigarette from behind his ear and lit it, causing a minute blaze of white. He had a bald spot on the top of his head.

"Can you back off, get down low and get a view of the man's face?"

"I don't want to do that. It's too heavily wooded and if I get tangled in tree limbs or a bush, that's it. Let's move on a little bit and see if we can find some open space."

The drone moved on, Kleiser concentrating on the tiny yoke screen, Josh on the laptop. The camera swept past the main house, then came back. Lights on both floors.

"See if you can see what's in that second-floor bedroom," Josh said.

The view gyrated, stabilized and zoomed in on a second-story window with blinds covering the upper third. An oxygen tank and part of a bed came into view. As they watched, a gnarled hand moved on the bed, gripped something, and the light in the bedroom changed.

"TV remote," Kleiser said.

"Any way we can see who's in the bed?"

"Not without flying in the window, but whoever it is, he's on oxygen."

"Old MacDonald," Josh said.

"That's what I think."

"Let's take a look at the barn."

The POV rose and tracked outward from the farmhouse until it came to the barn, a hulking structure with a cantilevered pole over the main entrance, which was wide open. The drone hovered low until it looked straight back into the barn from a height of ten feet. They saw a featureless Ford van and a pickup truck attached to a boat trailer. All they could tell about the boat was that it was made of aluminum.

"There's the boat. You wanna fly in there?"

"No."

"Fine. Let's keep moving."

The drone rose and looked around, zeroing in on row after row of neatly planted vegetables, including tomato vines, broccoli, pumpkins, gourds, peas and grapevines climbing on trellises.

Josh pulled out his spiral pad and a pen.

"Let's get a head count. That guy in the woods, we'll call him the Friar."

Kleiser piloted the drone in a grid pattern, up and down. There were two dudes between the farmhouse and the road, several more on the north and south perimeters. Josh made notes on his pad. There were nine: Friar, Rifleman, Cowboy Hat, Fez, Skullcap, Sandals and Jihadis 1, 2 and 3.

"There are probably more in the house," Josh said.

A fusillade of frantic barking split the night, followed by incoherent exhortations.

"See if you can find those dogs."

The drone rose and slowly rotated, fixing on Cowboy Hat dragging something through the dirt. The yard lights reflected off the conchos on his hat. He was dragging a dog by its tail. Josh wondered why the animal didn't cry out, then saw that its muzzle was taped shut. The image swept past a white blaze, swept back and zeroed in. At first the images were

214

indistinct due to turbulence, but the drone settled down and zoomed in on the action.

"Oh my God," Kleiser said.

The screen showed an enclosure approximately five feet across, made of hurricane fencing affixed to iron posts. Outside the enclosure three men were bent over several writhing forms—dogs, legs bound with duct tape, muzzles taped shut. A man grabbed a dog by its bound hind legs and hurled it over the hurricane fence into the ring. Another man poured gasoline on the dog, which immediately burst into flames, popped its muzzle tape in pain and terror and released a soul-shattering howl until it succumbed with a piteous wail.

Fez came out of the barn holding a cardboard box filled with puppies. Josh turned away.

CHAPTER 48

Documentary From Hell

"Jesus fuck!" Kleiser said.

Josh looked up, ashen. "Are you packing?"

Kleiser reached in his backpack and withdrew a .45 automatic. "I only got one. We can't go in there like this. They'd mow us down. I'm recording this shit. We'll turn it over to the sheriff. This is so bad. So bad."

"We can't," Josh said. "We're here illegally taping without permission."

"What do you mean illegally?"

"The park is open from sunrise until sundown."

Josh closed the laptop. "Let's get the fuck outta here before I do something stupid."

They packed up quickly and sloshed their way through the forest to where they'd left the car, a half mile away. Josh was in a state of shock. The images played against the inside of his skull. The devil was in there with a film projector. The images blurred together—the burning dogs, Dog Boy, the mountain lion he'd killed with a pocketknife, Stefan Prouse's headless corpse—a documentary from hell.

If this wasn't pure evil, what was? The image of Lebanon's captured pilot splashed across the movie screen in his head. They'd doused him with gasoline and set him on fire in an iron cage. Josh had never felt more violent. Right now, if he were dropped into the middle of the farm, he would tear them apart with his bare hands. He wished he'd brought his guns.

They got in the car and rode in silence back to Madison, Josh gazing out the window with hatred in his heart, Kleiser making every effort to be quiet. When they reached Josh's house, Josh stormed straight through and went out on the back deck, where Fig joined him, whining softly.

Kleiser sat on the front stoop and smoked a cigarette.

Josh put Fig in a headlock. "We're gonna get those fuckers," he whispered.

He was too upset to sleep. After a while he went back into the house, heard Kleiser taking a shower, went into his office and went online.

Dear Agent Stoeckle: I have returned from scoping Old MacDonald's Farm in Jackson County. You recall I believed there was terrorist activity. Well I was right. We counted nine jihadis. I don't know for a fact that they are preparing to wage jihad, but they were heavily armed and they were burning dogs to death. I don't know why they were burning dogs. I will send you the video in the morning. Right now it's past midnight and I can't sleep. I am holding my dog close and telling her I love her. I don't understand people who hate dogs. They may as well be an alien race.

Sorry for venting.

Yours,

Josh Pratt

Josh knew he wouldn't sleep. He wondered if he should send the video anonymously to local police agencies. He'd have to consult with Fleiss, the criminal attorney for whom he sometimes worked. He sat up, turned on the light and made notes while Fig lay with her head on his thigh. Finally, when he could stand it no longer, he got on his knees and prayed for guidance, for peace of mind, for the souls of the lost.

When the first shades of gray brightened the eastern horizon, he put on a pair of sweats and went running, pushing himself as hard as he could while Fig loped beside him. He did ten hard miles. When he returned home, Kleiser was still asleep. Josh showered and then, feeling exhausted as he always did after a hard run, went back to bed and fell asleep almost immediately. It was eleven when he woke, and Kleiser was gone but not before emailing him the contents of the video. Kleiser had edited out the irrelevant material, leaving five unbearable minutes.

Josh checked his phone and returned Stoeckle's call.

"Agent Stoeckle."

"Sir, it's Josh Pratt. I'm sending you the video we shot. I should warn you, it's pretty disturbing."

"Were they aware they were being filmed?"

"I don't think so. Why? Are there legal issues?"

"There might be but that's not why I ask. I just don't want to spook them before we get our ducks in a row. We'll assess the video and determine whether it represents an imminent threat. We're spread thin right now, as you can imagine. We're always spread thin."

"Sir, aren't the FBI, Homeland Security, Counterterrorism, Defense Intelligence Agency, the NSA and the CIA all concentrating on the same problem?"

The agent sighed, an uncharacteristic display of emotion. "If you're saying this is a clusterfuck, I can't disagree. There are six other agencies on the same thing, probably more I don't know about. However, we still have some professionalism. I appreciate your bringing this to our attention. It would be helpful if you could go back in there and catalog the extent of their arsenal. Can you do that?"

"Sir, isn't that the purview of the intelligence committee?"

"Of which you are a part. I see you're cashing the checks."

"Well I have to rely on my tech guy. He runs the drone. Surely you don't expect me to pay him."

"Did you pay him the first time?"

"No. My point is, my tech guy is taking a big risk if we go back in there. It might be worth a favor."

"What kind of favor?"

"I think he's on some watch lists."

"Get me faces and we'll talk."

"The faces are on the video. What if they are judged to be an imminent threat? What would you do?"

"Have a federal prosecutor draw up a warrant, probably go in with a pre-dawn raid."

"Sir, I understand there are dozens of terrorist training camps operating in the U.S. What you described, has that happened? To any of them?"

"No, and don't ask me why."

"If you do go in there, I'd like to come along."

"Ha!" Stoeckle barked. "Well, what the hell. Stranger things have happened. But don't sit around shining your boots. Like I said, were we to get the green light to go in and raid this place, it would be a first."

"What about Waco, sir?"

"I was speaking of alleged jihad. I see you're keeping busy. I assume your discovery has to do with this young lady you're guarding."

"It's more than that." Josh told Agent Stoeckle about the blackmail attempt on Kofsky.

"Send me Kofsky's contact info. I may want to talk to him."

"Will do."

Josh went into the kitchen, where Kleiser had left a pot of coffee on the stove, poured himself a cup and went out on the back deck. He called Fleiss, left a message. Fleiss called back twenty minutes later.

"What do you want?"

"Steve, we used a drone last night to film what may be a terrorist training camp in Jackson County. I'd like to send you the film, and you tell me if we can legally show it around."

"What am I, a lawyer?"

"You're a criminal attorney, Steve. You'll understand when you see it but I gotta warn you, it's pretty upsetting."

"Send it. Listen. I gotta go. I'm due in court in a half hour. I'll call you later."

"Thanks Steve."

It was one by the time Josh kicked out in Don's driveway. Don was at work but Polly called through the screen door, "Come on in!"

She sat at her drawing board in the living room, sunlight falling on an ink drawing of Doc Ock slugging it out with a giant octopus in space.

"It's a commission," Polly said.

"Do you have any forthcoming events?"

"Saturday I'm giving a talk on the Capitol Square at two on how to make comics. It's part of their "Culture on the Square" series. And the following weekend I'm marching in the Gay Pride thing at Orton Park, but I'll just be a face in the crowd. Look at this."

She turned to her laptop and in a moment showed Josh a letter from the City Attorney's Office: "Dear Ms. Furst: Due to past difficulties at public events where you've appeared, as a condition of your permit for the "Culture on the Square" series, the City of Madison requires that you post bond of $1 million for the security to be provided at your event this coming Saturday. Please respond by noon Thursday or we will withdraw your permit. Yours sincerely, Stephanie Coates-Ybarra, City Clerk."

"That's fucked. I'll talk to Steve about it. Please forward that letter to Fleisslawoffice.com." He spelled it for her. "Who knows about this event?"

"Everybody who reads, I guess. They have full-page ads in the *State Journal* and *Isthmus.*"

"Great."

CHAPTER 49

Cat and Dog

Josh checked his email on Don's front porch and found a file from Morris Lowenstein containing several pictures of Cat: vamping onstage in a high school production of *Guys and Dolls*; Cat in a gown with a handsome young black dude in a tux: prom time; Cat with a well-known Hollywood socialist. She was a brunette in all these pictures, but it was unquestionably Josh's Shelley.

Morris wrote: MY BROTHER ADRIAN IS A CORPORATE ATTORNEY. HE PROBABLY WOULDN'T APPRECIATE YOU CALLING HIM AT WORK. I GAVE HIM YOUR PHONE NUMBER AND HE SAID HE WOULD CALL YOU WHEN IT'S CONVENIENT.

Josh phoned MPD Detective Heinz Calloway. "Can I buy you lunch?"

"That is against our policy as you well know, but you can contribute a brat and a beer to the Policeman's Retirement Fund."

They agreed to meet Tuesday on the Union Terrace.

Josh got there early, plunked his backpack down on a table as soon as the previous occupants stood, and got a couple of brats and beers from the outdoor grill. He waved his ball cap when Heinz appeared in the cafeteria entrance. The tall detective heaved his old-fashioned barrister's briefcase up on the table and sat, wiping his brow with a handkerchief that he always carried in the breast pocket of his sky blue striped seersucker suit. Heinz was the best-dressed cop in Madison. His tie was a hand-painted mountain landscape.

"Nice tie," Josh said.

"My father was a barber and taught me the value of sartorial splendor. I checked with the Jackson County Humane Society. There has been an explosion of people reporting missing dogs."

"Did you watch that vid?"

"Sickening. I'm not a dog person but Ivy has two cats and treats them like family. As you know, that's not my jurisdiction."

"I think some of these attacks on Polly may have originated on that farm."

"That is a matter for the feds."

"The feds want me to go back there and film faces."

"What do you want from me?"

"Heinz, Polly has an event Saturday, teaching comics to kids on the Capitol Square at 2:00 p.m."

Heinz's one good eye found Josh. "Are you serious?"

"Yes."

"Farmer's market draws thirty thousand people. These crowd situations are among the most difficult."

"It would be helpful if you could tell the force about it."

"They're always on the lookout, but I will apprise them of this event. Who else is providing security?"

"Just me."

Heinz grunted. "You know, if they're really determined to kill your client, there's not much we can do if she insists on staying in the public eye."

"I know. Others have already advised her to change her name and go underground, like this is the fucking Soviet Union or something. Fuck that shit."

"Madison is a nice, quiet community. Your girl is causing a lot of stress."

"More stress than three hundred protesters taking over the Capitol, chaining themselves to the bannisters, screeching, 'We shall overcome' and playing bongos? How long were they in there? How much overtime did that cost?"

"A lot."

"The city wants my client to post a huge bond against damages."

Heinz quaffed his beer and set it down, leaving a light foam mustache on his face. "That is standard procedure."

"Mayor-for-Life ain't gonna like it if we take to social media and let people know."

Heinz shrugged. "Up to you. Personally, I don't think he has the balls to resist a popular protest movement, but your client isn't popular. In fact, she's decidedly unpopular."

"Only among a certain class of people," Josh said. "Most Madisonians would support her if they knew what was going on."

"There's a certain breed of Madisonian who, for want of a better term, I call Red Pampers Babies. They love to don their Guy Fawkes masks and march with upraised fists like a road company of *Les Mis* singing 'We Shall Overcome.' Stickin' it to the man! Up against the wall, motherfucker! 'The mere words "Socialism" and "Communism" draw toward them with magnetic force every fruit-juice drinker, nudist, sandal-wearer, sex-maniac, Quaker, "Nature Cure" quack, pacifist, and feminist in England.' Orwell. And these, unfortunately, are the mayor's constituents."

"Polly is one of his constituents."

Heinz smiled tightly. "I'm glad I'm not the mayor. The Policeman's Retirement Fund thanks you for the lunch." Josh rode across the square, kicked out in Steve Fleiss's postage-stamp-size parking lot on King Street and went up the stairs. Fleiss's receptionist, Marcia looked up from her tuna fish sub.

"He's in his office, Josh."

Fleiss looked up from his own sub.

"Subway today?" Josh said.

"What's up?"

Josh told him about the city's insistence that Polly purchase an expensive bond.

"That's illegal. Want me to write a letter?"

"Yes, please."

"I'm in court in a half hour and then I'm meeting with a client. Have Polly send me the city's demand and I'll have something for you tomorrow."

"Thanks, Steve."

"You free to deliver some paper next week?"

"I think so."

"Okay. I'll give you a call."

It was three thirty by the time Josh returned to Don's house in Middleton. Polly was still at her drawing board working through commissions. Josh looked over her shoulder. Shi was kicking Kabuki.

"Fleiss is sending a letter to the city attorney. We're just going to go and dare them to take action. Are you pushing this at all on Facebook?"

"Every day. I have people coming from Chicago and Milwaukee."

"Why don't you reach out, have them contact the City of Madison and tell them they are looking forward to the presentation and don't appreciate the city's attempt to shut it down?"

Polly pushed herself back from the desk and looked at Josh with a guffaw face and big eyes. "Wow. I can't believe you just said that! Josh Pratt, an enigma wrapped in a cipher wrapped in a riddle!"

Josh laughed. "I'm trying to move into the twenty-first century."

His phone rang, an unknown number. "This is Pratt."

"Mr. Pratt, this is Adrian Lowenstein. My brother contacted me regarding your query."

"Yes, Mr. Lowenstein. Thank you for calling me."

"I checked you out. Do you know, I was at Sturgis two years ago when you got into that beef with the Mastodons."

"You ride?"

"Got my first bike when I was seventeen. Read all about you. Morris told me you're involved with our sister, Cat. Tell me what this is about."

Josh told him of his two encounters. When he finished, he could hear Adrian breathing.

"Mr. Pratt, I believe you're a man I can trust. I'm afraid Cat has been irreparably harmed by our parents' lifestyle. It's a miracle Morris and I turned out as well as we did. We could very easily have become drug addicts or career criminals."

"I know the feeling, sir. I was headed on the wrong path until I came to Jesus in prison."

"I know about that and I respect you for it. Morris and I are secular Jews. We're too smart to believe in God, but lately I've been questioning my beliefs. We may have outsmarted ourselves."

"I will pray for you, Mr. Lowenstein."

"You can call me Adrian. When Cat was nineteen she took up with a streetwise black man named Terrence. I only met him once, seemed like an affable guy, but maybe he was just putting on a show for the white folks."

Said he produced rap artists and deejayed for a living. Excuse me. This is rather difficult for me."

"Take your time."

"Cat and Terrence got into a beef. While he was away she took his four-month-old pit bull puppy, put it in the oven, set the oven to three hundred degrees, jammed the door shut and left the house."

Josh felt a yawning ache in his chest. He wished he didn't know about these things. But this was his work—uncovering acts of evil and sadism. Self-disgust washed over him like a sewage tsunami. He'd found her so attractive. He still found her attractive, and it sickened him.

"Was she arrested?"

"Yes. I pulled some strings and she only had to do community service, but I told her I didn't want to have a thing to do with her after that."

"Thank you for telling me, Mr....Adrian. If she gets in contact, would you let me know?"

"Not gonna happen."

"All right. Thank you sir."

CHAPTER 50

Back to the Garden

"What's wrong?" Polly said, watching Josh's face.

"Nothing."

"You look sick."

"I'm fine. Has Don taught you how to shoot a gun yet?"

"Who has the time? Maybe next week. Relax. Nobody knows I'm here; you're doing a great job. Every time there's an incident I get new followers and readers."

"Are you gonna be all right here?"

Polly waved her arm. "Get outta here! Everything is copacetic."

"Call me if anything happens."

"Go."

Ten minutes later Josh kicked out in Dovetail's parking lot next to Kofsky's Tesla. The receptionist recognized him, handed him a lanyard and picked up the phone.

"I'm here to see Randall Kleiser, actually."

"Do you know where he is?"

"Yes, thanks."

Josh went back to Kleiser's office. He knocked on the closed door.

"Come in!" Kleiser sang.

The shades were down and the only source of light in the room came from the monitor, which displayed scrolling code. It looked like alien writing or a slow pan over a desert floor. Josh watched for a minute before Kleiser acknowledged him.

"Anonymous will launch an attack on Iran's computerized defense system in twelve hours."

"Not from here, I hope."

"I have nothing to do with it. I'm just providing technical support. What's up?"

"We have to go back to the farm tonight and film faces."

Kleiser turned from the monitor and picked up an open can of Red Bull. "You're kidding."

"No. I spoke to my NSA contact. They need this. If we get them faces they can check them against the lists, maybe find someone with a felony conviction or warrant. That gives them the right to raid the farm."

"I'm not getting paid for this!"

"The NSA will show its appreciation by withdrawing felony warrants on you."

Kleiser grinned, looking like Jeremiah Johnson. "Really? Suddenly at the ripe old age of thirty-five I'm about to join the establishment?"

Josh shrugged. "If you can't beat 'em, join 'em. Can you do it?"

"Sure. The trick is to not get caught and not fly the droid into a damned tree or something. I plan on installing mass detectors but that's going to take a while."

"My client has an event on the Square on Saturday. We have to do it before then. I was hoping to go back tonight."

Kleiser drew his palm over his forehead, smoothing back his mane. "Welp, looks like it's going to be another all-nighter."

"Go home and take a nap. I'll see you later."

Josh rode to West Towne, where Rocket Fizz, a candy and soda shop, had recently opened. The interior looked like a ten-year-old's Technicolor dream, where colorful candies and sodas marched the shelves in tight formation. Jujubes, Zero bars, jawbreakers, candy-pooping mules— Rocket Fizz had it all. Josh picked up two bottles of Lester's Fixins Bacon Soda, wrapped them carefully in paper bags and put them in his tank bag. Next stop was Walgreens, where he purchased two plastic spray bottles, the type used to moisten plants.

He took his own advice and took a nap with Fig, who was always down for a nap. Josh woke when he heard the front door slam. He looked at the bedside clock. It was five thirty. He went into the kitchen, where Kleiser was fishing in the fridge. Kleiser pulled out a bacon soda.

"Can I have this?"

"Nope. There's some root beer in there."

"Want one?" Kleiser asked.

Josh waved his hand. "No thanks. What about your drone? Worst-case scenario, they capture your drone. Can they find you from it?" Kleiser's mouth twisted in opposite directions. "I use a 4GHz spread spectrum. They can't track that. I custom-built the boards but there's nothing personal on them. I could encrypt it, but no, they couldn't. Not unless they dust it for fingerprints."

"Who has your fingerprints?"

"The feds. Back when Patty died I sorta lost it, said some things. That was actually the first time I came to their attention."

"Better wipe it off. I'll get a rag and some glass cleaner."

"Yeah. Good idea."

Josh went into the garage and looked at Fig's silver Super Hawk. *No, not gonna go there.* He found a rag and a bottle of Windex and took them into the house. Kleiser brought the droid in, set it on the coffee table next to the motorcycle motor and unfolded its appendages. Josh went into the basement, opened his gun safe and once again gazed with longing at his arsenal, inhaling the aroma of gun oil and burnished wood. He closed the door. There would be no gunfire.

Upstairs Kleiser wiped the rotors and the smooth, hard plastic of the nacelle, opened like a rose petal. Josh looked down at the bewildering array of circuits and wires. It really wasn't his business if Kleiser chose to carry a gun.

"I have a zoom lens that puts you in the subject's face from three hundred feet. I've also got a lens here looking straight down, so I could conceivably set the drone on a fence post or something to hold it steady, turn it with the blades."

"How'd you get into this racket?" Josh said.

"What, hacking? I studied computer technology for three years at CU before I dropped out, when Patty died. I'd go on Facebook or Twitter or one of those sites, zingin' shit back and forth—I type seventy words per minute—and all of a sudden everything would just stop. Drove me nuts. And this fucking banner appears over the top of the page—'a plug-in is not responding. Do you want to continue?' What plug-in? I didn't order a fucking plug-in. Or, 'a long-running script is slowing down your page.

228

Do you want to continue with the long-running script?' What the fuck! Who ordered the long-running script? So part of it was me just trying to backtrack that shit and fuck up their systems.

"I got pretty good at it. Anonymous got in touch and asked me to join."

Kleiser finished wiping and clicked the panels together, creating a black plastic lozenge with four little derricks at polar opposites. Josh threw balaclava, bug spray, Chigarid, gloves, sap, knives, protein bars, toasted and salted almonds and a rain poncho in his backpack. He carried a six-pack of bottled water out to Kleiser's car and put it in the back seat, moving aside boxes filled with electronic components, books and clothes.

As before, Kleiser parked in the unused entrance to a fallow field a quarter mile down from the tiny gravel parking lot for Black River State Forest. They were in place by eight thirty.

"I hate mosquitoes so much," Kleiser said, "I'm almost willing to forgo the bug repellant just to draw them into range. Imagine autonomous swarms of micro-drones the size of mosquitoes, with cameras that can home in on faces. They're almost here. Then we wouldn't have to worry whether they saw us or not. You could send in hundreds, thousands. Wouldn't matter if they knocked a couple out."

"If there's a repeat of last night, I don't know what I'll do," Josh said.

"Did you bring a gun?"

"I told you, I'm not supposed to have a gun."

"Riiiight."

The sun went down, the drone went up. Within minutes Kleiser found a sweet spot ten feet off the ground across the pasture from the barnyard and zeroed in on faces. Fez. Rifleman.

Skullcap. Friar. Sandals. Jihadis 1, 2 and 3. But not Cowboy Hat. Kleiser avoided turning the camera toward the crematorium.

Kleiser gained altitude, did a slow pan around the yard, the camera sweeping past a table just inside the barn.

"Wait," Josh said. "Go back."

The camera returned to the table and zeroed in on a selection of weapons, including several ARs and a long tube with a spindle-shaped projectile at one end.

"What's that?" Kleiser said.

"Take a still of it. Then let's take another look in Old MacDonald's window," Josh said. "Let's see if we can scope the guy."

Kleiser maneuvered the drone so that it hovered just outside the second-story bedroom window with no more noise than a hummingbird. He and Josh stared at their respective monitors as Kleiser slow-panned from an old, white-haired man sitting up in bed to a dude sitting in a kitchen chair. He had prominent cheekbones, a dark beard and hair partly covered in a keffiyeh. The old man had oxygen tubes in his nose. The window was open and they could hear the dark-haired man reading from an open book in his lap.

"The Lord hath decreed that ye worship none save him," the man read in a reedy voice with a Middle Eastern accent, "and that ye show kindness to parents. Lower unto them the wing of submission through mercy, and say, 'My Lord, have mercy on them both as they took care of me when I was little.'"

"Izzat the Bible?" Josh whispered incredulously.

"It's the Koran," Kleiser said. "I started reading it after Patty died."

CHAPTER 51

❧

Denial of Service

Kleiser uploaded the video in the car and sent it to Stoeckle. They were back at Josh's place by ten thirty. Josh sent Stoeckle a message in the morning but didn't hear back until five, when the agent called.

"We've been able to match three of the faces to our terrorist watch lists."

"Does that mean you'll go in?"

"No. But we now know more than we did, and we are getting a clearer picture of jihadist activities in the Upper Midwest. As I said before, we're spread thin, which is why we rely on auxiliaries such as you."

"Speaking of which, what about my friend? Can you do anything for him?"

"What's his name?"

"Sir, I'd better clear this with him first. It would be better if we could meet in person. Are you in the Midwest?"

"I'll be in Milwaukee tomorrow, which is Thursday. I could meet at three o'clock."

"Would you send me the dirt on the three you identified?"

"I'll do that. We need to fix you up with an encrypted server."

"Sir, I don't think that will be necessary. Wait until you meet my friend."

They agreed to meet at a Cracker Barrel in Waukesha.

When Kleiser arrived back from work, Josh told him the news. They went to the Rat Pack-themed Johnny's Italian Steakhouse in Middleton, with black-and-white photos of Frank, Dino, Sammy, Shirley, Joey, Ava and Angie on the wall, and Sinatra crooning "Fly Me to the Moon" as they entered. They sat beneath a photo of the Rat Pack cutting up onstage at the Sands.

The shapely waitress wore a black skirt and a white apron. "What'll it be, gents?"

"Jack Daniels and a Capital lager," Josh said.

"The nectar of the gods, baby!" Kleiser said.

"Excuse me?"

"Jack and a beer, just like him."

"Perfect," the waitress said.

Their drinks came and they ordered steaks.

"What would you take for that Hawk?" Kleiser said.

"It's not for sale."

"Why not?"

"It was Fig's."

Kleiser cut his steak. "Oh. Well, now I've got the bug again, thanks to you."

"Randall, if you haven't ridden since college, I would get some cheap little bike like a 400 or something and ride it around for a while. Don't spend more than five hundred bucks. It's a mistake for a first-time buyer to think he has to have something that weighs six hundred pounds and has a hundred horsepower."

"That bike I had in college was a CB650."

"Sweet bike," Josh said. "Wish I had one."

"You've got six bikes in there. Surely there's one you'd trust me with, just up and down the street."

Josh thought about it. Kleiser had made himself invaluable, not just to him but to Kofsky. "Maybe the Sportster. It's an 883 I picked up from a friend. I'd let you ride that, but I'm coming with you and you have to wear a helmet."

"What do you mean, you're coming with me?"

"On another bike, numbnutz. Did you send me that still from the farm? The weapons table?"

Kleiser pulled out his device. "Do it right now."

After dinner they returned to Josh's house.

Josh opened the garage door. "Want to go for a ride?"

Kleiser was like a little kid. "You bet!"

Josh checked the late-model 883's tire pressure and oil, and found an open-face helmet that fit Kleiser. "A few things. I know you rode a bike in college but you may have forgot. You follow me. Always use both brakes at the same time, with emphasis on the front. It does most of the stopping. No abrupt moves. Smoothness is the key to a safe ride. Leave a couple bike lengths between us. Ready?"

Kleiser straddled the Sportster wearing his sunglasses and the helmet and grinning like an idiot. "I was born ready!"

Josh rolled his bike out, keyed the garage door shut and led Kleiser west on Ptarmigan, out S, north on P to Observatory Road. The road ran past the university's rural observatory, untainted by the lights of the city, through gullies and forested valleys redolent of honeysuckle and cut hay, to Garfoot Road, which looped back toward Mineral Point past farms and grazing stock. As they began a long incline, a pair of sparrows attacked a goshawk, swooping and diving like World War I flying aces. They came to the stop sign on Mineral Point, and Josh headed back. It was just past eight when they rolled the bikes back into the garage.

"Whoa!" Kleiser exclaimed, removing his helmet. "I'd forgotten how great that is! Will you sell me that Sportster?"

"Sure."

"It's an entirely different experience to ride a bike than ride in a car. It's like you're part of the landscape."

"You ain't wrong. It reminds you of your mortality and how precious life is. In order to experience that rush of sensation, you must put yourself at risk. I'm always aware that each ride could be my last."

"Seriously?" Kleiser said, setting his helmet on the workbench.

"Not all the time, but it's there in the back of my mind. I can't tell you how many times I've approached a bend in the road and slowed way down, and come around the corner to find a truck completely blocking both lanes as it unloads something. Don't even ask about the deer."

They went inside and grabbed a couple of beers. Josh went into his office.

"I'm going to see if I can ID that weapon you sent me."

He went online and researched the device on the table. "Ho shit," he said. "It's an RPG-7 anti-tank rocket from Russia."

His screen went blank, then flashed a series of terrifying images—rows of orange-garbed Christians kneeling in front of their executioners, the crematoriums at Auschwitz, an iron cage filled with men being lowered into a lake, a pilot burned alive in an iron cage. The screen turned black. The ISIS symbol appeared above the words YOU'RE NEXT in red, followed by white noise.

"Randall!" Josh said. "Come in here, please."

Kleiser came into the room, took one look and said, "Get up." He knelt on the floor and pulled every plug he could find.

"Fuck. They know who you are."

Josh felt stupid. Of course they knew who he was. "Can you fix it?"

"I don't know. It might take a while. In the meantime maybe you should pick up a new hard drive and we'll transfer your secure files, if you have any left."

"If they hacked me they've hacked all my contacts," Josh said.

"Probably."

Josh phoned Stoeckle, and it went to voicemail. Josh recited what had happened, including the RPG-7. "Don't send me any emails. Talk to you soon."

Kleiser stood in the living room staring at his device with a stricken expression. "Shit," he said. "They got me too."

CHAPTER 52

Rites of Passage

Josh and Kleiser arrived at the Cracker Barrel in Waukesha at three fifteen and still beat Stoeckle, who arrived minutes later, driving a plain brown Impala that screamed government vehicle. They went inside and got a table.

"Roland Stoeckle, Randall Kleiser."

"I understand you've been providing Josh with tech support."

"Yup."

The waitress came and they ordered coffee.

"I understand you've traced these denial-of-service attacks to a rural address in Jackson County," Stoeckle began.

"You saw the video. It's a terrorist training camp," Josh said. "They've got an arsenal that includes Russian anti-tank missiles."

"Yes, we're familiar with the RPG-7. They've been used extensively throughout the Middle East since the seventies. Although they're several generations old, they can do a lot of damage against civilian targets, which is our main concern."

"Is your network secure?" Kleiser said.

"It is now. If you don't mind, Randall Kleiser is your real name?"

"Yup."

Stoeckle heaved his briefcase on the table, opened it and took out a thick sheath of printouts, which he flipped through. He paused ten pages in. "Black Widower. You've been on our radar for a while."

"Guilty."

"But now you're assisting us."

"I'm assisting him," Kleiser said, pointing to Josh.

"He may join Dovetail," Josh said.

"Dovetail does highly sensitive work. You'll need a security clearance."

"That's one of the reasons we're here," Josh said. "You give my pal Randall a security clearance and remove him from your terrorist watch lists, and he'll become an asset. Isn't that right, Randall?"

"That's right."

"Sorry to hear about your girlfriend."

"Yeah," Kleiser said. "Have there been any changes in TSA policy since that started? Like, you know, stop patting down random passengers and instituting profiling the way El Al does it? Do you know how many terrorist incidents El Al has suffered in the past twenty years?"

"You're talking to the wrong person. I share your point of view, but I don't work for the TSA."

"Sorry. It's kind of a sore point for me."

"I understand."

The waitress returned. "Will you gentlemen be ordering lunch?"

"No thanks," Stoeckle said. "Just the coffee."

"Are you working for Dovetail now?" Stoeckle said.

"Yes."

"Tell me why."

Kleiser looked at Josh.

"They were blackmailing Aaron Kofsky." Josh told him the story.

Stoeckle sat for a minute with his hands folded in front of him like a stern schoolteacher. "They are obviously probing for a security leak, which is how they came across your friend's dirty little secret. Why would he keep that stuff on his work computer?"

Josh shrugged. "He's supposed to be the security expert."

"Instead," Stoeckle said, "the security expert turns to a real security expert. Are you certain this threat originated at this farm?"

Josh told him about the tracking device. "As sure as we can be."

Stoeckle pushed his lips in and out.

"What are you going to do about this nest of vipers, Roland?" Josh said. "They might make a move on my client Saturday. We've got a public event."

"Don't go."

"You're a laugh riot, Roland. Will you notify local jurisdictions about those rocket-propelled grenades?"

"I will issue an alert. My job is to keep track of threats to our national security system. Right now we're dealing with a heightened alert that there will be an attack this weekend against malls. We've notified every mall in America to beef up security, and we've deployed our resources as best we can. The only agent I can spare is you, Pratt."

"How 'bout putting Randall on the payroll?"

"If he works for Dovetail, he's already on the payroll, isn't he? But you did good work. I'll see what I can do regarding your other request."

They got up, parted from Stoeckle and headed west on the interstate.

"Never thought I'd end up working for the feds," Kleiser said.

"Yeah. Real James Bond stuff."

"As a kid I always wanted to be a spy. Jet around, kill the bad guys, get the hot girls. Didn't you?"

"No. All I thought about was what a shitty deal I had. I used to think there was a secret handbook that told you how to behave. Everybody had a copy but me. My old man was an abusive drunk who dragged me around from job to job. Never even bothered to register me for school. I had to register myself. Finally he dumped me at a truck stop when I was fifteen, and I bounced around from foster home to foster home 'cause I was a little shit. Always fighting. Never grateful. I had to learn how to be a man by myself. Took me a long time."

"Is that why you became a biker?"

"That's part of it. I guess I was unconsciously yearning for a father figure, some group I could belong to. I'm sorta lucky I hooked up with the Bedouins. It could have been worse. At least they had a code. That was the only family I ever really belonged to, until Fig and Fig the dog. I think today's kids have it tough, especially kids without fathers. They have to make their own way in the world. On the one hand they have it too easy, so they invent rituals for themselves."

"Sports. Money. Martial arts. They need to feel something, some rite of passage. A hundred years ago, by the time you were twenty you had a wife and two kids, and if you didn't put food on the table you'd starve. Or you got drafted into the czar's army and spent the next two years tramping around. Today..."

Josh slapped himself. "Shut up, Josh."

"No, man, you're right. It's all good."

"That's the most I've spoken since I did coke."

"My folks are still around," Kleiser said. "We don't talk much, but we don't hate each other. I have two sisters who are disgusting overachievers. We love and respect each other but we don't have much in common."

"You talk to them?"

"Once or twice a year. Birthdays. Major life events. Patty and I were going to have kids."

"Don't give up, bro. God never dishes out more than you can handle."

Kleiser chuckled self-consciously. "I got no faith. I was raised Presbyterian!"

"Maybe you could come to church with me," Josh said.

"No thanks. But thanks for asking."

"May I preach a little?"

"Go ahead."

"My testimony is very short. I was a monster, and Jesus forgave me and changed me for the better."

CHAPTER 53

Strategy Session

Don had everyone over for a cookout Thursday evening, including Fig and Don's friend Dale. They sat around in the backyard drinking beer and watching Don turn the bratwursts.

"Randall," Josh said, "do you have any experience doing security?"

"No."

"I do," Don said. "I used to bounce at MacIntosh's in Milwaukee. That's a gay biker bar. Surprised you never came by, pretty man."

Josh next toasted Dale with his beer. "You have any training?"

"I'm a black belt in Brazilian Jiu-Jitsu," Dale said.

"Seriously?"

"I'm also a third dan at Salick's Karate and Fitness in Delafield."

"Would you be willing to help out Saturday when Polly gives her class on the Capitol Square? No rough stuff. Just keep an eye out for any wayward jihadis."

"Sure," Dale said.

"I'm in," Don chimed in.

Josh wondered if he should drag his friends from the Zhong Yi Kung Fu Academy into it. But no, Nelson Ferreira would be running his school at that time and had already done enough. He thought about Bricklin. She would probably be more than happy to face-plant some Muslims, but it wasn't fair to drag civilians into this mess, not without paying them.

"Maybe this is a bad idea," Polly said.

"Fuck that!" Dale said. "You can't let those creeps intimidate you. This is America, not East Fuckistan."

"That's right," Kleiser said.

"There's nothing offensive about my talk," Polly said. "I'm just going to teach some kids how to get started doing their own comics."

"Okay," Josh said, "let's all trade phone numbers. If you see something, tell me and then tell the nearest cop. Don't confront anyone unless they are about to get violent. And you'd better be sure, 'cause these guys know how to sue. Randall?"

Randall opened his backpack and dumped five burner phones on the table. "I taped the numbers of all the burners to the back so everybody has everybody else's number. Set your regular phones aside. Personally, I'd shit-can 'em just to be sure."

"If it starts to get ugly," Josh said, "pull out your phones and start filming. I guarantee they'll fade away."

Fig laid her snout on Josh's knee. He gave her a bratwurst.

On Friday Josh rode downtown and scoped out Polly's position on the Capitol steps. He went inside and climbed to the observation platform, which had a panoramic three hundred sixty-degree view of the isthmus and both lakes. Great place to plant a sniper. But of course a sniper had no place overlooking a popular, peaceful public gathering. The farmer's market had been a tradition for decades and regularly drew fifty thousand people on weekends. Not even the greatest sniper could fire into a writhing crowd with accuracy.

He phoned Katy Varner at WMAD. She was taping but returned his call fifteen minutes later as he was walking toward his bike in the Doty Street Ramp.

"What's up, Josh?" No mention of the filming debacle with Polly.

"Katy, did you know Polly Furst is giving a chalk talk tomorrow on the Capitol steps, for kids, on how to create their own comics?"

"I did not know that."

"There's a possibility we may have some protesters."

"Tomorrow is also the Crazy Legs Half Marathon, which I'm covering from ten until noon. What time is her chalk talk?"

"It's at one, at the top of State Street."

"I'll bring it up this afternoon. I can't promise anything. A lot of stuff is happening right now."

"Sure. I understand."

Katy hesitated. Dignity won.

"Thanks for the head's-up. I'll let you know."

"Thanks, Katy."

He saw that Kleiser had phoned while he was talking to Katy.

"Stop by Dovetail. I want to show you something."

Josh found Kleiser staring into his monitor in his darkened office, the monitor staring back.

"Take a look at this."

It was the recovered home page for oldmacdonaldsfarm.com, with a Currier & Ives print of a picturesque red barn in autumn, contented cows grazing in a glowing pasture.

> *Welcome to Old MacDonald's Farm, providing organic produce for over forty years! Here at Old MacDonald's, we choose only the finest strains of peas, beans, cereals and ginseng, untainted by GMOs, chemical fertilizers or synthetic light, because such would not be appropriate.*

"When did they take it down?"

"Six months ago."

"Damn," Josh said. "I'd love to get in there and talk to MacDonald."

"If he can talk. How much you want for that Sportster?"

"I'll take five."

"Done," Kleiser said. "I want to ride it downtown tomorrow."

"For what? You don't have any security experience. You don't even have a valid driver's license."

"I can go to the show, can't I? I want organic produce. That Old MacDonald's ad got me all revved up." Kleiser stood abruptly and shimmied. "Zucchini!" he sang. "Huh! What is it good for? Absolutely nothin'!"

"Okay, but you don't have a license, so don't get stopped. I'll see you back at my place."

Back home Josh went online, took Fig for a walk and checked out the Sportster. He topped the tires at thirty-five, made sure the oil was full and fresh and wiped it down. He was happy to let it go. Since the NSA had put him on their payroll, he could afford any motorcycle he wanted, but he was fiercely loyal to the bikes he already had, as he had been to the Bedouins. Sure he could blow eleven grand on the new Scout, but the experience wouldn't be that different from his modified Road King, on which he'd put a hundred thousand miles.

Kleiser entered the house counting up a wad of bills, which he handed to Josh. "Five Gs."

Josh signed the title over to him. "You always have that much cash?"

Kleiser winked. "I got no bank accounts."

"What about insurance?"

"HAH!" Kleiser barked.

"How do you expect to ride a motorcycle without insurance? What about your car?"

"I just have to be careful."

"Jesus!" Josh said. "You can't drive around without insurance! What happens if they pick you up?"

Kleiser raised a fist. "I know people!"

"The fuck you do. Listen. If you take that job with Dovetail, you'll have to become a legitimate citizen—Social Security, the whole nine yards. We can probably prevail on Stoeckle to get the IRS to overlook that whole tax thing, but that's a one-time deal!"

"Well now I don't know if I want to go legit."

Josh stared at him. Kleiser hit him on the arm.

"Just hossin', Josh!"

They went into the living room and watched the news. Scenes of devastation, body bags, ambulances, drowned immigrants washing up on Mediterranean shores, immigrants wading through a crowd of shocked sunbathers on Miami Beach.

A suicide bomber had detonated himself in a crowded Tel Aviv restaurant. The president was calling for calm. Governors and mayors were cautioning people not to blame all Muslims. Josh switched channels to a glowering chef browbeating a bunch of cooks.

"Fuck it," he said, getting up. He went into the kitchen, uncapped the two bottles of Lester's Fixins Bacon Soda, and poured one into each of the two spray bottles.

"What are you doing with that?" Kleiser said.

"Use your imagination."

CHAPTER 54

Saturday on the Square

Josh and Kleiser rode down at noon, left their bikes in the Doty Street Ramp and hooked up with Don and Dale at the head of State Street. Dale wore jeans, cowboy boots and suspenders over his *Star Wars* T-shirt. Don wore jeans and a Sturgis T. The Square was a party with thousands of people pushing baby strollers, stuffing hemp bags with produce, watching the jugglers and musicians and listening to the band that had set up on the Capitol lawn. It was a blue-sky day, temperature in the low eighties.

"Okay guys, let's walk around the Square. Randall and I will go clockwise; you boys go counter. Be cool, look hip, keep your eyes open. You see someone says trouble, take a picture. Be discreet. Don't let them see you."

"What about the cops?" Dale said.

Josh looked around and spotted two blue-uniformed city police officers chatting with a vendor on the sidewalk. "If you see something, say something."

He handed one of the spray bottles to Dale. "Here."

"What is it?" Dale said, bringing it to his nose and sniffing. "What the fuck? Is that bacon?"

Josh grinned. "To be used only in extreme circumstances. We meet back here at a quarter to one."

Josh and Kleiser walked down Mifflin Street past kiosks selling organic honey, stained glass, leather goods and essential oils, their eyes sweeping like lighthouse beams. At the corner of Mifflin and Pinckney, a white-faced mime juggled bowling pins. Hipsters in goatees and granny glasses pushed their spawn in prams while gangs of teenage girls giggled and texted. As they approached the northeast corner and the statue of Colonel Hans Christian Heg, Josh spotted a thin young man in cargo trousers, a beret and an olive drab tank top slouching toward the Capitol. The man's cargo trousers seemed unusually weighted. Josh looked around, spotted a cop at the curb and went over.

"Officer, I just saw this dude heading into the Capitol wearing green cargo trou and a beret and the pockets seemed awfully heavy."

"Oh yeah?" the cop said. "I'll let 'em know. What's your name?"

Josh handed him a card. "Josh Pratt."

The cop took the card and reached for his phone. "Yeah, okay. I'll let 'em know. Which door?"

Josh pointed. He and Kleiser resumed their walk.

"Probably nothing," Josh said. "But everything's so crazy now."

Josh looked up. Heads with binocs extended above the observation deck rail. You couldn't have a public gathering anymore lacking in security. Josh and Kleiser made it all the way back and walked up to where the Children's Museum had set up an easel with an erasable chalkboard for Polly's talk. Minutes later Don and Dale joined them.

"*Nada,*" said Don.

"I almost mugged that mime," Dale said.

Polly bounced up holding a big black portfolio over one shoulder as a yellow school bus pulled up at the head of West Washington. A stork-like woman led a platoon of eight- to ten-year-olds toward them, while others arrived with their parents or older siblings. A woman with Oprah hair wearing a Children's Museum XXXL T-shirt approached.

"Thank you for doing this, Polly," she said.

"My pleasure, Gillian."

"I have to tell you, Henry Park phoned me at ten thirty last night wondering if we should call it off. Because of the crazies, you know."

Polly turned to Josh. "Gillian, this is my secretary of security, Josh Pratt."

They shook hands.

"Polly!"

Polly turned toward the voice to see Melissa walking toward her with a cane. Polly hugged the older woman. "Melissa! What a surprise!"

"Yes, I surprised myself. First time I've been out in weeks, but I couldn't let my favorite cartoonist give her talk without seeing for myself."

Dale grabbed a folding chair from a stack leaning against the Capitol and set it back against the balustrade dividing concrete from lawn. He took a bottle of water from a cooler the museum people had brought, opened it and handed it to the older woman.

"Thank you, young man."

"Young?!"

"You're young to me."

Polly turned to find two dozen eager tykes seated on the concrete, the balustrade or blankets, their notepads and pencils spread before them.

Polly clapped her hands in delight. "Greetings, campers! I'm Polly and we're here to draw comics! How many of you are already drawing?"

Half the hands went up. Polly picked up a black marker and turned to her board. "There are lots of ways to draw a comic, but I always start by figuring out how many panels I want, and then drawing them on the paper."

She divided the rectangle into six squares. "Some people write their whole comic out beforehand, but we're not going to do that. We're going to be like the underground artists, and just draw the first thing that comes into our minds!"

Polly drew a cockatoo prancing on a pole in her first panel. "This is Snowball the cockatoo, working out to 'Another One Bites the Dust.'"

She drew a little word balloon above Snow Ball and wrote, "ooOOoo!" The kids laughed and squealed in delight.

"Now everybody draw something!"

Josh was looking toward State Street when out of the corner of his eye he saw two men edging their way around the side of the Capitol. One of them was the dude with the baggy cargo pants. He nudged Dale and as the men approached, Josh, Don, Dale and Kleiser stood tall and puffed up. Dale held phone to eye and snapped pictures. The two men turned abruptly and stalked off.

Josh said, "Two dudes, mid-twenties, maybe Middle Eastern, maybe Southeast Asian, camo cargo pants, brown shirts. One had a black beret." He looked around for a cop. A flash of red hair drew his attention.

No way. There were lots of redheads.

"This woman is a liar and a hatemonger!"

245

Josh turned. A middle-aged woman in a full-length skirt and tank top, with a buzz cut, stood in front of a stunned Polly addressing the kids.

"She has drawn a vile, blasphemous comic insulting the world's oldest and greatest religion! She has no business—"

Josh got in her face. "I've notified the police. They're coming to arrest you."

"For what?" she spat back. "Exercising my First Amendment rights?"

One of the kids started to cry. Others joined in. People began pulling their kids from the presentation.

"Please leave," Polly said.

The woman responded by wresting the marker from Polly's hand and kicking over the easel. Josh pulled his spray bottle and let her have it full in the face. For an instant she stood in gape-mouthed shock, eyes blinking.

"ARROOOOO!" she howled like a crazed wolf, rubbing her eyes furiously. "Water! Give me water!"

Josh sprayed her again.

A tall, thin teenager handed her a bottle of water, which she opened and poured on her head. Two cops hustled up.

"What happened?" asked the first officer, a diminutive Latina named Sanchez.

"This man assaulted me!" the woman shrieked.

"Is that bacon?" Sanchez said.

Dale held up his iPhone. "Officers, we can show you exactly what happened."

While Sanchez and her partner watched the video, two more cops arrived. They ended up arresting the woman, whose name was Clarion Mankiller-Rakovsky, for assault.

"That man sprayed me with bacon!" she raged. "Aren't you going to arrest him?"

"I'm hungry," Sanchez said as they led her away.

A crowd had gathered but it wasn't the crowd Polly wanted. The children had fled, replaced by curious onlookers, many of them holding their cell phones expectantly.

Polly turned to Josh with a big grin. "Well, that went well!"

"I'm so sorry," Gillian said. "People have no respect."

"Not your fault."

Polly went to Melissa and held her hand.

"I'm so sorry that fucking creep ruined my presentation. Why don't I come out and cook for you?"

"That would be delightful," Melissa said. "And bring your pals, especially this studly gent." She indicated Dale, who put his thumbs beneath his suspenders and stuck out his chest. When the old lady rose, he placed her hands on his forearm, escorting her slowly down the steps.

As Polly picked up her portfolio, Josh saw a man grinning at the edge of the crowd. He wore a black, green and yellow dashiki over tan Dockers and a cowboy hat encircled with silver conchos.

CHAPTER 55

Django

The preternaturally handsome black man in his mid-thirties with big eyes and an infectious grin came up to Josh and stuck out his hand.

"Mr. Pratt, I presume."

Josh shook. "Who you?"

"Django Mandingo Shabazz. Like to buy you a cup of coffee."

Josh turned to his buds. "Stay with Polly. I'll be in touch."

He followed Shabazz up the steps into the Capitol and through the rotunda, past the bust of Robert M. La Follette, the Kenyon Cox murals, beneath Edwin Howland Blashfield's glowing "Resources of Wisconsin," which covered the underside of the dome. They exited opposite, past the statue of Hans Christian Heg, down King Street, past the offices for *Isthmus*, "Madison's alternative weekly," to Ancora Coffee. Josh let Shabazz buy him a bottled orange juice, which they took out to King Street. They sat at a little round table with a Cinzano umbrella.

"What can I do for you, Mr. Shabazz?"

Shabazz smiled like a delighted child. "Mr. Pratt. You do not disappoint. Couple weeks ago, when you took out those sad clowns at FemCon, I said to myself, Django, that is one ballsy Caucasian! Then I did a little reading and oh my goodness! I swear if I were a woman I'd want to have your child."

"Did you know those sad clowns?"

"I did not."

Josh sipped his orange juice.

"There are remarkable parallels between your life and mine. I too came from a broken home. I never knew my father. I fell in with ruffians who led me astray. I served time in New Jersey's excellent Rahway state penitentiary. But with the help of my brothers in Islam, I saw the light, was able to reverse my anti-social tendencies, paid my debt to society and emerged a stronger and better person."

"Where did you read about me?" Josh said, annoyed.

"There was that article in *Madison* magazine by that TV reporter."

"Katy Varner."

"It is out of respect I seek you out, to urge you to urge your client to renounce her blasphemous comic, apologize and swear she will never again insult Islam."

"Or else?"

Shabazz took a pair of Gargoyles from his dashiki pocket and put them on, surveying the foot traffic. "I cannot be responsible for what happens."

"Where'd you get that hat?"

"Took it off a dead cracker."

Django's eyes followed a spectacularly endowed Latina with long black hair.

"Wouldn't you just like to troll her whole body between your legs?"

"What are you doing with those goat fuckers, Django? You're a hip guy. You've been around the block. You've drunk a little booze, snorted some blow, fucked a few women. You don't belong with them."

"Like you, I was lost and confused. Like you, I had to serve hard time before I awoke to the error of my ways. And like you, I sought guidance from a higher power. You chose Jesus. I chose Allah, blessed be his name. My mentor on the path to righteousness was Brother Ishmael Kabalarian."

"Mine was Chaplain Frank Dorgan."

"Islam, Judaism and Christianity honor the same prophets: Abraham, Isaac, Jesus."

Josh smiled. "Look. I'll talk to her. I don't think it's worth pursuing at this point. As far as I know, there are no more cons."

"She would have to renounce the comic and apologize. I'm not a thug, Mr. Pratt. I would prefer my brothers not take precipitous action, but as you can imagine, I'm a minority."

"They treat you like a brother?" Josh said.

"Let's just say they treat me a hell of a lot better than my white brothers have over the years. Or many of my black brothers, for that matter."

"Who we talking about? Does your group have a name?"

"We are a group of concerned citizens."

He doesn't know, Josh thought. *He doesn't know we scoped the farm.*

"Failure to renounce and apologize could lead to precipitous action."

"You said that."

Shabazz leaned forward with his elbows on the table. "America needs to understand Islam. We are the one religion that erases the race problem. Throughout my travels in the Muslim world, I have met, talked to, even eaten with people who in America would have been considered 'white,' but the 'white' attitude had been removed from their minds by the religion of Islam."

"What travels in the Muslim world?"

"That was Malcolm X, my friend. I have trained with my brothers-in-arms fighting for a worldwide caliphate. I have been to Algeria, Morocco and the Sudan."

"You know Arabs created the slave trade."

"'It's taken me all my life to learn what not to play.' You know who said that?"

"No."

"Dizzy Gillespie. What would it take for you to stop helping this harlot?"

"What about one of those Bugatti Veyrons?"

Shabazz's smile said, *Boy won't listen.*

"Name a figure."

Josh asked himself if he would give up on Polly for a million dollars. Before he went to prison, he would have. Not now. Besides, if the Ptarmigan Homeowners' Association kept upping the ante, he'd be at a cool mil in no time.

"Be a shame if you were lost as collateral damage," Shabazz said. "Such would not be meet."

"How 'bout a cool mil?"

Shabazz didn't blink. His big eyes showed white all around. "For that kind of money, we might expect a little help from you."

"Take it to your guys. See what they say."

"Time is short, my friend. I will get back to you within twelve hours."

"Pratt," croaked a familiar face.

Josh looked up at Calloway, who had his one good eye fixed on Shabazz.

"Detective Calloway, Django Mandingo Shabazz."

They shook hands. Josh took out his phone.

"Officer, would you take a picture of me and my friend Django?"

Josh slid over and put an arm over Shabazz's shoulder. Shabazz went stiff but the smile remained while Calloway snapped.

"Detective Calloway is in charge of Madison's Gang Unit."

"Boys," Calloway said, "I gots to gets some coffee." He went into the café.

Shabazz stood.

"How can I get in touch with you?" Josh said.

"You'll hear from us within twelve hours."

Shabazz fast-stepped east. Calloway came out holding a paper bag.

"Now where did Brother Shabazz go?"

"I think we saw him at the MacDonald farm. I think he's with the jihadis."

"I'll run that picture through the database. What did he want?"

"Wants me to stop protecting Polly. Wants her to apologize." Calloway sat down. "Where is your client?"

Josh told him.

"Ms. Clarion Mankiller-Rakovsky is with the Socialist Workers Party and Code Pink. She is in the forefront the free menstrual bleeding movement."

"Whatever that is," Josh said.

CHAPTER 56

Fisking Mandingo

It was five when Josh kicked out at Don's house behind Don's, Dale's and Kleiser's bikes. They were sitting on the veranda with Polly, drinking lemonade and passing a joint. As Josh stepped up to the porch, Polly sprang up.

"Take me for a ride, Josh!"

"Now?"

"Right now!"

Josh went inside, found a glass, filled it with lemonade and returned to the porch. "Okay. Just give me a minute. You boys notice anything peculiar? Were you followed?"

"Hell no," Don said. "We rode through the poles in the Arboretum. Hordes of spandex-clad bicyclists wearing helmets with little dentist mirrors cursed us and gave us the finger, but we weren't followed."

"Polly, do you have any more events this summer?"

She twirled like Julie Andrews in *The Sound of Music*. "I'm free! Freeeeeee! I'm just going to draw comics and listen to music."

"You got a helmet?" Josh said.

"Oh pooh! You don't wear one. No one wears them except those boys down on campus on mopeds."

Josh shrugged. "All right. We'll take it slow."

With Polly's hands wrapped around his taut stomach, Josh headed west on Old Sauk, down to Mineral Point, and when that ran out he freestyled west on zigzagging country roads that dove through cool glens past pungent farms. Josh loved Wisconsin. Because it was a dairy state, all the secondary roads were paved. They were endless and fascinating. The difference between driving a car and riding a bike was that on the bike, you were acutely aware of every smell. Pungent pine, freshly cut hay, pig manure, honeysuckle all combined in the perfume of the road.

As Josh slowly rounded a blind bend, they came upon a fawn and two does picking their way across the road. Josh stopped and shut off the bike, and they sat listening to the ticking of the breeze through leaves, the march of the cicadas, the distant hum of a tractor.

"It's magic," Polly said in his ear.

They traveled back roads until they rode by Taliesin, where Josh turned the bike around. On the way back they passed a yard filled with homemade metal sculptures—fantastic animals and birds cobbled and welded together from cast-off machine parts, car wheels, springs and colanders.

"Stop!" Polly commanded. "I want to take some pictures."

She pulled her camera from her pants and snapped away, stalking metal cranes. An old man came out of the ranch house, sat in a metal chair and fired up his pipe.

"Did you build these?" Polly said.

"Yup. Been doing sculpture ever since I was a kid. Why? You want to buy one?"

"I don't think we could get it on the bike," Josh said.

The old man looked past Josh with a wistful expression. "Useta have an Indian. I always rode until a few years ago, when I developed this darn back problem. Really miss it. I like to sit out here and watch the bikes go by."

"What about a three-wheeler? Like those Can-Ams?"

The old man spit on the ground. "Ain't the same thing."

They said goodbye and headed east. Josh pulled over on a lonely stretch covered by a canopy of old-growth trees.

"Hang on. I have to take a leak."

"Me too," Polly said, going into the woods opposite.

They got back on the bike. "One of the things I like about riding a bike is that I can stop and take a piss whenever I like," Josh said.

"I love you, Josh," Polly said. "Don't turn around. Not that kind of love. I love you because you are a good person, Josh."

"Thanks, Polly. I love you too."

"I want you to be happy, Josh."

"I am."

They rode without speaking, returning to Don's house at just past six. Don had fired up the back grill and was turning bratwursts with long-handled tongs while Mika's "Lollipop" poured from a boom box on the back deck.

Polly went through the house and came out with two beers, handing one to Josh.

Dale toasted Josh. "Don says you really worked that Road King over. What did you do to it?"

Josh took a deep breath. "Engine: 88 with oil cooler. Changed the cams to S&S gear drives with .510 lift. Took out the fuel injection and replaced it with an S&S Super E, Yost Power Tube, S&S manifold and Pingle high-flow petcock. S&S teardrop air cleaner cover with a K&N filter. Screamin' Eagle Hi-Performance ignition unit with a 6200-rpm rev limiter. Accell Super Coil, FireWire plug wires and spiral wound metal core wires. Accell platinum-tip plugs. Five-speed tranny with Barnett Kevlar clutch, self-adjusting hydraulic chain tensioner. Screamin' Eagle dualies. Progressive springs in front with higher viscosity, Progressives in back. Changed the rear swing-arm bushings to STA-BO nylon high density. SBS semi-metallic disc brake pads, and the brake lines are stainless steel braids. Went to tubeless wheels."

Don held out his hand.

Dale handed him a twenty.

Josh's phone chimed. His original phone, not the burner.

"Django Mandingo Shabazz," Calloway said, "a.k.a. Cedric Jones is on two terrorist watch lists because of trips to Yemen and the Sudan. Mr. Jones has been arrested twenty-four times, beginning at age thirteen for car theft, followed by assault, armed robbery, rape, drugs, you name it. Born in Newark, 1983, served four years for armed robbery, released in 2009. He was the Rahway middleweight champ for two years."

"He had a come-to-Allah moment?"

"Yesss," Calloway drawled. "Joined the Fruit of Islam. Arrested in 2012 for armed robbery, but the case was dismissed due to tainted evidence. Had a Fruit lawyer, Achmed X."

"Maybe you want to check a list of his cellmates and known associates against that bunch up in Jackson County, maybe show it to the feds."

"I'll do that. How's your client?"

"She's fine. We're at her uncle's house. Nobody knows we're here."

"I could ask the Middleton PD to keep an eye out."

"That would be fine, Heinz. Could you send me Jones's file?"

"Sure."

Josh rejoined the party. They ate brats and shouted about sports. Chicago-born Dale was a Bears fan.

"If you're born in Wisconsin," Don said, "you must support the Green Bay Packers. That's the law. Those born elsewhere are of course encouraged to support the Packers. Nobody likes the Bears. Their own mothers don't like them. Jay Cutler drops to the ground at the coin toss, just thinking of the rush."

"The drunk and sloppy cheeseheads of Green Bay are America's laughing stock," Dale countered. "Aaron Rogers is only semi-literate. I predict he will lead the league in interceptions this year."

Dale looked at Kleiser. "Don't you agree?"

Kleiser held up his hands. "I'm from Colorado, boys. I'm a Broncos guy."

Don and Dale snorted in disgust.

After dinner, Polly took Josh aside. "I've made up my mind. I want you to teach me to ride a motorcycle."

Josh swallowed. "Okay."

"I will ride my bicycle over to your house tomorrow morning so you can teach me. Is that okay?"

"Sure, what the hell!"

Polly threw her arms around his neck and kissed him. "Great! Thanks."

"What's she gonna ride?" Dale said.

Josh thought about the Hawk. "I got a 650 Super Hawk."

"Perfect," Dale said.

CHAPTER 57

Orange Glow

It was dusk when Josh and Kleiser pulled into his driveway to a fusillade of barks from inside. Josh gave Fig a treat and went to bed. In the morning he and Fig did five, then he showered and brewed a pot of coffee.

Kleiser came out of his room in X-Men boxer shorts, rubbing his eyes. An hour later he left for Dovetail and Josh went into the garage. He checked the Hawk's oil, filled the tires to thirty-five, rode it up and down Ptarmigan, put it up on its centerstand and oiled the chain. He looked up at the sign of a bicycle bell to see Polly pulling into his driveway in shorts, T-shirt, backpack, sunglasses and sunhat.

She wheeled her Trek ten-speed into the garage. "Oh wow! Is that the bike?"

"This was Fig's bike. You'd better not drop it."

"I won't!" Deep within her backpack her cell phone chimed. She dug around, pulled it out and went through the kitchen door into the house to talk. Five minutes later she returned with a somber expression.

"Fuck. I just lost a gig I thought I had, doing promo art for a chain of flower stores."

"Did they give a reason?"

"They said they decided to go in a different direction. Fuckers."

"You getting any comic gigs?"

"No."

"Okay," Josh said, pointing at the bike. "Take it off its centerstand and wheel it out onto the front lawn."

"The lawn?"

"The lawn."

Polly got on the bike, planted the balls of her feet on the concrete and rocked the bike forward. It took her two tries to get it off the centerstand, but she had no difficulty wheeling it around from a seated position. She rolled it into the middle of Josh's front lawn.

"Now what?"

"Get off and lay it gently in the grass."

Polly did as she was told, gently laying the silver bike on its side. "Now what?"

"Pick it up."

Smiling quizzically, Polly righted the bike and got back on. "Now what?"

"Congratulations! Roll it back into the garage and put it back on the centerstand."

Polly rolled it onto the concrete and got off. "How do I do that?"

Josh pointed to the pedal protruding from beneath the chassis. "You stand directly on that with your full weight and pull up on the handle." He moved around to the other side.

It took her three tries but she did it.

"Okay. Let's grab some drinks and go out on the deck."

"I thought we were going to ride!"

"Not yet, Grasshopper."

Josh got two cans of ginger ale from the refrigerator and went out back, followed by Polly and Fig. They sat in the Adirondacks and popped the tops. Josh explained how the gears and brakes worked, the importance of smoothness, how to be seen and how to avoid collisions.

"Do I have to wear a helmet?"

"Yes. I have one that will fit."

"Why do I have to wear a helmet? You don't."

"Cuz it's my bike, that's why. Now you're going to follow me down the road to a cul-de-sac and we'll practice going through the gears there. You understand about the gears?"

"Of course! I ride a ten-speed."

Josh went into the house and found a pink open-face helmet Fig had worn. Polly put it on and followed Josh as he wheeled his Road King down to the street, reached in his tank bag and shut the garage door.

"Start your engines!" he said.

The bikes roared to life.

"Slow and smooth!" Josh said, snicking into gear. He took off heading west on Ptarmigan, Polly about twenty feet behind. It was late morning and there was no other traffic. They traveled a quarter mile to White Oak Court, where Phil Bass lived, and turned left. The court was an exclusive enclave of million-dollar houses surrounded by shade trees. Polly followed Josh around the circle at the end, back to Ptarmigan, and they returned to Josh's house.

Polly took her helmet off and shook out her red hair. "Whooo! I love it! What's next?"

"Next you have to take a driver's safety course. They offer them at MATC, and after that you can apply for your motorcycle license."

"I need a special motorcycle license?"

"Do you think they let any fool ride a bike? Well they do, but only with a license."

"I don't suppose I can ride the Hawk home," she said.

"HAH!" Josh barked. "But if you're too lazy to pedal, I can drive you home and put the bike in the trunk."

Polly swung off the bike. "That would be swell, Josh!"

They stopped at the Capital Brewery, got brats and lagers and sat out back at a picnic table.

Polly slugged her beer and set it down with a thump. "I have to figure out my next career move. I think I screwed the pooch with the big comics companies. They won't hire me because they're afraid of getting bombed or beheaded. I've been thinking of going to chef's school."

"You can't be serious," Josh said.

"What? Why not? Why shouldn't I have my own kitchen? Odessa does."

"Look. I'm no expert, but you've obviously got talent. A lot of talent. You draw better than half those jokers who are drawing *X-Men* or *Superman* or whatever. It's what you want to do. You're not going to let a bunch of camel jockeys scare you off, are you?"

Polly regarded him with hero worship. "You're right, dammit! And when you're right, you're right!"

Josh took the front wheel off Polly's bike and stored the whole thing in the trunk of his Chrysler. It was two o'clock when he dropped her off at uncle Don's house in Middleton. When he got home he worked with Fig in the backyard, using a hollow ball filled with a sliver of C4. Kleiser arrived at six with a Godfather's pizza the size of a tractor wheel, which they ate on the back deck. Fig got the last piece. Although it was Sunday, Kleiser had just come back from Dovetail.

Josh was used to living alone, and Kleiser was beginning to get on his nerves. Just having another person there interrupting his train of thought with questions and comments was irritating, and Kleiser was not an annoying personality. If Kleiser accepted the Dovetail position, Josh would suggest he find his own place.

After dinner, Kleiser talked Josh into watching *Dancing With the Stars*. During a commercial break, a woman who looked like Honey Boo Boo's mother said, "I got hit by a car and the insurance company only wanted to give me $2,000. So I went to Steve Fleiss and he got me $350,000!"

Fleiss appeared with a determined expression. He looked like the missing link between

Gary Shandling and Russ Feingold. "Of course I can't guarantee you $350,000, but if you've been in an auto accident and the insurance companies are refusing to pay up, come see me, Steve Fleiss, The Hammer!"

Kleiser turned to Josh. "Isn't that your guy?"

"That's my guy."

They went to bed. Josh was dreaming that he was driving a Jaguar when Fig's barking jarred him awake. He looked around. Fig was at the front door. Between barks he heard a tap on the door. Putting on a pair of jeans, he padded through the living room and opened the door. Polly stood there with her bike.

"I'm so sorry to bother you! I left my phone here and I need it really early. I wasn't going to wake you up, but the front door is locked."

"What time is it?" Josh said.

Polly looked at her watch. "It's twelve thirty. I know. I'm bad."

A dull whump rolled over them from the northeast. Josh stepped outside into the warm night air. "What was that?"

They both looked toward Middleton as an orange glow insinuated itself into the sky, reflecting off the bottom of a cloud.

CHAPTER 58

Inferno

Josh grabbed a shirt and his keys. "Leave your bike," he said. He and Polly got in his car and drove north. Within minutes they heard the wail of sirens through open windows. As they approached Don's house, the glow in the sky became pervasive, along with the whoop and wail of emergency vehicles. Elmwood Avenue was blocked by police and ambulances. Don's house was a roaring inferno casting sickly flickering yellow on the undersides of branches. A handful of people stood opposite and down the block in bathrobes and pants, staring in disbelief. Josh saw a young family, baby in stroller, another in mother's arms, hastily exit their bungalow and walk toward the police.

Cops began evacuating people. Josh parked as near as he could and walked two blocks with an anxious Polly.

A Middleton cop fronted them. "No one beyond this point."

"What happened?" Josh said.

"We don't know. Some kind of explosion."

"Officer, I'm Josh Pratt and this is Polly Furst. That's Polly's uncle Don's house. She's very upset. She's in a state of shock."

"I was living there," Polly said.

"Know anybody who would do this?" the cop said.

"I think they were trying to kill me," Polly said blankly. "I do a comic called *Muhammad*."

"Oh," the cop said with a hint of disgust. He turned away and spoke into his shoulder mic.

"Yes, we're aware of your recent activities. Who do you think might have done this?"

"Muslims," Polly said. "I've been getting death threats since I announced the book, and there have been several attacks. That's why I hired Josh as a bodyguard."

"So you think the house was targeted because they thought you were in it."

"That's my guess," Josh said. "Are there any survivors?"

"We won't know until we can get in there. Doubtful. I mean, look at it. Right now that fire is out of control. We're evacuating the whole block and everyone around it."

A cop with a walrus mustache came up. "I'm Chief Bill Roberts. You're Polly Furst?"

"Yes."

"Let's go sit in my office."

They followed Roberts to his Dodge and sat in the back seat with the doors open while the chief sat in front. Chrysler had designed the Dodge to intimidate, knowing it would appeal to police. It was the automotive equivalent of Brock Lesnar. Roberts set a small recorder on the center console next to an open laptop.

"Who knew you were there?"

"Don, Josh and Don's friend Dale. That's all."

I wrote the address on my notepad, Josh thought. *The notepad in my vest. The vest in my hotel room.* He felt sick.

"Do you have any specific suspects in mind?"

"Sir," Josh said, "we've been looking into a farm in Jackson County. Old MacDonald's. They sell organic produce. We believe it's being used as a terrorist training camp."

"Have you alerted Jackson County?"

"We've told them, the Madison police, the FBI and the National Security Agency."

"And?"

"Nobody has the manpower to investigate, and they have no grounds to investigate. We shot some footage with a drone that shows a Russian RPG-7 and at least seven heavily armed jihadis. That's a shoulder-mounted anti-tank weapon. We forwarded it to those agencies."

"Seems to me more than enough to get a warrant."

"Sir, the footage is inadmissible and can't be used for a warrant because we shot it on private property without their permission."

"Seems to me the sheriff could find a way in there. Do you know who the sheriff is?"

"Francis LaBute."

Roberts made a note. A patrol officer approached.

"Chief, we just talked to one of the neighbors. She was out walking her dog about an hour ago and noticed a Ford van parked around the corner on Middleton Street."

"Did she get a license number?"

"No."

"Sir," Josh said, "I've seen a Ford van entering the MacDonald Farm. It's white with rust spots. I have the license plate."

He dug out his phone and found the still he'd saved from the surveillance footage. Roberts copied it down.

"Give me your email and I'll forward the videos."

Roberts and Josh exchanged cards, and Josh dialed up the videos and sent them. A half hour later the cops cut them loose and they returned to Josh's house, passing more screaming emergency response vehicles and a WMAD news van. Josh wondered if Katy was in it.

"You can sleep in the basement. There's a fold-out bed."

Polly had not stopped weeping since they left Middleton. The ruckus roused Kleiser, who came out wearing jeans and a T-shirt.

"What's going on?"

Josh told him.

"Jesus! I'm so sorry, Polly!"

"Can you print out those aerial views of MacDonald's? Can you make a map?"

"I can do that. What do you want them for?"

"For the cops if they ever get off their asses and go in there. In the meantime, we're going to have to clear out of here. These guys know where I live, and when they find out they missed, they're going to come here."

"You're shitting me," Kleiser said.

"I'd tell the cops but we can't take a chance. We're going to have to find some other place for the next couple days."

"Where?" Polly said.

"I have an idea. I'll make a few phone calls in the morning."

"All my artwork is gone," Polly said.

Josh put an arm around her. "You'll make more."

He led the way into the basement, put fresh linens on the sofa. "I have to tell you something."

"What?" Polly said, wiping her nose with her sleeve.

"I think Cat Lowenstein got Don's address from my notepad the night she drugged me."

"Who's Cat Lowenstein?" Polly snuffled.

"Black Widow."

"It's not your fault! You didn't kill him!"

Josh went to bed knowing he wouldn't sleep. He'd been careless. And now Don was dead. He envied Fig, who was snoring softly and dreaming she was chasing squirrels. Josh drifted off around three and fell into a shallow, restless sleep peopled with crazed jihadis chasing him across a field. In front of him an angry bull pawed the ground, lowered its head, snorted and charged.

The two opposing forces inexorably closed in, with Josh between them. He woke as they were about to clash. Fig lay on her back with her legs in the air, snoozing softly. Josh blinked, looked at his watch. It was eight thirty.

Josh swung out of bed. "Come on, you lazy mutt. Let's go."

Fig leaped to the floor wagging her tail. They went for a run. By the time Josh returned, showered and made coffee, it was almost ten. Josh knew of a farm in Richland County, the scene of a former commune called the Collective that had been home to a federal judge, a professor and a killer. In fact, they were all killers.

CHAPTER 59

Feds

The farm belonged to Mrs. McIntyre, a widow, who rented the acreage to a neighbor. The house and barn had long stood dormant, and the barn was falling apart because of Josh's fight with the Jesuit. The Jesuit had a brother who was a member of the bottom-feeding Insane Assholes MC, whose colors showed a middle finger rolling on two wheels. Josh had rousted the Jesuit's brother for snorting coke off the table at a bar where Josh bounced. The brother and his fellow Assholes had arrived on Josh's property coked to the gills, drunk as skunks, heavily armed and screaming for payback, and were duly mowed down by the cops. The Jesuit blamed Josh and vowed revenge.

The Jesuit was a retired CIA spook and wet-work specialist. Josh killed him with a pitchfork, but not before the Jesuit inflicted grievous harm on Fig, the real Fig. Fig's ashes rested on the mantel in her father's house. Her motorcycle was in Josh's garage. Her scent and touch were with him always, the standard by which every future woman was doomed to fall short.

Josh went into his office, found his notebook from that period and looked up Mrs. McIntyre's phone number. She answered on the second ring.

"Mrs. McIntyre, this is Josh Pratt. You remember I was out there last year?"

"I remember."

"Ma'am, are you aware of the recent troubles in Madison, with jihadis attacking my client Polly Furst?"

"Yes. I think it's just terrible! Who let them into the country? John Kennedy would never have let them into the country."

"Yes, ma'am. I have a favor to ask."

"Mr. Pratt, you are a good and godly man. Whatever you'd like, I would be happy to help you."

A weight lifted off Josh's chest. He hadn't realized how anxious he'd been about the phone call. Asking brother bikers for help was one thing. Asking a seventy-eight-year-old widow with whom he had a tenuous relationship was another. He'd killed a man in her barn.

"Ma'am, I'd like to use the empty farmhouse next door. Just for a couple days."

"Well of course, Josh, as long as you need. There's no electricity but I believe the water is on. Am I in any danger?"

"No, ma'am. Not unless they nuke us from orbit."

"Nuke you from orbit? I don't understand."

"It's a joke, ma'am. I'll loan you my *Aliens* DVD. Do I need a key?"

"I will go over this afternoon and leave a key for you under the doormat."

"Thank you. I'll let you know when we're coming."

Josh went back to the kitchen and saw Polly in one of his bathrobes sitting on the deck sipping coffee, with Fig's head in her lap. Josh got a cup and joined her.

"Okay. We're moving to a farm this afternoon. Is there anything you need?"

"Everything! I have no clothes! At least my original art is still back at the Alhambra. Can we stop back there so I can get some stuff?"

"Sure. I'll drive. Let me know when you're ready."

"I need to take a shower and I need to borrow some clothes. Some T-shirts or something."

"I have some things that belonged to Fig. They should fit."

Polly stroked the dog's head. "What about this Fig?"

"I'll leave her with the neighbors. It's not a problem. In fact, let me do that now."

Josh rose and whistled, and Fig followed him into the house. He caught Louise Lowry as she was backing her Murano down the long blacktop. She stopped and opened her window.

"What's up?"

"Louise, I have to go out of town for a few days. Could you watch Fig?"

"Of course. The gate is unlocked; just put her in with George and Gracie."

"Thanks! I'll bring some dog food over."

"No need. We'll just open up four cans of Fancy Feast for her."

Josh whistled and Fig followed him to the gate to their fenced-in backyard. He opened the gate and Fig bounded in and was immediately faux-attacked by George and Gracie, the Lowrys' two schnauzers. Polly was in the front yard as Josh crossed the street. "I just spoke to the cops. They found one body, which they think is Don's. Dale called. He wants to kill every motherfucker involved. My car is okay. I parked it down the street. I want to go get it. Can you give me a ride?"

"Sure. What's Dale's phone number?"

She told him.

Josh's phone buzzed. It was Stoeckle.

"I'll be in Madison at one o'clock. I'd like to meet with you then."

"What about?"

"We've identified several of the people in your video. It's not something I feel comfortable telling over the phone. Can you meet me at 8215 Greenway Boulevard, in Middleton?"

"What time?"

"One thirty?"

"Okay."

Josh looked at his watch. It was almost twelve. He and Polly drove to the Alhambra and went up to her apartment. The police were gone. Polly used her key to let herself in. Most of her stuff had been packed into cardboard boxes, as the manager was renovating the unit. It smelled of fresh paint. Josh and Polly made three trips, taking down boxes. They drove to Middleton where Don's house had burned to the ground and was surrounded by yellow police tape. Polly's Beetle was grimy with soot.

Josh waited until she'd unlocked it, started the engine and pulled out before he left. It was just past one thirty when he pulled into the FBI's parking lot outside its regional office, housed in a faux-Bauhaus white-and-glass tower.

The office was on the second floor and looked west toward the Town and Country Golf Course. The agent at the front desk was an earnest young man with sideburns.

"Sir, please leave any personal electronic devices with me. You can retrieve them when you leave."

Josh handed over his cell phone and followed the agent's directions down the hall to a conference room. Looking rumpled, Stoeckle rose from behind the conference table and shook Josh's hand. He hadn't shaved in several days.

Josh sat opposite in an Eames chair as Stoeckle tossed a legal folder before him. Josh picked it up. Inside were black-and-white mug shots of five sallow, surly men, three with beards. They were: Friar—Abu el Salaam, Pakistan; Fez—Hasaan Al Rahman, Saudi Arabia; Sandals—Khalid Al Wahaab, Saudi Arabia; and Jihadis 1 and 2—the brothers Amal and Emil ibn Saud, Saudi Arabia.

"Don't forget our friend Django Mandingo Shabazz, a.k.a. Cedric Jones."

"We're looking for him."

"Look for him at the farm."

Stoeckle wiped his forehead with a handkerchief. It wasn't that warm in the room. "We don't have the resources. Haven't you heard? It's jihadist week. There are terror alerts from sea to shining sea. Homeland Security is asking all malls to beef up security. The Giants and Bills called off a pre-season game in the Meadowlands. They're worried about a *Black Sunday* scenario."

"So what do you want me to do?" Josh said.

Stoeckle folded his hands and looked across the desk. "Since you brought us this data, I thought you should know who they are."

Josh picked up the folder. As he walked out, the agent handed him his cell phone. Josh drove home. Kleiser's car was there but no Beetle. Josh went into the house.

"Where's Polly?"

"I don't know. I thought she was with you."

Josh felt a yawning void in his gut. He pulled out his cell phone and saw that the agent had turned it off. It seemed to take forever to power up and when it did, there was one missed call: Polly.

"Josh, Melissa just called. I have to go out and see her. She needs me. I won't be more than an hour so don't worry! No one even knows where she lives."

Josh ran to the basement, unlocked the gun safe and grabbed the .45. A puzzled Kleiser waited in the kitchen.

"What?"

"Grab your piece and come with me."

CHAPTER 60

"Be happy, Josh."

Josh headed west on 14, Valentine fuzzbuster glowing on the dash. Just east of Cross Plains it went off, and Josh quickly slowed from eighty to sixty. Too late. The flashing lights appeared in his rearview, but just as he was about to pull over, a car came around the curve heading east at over a hundred miles per hour. The county Mountie waved Josh off, did a Y-turn in the middle of the highway and went after the other guy.

Josh slipped back into gear and took off. Kleiser clung to the grab handle with both hands. They turned north off 14 and ran into a construction site with a woman in a yellow hard hat holding a stop sign, while behind her a steamroller rolled blacktop. Josh wished he had an AK-47 to blow them out of the way. After what seemed like an eternity, the woman rotated her sign revealing SLOW. They crept forward past men in hard hats and coveralls, followed by a couple of vehicles.

Once free of the construction zone, Josh accelerated to ninety, slowing at the last moment for the turnoff. As he peeled into the cul-de-sac, the rear end swung loose. Josh over-corrected and the big car momentarily swung from skid to skid until all four tires bit. He screeched to a stop in Melissa's driveway, grabbed his gun off the floor and ran toward the house, Kleiser right behind him.

The front door was open. Josh tore the screen door off as he ran into the living room and stopped dead, staring with incomprehension.

Polly lay on her back, legs splayed, hands clutching the hilt of a butcher's knife buried in her chest. Her eyes twitched. Josh sank beside her, wanting to take her head in his hands but afraid to touch her. This was on his head. How could he be so stupid?

You killed another one, you dumb son of a bitch!

Kleiser took one look and pulled out his phone.

"Polly," Josh croaked. "Polly, can you hear me?"

She focused on Josh, green eyes swimming in pain. "Josh...I was dumb...I shouldn't have come..."

"Hush. An ambulance is on the way. You're going to be all right."

She grinned. There was pink foam on her lips. "I fucked up."

"Who did this to you, Polly?"

"Black dude in a cowboy hat."

A hand reached into Josh's gut and squeezed. His kidneys ached from the pressure. Out of the corner of his eye he was aware of Kleiser going through the rest of the house.

Josh stared at the knife. He knew if he withdrew it he would probably only hasten her death from internal bleeding. He felt as helpless and useless as a child.

Kleiser re-entered the living room clutching his gun, shaking his head. "Don't go in there. She's dead."

"Did you call 911?"

"They're on their way."

Josh couldn't tear his eyes from Polly even as her gaze slipped to the ceiling. She let go of the knife and reached up with a bloody hand. Josh took it.

"Listen, Josh..." she said in a dry whisper.

Josh leaned over her ear. "Yes?"

"Be happy, Josh. I want you to be happy."

She croaked deep in her throat and was gone. Josh put his ear on her lips. He pinched her nose, put his thumb on her tongue and breathed into her. Kleiser kneeled opposite and watched for a minute.

"Forget it, Josh. She's gone."

They knelt opposite each other over Polly surrounded by finished and half-finished paintings. Josh shut his eyes and prayed.

"They cut off her head," Kleiser said. "In the bedroom."

Sirens filled the air. Kleiser must have got through to a Cross Plains first responder. The sirens grew louder until they were right outside the door and then they stopped. A Smokey-hatted sheriff's deputy appeared in the doorway gripping his pistol in both hands. He entered the room in a stance and looked around. He pointed at Kleiser with his gun.

"Set the pistol down and slide it over to me."

Kleiser did as the deputy said.

"Now both of you get down on your bellies and clasp your hands behind your heads."

Kleiser and Josh both did so.

"Officer, I'm the one who phoned this in," Kleiser said.

"I would appreciate you gentlemen just staying there for a minute while we get this straightened out. Now which one of you is Pratt?"

"I am," Josh said, his cheek against the Victorian rug.

"Please pull out ID, gentlemen, very slowly."

Two paramedics entered and went to Polly. "You boys're gonna have to move," one said.

"Gentlemen, you may sit up and lean back against the wall." Kleiser and Josh followed instructions and sat with their backs against one wall. Josh had to push an easel out of the way to make room. He looked up. It was a painting of a sailing ship battling colossal waves off a rugged coast. A tiny color photo was pinned to one corner.

Two Cross Plains cops entered. The deputy finally holstered his weapon and picked up the wallets, pulling out the IDs.

"What happened?" he said.

Kleiser looked at Josh.

"You know about Miss Furst's troubles?"

The deputy nodded. "Yes. What's she doing here?"

Josh explained about Polly's relationship with Melissa.

"Everybody knew and loved Melissa," the deputy said. "Did she tell you anything before she died?"

"She said it was a black dude in a cowboy hat."

"Any idea who he might be?" the deputy asked as police quickly searched the house and poured into the backyard.

"The black guy may have been Cedric Jones, a.k.a. Django Mandingo Shabazz...I think they came from the MacDonald farm in Jackson County."

"Wait, wait, wait," the deputy said, pulling out a spiral pad and a pen. Josh spelled the name as two more EMTs entered with a collapsible stretcher and went down the hall toward the bedroom.

"Holy shit," one said from the room.

The sheriff arrived, escorted Josh and Kleiser outside. Sheriff Clarke took Kleiser to his car while Deputy Lutz, the first responder, questioned Josh on the porch. Josh told him everything from his and Polly's first meeting. The deputy told Josh he was free to go and that the police would be in touch.

Josh went to his car as a female deputy backed out and turned off her flashlight. She turned toward him with a smile.

"Just checking."

Josh sat in his car and stared through the windshield. He lowered his head and put his hands together.

Lord, where do I start?

No one had asked him about the pistol.

CHAPTER 61

Clean Them Out

Josh was still sitting there staring into space when the sheriff came over. "You're free to go."

"What about Kleiser?" Josh said.

"There's a federal warrant out on him."

But I need him.

"All right. Thank you sir."

As soon as the sheriff turned away, Josh called Stoeckle, who answered on the second ring.

"I heard," he said. "I'm on my way."

"How long?" Josh said.

"At least three hours. We're just pulling onto the interstate now."

"Call me when you get to town. I'll be at my place."

It was five thirty by the time Josh arrived home. After her effusive greeting, Fig shoved her muzzle into Josh's hand and whined. Dogs knew things. Josh fed Fig and paced in the living room with the television on. There was nothing about the shooting on the six o'clock news. Josh looked at Melissa's painting hanging over the fireplace. He'd taken Biker Girl into the garage to join the tin Indian and Elvis signs on the wall.

Josh wished he could dive into that landscape, where he would find Fig Newton, Polly and Melissa. He went into his office, where he ghoulishly followed world news. Things were going to hell all over. Middle Eastern refugees flooding European countries by the tens of thousands, driven out by the fighting. Two cops gunned down in the past twenty-four hours.

He checked the status of the jihadis he'd fingered. There were no updates. He phoned Calloway.

"I can't talk now," the detective said. "I'm driving."

"Heinz, just before Polly died, she said it was a black dude in a cowboy hat."

"Yeah. I'll call you back."

Josh looked down at Fig's worried eyes, her snout on his leg. He got up, went to the basement and opened the safe. A half hour later he drove to West Towne and purchased a six-pack of bacon-flavored soda. He went into his office, pulled out Stoeckle's files and stared at the photographs until he had memorized them.

He heard the front door open and close. It was nine o'clock. Josh went into the living room, where Kleiser was holding a paper bag, which he set on the table with a thump.

"I told them both those guns were mine."

"And they gave them back to you?"

"Neither one was fired. They had no reason to keep them."

"Are they going into the farm?" Josh said.

Kleiser shrugged. "I have no idea."

Josh phoned Stoeckle.

"Stoeckle," the agent answered.

"Are you gonna raid that farm?"

"That's not my decision. I've brought it to my superiors' attention. That's all I can do."

Josh hung up. He phoned Zlatko.

"Alhazred," the cartoonist answered.

Josh went out on the back porch and spoke to him. When he was finished, he phoned Don's friend, Dale. Finally he phoned Bricklin.

"What's going on?" Kleiser said when Josh came back in.

"We're gonna clean out that viper's nest. Are you in?"

Kleiser looked worried. "What do you mean?"

"I mean the fucking feds are going to sit around with their thumbs up their asses until we're all blown to hell and gone. Now they've murdered my client. How am I going to get any work if I let this go?"

"What do you mean, 'clean out'?"

Josh headed for the basement. "I mean we're going to kill them. You can't have a wasp's nest hanging on your porch."

Kleiser followed him into the basement, where Josh pulled things from the gun safe. "Are you serious?"

Josh looked at him. "When's the last time I made a joke?"

"What the fuck is that?" Kleiser said, pointing.

Josh hefted the weapon. "Armsel Striker. It's South African."

"Where the fuck did you get something like that?"

"Why?" Josh said. "You want one?"

"Can I hold it?"

Josh passed the heavy fully automatic shotgun to Kleiser, who brought it to his shoulder, squinted across the sights and went, "PCHEW PCHEW PCHEW!"

"I'm going to try and grab some kip. Dale, Dzelko and Bricklin will be here tomorrow at six. We're going in Tuesday morning. The cops have until then to get their shit together."

"I'm in," Kleiser said. "I've been wanting to do something like this since Patty died."

"Randall, you don't have to go. This is a volunteer mission. Nobody's going to hold it against you if you hang back. But we could use some tech support. Could you take their computers offline?"

"Yeah," Kleiser said. "I'll give 'em my Miley virus. I haven't tested it yet, so this should be a good opportunity. But I want in. I've been holding in a lot of rage, y'know?"

"Yeah," Josh said.

They bopped fists.

Kleiser went to his car and returned moments later carrying a fat black folder. He grabbed his laptop and sat in the living room. Josh took a shower. When he came out, Kleiser was folding up his laptop.

"It's done."

"Did it work?"

Kleiser grinned. "They should be panicking just about now."

"Good," Josh said.

He knelt next to his bed and clasped his hands.

Forgive me.

Fig whined and thrust her snout at him.

He lay down with Fig beside him. His phone rang. He picked it up, not recognizing the number. "Hello?" he said. He thought he heard someone breathing, and then it went silent.

He didn't think he would sleep after that, but sleep snuck up on him and when he woke, the sun was shining through the window and Fig was licking his face. He glanced at the bedside clock and saw that it was almost nine. Josh fed Fig, made a pot of coffee, lifted the S&S motor off the living room table and set it in the fireplace, and compiled his kit for the coming raid. In addition to the .45 and the Striker, he put out a pair of Armasight Vega night vision goggles.

He searched every news network looking for reports on Polly's murder. Nothing. There was nothing on the noon news either. His calls to Stoeckle and Phillips went unanswered. Only Calloway returned his call.

"There was nothing at that house pointing to this farm in Jackson County. We're waiting on the feds."

"She practically named Django!"

"She said it was a black man in a cowboy hat. Can you imagine the shitstorm if we tried to use that as a basis to raid that farm? On what evidence? Sit tight, my man. There's nothing you can do."

Josh thanked him and hung up.

That's what you think.

276

CHAPTER 62

The Cat Came Back

Josh went into the garage, picking up shit and wheeling the bikes over to one side to make room for Zlatko's car. He didn't want anyone running the plates. He drove to Woodman's and got three pounds of ground beef, black beans, Liquid Smoke, onions and canned stewed tomatoes. At home he whipped up a mess of chili.

The Mad Arab arrived at three in the afternoon dressed for hunting in camo cargo trou, top and vest. Josh waved him into the garage and shut the door behind him.

They went into the house. Zlatko was a live wire. He went down on the floor and wrestled with Fig, then bounced up. He was happier than a pig in shit.

"What's the plan, man?" he said, rubbing his hands together.

"Let's wait until everyone is here."

Dale arrived in a Ford F-150 Super Duty carrying a backpack that clanked when he set it down. Bricklin pulled up on her Indian and hoisted a leather satchel from her saddlebag. Josh, Bricklin, Dale, Zlatko and Kleiser sat around the living room table, on which Josh had placed a printed-out aerial view of the farm.

"I have no right to ask any of you to participate. What we're about to do is a felony, and there will very likely be serious repercussions. Some of us may not survive. With me it's personal. This is something I have to do."

"It's personal with all of us," Dale said.

Bricklin reached into her satchel and pulled out an Uzi.

"Where the fuck did you get that?" Zlatko said.

Bricklin smiled. "I have friends. I also got this." She pulled a revolver with an unusually long cylinder. "Taurus Judge. Holds five .410 shells."

"Here come de *judge*!" Zlatko chanted. "Huh! Good God!"

Josh passed out pages with black-and-white mug shots of every known jihadist at the farm. "I'm going in first. I'll signal you via cell. I need to know if MacDonald is still alive and if there are any innocent people at the farm."

"I'll go with you," Zlatko said.

"No. If you don't hear from me by six, you go in. I checked the weather, and sunrise is at ten past six. It's supposed to rain, which is good for us. They don't have motion detectors, because there are so many of them moving all over. There might be a couple around the house but I doubt it. I think they think they're pretty secure. They've been running ops out of this farm for at least three months, maybe a lot longer, and they're pretty confident law enforcement doesn't give a shit."

"We know they don't have dogs," Zlatko said.

The spark of rage in Josh's soul flared anew but he kept a lid on it, unconsciously reaching to stroke Fig. "Be certain of your targets. We don't want to shoot each other."

"What if they surrender?" Bricklin said.

"I'll bring some wire harnesses so we can tie them down. I don't expect anyone to surrender. These are jihadis. Except for this guy."

Josh circulated a photo of Cedric Jones. "Cedric Jones, a.k.a. Django Mandingo Shabazz. I'd like to take him alive."

"Django Mandingo Shabazz," Zlatko said with lip-smacking exactitude.

"There's chili and beer in the kitchen. Help yourselves. Don't make a mess."

Polly's and Melissa's murders led the WMAD evening report—Katy Varner stating, "Police are treating the double homicide as a home invasion. They declined to offer descriptions of the perpetrators but say they are working on several promising leads. Cross Plains Mayor Janet Sullivan is pleading for calm."

Cut to the mayor, a middle-aged woman with a tight cap of white curls, expressing shock.

Josh interrupted the news. "I put a futon in the basement and one in the office. Brick, you can take the office. Let's get some sleep, because we're outta here at four thirty in the morning."

"Can I get the dog?" Bricklin said.

"If you can persuade her to join you."

Bricklin bent forward. "Come here, sweetie."

Fig approached for rubbing and scratching.

Dale took the basement. Zlatko took the sofa. Bricklin coaxed Fig into the office but as soon as Josh turned in, Fig whined to get out, joining him on his bed. Josh lay awake all night glancing at the clock from time to time, rising at four to make coffee. The smell of coffee brought out Zlatko and Kleiser, soon joined by the others. Nobody spoke as they gathered their wits. Outside, the wind howled and the first splatters of rain hit the roof and windows.

"Great!" Josh said. "Everybody check your gear. I got extra rain ponchos."

Dale raised his hand. "I'll take one."

"Good," Kleiser said. "No fucking mosquitoes."

Bricklin and Zlatko followed suit. Josh handed out plastic packets marked VICTORY MOTORCYCLES as the room filled with metallic clicks and the smell of gun oil. They headed northwest in silence, rain pounding the roof, windshield wipers sweeping, the hum of the tires penetrating the cab.

Zlatko hummed "The Flight of the Valkyries." Within seconds everyone was humming. It was black as pitch when Dale pulled off into a field entrance a quarter mile from the state forest parking lot. Josh, Dale and Bricklin put on their night binocs and checked them out. Josh led them down the path toward the creek, where they huddled beneath the boughs of an umbrella oak.

Josh handed the Streetsweeper to Zlatko. "You know how to use this?"

Zlatko took the heavy gun, grinning wolfishly. "Spent a week in Tel Aviv training with the Israeli Army on these things."

Josh looked at his watch. "Give me a half hour. If you don't hear from me by five thirty go on in. Be sure of your targets. I'll phone when I want you to move. Don't answer. Just move."

"Godspeed, brother," Dale said.

"A-fuckin'-men," Zlatko said.

Wearing a black rain slicker, Josh sliced through the dripping gorse toward the creek, carefully picking his way across on a few boulders. He paused at the edge of the tree line and scanned the horizon through eerie green light for long seconds. He saw no sentries. They'd grown complacent, confident in Western sloth and credulity, protected by their rights.

Josh's first order of business was to ascertain if Old MacDonald was still alive, and if there were any innocents in the house. Applying tenets he'd learned the previous year from an executive security class, he slunk through the shadows, worked his way around the barn and paused in the baleful glow of the barn lights, which illuminated the yard between barn and house 24/7. He backtracked around the barn and approached the house in shadow, from the north, the rain a steady drumbeat on his head. He crept up to the edge of the west-facing veranda. A man with an AK-47 slung over his shoulder sat in a chair tilted back against the wall. Josh watched him a while. The man appeared to be sleeping.

Josh boosted himself over the railing, sound masked by the rain, took out his .45 and smashed the butt into the man's temple full force. The sentry went down sideways and stayed there. Josh leaned down to ascertain if he was still alive. He was. Josh removed the hunting knife from its ballistic scabbard and slit the man's throat ear to ear.

With the delicacy of a surgeon he tried the front door. It was open. He slipped into the darkened living room, becoming immediately aware of a man sawing logs on the sofa to his left. Josh crept up to him and drew his knife.

Lord forgive me.

Wiping the blade on the sofa, he searched the first floor. There was no one else. The door to the basement was open in the kitchen. Night lenses activated, he crept down the stairs, standing next to the wall to avoid making any sound. The storm drowned everything out. The basement rec room hosted two jihadis, each sleeping on a separate sofa, their weapons lying on the end tables. Josh did what he had to do. Four down, God knows how many to go. He glanced at his watch. He had fifteen minutes.

Josh crept up the hardwood stairs to the second floor, which housed four bedrooms. One of these had an open door and had been turned into an office. Three computer terminals glowed softly. It was empty. The second had a padlock. Weapons room, he guessed.

The third extruded a pale light from within. Josh turned the knob and stepped inside, gripping his pistol. Cat Lowenstein looked up, startled, from where she sat Indian-style in bed, poking at her phone. She wore a Che Guevara T-shirt. The sight and scent of her delivered a jolt straight to Josh's groin.

Down, rough beast.

Cat put her hands to her mouth, but before she could take any other action, Josh grabbed her by the hair, yanked her upright and got his arm around her neck, with her throat in the crook.

"Make one sound and I'll kill you," he hissed.

CHAPTER 63

Old MacDonald

"Now," he hissed in her ear. "Very softly. How many jihadis here, including your boyfriend?"

She tugged at his arm. "Sixteen," she croaked.

"Why so many? What's going on?"

"I don't know! I swear! They won't tell me! I'm just a girl!"

"Where's your boyfriend?"

"They've got bunks in the barn. Sometimes he sleeps with the guys. Are you going to kill me?"

"You gave them Don's address, and Melissa's. You slipped me something and copied my notebook, didn't you?"

"So what? She's a blasphemous bitch."

Josh lifted Cat off the ground with his grip. Her legs thrashed. He let her down. "And the old lady too. Did you give them her address? Just nod."

Cat nodded, gasping against his grip. He loosened it so she could breathe.

"Are you going to kill me?"

"It depends on the next few seconds. Anyone else up and about?"

"There's a dude on the front porch, and there's supposed to be someone in the loft."

"If I turn you loose, will you run off? Just put on some shoes and go. Don't take a car. Just get your ass out of here and get as far as you can get."

"Yes!" she said. "Just let me go! Please, Josh! I thought we had something."

Josh let her go, swung her around by the shoulder and punched her as hard as he could on the point of the chin. She went down like the Twin Towers.

"You lying bitch."

He checked her pulse. Steady as she goes. Taking a roll of Gorilla Tape from his cargo pants, he wrapped her thighs and her elbows behind her back before taping her mouth. Josh let himself out and crept down the hall to the master bedroom, the room they had spied through the window a few days ago. It seemed like an eternity.

Josh let himself in, the creak of old hinges lost in the steady drumbeat against the roof and windows. The old man lay in bed propped up on some cushions, table lamp on, a book open on his lap, hands at his sides, wide awake. He stared at Josh in surprise.

Josh sat on the chair next to the bed. "Sir, I'm Josh Pratt. I'm a private investigator. No one's going to hurt you. Can you speak?"

"I can talk," the old man said in a phlegmy voice. Oxygen tubes went into his nostrils from a green tank next to the bed.

"Sir, you know all these guys are jihadis, right? The same gang that attacked us on 9/11?"

"They were driven to attacking us by American aggression."

"How did they get here?"

"Few years ago I advertised for some help. My wife died in '06. Salim answered, he and his brother. They proved to be good workers, so when they asked if I would admit their relatives—no pay; they would operate the ranch and do chores as payment—I agreed. These are good people. They take real good care of me, better than any Christians I know, that's for damn sure."

"Sir, have you converted to Islam?"

"Hah!" the old man spat and broke into a paroxysm of coughing. Josh handed him the bottled water with a straw in it from the bedside table. Thunder rattled the windowpanes.

The old man sipped. "Hell no! I'm an atheist. But if you've got to have religion, I reckon Islam's as good as any."

"Are you aware they've been murdering people?"

"So you say."

There was a phone on the bedside table. Josh ripped it out of the wall, then searched the bed and the side table for a cell phone or weapons.

"Sir, stay here and you'll be okay. The police are coming."

MacDonald stared balefully. Josh let himself out, shut the door behind him and phoned Kleiser. He let it ring once and then he was down the stairs, over the rail, working his way to the back side of the barn. He switched on the night goggles and crept in low to the ground. Lightning flickered through the dirty windows, illuminating four men sleeping on futons on the hardwood floor. A bearded man wearing a watch cap and smoking a cigarette leaned against the rear wheel of a Mahindra tractor. Thunder rumbled, and the steady drumbeat of rain hid any sound Josh might have made as he came around the back of the tractor and kicked the man in the face with his leather boot, bouncing his skull against the metal wheel rim. The man slumped forward, unconscious.

Gunshots penetrated the barn, muffled by the rain, flurry followed by flurry. Two of the three sleeping men stirred and sat up, reaching for their weapons. Josh drew his auto and shot them both twice. The third rolled to his side beneath the van. Josh ran around the back of the van but the man was gone. Or he was still under the van, which had recently been painted and now sported a rainbow on the side, ending in a pot of gold labeled LGBTQ.Josh leaped as high as he could, drawing his knees up, as a fusillade of shots erupted from under the van. He took off as soon as he landed, ran around the front of the van and threw himself atop a wood bench. He lay on his belly holding the big auto upside down with his pinky finger on the trigger and fired three shots parallel to the ground beneath the van. His second and third shots dug into the wood floor. He caught a glimpse of shadow as the jihadist bolted from the barn into the yard.

What about the one in the loft?

Josh rolled to his side as bullets penetrated the heavy workbench and reverberated through the wind. Chips flew. Josh rolled beneath the bench as gunfire impacted the surface. With every shot, the bench jolted a half inch.

A spray of gunfire vomited from the front door, where Bricklin stood in her slicker holding the Uzi in both hands like a vicious bulldog. A body tumbled to the floor with a thump.

"Where are the others?" Josh shouted over the storm. A dull gray was creeping behind the tree line to the east.

A series of percussive explosions sounded outside the barn. Recognizing the Streetsweeper, Josh stuck his head out down low to see

Zlatko firing on three men approaching in an arc, the shotgun's muzzle gouting flame. One of the men went down but the other two advanced, firing AKs from the hip. Zlatko danced like a marionette and went down firing at the sky. Bracing one arm against the doorframe, Josh squeezed off two shots but couldn't tell if he'd hit his target. Something impacted the doorframe, and a sliver of wood buried itself in Josh's cheek. He pulled back as bullets penetrated the thin wood wall, forcing Josh to take refuge behind the tractor.

A pause, followed by gunfire and the metallic careen of ricochets.

"Stop firing!" someone shouted from outside. "You'll hit the van!"

The white noise of rain filled the air as Bricklin tipped over the heavy workbench and took shelter, dropping the spent mag and slamming in a new one. She pulled out her Judge, turned toward Josh and grinned. She looked like a demented Annie Oakley.

An unintelligible babble from just outside. Men talking. Bricklin winked at Josh and cupped her hands around her mouth.

"HEY YOU PUSSIES! THIS HERE'S A WOMAN KILLIN' YOU!"

"*ALLAHU AKBAR!*" one of the jihadis cried, filling the barn door and sweeping his AK from side to side. He paused for an instant and Bricklin rose and let him have it with the Uzi, holding the Judge for another jihadist who was lurching in from the opposite side. She got him too but not before he clipped her left bicep. Bricklin sat down hard, dropping the Judge and clapping her hand over the wound.

For an instant there was silence. Josh sat next to Bricklin, replacing the clip in his .45.

"How you doin'?" he said.

Bricklin grinned. She had big teeth. "Ah, pleasant memories of Kandahar. Nineteen troops, two women. Gwen Buva was twenty when she signed up. Slim blond. I begged her not to go on that patrol but she insisted. She got cut off from the main patrol along with two other guys. The Muzzies killed the men and raped Gwen to death. Part of the reason I'm here."

"I can dig it."

Josh pulled a rolled bandage from his cargo pants and wrapped it around Brick's wound.

"Looks like it went right through. Made a big hole."

"I can fight. Load that Judge for me. Shells in my right vest pocket."

As Josh reached across for the shells, a fat bullet whizzed by his ear. A split second later Bricklin's head exploded. Josh grabbed his gun and rolled, swinging the heavy workbench between him and the shooter. Through the crack between boards he saw Django pop up momentarily from behind the tractor, wearing that cowboy hat with the conchos and holding a long-barreled revolver.

CHAPTER 64

Nest of Vipers

"Whassup, my brother?" Django sang from behind the Mahindra. "Give it up, Django. The cops are on their way."

"How you know that? We're in the boonies, my brother! Could be just a little night practice."

"Everybody's dead but you."

"Maybe. Maybe not. I'm not going back in the joint. This is it, my brother. Django's Last Stand. And I'm not going alone. You're coming with me."

Josh peered through the crack in the bench, thought he could make out Django's legs crouched behind the tractor, but it was so dark it could have been anything.

Where were Dale and Kleiser?

"Did you kill Polly?" Josh said.

"I did the deed, my brother! I killed the blasphemous Jew bitch and the old lady."

"Why don't you just eat your gun?" Josh said.

"Too easy, my brother!"

"What's in the van?"

"That's not for you."

Josh glanced at the van as lightning illuminated the yard and God clapped his hands together over Josh's head. The van was for the Gay Pride event.

"You should join me, brother. Would ten thou buy me a ticket out of here?"

"Where do you get ten thou?"

"Old MacDonald. We cashed in some of his annuities."

Lightning struck the rod on the barn, followed by an ear-shredding rip as the universe tore itself apart. Josh lay prone and fired three shots at what he thought were Django's legs. At least one hit but the shadows didn't move. They weren't legs. For long seconds Josh remained where he was, trying to listen between peals of thunder. Useless.

White noise filled the barn.

Two shots and a shout rang out from the yard. Sticking to shadow, Josh hunched toward the door and crouched just inside. He looked out. Django, rain pouring off the brim of his hat, stood over a figure in the mud, pointing a long-barreled revolver. Josh aimed with both hands and squeezed. A *splang*, a spark and an explosion and Django's gun went flying.

I hit the fucking gun, Josh thought. *What are the odds?*

Django jumped around bent over with his hands between his knees, and Josh brought his pistol up. The world did a 360 as he blacked out and slumped to the floor. He came to almost immediately and looked up with a pulsing pain emanating from the back of his skull. Cat Lowenstein was aiming his own gun at him. Josh hooked her heel with his right foot and swept her, slamming her head into the wood floor as she came down. He reached for the pistol.

"Let it go, my brother."

Josh looked up.

Django stood just inside the door holding an automatic. It might have been Dale's.

Josh looked up from his knees.

"Tell me something."

"What?" Django said.

"Why did you burn the dogs?"

Django grinned nervously. Some cultures did that when they were embarrassed or humiliated.

"Hashim Rashad has declared a jihad on dogs. The brothers insisted. I know it's crazy but that's the way it is."

"But why burn them alive? Why not just shoot them?"

Django shrugged. "I didn't get that."

"But you went along with it."

A ripple of rage passed across Django's face. "Who are you to judge me? What are a few fuckin' dogs compared to the lives of my people?"

"Who are your people?"

That grin again. "I can't pull that race card with you. You've been in the belly of the beast. You had it bad. Maybe even badder than me. I like you, Pratt. That's what sucks. I really like you."

"You're just afraid to fight me."

Shock popped on Django's face. "You have got to be shitting me."

"I can see it in your face. You're afraid of me."

Django laughed. "Tell you what. You give me your word you'll let me go if I beat your ass, I'll set down this gun."

"Deal," Josh said, slowly getting to his feet.

Django grinned, pointed the gun and tossed it behind the tractor. He held his hands up open-palmed in front of his face. "Come on, white boy. Show me what you got."

Bouncing on the balls of his feet, Josh faced him sideways. Django darted forward with astonishing speed and hit Josh with an invisible jab that buckled his knees. Josh instinctively looped his head left to right and threw an overhand right that clipped Django on the temple. Django stepped back smiling, touching the side of his head.

They jockeyed a little and clashed, Django throwing a barrage of hard punches that forced Josh to cover up and spin from side to side on the balls of his feet, suddenly leaping and twisting in mid-air with a spinning reverse side kick that caught Django in the bread basket, setting him on his ass.

Still smiling, Django sprang back up in a fighter's crouch. "A-huh. Okay."

He darted forward, faked high, aiming his kick for Josh's crotch, but Josh turned sideways and caught the point of Django's heavy work boot on his thigh. Like being rammed by a shark. It would swell up and become immobile later. Josh threw an elbow but Django went low, threw his arms around Josh's midriff and tripped him. They went down hard, Django scrambling to maintain top position as Josh twisted and lashed out with his knee. Josh grabbed a handful of sawdust and threw it in Django's face, scrambling backward on his ass until he was able to get to his feet. Django stood and dove forward, leaping and landing on his hands in a cartwheel, striking Josh in the head with his foot. Pain exploded in Josh's nose. Blood splattered the ground.

Before Josh could react, Django's right leg went around Josh's left, and Django brought him down, seizing Josh's ankle and hugging it to his belly in a heel hook. Josh reacted with furious thrashing, pulling one leg free and pistoning his heel into Django's chin. They rolled apart and got to their feet, panting. Django bobbed, weaved, feinted and fired a hard right that caught Josh on the side of the head, knocking him sideways. Josh turned his wobble into a spin and lashed out again with a spinning reverse right side kick, but Django spun clockwise away from the kick and slammed his elbow into Josh's head. Django pumped a hook into Josh's torso, and Josh felt his ribs crack. Django grabbed Josh by the back of the neck and pulled him into a knee.

Django stood over Josh, grinning. "Now omma take my leave, my brother."

A flame erupted from the barn entrance so loud and piercing that Josh thought lightning had struck the barn. Django made that surprised face and slumped to the ground. Josh looked up. Kleiser stood just outside holding his .45 in a horse stance. The pistol waved in his grip. Painfully, using the tipped-over workbench for support, Josh got to his feet.

"I think you got him, Randall."

Josh looked around. Cat was gone.

CHAPTER 65

Aftermath

The sky looked like pewter as rain dimpled the muddy yard. Josh's boots pulled free with a sucking sound as he ran in slo-mo toward the figure lying on the ground. It was Dale, eyes wide open, letting the drops hit him in the face. Josh bent down and put a finger to his carotid.

"You okay?"

"I'll live," Dale wheezed. "Bullet went clear through—broke a rib— hurts like a motherfucker every time I breathe."

"Hang on," Josh said. "We'll get an ambulance." He turned toward Kleiser but the programmer was already punching numbers.Kleiser stuck his phone in his pocket. "They're on the way. More cops than you can shake a stick at. Someone else heard the shots and phoned them."

"All right," Josh said. "We've got to get Dale out of the rain. Let's find something we can carry him in."

"I thought I saw a wheelbarrow in the barn."

While Kleiser returned to the barn, Josh took off his rain poncho and held it over Dale's head. Kleiser returned driving one of those off-road 4x4s with a tiny pickup bed. They carefully placed Dale sideways in the bed and drove slowly toward the house, where they lifted him out and carried him up the porch stairs into the kitchen.

"I can stand," Dale grimaced, one arm thrown around Josh's shoulder. They helped him into the living room, where he collapsed on the sofa with a dead jihadist at his feet. Josh went upstairs to check on the old man.

291

MacDonald was sitting upright in bed clutching a twelve-gauge shotgun, which he aimed at Josh.

"Stop right there, sonny!"

"Sir, the police are on their way. Please put that gun down. You're not going to shoot anyone."

After a long minute MacDonald set the gun on the bed.

"Sir, did you give your guests access to your bank account?"

"So what if I did? I trust them. Why? What do you know about it?"

"I would check with your financial institutions to see if you have any money left. I believe they've been using your power of attorney to finance jihad."

"They promised me they wouldn't do that."

The first faint wail of a siren penetrated the old house.

"Did you know Django?" Josh said.

"Django? Fine man. Does a lot for me. Why? Where is he?"

"I'm afraid he's dead."

The old man stared balefully with cold blue eyes for a minute.

"They're all dead, aren't they?"

"A lot of them are dead, yes."

Air left the old man like a collapsing balloon. "I feared it would come to this."

"Do you know Cat Lowenstein?"

The old man blinked. "Who?"

"Stunning redhead. You couldn't miss her. She was here when I arrived."

"I never...no! I told them not to bring girls to the house! My late wife Adrienne's the only woman I ever trusted. She'd roll over in her grave if she found out."

"Sir, I know of only one girl. Can I help you get some things together? They're probably going to take you to a hospital."

"Why? What for? This is my home, dammit. What makes them think they can just come in here and cart me off..."

He stopped, looked puzzled and put a hand to his throat. He made a weird ratcheting sound in his throat. Josh was at his side but he didn't know what to do.

"Can you breathe?" he asked.

MacDonald leaned over, rattled and slumped face first on the old duvet. Josh felt for a pulse. There was none. He pulled MacDonald down by his feet so that he was flat and then, stifling his revulsion at the old man's rotten breath, he put a thumb on the farmer's tongue and began mouth-to-mouth. After a few breaths the old man gargled, coughed and began breathing again, so Josh went into the bathroom and found a bottle of Listerine.

Red and blue lights strobed the bedroom windows from outside. Josh looked out the window as Sheriff LaBute got out of the lead car. He wore a yellow slicker with a hood, JACKSON COUNTY SHERIFF in black letters on the back. His driver approached a body in the mud, gun drawn. As Josh watched, vehicles continued to arrive, including an ambulance. He went downstairs, entering the kitchen as the sheriff opened the door from outside, came in and stamped his feet on a jute mat.

Josh stood with his hands at his sides. "Sheriff."

"What's going on?" the sheriff said.

"We had reason to believe that a woman named Cat Lowenstein was being held here against her will. We entered and were fired upon and returned fire."

"Who's 'we'?"

"Me, Randall Kleiser, Dale Costigan, Bricklin Beasn and Zlatko Dzelko. Beasn and Dzelko are dead."

A deputy entered behind the sheriff. "We have six dead bodies in the yard and in the barn, Francis."

"Sir," Josh said, "that van in the barn may be filled with explosives."

LaBute snapped his fingers at the deputy and pointed toward the door. The sheriff squinted at Josh. "Is this a vigilante operation?"

Suddenly Josh felt weak. He pulled out a wooden kitchen chair and sat. "Sir, we have repeatedly asked every law enforcement agency from the local to the federal level to investigate what we believe is a terrorist training camp. You'll find that the men we shot were all heavily armed and may not be in the country legally. Knowing time was of the essence, we thought it prudent to act. Have you met Federal Agent Roland Stoeckle? If you phone him, he'll vouch for us."

"Maybe," the sheriff said. "In the meantime we're going to place you and any other survivors under arrest. We can sort it all out in the morning."

"I understand. I have Agent Stoeckle's phone number, if you'd like."

"Write it down for me."

Josh removed his soggy spiral pad, wrote it down, tore the page off and handed it to the sheriff.

"Wait here. I don't want to have to cuff you."

"Yes sir," Josh said, folding his hands on the table in front of him.

The sheriff went outside. Deputies entered the house wearing gloves and baggies on their feet and searched, followed by crime technicians with cameras. More vehicles arrived outside, including two more ambulances. A half hour passed. LaBute returned.

"We've got twelve bodies so far, including Beasn and Dzelko. Some of these guys have no identification. It may be days before we know who they are. We found a cache of weapons including Semtex, anti-tank rockets and factory-fresh AK-47s. We got a bomb-sniffing dog who howls at that van like it's a cat. I spoke to Agent Stoeckle, and he won't confirm or deny whether you work for him or not. He's on his way. He'll be here in a couple of hours. In the meantime you're going to give me a statement. I have a deputy bringing coffee and Egg McMuffins."

The sheriff pulled out a wood kitchen chair with a screech on the worn linoleum, sat down and dragged his mitt over his face. He looked like he hadn't slept. He pulled a recording device out of his pocket and set it on the table.

"Let's start at the beginning."

CHAPTER 66

Bucket List

Agent Stoeckle arrived shortly before noon with another man in an institutional gray Chrysler. Josh watched through the kitchen window as Stoeckle talked with Sheriff LaBute, their expensive shoes covered with straw and mud. It was a gloomy, overcast day. LaBute pointed at the farmhouse, and the three men headed toward it.

The kitchen's ancient Bakelite GE radio was tuned to Wisconsin Rapids, mostly farm reports interspersed with old-time country. Glenn Campbell. Buck Owens. Merle Haggard. Patsy Cline. As Stoeckle, LaBute and the other man reached the back door, the news came on.

"We've just learned of a mass shooting at a farm in Jackson County. We have no details, but it appears to have been some kind of domestic dispute. We will keep you updated as we learn more."

The third man had fed written all over him, from his Jos. A. Bank suit to his icy demeanor to his crewcut coconut head. Josh stood and shook hands with Stoeckle.

"Josh, this is Federal Agent Rio Herrera. The FBI is sharing the investigation with us."

"Am I under arrest?" Josh said.

"No," Stoeckle said. "We've made it clear you were acting on federal orders."

"I'll need to see that in writing," LaBute said.

"It's coming. We've ID'd Cedric Jones. I understand you've sent photos to Washington?" Stoeckle said, looking at LaBute.

LaBute nodded.

"We've called in a bomb disposal unit to deal with the van. Looks like they were planning to light up the Gay Pride event in Madison next week."

"Any trace of Lowenstein?" Josh asked.

"No. Do you have any photos?"

Josh pulled out his cell phone. "I'll forward them. They're several years old. She's dyed her hair red."

"One thing I don't get," LaBute said. "If you came here to save her, why is she on the run?"

"She must have freaked out," Josh said. "I imagine she was in quite a state."

Stoeckle looked around. "Boys, I need a few moments with Josh. You too, Rio."

The cops shuffled into the living room. Scuffling feet and muted voices filtered down from the ceiling.

"How you doing?" Stoeckle said. "You look pretty banged up. Do you need to go to the hospital?"

"I'll live."

Stoeckle pulled out a chair, sat, bent forward and spoke softly behind his hand like a kid in grade school.

"Between us, you did a good thing but there are elements that want to hang you out to dry. The administration has launched a pogrom against anti-jihadist factions, and there's even talk of charging you and your friends with murder. That's dead for now. I went out on a limb for you. Fortunately, there are still enough people at the federal level who see what you did as a good thing. You did what many of us have been advocating for years. This story that they were holding this woman hostage, is it true?"

"No sir. Cat Lowenstein is a terrorist sympathizer and Cedric Jones's girlfriend. If you examine those drone tapes we made, they should show all the vehicles in the yard. She may have taken one of those. Just see which one is missing."

"Will your story hold up?"

"Don't know. She's likely to say anything. She's a damn good liar. Who's gonna say she was Django's girlfriend? Not Old MacDonald. He didn't even know she was here."

"Didn't you bang her in San Diego?"

A red tide rose up Josh's neck. "Yeah. I was so fucking easy. I should have known a broad like that would never go for a man like me."

"Women love the bad boys, Josh. You'd better check with your doctor."

"Oh fuck," Josh said. "I hadn't thought about that. What about this story I was acting on your orders?"

"What else am I going to say?"

"Sir, if you're claiming me as one of yours, maybe you ought to supply me with some identification."

"It's coming. Kleiser too. You boys did what we only dream of doing."

"Yeah. How come you ain't all over these camps like white on rice?"

"You know why."

They heard footsteps tromping down the stairs. Josh turned and looked down the hall to see two burly EMTs carrying MacDonald out the front door on a stretcher swaddled in blankets and strapped to a board.

"The old man's a bit of a crackpot," Josh said. "Libertarian. Oddly enough, since he gave these scorpions shelter, they've been taking care of him real good."

"The Feebs are probably going to charge him with aiding and abetting a terrorist organization."

"He didn't know shit," Josh said. "Check his bank accounts. I'm betting they drained him dry. Better check on his credit cards too. We don't know who all was staying out here. Some may have been away when the shooting started."

"Good idea," Stoeckle said, reaching for his phone.

Dale had been transported by air to University Hospital in Madison. One of the jihadists was alive but unconscious. He had ridden in a Blackhawk to Volk Field Air National Guard in Juneau County. At 2:30 p.m., Josh and Kleiser got in the back of Stoeckle's car for the drive to Madison. Stoeckle and Herrera sat in the front. It was the first time Josh had seen Kleiser since the shooting had ended. Covered with mud and all scraped up, Kleiser nevertheless had the look of a man who had just won a world championship. He was grinning like a dog. He could not stop grinning.

"You all right?" Josh said.

"Me? Never better. Scratch that off the bucket list."

Herrera turned around and looked at Kleiser.

"Why are you so goddamn happy?"

"Jihadis blew his girlfriend up," Josh said. "What was it, five years ago?"

A trio of cops manned the farm entrance off Ralston Road. Josh saw the cops had set up barriers a hundred yards apart and were diverting traffic. Beyond the barriers were several news vans. Josh recognized the distinctive colors of WMAD, Madison. As they approached the barrier, a cop moved the sawhorse aside to let them through. Katy Varner, wearing a curve-hugging knit burgundy dress, pointed at them as her cameraman dutifully zeroed in.

"Josh!" she shouted as the car eased through. "Can you tell us what happened?"

Josh kept his eyes straight ahead.

CHAPTER 67

Run Run Run Away

"Pratt, whose previous client also died under bizarre circumstances, claimed that the alleged kidnap victim phoned him the previous night and begged him to save her. Police have declined to name the alleged victim, or any of the deceased. Locals were not so reluctant."

The camera cut to a middle-aged man in OshKosh coveralls and a Renk Seed cap. "Bunch of A-rabs. Don't know what Old MacDonald was thinking. He was always...different. But this, this is crazy."

Cut to a medium shot, exterior daylight, Katy Varner in jeans, huaraches and a work shirt, holding the microphone toward two young women, each with a baby stroller.

"What's your reaction to the events at MacDonald's farm yesterday?"

A plump blond said, "It's weird. We'd see these creepy-looking guys in town sometimes."

The camera turned to the other, a tall brunette. "I was at the Red Owl when one of those guys walked up right behind me and rubbed his [*bleep!*] against my [*bleep!*]."

"What did you do?" Katy asked.

While the blond grinned, the brunette made a fist. "I kicked him in the [*bleep!*]. Then I told the manager, but by the time the cops came he was gone. Some of his greaser buddies came in and got him."

Katy addressed the camera. "This is not the first time Josh Pratt has been the center of controversy. Last year he was involved in a shootout in his driveway with four members of the Insane [*bleep!*] motorcycle gang.

Police killed all three. Nor is this the first time he has lost a client. Last year, his client Charlotte Newton died under bizarre and tragic circumstances."

Josh got off the institutional cloth sofa, walked to the big flat-screen TV affixed to the wall and looked for a shut-off switch. The screen went blank. Josh turned and faced Agent Herrera, who was holding the remote.

"Thank you."

Josh returned to the sofa in the beige-colored meeting room at FBI HQ in Middleton. One wall was floor-to-ceiling windows looking north across the boulevard toward green hills in the distance. Josh sat down next to Kleiser, who had a white bandage across his forehead. He'd cut his hair, and he looked like any bright young techie. Agents Herrera and Stoeckle sat at a lozenge-shaped maple table with a small, middle-aged Asian woman, National Security Advisor Margaret Yee. She turned her smooth porcelain face toward Josh.

"The president is extremely grateful to you, young man, for averting what would have been a tragedy. He will want to thank you personally. You too, Mr. Kleiser."

Josh smirked.

"Mr. Kleiser, you've been approved for Level B clearance and are now an independent contractor on retainer with the NSA. Rio?"

Herrera sailed laminated ID cards across the smooth surface of the desk, launching them into space. Josh snagged his out of the air. Kleiser was a little slow and his fell to the ground. The card showed a photo of Josh, taken the previous day, along with the NSA seal and lines of coded information.

Kleiser rubbed thumb and forefinger together. "What's it pay?"

"A hundred eleven thousand per annum," Yee said with a slight smile. "We prefer direct deposit if that's all right."

Josh nudged Kleiser with his elbow. "Now you gotta open a bank account."

"Fuck," Kleiser said.

Stoeckle pointed at the TV screen, which now showed a slow scroll of mug shots and bios. "We've identified all but one of the deceased. All save two are on State Department terrorist watch lists. The two who are not on our list are on a list the Russians gave us several months ago. They come from Chechnya and Pakistan. We have issued an APB for Cat Lowenstein.

She won't be able to use a credit card or enter a bank without us knowing about it."

"It's been forty-eight hours," Josh said.

"We'll get her," Stoeckle said. "With modern face recognition technology, it's only a matter of time."

Josh stood. He wore clean khakis, a black silk T-shirt and a black cotton jacket. "We got a funeral. You coming?"

Stoeckle remained where he was. "Nope. Again, thank you gentlemen. We'll be in touch."

Kleiser stood and followed Josh out of the room. He wore a black jacket over a black shirt over jeans.

Downstairs they got in Josh's car, got on the interstate and headed toward Milwaukee. It was just past eleven. The funeral was due to start at 2:00 p.m. at Hillel Sanctuary Temple in Fox Point. Neither man spoke. After a while, Josh turned on the radio and found a blues station playing Otis Rush. They rode right downtown and took 43 North to Fox Point, turning east toward the river.

They found the temple without difficulty in a hushed and shaded neighborhood filled with million-dollar homes. It was a stucco building of quasi-Moroccan design set back behind a lush green lawn. The parking lot was filled with expensive cars. Josh found a spot at the back, and he and Kleiser walked toward the building, joining a steady migration of somber and well-dressed people of all ages. A stout man in a black suit and yarmulke checked purses at the entrance. Inside, it was SRO. Josh and Kleiser took their places against the back wall. Josh counted people by pew. There were at least two hundred fifty in the big room.

The rabbi was surprisingly young, with a red beard. He took his place behind the podium.

"I first met Polly in fourth grade. We both attended Thomas Jefferson Elementary School, and we both went to Fox Point High. I lost touch with her when she went to school in Madison, but we found each other again over Facebook..."

Muted laughter.

"And we got back together at least several times. I don't have to tell you what she was like. Bright, funny, kind, caring, always ready to help someone else. We all knew she was going to be an artist, even before she did. She drew compulsively in the margins of her schoolbooks, driving her teachers nuts. She'd make little flip books out of the margins, mostly starring her creation Ed 'Big Daddy' Sloth."

Josh couldn't take any more. He lurched off the wall and headed for the exit, keeping his head down. Several people patted him on the shoulder as he went by. He barely made it outside before he burst out sobbing, walking quickly away from the door around the corner near the service entrance, where no one could see him.

He dug around in his pocket and found a napkin from the drive-through, honked into it and dabbed his eyes. He'd seen guys die in the joint, bleed out on the shower floor, and it hadn't fazed him.

A shadow preceded the intrusion. Josh looked up as Katy Varner came around the corner holding her mic, with her cameraman following like a well-trained dog. She held the mic out to Josh.

"Josh, could you tell us what happened at the MacDonald farm?"

Josh gaped in disbelief. He turned to walk away but Katy and the cameraman followed, as if daring him to assault them. He was about to run when someone called out from behind.

"Hey! Hey! Leave that man alone!"

He stopped and turned, along with Katy and her cameraman, who sensed news. Jade Kamal was striding purposefully their way, wearing a floor-length black knit dress that clung to her curves like a mountain road, and long black gloves.

Jade rounded on Katy. "Have you no decency?"

Katy held out the mic. "Ma'am, who are you and what was your relationship to the deceased?"

Jade looked over Katy's shoulder and flicked her eyes. Josh didn't need an engraved invitation. He ran.

Acknowledgments

Once again, I'd like to thank Lou Anne Yee for her proofreading, and John Loveall and Jamie Leben for their technical assistance. Also Jay Merwin for his meticulous, some might say fanatical, editing skills.

About The Author

Mike Baron grew up in South Dakota where he fell in love with comics courtesy of Uncle Scrooge. After graduating from the University of Wisconsin he moved to Boston to write. His first job: smoking dope for the government. He wrote about it and landed a position with the *Boston Phoenix*. Mike returned to Madison in '77 and took a job at an insurance company. That lasted until he met Steve Rude, with whom he created the award-winning and groundbreaking science fiction title *Nexus*. He has also written *Punisher, Flash, Star Wars*, and his other creation, *Badger*. Mike moved to Colorado in 2003, but it wasn't until 2011 that he finally figured out how to write novels. Mike's a slow learner. But now he gets it. *Biker*, about reformed motorcycle hoodlum Josh Pratt, was his first published work followed by *Helmet Head*, about Nazi biker zombies, *Skorpio*, about a ghost who only appears under a blazing sun, and *Whack Job*, about spontaneous human combustion and alien invasion. This is his fourth novel featuring Josh Pratt (following *Biker, Sons of Privilege*, and *Not Fade Away*) and he has finished two more Josh Pratt novels to be published by Liberty Island in 2018. He lives in Colorado with his wife and some dogs, rides motorcycles, and trains at Karate West.